TALES OF GALLOWAY

TALES OF
GALLOWAY

ALAN TEMPERLEY

MAINSTREAM
PUBLISHING

Copyright © Alan Temperley, 1979.

First published, 1979.
Second impression, 1979.
Reprinted, 1992.

This edition published in 1986 by
MAINSTREAM PUBLISHING COMPANY (EDINBURGH) LTD.
7 Albany Street,
Edinburgh EH1 3UG.

The publisher acknowledges subsidy from the
Scottish Arts Council towards the publication of this volume.

Illustrations by pupils of Kirkcudbright Academy.

ISBN 1 85158 026 3

Printed by HarperCollins Manufacturing, Glasgow.

Contents

Preface

Galloway is sometimes called the Garden of Scotland, and justly so. The region, covering the County of Wigtown and the Stewartry of Kirkcudbright — 'from the brig end o' Dumfries to the braes of Glen App' — lies on a south-facing slope with its feet lapped by the Solway and its shoulders propped against beautiful ranges of mountains. From these uplands broad silver rivers wind south through undulating pastures and tracts of woodland, wonderful farming country, to run at length into the Solway Firth. And far off across the water, or miles of rippled sand when the tide is out, are the blue hills of Cumbria.

It is a region of dramatic history. The maps are thick with references to the sites of battles, towers and ruined castles, ancient stones, burial mounds, smugglers' bays and the graves of martyrs. Each has a tale to tell, though sadly many have been forgotten. And where the map is bare, where today the passer-by sees only a ploughed field or scrubby wooded hillside, until recent years an ancient village stood. Our present towns had not been built and some of these vanished villages and clachans were local centres. The land was rougher and more wild. A scarcely distinguishable ribbon of level moorland or meadow is all that remains of a potholed main road that for centuries took all the foot travellers and horsemen and rattling carriages of that district. The wonderful old railway lines, so recently closed, are already sinking back into the land from which they were hewn.

But there are many histories: this book is an entertainment. My aim in writing it has been to present a simple selection of the old traditional tales of the area. They tell of witches and colourful rogues, family feuds and smuggling escapades, rustic comedy and murders descending into horror, wicked landowners, monsters and fairies. And there are, too, a good number of historical adventures.

Many of the tales were told to me orally, others I have found in old books. Though I have sought to tell the stories simply and directly, it was seldom that they were found so. In every case where it was possible I travelled to the location and enquired locally. Sometimes, in this way, three or four versions of the same story emerged. The one I have recounted seemed to me the most commonly accepted and acceptable, and in many cases I have written or indicated a second and even third account also. There is, of course, bound to be disagreement, and I am glad, for that indicates a living interest. I can only say that I have done my best to be thorough and tell the tales truthfully.

So far as the historical stories are concerned, I have found great disagreement in published sources. Five quite separate fates, for example, are allocated to the Fair Maid of Galloway during the siege of Threave Castle — if she was there at all: Mons Meg is bound to the region by strings of historical myth as tangled as barbed wire: Galloway is described as being both in the vanguard and rearguard of agricultural change. It has not been my brief to hunt deeply among ancient archives and historical papers to ferret out the truth or otherwise of an old tale. On the other hand, it would not do in print, I feel, to show a sublime disregard for historical fact in the manner of the old storytellers. One is on the horns of a dilemma. In many of the old stories, of course, myth and fact are inextricably entwined. I have tried, in recounting these historical tales, to be as accurate as possible, and there is no fact for which I cannot account on good authority. But pure history and traditional legend, of course, rarely make the happiest of marriages.

Another problem has been the Scots language. I need make no apology for the fact that whilst generally characters speak in plain English, they sometimes use broad Galloway Scots, and the occasional Scots phrase is used where it is appropriate in the narrative. To have omitted the Scots would have been to deprive certain speeches of their force and even fame. It is untranslatable. On the other hand, to have maintained it throughout would often have made the dialogue hard to read, have held up the story, and in my opinion would have been artificial. Certainly it would have been artificial for me to attempt it.

The most important reason for writing the book was to present a selection — and it is no more — of the local tales for the people of the district, for those who love Galloway and are absent, and for those who travel here. Also I hope it may remind people in all parts of the country of their wonderful heritage. These stories, which grew over the centuries and are now almost entirely forgotten or ignored, present a glimpse of the life that flourished in the south-west until comparatively recent years. Farms and villages were isolated by the poor roads and limited means of transport: many people did not move more than a few miles from home throughout their entire lives. The stories were told in cottages for entertainment. They grew up out of the history of the land and the lives of the people. And they are as alive today as when they were first told. But now, in the manner of our time, we switch on television, and instead of absorbing the stories of an honourable past, we are battered by the sham and slick drama of the great cities. I would like to think that this collection might do at least a little to redress the balance.

But in most cases we do not read a book of this nature for some objective reason, we read it for entertainment. And it is my hope and belief that these old stories, written by the past and the land and the people of Galloway, will be enjoyed today.

Alan Temperley
Rhonehouse, 1979

Acknowledgements

My thanks are due to the hundreds of local people who have so readily and with such interest told these stories to me, and so unfailingly helped my enquiries. It sometimes seemed strange, standing in the doorway of a barn with the rain sweeping by, talking to a farmer in wellington boots about witches and fairies; or having introduced myself to a quiet old lady, plunging at once into stories of bloody murder and pillage. I would like to express my gratitude also to the many people who lent me books that were precious to them, and sometimes quite irreplaceable. More particularly I wish to thank Miss Jean Slaven for her great help and encouragement; Mr. James Manson, Rector of Kirkcudbright Academy, for his enthusiasm and readiness to allow the young people to participate; Mr. Robin McLeish and Mr. Tom Collin, Honorary Curator of the Stewartry Museum, Kirkcudbright, for reading the manuscript and giving me the benefit of their opinion and knowledge; the Dumfries and Galloway Regional Library Service, and in particular Mrs. Jo. Laurie, Mrs. Mary Kirkpatrick and Mr. Martin McColl of the Castle Douglas Library, for their kindness and great assistance; and The Scots Magazine for permission to publish substantial extracts from my articles 'The Boy and the Adder' and 'The Yule Beggar'. Finally I wish to acknowledge with appreciation the award of a writer's bursary from the Scottish Arts Council.

Aiken Drum –
the Brownie of Bladnoch

Roun' his hairy form there was naething seen,
But a philabeg o' the rashes green,
And his knotted knees played ay knoit between:
What a sight was Aiken-drum!

On his wauchie arms three claws did meet,
As they trailed on the grun' by his taeless feet;
E'en the auld gudeman (Satan) himsel' did sweat,
To look at Aiken-drum.

"I lived in a lan' where we saw nae sky,
I dwalt in a spot where a burn rins na by;
But I'se dwall now wi' you, if ye like to try –
Hae ye wark for Aiken-drum?"

William Nicholson

Darkness spread over the land, the last traces of sunset faded over the Machars. It was All Hallows Eve.

One or two women, shawls drawn about their shoulders against the advancing chill, gathered at the gates and in the doorways of cottages before they should retreat indoors for the night. Children played along the lane.

From far down there came a scream, then a hubbub of cries, and the children came racing and scampering back to the houses, looking behind them with terror as they ran. Way up the lane, dark in the fading light and too far off to see distinctly, a hunched form came stalking towards the houses.

The women in the lane ran to their homes and shut the gates. Calling their men they stood back in the doorways.

The figure drew closer, bare feet slapping on the ground, moaning and humming and uttering fragmentary words beneath his breath: "Aiken Drum ... no fee ... till your fields for a dish o' brose."

The young wife who lived in the first cottage gave a loud cry of fear and slammed her door.

The figure that trudged towards them was truly terrible, more like a

1

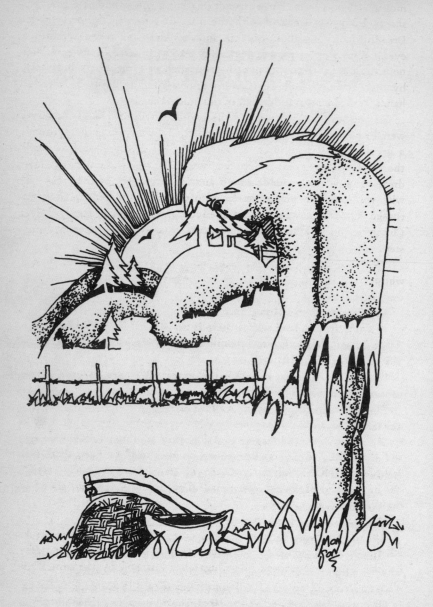

monster than a man. He wore nothing but a rough kilt of rushes, his shaggy body was smeared with the mire of the deep Galloway bogs. Dreadful hair hung about his face and shoulders, and at the glare of his eyes a good woman passed clean away into her husband's arms. He had no nose, and for a mouth only a hideous gash that might have been torn by the horn of a bull. His clammy arms, ending in knotted claws for hands, trailed almost to his feet in the mud of the lane.*

By the time he had reached the middle of the village all the doors were locked and barred save one. Frightened, but standing their ground, a goodwife and her husband watched as the creature came towards them and stopped only a few feet away. Unable to stand it, the man drew a swift circle around himself and made the sign of the cross. His wife was too terrified to move a muscle, then suddenly recovering, rushed into the house and grabbed up the big black family Bible. Clutching this to her bosom she ventured once more as far as the doorstep.

"What do you want?" said the man, his voice little more than a whisper. "Tell us, in God's name, from where you come, and what you want here with us."

The monster gave a groan, his dreadful mouth moved.

"I come from a land where there is no sky, no water. No home! ... Aiken Drum, they call me: Brownie of the Bladnoch. ... Work! Have you work for Aiken Drum?"

"No! No!" Again the man crossed himself. "We have no work. Leave us. Leave us in peace. We have no work for you."

"I seek no wages, no bond, no fee. All I ask is a dish of brose and a clear well, to drink and see my face. I can leap the burn when it is in spate, and milk the cattle, and plough the fields. I can churn the butter, and thresh the corn, herd the sheep on the hills and keep them safe from foxes, lull the children to sleep with songs they have never heard." His head lolled backwards, his dreadful eyes, full of anguish, glared at the sky.

"No, no! I tell you we have no work."

But the goodwife thought of their crops still on the fields unthreshed, the autumn ploughing, the decimation of their flocks and poultry by the foxes and wolves. She caught her husband by the arm. "His

* Aiken Drum was given the rush kilt by Nicholson, and this is now accepted. In the original tale, however, he was naked. This more readily explains the gift of the proper young wife — 'a mouldy pair o' her ain man's breeks'. It also gives a second explanation for his departure, for brownies were generally considered spirits too free to be fettered by human clothing.

3

speech is fair, he seeks no harm. We have plenty of meal. Let us give him a trial for one week."

When the other wives and men saw that their neighbours were unharmed, that they were not attacked and devoured by the terrifying creature, they crept from their doorways and ventured closer. But when they heard that he was to stay among them and work for his living, they raised their voices in horror.

"No, he must not stay. His very looks make us faint with fear. And who will ever come to the village when they know that Aiken Drum is living among us? He is dreadful, a foul ghost. His presence will blast the village."

But the goodwife silenced them with a reminder of the work that was unfinished — for they were not industrious villagers — and what must yet be done if they were to survive the following year.

So Aiken Drum stayed. The goodwife had made a good bargain, for the brownie did the work of ten men. By the gleam of the northern lights, and the light of the moon and stars, the fields were ploughed and furrowed, the corn was threshed and later sown, the sheep were tended and herded into folds on the hills.

(One evening, the tale is told, a farmer had requested Aiken Drum to drive his sheep from the hill and pen them in a fold at the end of the village by an early hour. Before breakfast the following morning he went along to see if the job was well done. So conscientiously had the brownie done his work that along with all the sheep from the hillside he had driven down the hares and rabbits also, and they were running about among the sheep's legs and jumping up the walls of the fold. Not a single sheep was missing. The farmer congratulated Aiken Drum on the excellence of his work. The brownie replied: "Confound they wee grey devils! They cost me mair bother than all the lave o' them!")

Soon the villagers grew used to his awful appearance, and the children came to love him, for he sang strange gentle songs to them when they were fretful and could not sleep; and at other times he played and showed them fairy games that they loved. Wherever he was, the children were merry and content. In the evenings, when he started work before their bedtimes, they followed him into the fields.

And all he asked was the wooden bowl of brose that the goodwife left for him on the doorstep every night, and a drink from her clear well. No-one ever saw him eat the brose, but in the morning it was gone. He never even asked for a spoon. And so anxious was he to be helpful that a word, or a wish, and he was there, his gash of a mouth twisted into a smile. Only when the sun was out did he slip away. Also, though the Bible held no fear for him, he could never bear to look upon a certain communion cup of the district.*

For a long time the brownie worked for the villagers and unfailingly did his best. At length the act of a young wife drove him away. She was a newly-married girl, and very aware of the proprieties and decencies. It offended her sense of decorum that Aiken Drum should go around in no more than a ragged kilt of rushes. So one night she left a pair of old, mouldy britches, discarded by her husband, by his clean dish of brose.

She did not know — perhaps no-one in the village knew — that any payment for his labours infallibly drives a brownie away, even a gift so poor as a pair of rotten breeks. So Aiken Drum, who needed a place of work and a home, and was so happy among them in his brownie way, had no alternative but to depart. Their bond was broken.

And in the night some were woken from their sleep by his loud cries of distress when he found the breeks by his bowl of brose. Peering from their curtains they saw his hairy form shambling flat-footed away down the lane through the village. Soon he was gone into the darkness and his moans and sighs faded into silence. He never returned.

Some time afterwards his voice was heard by a shepherd up in Penninghame, a few miles to the north. It came from the heart of the bogs in the miles of no-man's-land before the old Penninghame Forest, but in the darkness the shepherd could discern nothing. The brownie was grieving: "Aiken Drum. Oh, Aiken Drum! Fee and leave! ... Weep now, weep! No home! ... No home for Aiken Drum!" And as he passed, the shepherd heard the splash of his big feet in the bogs.

But still, they say, when the wind is in the trees, when the Bladnoch Linn is in spate and the water roars through the rocks, if you listen carefully you may make out the voice of Aiken Drum. And children in their beds smile, for they hear him clearly, singing them to sleep as he did so long ago.

---

* McMillan's Cup was used as a test of orthodoxy. It had originally belonged to John McMillan, founder of the Reformed Presbyterian Church, who was deposed in 1703 from the Established Church of Balmaghie for his nonconformity. The cup was treasured by a follower in the parish of Kirkcowan, the eastern boundary of which is the River Bladnoch. If, upon holding it, the man under examination trembled or showed any other sign of agitation, he was denounced as 'having bowed the knee to Baal, and sacrificed at the altar of idolatry.' Small wonder that Aiken Drum found the cup intimidating.

MAP BY MARTIN ROSINDALE

The Mermaid of Barnhourie

On a clear, cool night in early April, a little Dalbeattie lugger, home-ward bound from Whitehaven, drew in towards the mouth of the River Urr. The moon was full, and as the young seaman adjusted the sheet and tidied the deck, the moonlight shone on his dark curls and the side of his face and shoulders. A little distance away the waves curled and broke on the treacherous sandbanks of Barnhourie.

Gazing along the moon's track the young seaman saw the silhouette of what he took to be a seal's head dark on the water. He watched and whistled; then whistled again, trying to tempt the animal closer. From further aft the captain shouted: "You should know better than to whistle on a boat — especially with the banks so close." Looking away and breaking into song, the seaman continued with his work.

The head, however, was not that of a seal. It belonged to the mer-maid of Barnhourie, who was utterly in love with the young man. Whenever he returned home, or went fishing along that stretch of coast, she followed his boat, and when she thought it safe, she watched him from the shelter of rocks or some patch of weed. Now, as the Galloway coast came closer, she swam easily, parallel with the lugger.

Soon they shortened sail, and drew neatly into the channel that led up to Kippford at the mouth of the river. In less than half an hour they were moored in one of the narrow creeks.

The young sailor jumped ashore, barefoot in the mud, carrying his clothes and few possessions in a small bag slung over his shoulder. Then he set off up the rough road that led five miles into Dalbeattie, where his pretty wife and children lived.

The mermaid saw him vanish behind a clump of trees, then turned sadly and swam back down the channel between the muddy banks, out into the open water of the Solway. Rocking in the comforting waves, she swam eastwards along the shore to the Needle's Eye, a high narrow fissure through an outcrop of rocks beneath the crag. It was her favour-ite spot. There she sat on a weedy stone with the sea lapping about her beautiful tail. The moon moved across the sky. Slowly the tide ebbed, showing the top of the long lines of stake net set in the sand a little distance off-shore. When the water had sunk so far that barely sufficient remained for swimming, she slipped once more into the waves and made her way over the miles of rippled sand to the deeper channels between the Mersehead Sands and Barnhourie Bank.

Further out, in the depths of the Solway, lived her father, a merrow from the Irish coast. Despite his dreadful green body and face — the black beard topped by a nose like a red thorn and little piggy eyes — he was a kindly fellow. The mermaid of Barnhourie, his youngest daughter, had inherited her gentle nature from her father. Her sisters, however, though wonderfully beautiful were avid and cruel, always seeking to lure sailors and fishermen into watery graves with their sweet singing and wiles.

For many months the mermaid had been in love with the young seaman, and the morning following his return from Whitehaven she swam back to Kippford. He was working on the boat with a pot of pitch in his hand. On the shore nearby he had built a little fire to melt the pitch down, and his children were playing around it. Keeping against the hull of a vessel moored a few yards away, where she was sure she would not be seen, the lovely mermaid watched him working. Then she turned her eyes to the children, laughing and calling as they clambered aboard one of the boats drawn up on the shore. An old man called, holding out something in his clenched fist, and they ran across to him. When the mermaid looked back at the lugger, the young seaman was watching her. In his eyes was a look of surprise combined with an expression of wonder that was to remain with her for many months. For a moment she regarded him with some fear, then quietly slipped below the surface.

She swam away, but before she had gone far she paused, then turned and swam back. Clinging to the mooring rope of another vessel, she watched him from behind the stern. He had come to the rail and was scanning the water with his dark eyes. In a minute or two his children joined him, holding out their little hands to show him something, and he gave them his attention.

Less than a week later the lugger sailed. He was gone for three months.

During the shortening spring nights the mermaid sat on the rocks at the Needle's Eye. When she sang, the fulmars and jackdaws which cawed on the rocks were silent, the moon grew pale — unlike her sisters, for at their song the moon turned red and the stars dripped blood upon the water.

At the end of June there was a great storm. The sands of the Solway were stirred and Barnhourie Bank shifted. A few days later the young seaman returned.

The sea was still rough and the crescent moon showed briefly

between ragged tails of dark cloud. The captain of the lugger kept his eyes on the beacons of Southerness and Heston Island, and the diamond glittering on the summit of Criffel.* The wind roared in the rigging, the waves whipped across the deck. No-one knew that Barnhourie Bank had shifted further west than had ever been known before. The lugger was into the broken water before they even saw it. Swiftly the captain flung the helm across and called on his crew to trim the sails. But the following wind drove them onward, and barely a minute later, with a massive lurch, the keel struck the sandbank. Briefly the lugger lifted on the crest of a wave, then struck again, swung wildly as the sea caught her on the beam, and settled with a final splitting shudder on the clinging bank of sand.

The waves broke clear across the sails and soon they were hanging in shreds. The yard-arm snapped like a splinter and fell across the rail. In the wash that swept the deck the captain and other members of the crew were carried away. For a while the young seaman clung to the rigging and the broken spar, then his grip was broken and he, too, was flung into the wild water.

His cries were instantly swallowed up in the wind, but they reached the ears of the mermaid, who sat with streaming hair on the rocks beneath the Needle's Eye. Her own cry answered his. In a moment she had slipped into the foaming sea and was making her way through the curling masses of water towards the treacherous sandbank.

Already the lugger was being broken up. When she reached him the young seaman was unconscious, tumbling over and over along the sandbanks of Barnhourie. With her slim arms about his waist she bore him to the leaping surface of the sea. He coughed salt water, and the sweet air struggled into his lungs. Soon he was breathing, his dark head lolling on her breast. As consciousness returned they were still a mile from land. He felt her arms, her long hair trailing about his face, the strong sweep of her tail.

Soon they were ashore, on the foaming rocks by the Needle's Eye. From the blackness of the sea the waves bore in and climbed hungrily up the rocks as if to pluck them back. The roaring south-west wind struck cold through his heavy, sodden clothing. They moved to a small cave nearby, and there, on a bed of bracken, out of the wind, they passed the remainder of the night.

* Criffel is the highest mountain in the district and stands just above the shore. A large diamond is said to shine from the summit in rough weather to give a lead to seamen.

11

The stars moved round, the tide swelled and sank back, and at length the first light of morning showed in the sky. There was barely enough water in which to swim. Bidding her young lover a reluctant farewell, the mermaid slithered to the shore. Like an eel in a marsh, she splashed and squirmed for a mile, desperately trying to reach deeper water before the tide was gone altogether. At length she succeeded. From the shore the curly-headed sailor saw her rise and vanish like a porpoise, then rise again and splash briefly in the early sunlight.

Beyond her, its mast smashed, already a hulk on the sandbank, lay the wreck of the lugger. Caught in the long, long webs of stake-net, two or three hundred yards off-shore, he saw and recognised the body of one of his shipmates. With the water to his calves he splashed out and brought the man ashore. Then, choosing to wade rather than climb the crags, he splashed half a mile along the shore until he came to a steep meadow. From deep water the mermaid saw him, a tiny figure, climb through the banks of bushes and shrubs and at length vanish above the rim of the hill.

He had fallen in love with her, and throughout the summer he returned to the little cave by the Needle's Eye. For whole days he neglected his work, and he and the mermaid lay among the wild flowers, with the lichen-yellow crags above them, the birds swooping overhead, and the fresh wind blowing in from the Solway. So completely did she trust him that she stayed while the tide retreated, until the miles of bare sand stretched out from the shore to mingle with the sky against the hazy, mountainous Cumbrian shore twenty miles away.

Sometimes they swam in the glassily calm or wind-rippled pools the tide had left in the shingle beneath the rocks, and she laughed at how clumsy he was, though in fact he swam well. Then he left her stranded and walked back across the sand until he relented and carried her to the grassy hillside in his arms, her long tail gleaming and shining in the sunlight. They were idyllically happy.

But at length he had to return to the sea once more. There was no money, and though he could always get food from the land and sea, his wife and children were becoming ragged and needy. For one last beautiful September day they lay together above the shore. Then he turned away and began to climb the track that he had made for himself towards the summit of the cliffs. Heartbroken the young mermaid slid into the warm autumn sea. Neither looked back, they could not bear it.

The following afternoon, at high tide, he sailed once more from Kippford, bound for Whitehaven and a ship that was to take him to the Americas.

The following April the mermaid's baby was born. He was a beautiful child, with his father's dark curls and merry manner, and his mother's black eyes, webbed fingers and long silver tail. From the first he could swim like a fish.

The young seaman was away for twenty months. It was May when his schooner returned from the West Indies. They had traded among the islands and done well. Alas on the return voyage a fever had broken out and a number of the seamen, including the captain, had died. But now in the first light of dawn the sailors, brown as monkeys, gathered in the shrouds and on deck and looked out once more towards the Cumbrian shore. They had all bought trinkets and presents for their children and loved ones. Their kit bags were already packed in the foc'sle. They looked forward very much to being home. On the port side the Scottish seamen gazed across the Solway to the distant mountains of Galloway.

The mate was on the bridge as they drew in towards St Bees Head. He was a man who had joined the ship during the voyage and did not know the coast well. Sails set, green bow-wave curling as they sped through the dancing waves the last few miles to home, he drove her full upon a submerged outcrop of ragged rocks. For a full third of her length the bottom timbers were ripped open. Instantly water flooded into the holds. The suck of the waves carried the schooner back off the rocks into deep water. Within minutes she was floundering. Then she was gone. In the swirl that remained on the surface a single ship's boat spun slowly round and round, crowded with survivors. The young Dalbeattie sailor was not among them.

Deep in the Solway off Barnhourie Banks, a second time his cries reached the ears of the mermaid. Leaving her baby son in safety, she swam off in a panic of haste. The rippled sands sped by beneath her, with weedy rocks and fish, and the barnacled ribs of old wrecks. But it was a long swim and nearly two hours had passed before she reached the scene of the tragedy. Two or three drowned sailors floated by her, drifting slowly in the eddying currents above the banks of sand. She passed them without caring. Then there before her, on its side, lay the wreck of the lovely schooner, the sails still set, but torn, and the mainmast spars broken.

Desperately she hunted through the watery cabins for her lover, but there was no sign. Then she quartered the whole area of seabed round about, her tail glinting in the moving fingers of sunlight, but he was not there either. She stopped and listened, but all sounds and signals from him had ceased. Then she knew that he was dead.

For many hours she searched on, while the long day passed. At last she knew that there was no chance of finding him there, so far from her own banks, for the tricks of the tides were unknown to her. Slowly, distressed, she returned to her son at Barnhourie.

The following morning at low water, rising from the clear green depths of her home to look towards the Galloway shore, she saw a huddled bundle dumped by the tide far away across the miles of dappled sand. It was too far off to distinguish, it could have been a heavy skein of seaweed, and yet she knew, at once, that it was not. She swam to the edge of the sandbank, and pulling herself from the water struggled across the wet brown sand, leaving a shallow trench in her wake. As she drew close she saw his dark monkey-jacket and wide seaman's trousers. Then at last she was with him. He looked very young, and as handsome as ever, as though he was asleep. She knew what she must do.

The tide was flooding, brimming white-edged across the sands with the speed of a running man. Soon it was about them, and in less than an hour she had brought him to the shore. Then, from the hillsides about the Needle's Eye, she gathered specific herbs and wild spring flowers and weed from the shore rocks. Carefully she mixed and crushed them, and then pressed them between the young man's lips. Her tears fell upon his eyes, the clear, saltless tears of a mermaid.

With a deep, convulsive sigh, he began to breathe, and in a little while his eyes opened.

He was weak, but lying on the bank in the warm May sunshine, soon his strength began to flow back. And at length they lay once more in each other's arms among the flowers beside the Needle's Eye.

Although he lived, however, he was not as he had been before. He had drowned, and the mermaid's love and power were unable to restore him to his full humanity. Instead, as they descended to the water and the tide washed about his legs, he felt a thrill that he had never known. She left his side and plunged into the sea. Without a thought he followed her, gliding through the sunlit bases of the waves as no man had ever swum before.

Down in the clear depths beyond Barnhourie, in the mermaid's world, he found his young son. And when daylight was fading all three swam back to the rocks at the Needle's Eye, and looked out towards the distant lights of Southerness and the stars shining above the glinting waves of the Solway.

Occasionally he returned to the land, for he was anxious about his

14

children. The owners of the schooner, however, were caring for his family, and a year or two later his pretty wife remarried.

Down in the depths of the sea, never growing old, the mermaid and the young Dalbeattie sailor had many children, all with long silver tails like their mother, and curly hair and merry ways like their father. They were very happy. And as the years passed they grew famous among the fishermen and seamen of the Solway, for warning them in storms, and guiding them from danger on the treacherous sandbanks of Barnhourie.

Billy Marshall -
King of the Galloway Tinklers

"Can you jas to stariben?
Can you lel a kosht?
Can you besh under a bor?
Can you kel the bosh?
Misto! Romani-chal,
Del les adre his mui!
S' help me, diri datchen,
You can kur misto,"
Said the Romani chai to the Romani rai.*

'Romano Lavo-Lil' — George Borrow

Billy Marshall — tinkler, gipsy chief, the Caird of Barullion, king of the randies, claimed by some as the last of the Pictish kings — was commonly accepted to be 120 years old when he died on 28th November, 1792. Many believed that he was older than this, and he himself sometimes claimed that he was born in 1666. In almost every respect he was a remarkable man, and many parishes have claimed the dubious honour of his birth in a gipsy encampment: the most likely, however, seems to be Minnigaff in the Stewartry. He was married seventeen times, most notably to Flora Maxwell, the main prototype of Meg Merrilees, and had many other liaisons in addition. His offspring were very numerous — the precise number is not known, but may be imagined, since three or four were born after his hundredth year.

As a young man he enlisted in the army, and at the age of eighteen was a mercenary fighting with William of Orange at the Battle of the Boyne. He enlisted with the Scots Greys and served in a number of

* "Can you go to prison?
Can you gather sticks?
Can you sit under a hedge?
Can you play the fiddle?
Well done! Gipsy man,
Give it to him in the face!
So help me, dear father,
You can fight well,"
Said the Gipsy girl to the Gipsy gentleman.

16

campaigns. More than once he was in Flanders under Marlborough. Seven times, altogether, he enlisted or was pressed into the army — and deserted as often. His principal reason for leaving was that he wished to be home in Galloway for the great Keltonhill Fair, the highlight of the gipsies' year. He claimed, and there is no reason to disbelieve it, that he attended every summer, without once being absent, for more than a hundred years. The tale is told that once being stationed in Flanders he entered the tent of a senior officer who came from the Stewartry — a McGuffog of Rusko — and enquired whether he had any messages he wished carrying to friends back home. When, with some surprise, the officer asked him why, Private Marshall informed him that the Keltonhill Fair was at hand and he planned, as always, to be there. The officer laughed, knowing his reckless character, but took no steps to have him arrested, since they were so far from home. The following roll-call he was gone, and duly turned up at the Marshalls' encampment in time for the fair.

He was in his early forties, though seeming more like a young man in his twenties, when finally he quit the army and returned to the tinklers. Shortly afterwards he became king, and according to strong tradition, it was brought about by a bloody and murderous act. One day, in private, he bought from a visitor or junior member of the clan a fine knife, which he had purchased at the fair in Ayr the year before and was easily recognisable. That night he used the knife to murder one of his wives and Isaac Miller, at that time the tinkler king, since they had indulged in some amorous adventure. The following morning, by chance, the previous owner of the knife went to rouse the king in his tent, and found him lying on a pallet greatly messed with blood. His

body had been stabbed many times, and the long knife lay among the bedding beside him. Realising his implication he took the knife away. With the evidence gone it was given out that the king had killed himself, and he was buried secretly in the hills, in the vicinity of Cairnsmore of Fleet. The murder may have been planned some time in advance, since for a while Billy had been hinting at a close relationship with the chief on his mother's side. In any case, he then assumed the position, and maintained it magnificently for between seventy and eighty years.

Billy Marshall was ambitious, and a year or two after his election he determined to extend his territories, which ran from the Brig-end of Dumfries to the Braes of Glen App.* He sought to drive further to the north-west, but at the Newton of Ayr he was driven back by an army of tinkers from Argyle or Dumbarton, supported, he afterwards claimed, by Irish sailors and Kyle colliers. Many of the Marshalls' ponies and donkeys were driven into the river and drowned, and in the retreat they were compelled to abandon great quantities of baggage and equipment — tools, creels, cooking utensils, crockery, pigs, poultry, pots and pans, horns, tents, blankets, and so on. More important, several of the clan were killed, others badly wounded, and some disappeared. Reinforcements arrived, however, and a pitched battle was fought somewhere near Alloway Kirk. Both sides claimed the victory for this, but so great was the loss and distress that Billy Marshall's territorial ambition was duly curbed, and for many years comparative peace reigned between the rival clans.

The Marshalls and other tinklers were distinctive among the folk of Galloway. Though commonly clad in old clothes, they wore them with a certain air. Many liked to adorn themselves with a bright scarf at the throat or waist, a nosegay, or some bright trinket — familiar in the dress of later gipsies. Billy, it is said, customarily wore a wristlet of lamprey skins. They lived, of course, in encampments, moving from site to site with the seasons, and as local fairs, grazing, whim, and their changeable fortunes dictated. Alone, at festivals, the Marshalls sometimes painted their faces with ruddle — perhaps a direct link with their Pictish past.

Billy's personal trade was that of a horner, making all sorts of spoons, beakers, combs and ornaments.† He also made bagpipes, flat-irons, brass and silver brooches, tins, besoms and bee skeps: the years of the tinklers as tin and tool workers and repairers of pots and pans, were yet to come. Also, though it is not known with what degree of

---

* A common phrase meaning from end to end of Galloway. Glen App lies to the north-east of Loch Ryan.
† Several examples of his work are to be seen in Kirkcudbright Museum. Principal among them is a fine horn beaker, with a delicate twist handle at the top. It is engraved 'W x M 115 1788': his initials, age and the date. The 'x' is a personal mark, mentioned later.

success, the gipsy chief tried his hand as a coiner. And he dealt in horses.

These, generally, were the legitimate activities of the tinklers, and upon them they depended for their living. In addition, however, there were the lawless pursuits that often landed them in jail, or on prison ships that transported them to the colonies. For Billy's followers were thieves and pickpockets, highway robbers, cattle thieves, poachers and smugglers.

At Keltonhill Fair, rather over a mile from Castle Douglas, the gipsies moved with familiar ease among the thronging booths. They were there with horses, ponies and cattle; up to a hundred tricks to cover a defect. The tinkler women, with deft brown fingers, stole from the stalls and removed scarves, kerchiefs, pins and wallets from the fair-goers. The men, with sharp knives, sliced the thongs of purses and were gone into the swirling crowd. And at some time during the day, Billy Marshall would be found in his round-topped tent, on the ground or the back of a cart, where they camped at Bridge of Dee a mile away. There he sat, receiver of stolen goods extraordinary, with two or three of the tinklers' swarms of dogs — half mastiff, half lurcher — lying nearby, and the ground and his pallet strewn with takings. It was said that anyone who had been robbed, bold enough to make his way to the tent at this time, would in a good-humoured way be asked to pick his belongings from the pile: there was so much that a single wallet or cane was never missed. It was Billy's delight to cause a ruction in the drinking tents. Sending his followers inside to inflame the ensuing trouble, he bent beneath the loaded drinking table from outside and sent it crashing to the ground, with a fine spray of beer and splintering of glasses and bottles, bringing the whole assembly into a turmoil.

He was deeply involved with the smuggling trade, and friendly with Captain Yawkins, the most notorious of the smuggling skippers. Often Billy Marshall was there to meet him when the 'Black Prince' sailed into Ravenshall, Balcary Bay, or one of the other smugglers' coves. Sometimes they sat in Dirk Hatteraick's Cave, yarning, drinking and smoking in the lamplit gloom, while the boat was discharged, casks were lowered on ropes, the pigeon holes filled with liquor, and on the beach swarthy lingtowmen loaded ponies for transport inland. Strings of horses were at his command. Not just four or five, but up to eighty might be seen wending their way through the Marshalls' territory, bearing the Isle of Man tea, spirits and tobacco to Edinburgh and the markets of the Clyde valley.*

* See Billy Marshall and 'The Fairy Pipers of Cairnsmore' in 'Smuggling in the Solway'.

Billy Marshall was one of the most famous leaders of the Levellers in the 1720's. Along with the poor farmers and crofters, the tinklers grazed their animals on the moorlands, and resented their fencing off by the improving landlords. They joined in bands to knock down the new dykes. Billy led a large force of farmers and land workers, as well as his own tinklers. With a wealth of military training behind him, he drilled them in the fields and led them to quiet hillsides for rifle practice. It suited him not to drive the dyke-building labourers away, for in· them he found a ready market for the raw spirit his men were distilling in caves and shielings on the Still Brae, among the mountains nearby.*

In common with many gipsies — and good-blooded Scotsmen — he liked the whisky himself, and hearing it once denounced as slow poison, is said to have remarked: "Aye, well it maun be damned slow, for I ha'e been drinkin' it for a hunner years, an' I'm livin' yet."

A man of necessity so much on the move, he had many homes, ranging from cottage and tent to caves and shelters where he could rest overnight. He spent quite a lot of time in Minnigaff, where he may have been born, for in the market and district there was good trading. There was a time, it is said, when every second cart and tumbril that rattled along the rough road to the town belonged to the Marshall gang. The location suited him well, for it lay between the smugglers of Wigtown Bay and the mountains where many of his followers lived, and into which he could vanish when he was in trouble. Rarely did he leave his people in Minnigaff with more than a couple of companions, but the following day would find him escorted by a gang of thirty or forty from another settlement.

It was well known that Billy headed 'a body of lawless banditti'; and many would have agreed with the man who wrote that 'with the exception of intemperate drinking, treachery, and ingratitude, he practised every crime which is incident to human nature, including those of the deepest dye.' But he had many generous, humorous, redeeming features also, high among which were his impudence, reckless flaunting of the law, and wonderful sense of style. Although he was notorious, he was regarded with an alarmed admiration by the people of Galloway. Many anecdotes surround him. How far they are true we will never know, but undoubtedly he was of the stuff from which legends are made.

On one occasion a Mr Douglas, of Little Park on the Palnure Burn, was returning home in the evening when he was astonished to be

* See Billy Marshall in 'The Levellers'.

20

passed on the rough road by seven racing, shrieking women, pursued by Billy, brandishing a large knife and clad in nothing but his shirt. They were his wives. For a moment he paused to speak to Mr Douglas, observing with simple regret: "I wonder that they canna agree; I'm sure there's no' that mony o' them."

The most famous of his wives was Flora Marshall. Billy said of her: "I'd raither hae yin rake o' Flora thro' Ayr Fair than a' the ithers put thegither." Another was called Langteethy. One day as she was going along the road she came upon two men trying to place a huge granite stone on top of a dyke. For a time, with growing disdain, she watched their efforts. Finally she laid down her bundle and crossed to the dyke. Crouching, she held out her forearms, saying with scornful brevity, "Lay't there." With some effort the men managed to do so. Then she straightened and set the stone on top of the dyke where they wanted it. As she took up her bundle again she called from the road: "Ye lazy good-for-naethin's; ye're no worth yer meat!" Then, breaking blithely into song, she continued her journey.

Whilst generally easy-going among the Marshalls he led, there was no doubt that Billy was king, and when necessary he made his feelings known very forcefully. As he was going along the road one day he met a poor tramp in considerable distress. When he asked the trouble, the tramp told him that he had been set upon by two gipsies, who had beaten him for no reason only minutes before. Dragging the tramp with him, Billy set off in pursuit, and soon came upon the two men, both Marshalls, the only cowards in the gang. First Billy made the tramp beat them in return, then cutting a strong ash stick from the hedge, he thrashed them all the way back to the camp.

On another occasion, as must have happened frequently, his wives were quarrelling. They were a small party at the time, descending a hill road somewhere in Kells. The bickering had gone on for hours, he had had enough. More than that, two were picking on Flora, and hardy though she was, this time she was getting the worst of it. Suddenly overcome with impatience and anger, Billy flung down his load, and with an oath seized one by the legs and the scruff of the neck and pitched her headlong into a deep quagmire at the side of the road. Whether or not they tried to rescue her is not related, but in any event the quarrelsome woman drowned.

One wintry night, with the clouds full of snow, the tinkler chief came to a lonely clachan, and calling at the largest house asked for shelter until the morning. Not wanting such a disreputable character beneath his roof, the landlord refused. Hot words were exchanged. Then flaring up in anger, Billy Marshall threatened to set fire to the house. The landlord roused all the strong young men in the surrounding cottages and they pursued the tinkler across open ground until he found his way barred by a loch. The men were closing in. Despite the bitterness of the night, Billy took to the water, but as he did so, one of the pursuers caught hold of his jacket. The icy loch swirled about their knees. Dropping his head, Billy Marshall bit the young man's thumb right off. Taking it with him as a souvenir, he made out into deep water, and in the darkness swam to safety.

Travelling on horseback down a remote stretch of the Edinburgh road, a young McCulloch from Ardwall was approached by a hunched beggar. Looking up sideways the beggar whined, "What's the time, sir?" But the sing-song voice and crippled physique did not for a moment fool the young gentleman. "But is it not my old friend Billy Marshall?" he said. For a moment Billy did not recognise the young man, but discovering that it was the son of his good friend from Ardwall, the stoop vanished. Reaching into his pocket he produced a whistle and blew a shrill blast. Up and down the road hidden figures emerged from ditches and behind bushes. Summoning a trustworthy man, Billy instructed him to accompany the young traveller to the inn that was his destination, and ensure that he arrived safely.

He was a canny man. Once when he was at a farm, busily engaged in carving a set of horn spoons, the question of strength arose and the farmer challenged him to a wrestling match. Before a crowd of the farmer's friends they took off their jackets and set to. Very soon Billy was vanquished, flat on his back on the ground. The farmer was very pleased with himself, for Billy was a stocky, powerful man, and of course well known in the district. A while later, as he was leaving, the tinkler chief challenged the farmer to have another wrestle. Almost immediately, as they took their stances, strong legs set well apart, the farmer found himself flung to the ground — three times in a row. He was very surprised and asked, "Why couldn't you do that before?" "Ah, well," Billy replied, "ye hadna peyed me for the spunes then."

Frequently Billy advised those he met to "tak' care o' their han's", by which he meant to ensure that they did not dishonour the families from which they came. His own hand was notable by displaying a deeply lined cross upon the palm. This was a distinguishing feature of many of the Marshalls and his own descendants. Billy was proud of it, and used the cross as a personal mark on some of his hornware.

The cross is, of course, a symbolic figure also, and the tinklers were deeply superstitious people. The Marshalls, however, did not accept the gipsy tradition that the cross was a mark set against them by God, as a permanent reminder that it was a gipsy who had forged the nails for the Cross.

As a young gentleman, travelling with older companions, James McCulloch of Ardwall met Billy Marshall briefly in 1789, when he was 117 years of age. In his own account he describes how driving in a carriage to Bargaly in the Palnure Glen, they passed close to the old tinkler's home three hundred yards above the Mill Burn falls. They called, to renew an acquaintance, and Billy walked firmly to the carriage. His eyes were not quite what they had been, but upon being introduced to the young man, Billy shook his hand and admonished him, as has been said, to 'take care of his hand, and do nothing to dishonour the good stock of which he was come' — for the tinkler chief had always been on good terms with the Ardwall family. The older gentlemen then gave Billy a sum of money, which he graciously accepted. Returning between ten and eleven o'clock that evening they found the gipsy encampment singing wanton songs in the wood, having bought drink with the unexpected windfall. Billy approached out of the darkness, and in reply to observations about his age said that he feared none of them would see their beds that night, for they were well set in their merry-making and were taking to the countryside in the morning.

He died in Kirkcudbright. When in his last illness someone suggested that he might at last be approaching his time, he replied: "Na, na; every pin in my auld tabernacle's o' richt gude aik; feint a fear o' me this time yet." So great was the interest, not to say respect, in which he was held, that no less a person than the Earl of Selkirk, who had assisted him in old age, acted as chief mourner at the great funeral, and with his own hand lowered the gipsy's head into the grave.* He was buried in St Cuthbert's Churchyard, on a wooded hillside on the outskirts of Kirkcudbright. The headstone, only two and a half feet square, is plain and dignified, easily seen among the larger, red sandstone memorials which surround it. The inscription, deeply chiselled and dark on the plain stone, bears no religious message. It reads, simply:

*There is some disagreement about this. It is believed that the honour of laying his head in the grave would rightly have been claimed by one of the tinklers — indeed, that nothing else was imaginable.

The remains of
WILLIAM MARSHALL,
Tinker, who died
28th Novr 1792,
at the advanced age of
120 Years

On the back is a plain and distinctive scutcheon — two tup's horns above two spoons crossed.

Billy Gives Evidence*

A gang of the Marshalls, from several settlements, were on a foraging expedition, and in the afternoon they killed a cow. It was cleaned where it lay, and the carcass was divided between the parties. Leaving the tinklers from his own encampment to carry the bloody haunch home, Billy set off along the road in another direction, for he had business to attend to.

On the way he encountered a gamekeeper, who previously had attempted to have Billy imprisoned for poaching. Even at the sight of each other they bristled like a couple of dogs. Violence was not far behind their heated exchange of words, and in the inevitable fight that followed, the gipsy killed the gamekeeper. He was lugging the body by the jacket, in the act of dumping it over the dyke, when it occurred to him that the keeper's jacket was much better than the one he was wearing. Propping the dead man up for a moment, he stripped off the jacket, then tumbled him over into the rocky bracken behind.

The jacket fitted him to a T. Smoothing the lapels, he greatly admired his smart new appearance. Then, transferring the bits and pieces from his pockets, he set off along the road, leaving his old jacket slung across the dyke.

His business detained him, and he had not gone more than a couple of miles from the scene of the murder when he was overtaken by darkness. Though there would have been a grand feast at the encampment that evening, he decided not to continue, and put up for the night at a common lodging house in a village.

Shortly after his fight with the gamekeeper, a tramp came along the same road. Seeing Billy's jacket on the dyke he put it on, and left

*This story was told a century after Billy's death by a Galloway tinkler.

24

his own ragged affair in its place. It was a little windfall for him. And as
luck would have it, he put up for the night in the same lodging house as
Billy Marshall. Seeing the much newer coat that Billy had left on the
back of a chair in the parlour, the tramp made a point of rising early,
and with the gamekeeper's jacket on his back, set off on his travels.

Discovering his smart jacket gone and the old one in its place, Billy
was perturbed. He did not like to enquire too closely, however, and
having made his breakfast, set off for the encampment.

The tramp had not gone very far when he was overtaken by two
sheriff's officers who had come out from Dumfries to investigate the
gamekeeper's murder. There seemed little doubt of his guilt, for he was
wearing the keeper's jacket and his own had been found at the scene of
the crime.

He was taken to court, and though the evidence was circumstantial,
he had no established reputation and no respectable friends to speak
for him. The jacket alone, it seemed, was going to be sufficient to hang
him. In vain did he protest the unlikely truth. Where, they asked him,
was the coat he had taken from the dyke, and where was the man to
whom it belonged?

Then from the back of the court stepped Billy Marshall, the old
soldier, resplendent in knee breeks and a long blue coat with huge
silver buttons. Presenting himself to the judge with a military salute,
he craved their honours' pardon. What his friend the tramp had told
them, he said, was perfectly correct. He was the man whose jacket had
been left on the dyke. This was the very garment in his hand. In every

25

respect his evidence corroborated the tramp's tale. He had been walking along the road on a matter of business when he found a good jacket discarded on the wall. He had taken it and left his own behind. That same night his new jacket had been stolen — he wished to make it plain to their honours that he pressed no charges — and his old one was left in its place. It had been a complete mystery to him until that moment. If their worships would send his friend and himself to the plantations simply for lifting a discarded jacket from the wall, then so it must be, though he had come forward of his own accord from the back of the court to give evidence.

Everything he said was incontrovertible, and the tinkler chief was not on trial. The court had no option but to release the tramp, who without Billy's intervention may very well have ended on the gallows.

A similar story was told of Billy Marshall by Sir Walter Scott.

It was the gipsy chief's practice to walk the highroads on the chance of meeting a traveller who might with a little prompting be persuaded to part with his purse and valuables. One day he encountered the Laird of Bargaly* on the high hill road between Carsphairn and Dalmellington. The laird put up a struggle, during which Billy Marshall lost his remarkable bonnet, and was obliged in the end to escape, leaving it lying on the road behind him. Bargaly hurried off to round up some helpers and apprehend the villain. While he was away the farmer of Barstoberick, an entirely respectable man, came along the road, and seeing the bonnet lying on the ground, picked it up. Briefly he examined it. Since the bonnet was clean and there was no owner in the vicinity, he put it on his head and continued his journey.

He had not gone far when he was seized by the Laird of Bargaly and his assistants from nearby cottages. There was no doubt of his guilt, for the bonnet was unmistakable, and like the gipsy chief the farmer was a square, powerful figure. Despite excellent references to his character, Bargaly was convinced of the farmer's guilt and persisted in the charges.

When the case came to court, things indeed looked black for the unfortunate man. Then Billy Marshall rose and pushed his way to the front of the court. Taking the large and strangely-shaped bonnet from the bench he pulled it on his head, and thrust his face towards the laird.

* I suspect Scott has got the name wrong, since Billy Marshall and the Laird of Bargaly lived within a mile of each other in the Palnure Glen, and for some time at least, the tinkler chief was in receipt of favours from the laird.

"Look at me, sir," he said, "and tell me, by the oath you have sworn — am not *I* the man who robbed you between Carsphairn and Dalmellington?"

Bargaly was amazed and thrown into confusion by his sudden appearance. "By heaven!" he exclaimed. "You are the very man!"

Billy Marshall turned to the judge and held out his hands. "You see, sir, what a memory the man has. If you were to put the bonnet on your own head, my Lord, I have no doubt he would swear that it was you who had attacked him on the road."

The court laughed. The Laird of Bargaly was both mocked and condemned, and the farmer from Barstoberick was unanimously acquitted.

During these proceedings, it is said, Flora Marshall contrived to position herself behind the judge's chair and detach the hood from his gown. For this crime, together with her presumptive guilt as a gipsy, she was banished to New England, from where she never returned.

The White Snake

The mote of Dalry stands on the rising east bank of the River Ken, between the town and a deep pool known as the Boat-Weel. Long ago, it is said, a great crock of gold lay at the bottom of this pool, protected from treasure seekers by a devil — but that has nothing to do with the present story. The mote is surrounded, save on the river side, by a ditch, and rises twenty feet above it. Originally, when it was built in the twelfth century, it was surmounted by a wooden look-out post, with walls high and stout enough to deter attackers. Now it is reduced to a strange, circular hill with regular sloping sides and a flat top thirty-five yards across, thick with bracken — a splendid view-point above the beautiful valley of the Ken.

Back in the mists of time, it is said, a great white snake, like a dragon, took possession of the mote. It curled itself around the hill, cradling its body comfortably in the ditch. It was so long that its tail trailed down the hillside into the river at one end, while at the other its head floated in the Boat-Weel, gazing with contemplative reptilian eyes at the frightened people as they hurried past on their business.

Every day, at the same hour, the snake raised its head to the top of the mote and rested its throat in the soft bracken while the people poured bucket after bucket of milk into its mouth. This was followed by a few sheep or one or two cattle for the main course. If they forgot, or were short, then the snake just uncurled itself from the mote and slid up through the clachan. Reaching its long neck over into the fields and through cottage doors, it crunched up a few villagers until it was satisfied.

With such rich feeding the snake grew and grew. Soon it was so big that it did not bother to chew up the sheep and people at all, but just swallowed them whole. Anything smaller than a full-grown ox went straight down its throat.

One day a local blacksmith by the name of Michael Fleming discovered that the snake had unearthed his wife from the churchyard and devoured her. He was very angry, for he had gone to a lot of trouble and expense just the previous day to have her nicely buried. Things had gone far enough, he decided. It was time to put a stop to the carry on.

28

So he made himself a suit of armour, covered all over with long
sharp knives. Like a hedgehog's quills they lay close to his sides, but
when he began to struggle and fight they erected themselves and stuck
straight out as sharp spikes. Arming himself with a pair of long gully
knives, he clashed down to the mote to confront the snake. Looking
from their windows the villagers saw him pass by. Clearly something
was in the air. Hurriedly they put up the shutters and locked and bolted
all the doors.

The snake was asleep when the blacksmith reached it. He gave it a
kick to wake it up, but it did not stir. Then he gave it a sharp poke
between the scales with one of the long knives. Blinking, the white
snake raised its head from the Boat-Weel and gazed at him sleepily from
beneath lowered lids. Then seeing his threatening gestures it woke up
fully and roared. And the next moment, before Michael Fleming could
move, it had darted its head towards him and he was tumbling down
the long, hot gullet towards its deafening stomach.

For a moment, when at last his dizzy fall was ended, he thought he
would be stifled with the moist heat. It was utterly black, rumbling like
an avalanche. Then he began to struggle, and all the razor-sharp blades

29

stuck up from his armour. Like a warrior he slashed about him with the long gully knives. The snake roared and threshed about until the Boat-Weel was lashed into foam and threequarters empty, and great gouts of water sloshed over the thatch of the houses in the village.

At length it lay dead, and the blacksmith carved his way out into the sweet sunshine. Then the villagers came creeping from their houses. When they saw the great snake lying lifeless in slack white coils all up and down the banks of the river, they raised a loud cheer. And when Michael Fleming had taken off his bloody armour, they raised him to their shoulders and carried him in triumph through the village.

Together the people of Dalry cut the snake into lengths and sent it down the river in a spate which followed shortly afterwards.

Some of its bones, they say, still lie among the ooze in the depths of Loch Ken.

Sealed with a Handshake

Many centuries ago, when family and clan feuds were endemic in the lands of the south-west, freebooters — rebels of the woods owing allegiance to no-one — threw in their hands with any group which offered them chance of gain, and by their daring and bloody reckless-ness often swung the tide of affairs. Certain bands of freebooters, growing strong, became raiders on the grand scale, and whole tracts of the country were threatened by their depredations. Sometimes for years, until united resistance was offered by the landowners or a major force was sent by the monarchy, the countryside and normal commerce declined into a state of anarchy.

One ruthless freebooter, by all accounts a scoundrel with endless cruelties to his discredit, was called Graeme. His name and reputation were reviled along the whole northern shore of the Solway.

On one famous occasion, however, he met his match. He had planned to plunder the castle and lands, not easily protected, of Gordon of Muirfad. Word of the projected raid travelled ahead of him and came to the ears of the old laird, who was not prepared to submit without a fight. Gathering all his friends and followers together, he prepared a great ambush for the company of freebooters.

It was a deadly repulse. Taken completely by surprise, many of the desperadoes were slain. Graeme himself was seriously wounded. But though his body was injured and gave him pain, much more so was his pride. And as Graeme with savage determination made good his escape, he vowed that soon he would be revenged upon the old laird who had so humiliated him.

He was not a man to wait upon the act. No sooner was he recovered than he made plans for the return raid, recruiting villains and raiders from far along the disputed lands.* The raid was anticipated, but so cleverly was the attack timed and executed that Muirfad was taken completely by surprise. There was barely time to retreat within the castle before Graeme and his outlaws were thundering at the doors. Then standing back and staring up at the stone walls, Graeme roared

* These were the border lands between England and Scotland that were almost perpetually under dispute and subject to incessant raids from either side.

his demands for admittance, uttering the most dreadful curses and threats.

Those within did not know what to do. The outlaws piled wood against the door and prepared to set fire to it. It seemed only a matter of time before they were within the walls. The old laird, hoping desperately that some deal might be made, called for a parley through the grille of the door. Graeme approached him. Muirfad was not really in a position to do much bargaining and soon an enormous sum of money was agreed upon, as a guarantee of present safety and future peace.

With unspeakable relief, for himself and all within the castle — women and children among them — the old man peered through the grille. Graeme came close, observing that since all was now satisfactorily concluded, they might as well be friends. He held out his hand. Apprehensively, fearing perhaps a knife or sword, the laird regarded it. His position was weak: to ignore the hand was to offer further insult. He stretched his arm tentatively through the door.

No sooner did their fingers touch, however, than Graeme seized the weaker hand in his own and quickly threw a noose of chain around the

S·McNEIL

wrist. Holding it tight, with the laird's shoulder pulled right to the door, he coupled the chain to an iron staple in the wall.

Laughing ferociously then, Graeme called for a brand and instantly set fire to the pile of brushwood and logs that was against the door. Gordon of Muirfad was burned alive, and the castle and all within it were destroyed.

The Devil
and the Highlandman

Tam Campbell was a Highlander and he jumped ship in Wigtown, for he fell for a girl of that part and they ran away together. They did not run very far, only to Glenluce. There Tam set himself and the girl up in a little cottage at Crows Nest Bay along the shore road, and took a job with the Glenluce blacksmith. Soon the girl married him, though he never liked her quite so well after that, and within the space of three or four years they had three or four children.

He was a big chap, with hairy arms the thickness of oak branches, but he was careless and easy-going, and had the slow soft speech of the part he came from. Always, from the start, he had a great liking for the drink, and soon got the reputation of being a bit wild, for with the drink and his easy-going ways he was always getting into trouble.

One night he was wending his way home from the inn. The shore road was deserted and he sang a quiet song or two to keep himself company. Every now and then he stopped to have another mouthful from his bottle, and look wonderingly at the moonlight rippling on the water as it flowed up over the sands from Luce Bay. Suddenly he was startled by what seemed like a black flash and the Devil appeared in the road a few yards away, between himself and the dunes. He was covered in shaggy hair and had a long pikestaff in his hand.

Now at the time the Devil had sent a great plague to the district. The people were dropping like flies. None of Tam's family had caught it, however. "All you want is a wee drop of Highland blood, and you'll be right as rain," Tam told his cronies in the inn. "And maybe a few drams, just to be on the safe side."

The Devil flourished his staff at the drunken young smith. "I'm going to blight you with the pox!" he cried dramatically. "Let that teach you not to make fun of me."

"Rubbish!" Tam said. Rubbing the neck of his bottle he passed it across.

The Devil took a drink, tossing his head back so that his black horns shone in the moonlight.

"Here, steady on," Tam said. "Leave a bit for me."

The Devil rubbed his lips with the back of his hand, wheezed, and passed the bottle back.

"I'll tell you what, then," he offered. "Fair play. You say I can't touch a Highlandman. I'll wrestle you for it."

The neck of the bottle smelt a bit sulphury. Tam rubbed it again on his sleeve before taking another mouthful.

"Na, na," he said. "That's not fair. I'll tell *you* what. I'll wrestle you for all the plague in Glenluce. If I lose you can give it to me," — for he knew fine that with his Highland blood and another half bottle or two he would throw it off with no trouble. "But if I win, then you tie it all up in a poke and give it to me right now."

Instantly the Devil agreed, for he was an arrogant fellow with complete faith in his own powers. He laid down his pikestaff and flexed his thin arms.

"Here, you'd better have another mouthful to set you up," Tam offered.

Again the Devil poured the flaming spirit down his throat.

Then they set to, both of them half drunk, for the Devil was not used to the fiery spirit they sold in that part. This way and that they staggered on the rough, moonlit road, locked in each other's arms. Then they were off the road, rolling in the sand dunes and down the beach into the edge of the sea. Feeling his hair all wet the Devil let go, and Tam, feeling the salt water cold against his back, let go also. Both panting, they retreated a few yards up the sands and sat down on two boulders.

"Well, I think I had you," the Devil said, when at last he could speak. "Do you give in?"

"Give in — me? Another minute and you were flat on your back!"

The Devil knew the truth of this and did not argue the point lest Tam should insist they took up where they had left off.

"A dead heat, then," he suggested.

Tam agreed.

"Something else," the Devil said, holding his hand out hopefully for the bottle, still somehow intact in Tam's inside pocket.

After another swig himself, Tam passed it over. The Devil poured the last couple of fingers down his throat and tossed the empty bottle against a rock where the broken glass would cut the children's feet.

"A piping contest, then," he said, for he was very proud of his piping. "How about that?"

"All right," Tam said, "but my pipes are in the house."

35

"No problem at all," said the Devil. He waved his hand in the air and suddenly a set of bagpipes appeared. "I don't know what they're like, mind," he added.

Rising to his feet he inflated the bag and forced the first droning notes with his elbow. He need have had no fear, the pipes were magnificent.

The Devil played first, pacing to and fro on the sand. The brilliant, dancing notes floated across the water to the ears of those people who were still out of their beds in the town. It was a wonderful performance.

Fully appreciating all the finer points that the untutored ear might miss, Tam listened, and when the Devil was finished greatly praised his playing. The Devil was pleased — indeed he was quite smug about it.

Then Tam took the pipes, warning him to play no dirty tricks with their tone. First he played a wild march that made the Devil's eyes shine, his nostrils flare, and his breast heave with martial passion. Then he played a merry dance. The Devil's face was transformed with delighted laughter. He swung his leg and clapped his hands and tapped the time with his hoof on a stone. To conclude Tam played a lament. The laughter left the Devil's face and in a minute the tears were coursing down his cheeks.

As the drunken blacksmith laid down the pipes the Devil rose and embraced him.

"Tam, Tam," he said. "My friend! You're a piper!"

Wiping the tears from his face the Devil turned up the bay to face Glenluce. Stretching his arms to their widest, he drew his gathering hands inwards across the countryside, and pushed something that seemed like a dark, swirling fog into a long canvas poke that appeared in his hand. He drew the neck together and bound it tight with a strand of hair from his tail. Then he handed the bag to Tam, light as a feather, but bulging and swelling with whatever moved inside.

Tam took it and stood waiting on the beach while the Devil collected his staff from the side of the road.

"There you are, my friend," the Devil said, "the plague. Goodbye. You may hear of me again."

Tam took the hairy hand that was extended towards him. Then the Devil reached towards the moon with his staff, and with a soft pop and a second flash of darkness, he was gone. A faint whiff of sulphur lingered for a moment in the sweet air that blew in from Luce Bay.

For a few minutes Tam sat on the rock, holding the bag that writhed so ominously in his hand, uncertain what to do with it. At length he decided that this was a job for the minister. Tucking in his shirt tails, he walked the mile or two back along the edge of the bay into Glenluce.

The minister was not at all pleased to be called from his bed at such an hour, especially by such a notorious drunk as the blacksmith's assistant. Even now he smelled of spirits. Standing on the doorstep Tam told his tale, while the minister looked askance at the ballooning poke in his hand. Telling him to wait there, the minister shut the door hastily and hurried upstairs to dress. Seizing the opportunity Tam ran along the road to the inn, where they were drinking late, and bought himself another bottle of whisky on the slate. Not wishing to create a bad impression he hurried back to the minister's door. Soon the incongruous pair were making their way swiftly along the moonlit lanes that led to Glenluce Abbey, for the minister felt that this was too dark an affair for him to deal with alone. As they approached the magnificent abbey the movement within the bag grew agitated, and Tam held it tightly in his hand.

A monk admitted them through the great doors, and when he heard the story called the abbot. The abbot led them down into the vaults where there was a grey chapel lit with candles and lanterns.* They were followed by what seemed a host of silent monks in white habits. It was very strange and holy, and Tam could feel the bottle of whisky pushing out the breast of his old jacket.

The abbot took the bag from him and laid it on the altar. Then taking the great abbey Bible, he began a tremendous series of readings and prayers to destroy the forces that moved within. It seemed as though the bag must burst asunder, and noises as of rushing wind and children's tears and confused subterranean screaming grew louder and louder. They reached a crescendo, and the monks prayed in unison, their deep voices rising above the unholy sounds that issued from the bag. And then the noises began to fade; the movements became less agitated. At length the bag lay still.

The prayers were concluded. The white procession, with the wide-eyed blacksmith and minister in its midst, left the chapel and rose to the abbey above. The abbot turned to Tam Campbell.

"The spirit is dead," he said. "Now take the bag whence you received it, leave it there, and tamper no more with Satan and the works of Hell. Things have turned out well on this occasion, but the Devil is ever among us, seeking whom he may devour."

* In a different version of this tale the plague is imprisoned in a casket by Michael Scott, the famous Border wizard, and locked away for ever in the dungeons of Glenluce Abbey.

As soon as he was alone in the streets of Glenluce, Tam uncorked the bottle and had a few good swallows to steady the shaking in his legs and recover some semblance of normality. Then he set off down the road as the abbot had directed him.

But as he walked above the shore in the early hours of the morning, he thought he detected a slight stirring within the bag in his hand. He stopped, and held the bag still. There was no mistake, for it moved again: it shivered, as with a tremulous laughter.

Tam was very angry. This time, he decided, he would deal with the spirit in his own way.

He was nearly at the spot where the Devil and he had wrestled, and dropping down to the shore he soon found the place where they had paced to and fro on the sand. Quickly he searched along the rim of the tide until he found a heavy stalk of seaweed. Then he carried the bag and the stalk up to the flat rock where the Devil had sat. The spirit within the bag was livening up, swelling and bulging once more; and above the soft noise of the wind and sea, Tam thought he could detect low laughter. It was too much! Pulling the bottle of whisky from his pocket he had another mouthful, just to keep himself going, then laying the bag on the flat stone, he poured the rest over the top — nearly threequarters of a bottle. Then, with the great stalk of seaweed, he set about it, giving the bag such a thrashing as had never been heard of before.

Dreadful cries and groans came from within, but Tam did not relent. Soon, once more, the bag lay still, but this time it was not good enough for Tam, and he continued with the thrashing. When the stalk of seaweed broke, he sprang up on the rock and jumped on the flattened bag, and pounded the heels of his old boots into it.

Then with another pop the Devil was beside him once more. Angrily Tam jumped down to face him, but before he could get his hands on the Devil's mane to teach him a lesson he would never forget, the Devil seized the bag, and vanished.

Tam stood alone on the seashore.

And at that very moment the last of the plague left the district. The babies and young wives and old men turned in their beds and breathed more easily, their fevers began to subside.

And from that time onward only once did the Devil dare to visit Glenluce while Tam Campbell lived. But that is another story.*

* See 'The Rope of Sand'.

In Cold Winters
when the Ice was Thick

The Seven Sons of Morrison

The winter was long and severe. The frost held for week after week with brilliant days and black bitter starlit nights. On the lochs of Galloway the curlers gathered for their bonspiels, and skaters with trays sold pies and hot potatoes.

On Edingham Loch, a mile from the present town of Dalbeattie, a match was in progress. The ice was thronged. Among the laughing, red-cheeked curlers were three families of Morrison, each of seven sons, from the neighbouring farms of Cocklick, Culloch and Drumlane. Beneath their boots the ice was thirty inches thick.

Daylight faded, it was time for everyone to return home. Pushing their stones, reluctantly, into the stiff rushes at the edge of the loch, they left the ice and began the walk back to their farms, through the deep snow that cloaked the little fields.

But before they had gone half a mile they heard the ice once more ringing with the cries of curlers, and looking back down the gentle slope beyond the rough hedges, saw that crowds of fairy revellers in clothes of green had taken their places now that the night was come. Their voices rang back from the hillside, merry and clear.

The curlers returned to the shore and watched. On the darkening ice the fairies were having a wonderful time. Goblets of wine were being quaffed. Fairy maidens with dancing eyes and flowing hair swept by on skates, filmy dresses fluttering behind them. Restlessly from the shore the young men wished to join in, but dared not.

Then one brother cried, "Lads, here's adventure, wha's game?" and buckling on his skates sped off across the ice to join the revellers. Not wishing to seem laggardly or miss out on anything, his brothers and kinsmen, all fine young fellows noted for their high spirits, soon followed him. All three sets of seven brothers joined the fairy throng in the middle of the loch. Yet strangely not one of their friends dared venture. All remained watching with envy from the shore.

Suddenly above the laughter and merry voices came a great crack, and from end to end of the loch the ice split open. In an instant the fairies had vanished and the twenty-one young Morrisons were plunged into deep black water. Almost before the watchers on the shore had realised it, they were gone. Thick ice floes covered the surface of Loch Edingham.

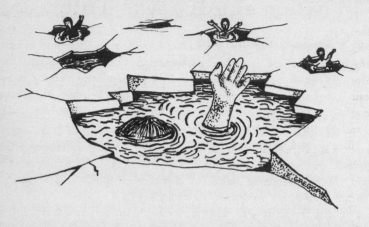

But afterwards, in succeeding centuries, travellers passing the loch near the midnight hour have seen the rippling water thronged with dancers clad in green, and among them the three times seven sons of Morrison on steeds of milk-white foam. Happily they gallop among their fairy fellows with spears of sedge and swords of rush. Before morning they have gone, no blade of grass crushed nor dew-drop spilled by the feet of their prancing steeds.

The Robber Laird with Nine Daughters

In ancient days a wild laird had spent his entire fortune in the construction of Cardoness Castle. Though the walls were magnificent, it was roofed with heather: there was money for no more. His neighbours were amused, and enemies set fire to it with flaming arrows. Seeking to fill his coffers once more, the laird joined a band of reivers — thieves and border raiders who acknowledged no law. He was as fierce as the best of them, and soon his chests were filled with gold and silver coin, overflowing with rich communion cups and ropes of pearl and other plunder.

Once he had enough he bade farewell to the band of robbers and retired to his great estate. The building was completed; his creditors —

those bold enough to insist — were paid; he was lord of all he surveyed.

Though everything should now have been happiness and plain sailing, it was not. He longed for a son, but as year followed year his wife presented him with an endless succession of daughters. There were nine of them — sometimes it seemed like ninety.

Then a tenth time his wife was with child, and yet again his hopes rose.

One morning in January, just before his wife's confinement, he burst into her room, and with the passionate ferocity of his reiving days informed her that if this time she did not present him with the son he desired, he would take herself and the baby and the other nine useless daughters, and drown the lot in the deep Black Loch on the estate. Then he would find himself a wife who knew how to have sons!

His wife was terrified, for she knew that he was perfectly capable of doing what he said. How great was her relief when this time her prayers were answered, and two or three weeks later the howdy (midwife) who was attending her held up a wriggling baby son.

The robber laird was delighted and his joy infected the whole neighbourhood. By way of celebration he ordered a great midwinter feast to be prepared on the thick ice of the Black Loch. Everyone was invited.

On a bright Sunday morning, with the air biting cold though the sun shone cheerfully, the festive crowds converged on the loch through the snowy trees. The laird was there with his wife and baby son, and all his daughters save one — who was ill and had to be left behind at the castle in charge of a nurse. Servants carried heavy salvers of roasted venison from the shore, ale was mulled by glowing braziers, musicians played, young couples danced, fat farmers' wives fell to the ice with shrieks of merriment.

Suddenly, when the gaiety and feasting were at their height, the ice snapped with a fearful ringing, splitting sound, and all those at the heart of the throng vanished from sight into the loch — the wicked laird, his wife and son, and every one of the daughters. For a moment, as guests scrambled madly for the safety of the shore, the faces and bonnets of the laird's family were glimpsed in the icy, tumbled water. But when they looked back from the snowy brink the loch was empty, save for the shattered grey ice and the remnants of the feast.

The entire estate fell to the single surviving daughter — one of those so contemptuously dismissed by the laird. Several years later, when the girl had grown into an attractive young woman, she married a man named McCulloch. Thus it was that the splendid castle and rich lands of Cardoness came into the hands of that great Galloway family.

FOOTNOTE

Cardoness was often called 'the castle of ill-luck'. Another traditional reason for this name is that the building of the castle exhausted the resources of three successive lairds, none of whom was able to finish it. The fourth managed to complete the walls, after which he was reduced to such poverty that he could not even afford to pay a man to gather heather for the roof. He had to pick it himself on Glenquicken Moor and carry it on his back all the way to Cardoness, then for months risk life and limb clambering about the high walls. He was not a very good workman, for every time it rained the roof leaked like a seive. Most of the time he lived in a little hut.

The Covenanters *

Blows the wind today, and the sun and the rain are flying,
    Blows the wind on the moors today and now,
Where about the graves of the martyrs the whaups are crying,
    My heart remembers how!

Grey recumbent tombs of the dead in desert places,
    Standing-stones on the vacant wine-red moors,
Hills of sheep, and the howes of the silent vanished races,
    And winds, austere and pure.

R. L. Stevenson

The story of the Covenanters, in retrospect at least, is romantic. The fabric of their history is woven of such strands that it is well-nigh irresistible: brave, simple Covenanters on the run in the heather; tremendous chases and flight through bog and swollen torrent; secret services in lonely cottage or hollow of the moor, with circling curlew and psalms rising on the wind; troops of dragoons, led by notorious officers, mounting the hillsides in pursuit; scores of martyrs shot in cold blood, unflinchingly true to their faith and pure ideals; moral declarations of war in market places by small, hungry bands of men, against the whoring, bloody-handed and absolute king; pitched battles between ragged, poorly-armed countrymen and government soldiers; leaders with a price on their heads.

More prosaically, it is the story of brave and good Scotsmen fighting for the freedom to worship God as they chose; the story of Presbyterian resistance to the pressure of government to force Episcopalianism upon them, if necessary with force of arms. Also, however, it must be confessed that from another point of view it is often a story of religious extremists who would die rather than bend, and unquestionably sought, when they were in a position to do so, to impress others into their belief with a force as intransigent as that they resisted. But although the accusations of intolerance, spiritual pride and fanaticism cannot be denied, there was also an austere passion, a fierce honour, and courage in the highest degree. From beneath the blanket of religious repression

* See 'The Pentland Rising'; 'The Wigtown Martyrs'; 'The Martyrs of Kirkconnel'.

and military rule of great cruelty, astonishing numbers rose to the heights of heroism.

The Covenanters wished to worship God freely and directly, unhindered by the intervention of king and bishop between man and his Creator: they wished their worship to be pure, based solely upon Holy Scripture, free from the contamination of ceremony, prayer-book, and an established form of service: they abhorred all form of religious patronage, and wished to appoint their own ministers. They did not wish, simply in order that the king might rule a united church in a united country, to be brought into line with Episcopal England.

The history, of course, is rooted in time, in the bleak and fiery doctrines of John Calvin and John Knox. The Covenanters themselves, however, were close to the heart of the religious and political turmoil of the seventeenth century — and so far as this account is concerned, primarily the 1680's. It was in the wild and independent south-west that the resistance to king and government, in religious matters, was most determined. Here, consequently, military pressure was most energetic — and ultimately savagely repressive.

It is necessary, I think, to look briefly at the earlier history. In 1618 the Five Articles of Perth were presented to the Scottish church. Among other matters, they insisted upon confirmation by bishops, kneeling at communion, and the observance of certain religious festivals — all of which smacked far too much of Roman Catholicism for the Presbyterians of Scotland. Seven years later, upon his accession to the throne, Charles I insisted upon an absolute monarchy, and it was primarily as the King of England that he looked north. In 1637, desiring to 'improve' the Scottish church and advised by Archbishop Laud, he introduced a Book of Canons, shortly to be followed by the famous Prayer-Book with its established forms of service and ritual, which caused a great explosion of anger throughout the country.

As a consequence the National Covenant was drawn up the following year, declaring that the purity and freedom of Scripture alone must be the central matter of religious services. Copies were sent about the country. From remote croft, manse and lodge, from every walk of life, people flocked to sign the Covenant. Many, showing an access of passion and zeal that was to be typical of the whole period, signed it with their own blood.

In November, 1638, a General Assembly of ministers and elders, many armed, met in Glasgow Cathedral. The Five Articles of Perth, the Book of Canons and Archbishop Laud's Liturgy were all condemned, and the bishops were deposed. Charles, under pressure, had given permission for the assembly, but this was open defiance. In view of the intractable position taken by each side, military action was inevitable.

Before the 'Bishops' War' broke out, however, the General Assembly of the Church of Scotland made compulsory the signing of the Covenant. Like the Roman Catholic Church, which it detested, the Church of Scotland would tolerate no heretics. Trouble increased on all sides. In England Charles found himself involved in civil war with the Puritans: on the borders the Presbyterians also faced Royalist forces: in the north-east of Scotland Episcopalians resisted the Covenant.

In England the war went badly for both sides. Royalists and Puritans sought help from Scotland. Unaccustomed to being wooed, in the end the Presbyterians did a deal with Cromwell. In return for compulsorily establishing Presbyterianism throughout England, Wales and Ireland, and rooting out popery and prelacy from the whole land, the Scots promised to send 20,000 men to aid the Puritan parliamentary party. This was the 'Solemn League and Covenant' of 1643.

It was at this juncture that many Scots, like the Marquis of Montrose, found themselves with divided loyalties. Politically it was impossible to remain loyal to the king and true to their religious ideals. The brilliant Montrose, of course, already a Covenanting leader, felt that the Scots were pressing their demands too far, and his loyalties lay with the king. Thus with Covenanting sympathies he led the Royalists to a series of magnificent and bloody victories in Scotland. But in September, 1645, with Scotland at his feet, the troubled and depleted Royalist army was routed at Philiphaugh, near Selkirk. After hiding for some time in the Highlands, Montrose escaped to France.

The following year King Charles surrendered to the Scots at Newark. Even though a captive, he could not promise to establish a Presbyterian church in England. Consequently he was handed over to the Parliamentary party for the sum of £200,000, which was used to defray the Scots' considerable expenses. Three years later King Charles was beheaded, an act which caused great revulsion throughout Scotland.

Immediately, at Scone, Charles II was proclaimed king by the Scots. Readily he subscribed to the National Covenant. Thus, when he was restored to the throne in 1660, the Scots had great hopes that their religious ideals would at last be recognised.

In the Scottish parliament of 1661, however, members were required to sign an oath of allegiance recognising the king's supremacy over 'all persons and clauses'. In that same March an act was passed which cancelled all legislation since 1633. Consequently Episcopacy – with, of course, the bishops – was re-established throughout the country. It was seen as the great betrayal. After all the fighting and political manoeuvring they were virtually back at square one.

Established Presbyterian ministers were required to seek re-admission to their churches and parishes from the bishops. One third of all the ministers in Scotland refused to do so. In Galloway the proportion was much higher, nearly all refused, and twenty-five ministers were deposed from their parishes and churches. In their places curates were appointed, often hastily-trained and not very competent young men, described even by Archbishop Burnet of Glasgow as 'a disgrace to their order and the sacred function.' The appointments caused riots in many places. The curates were mobbed. Some churches were almost empty. Many of the ministers, rather than forsake their charges, remained in their parishes and conducted services in the open air. To discourage this, and in an attempt to compel the people to the services taken by the curates, the king levied fines against those who refused to attend. A roll of parishioners was called at every service to discover the non-attenders. It was known as 'the Bishops' Drag-Net'. Troops were stationed in areas where it was expected there might be trouble. Like all the king's men north of the border at this time they were themselves Scots. Frequently they were quartered on the unfortunate and unwilling parishioners. In addition to food and lodging, the soldiers commonly demanded money from their hosts, and by their depredations reduced many to real poverty.

One such place was St John's Town of Dalry. In 1666 four local men, who had been hiding in the hills, discovered troopers about to torture an old farmer who had not paid his fine. They attacked them and made the soldiers prisoner. Fearful of reprisals they immediately took the initiative and marched on a small force billeted nearby. The word spread like wildfire. Soon they had swelled into an army of the Covenant, with military leaders, large enough to march on Edinburgh. Alas, for their own sakes and those who espoused their cause, the further east they went the less physical became their support, and at Colinton, only three miles short of the city, they were forced to halt. In retreat they were pursued by Dalziel with Royalist forces, and at Rullion Green, low in the Pentland Hills, they were forced into combat. Outnumbered by three to one, poorly armed, worn out by hunger and the unremittingly dreadful weather, they were easily defeated. To discourage further such uprisings, those captured were cruelly punished.

Many were put to death and displayed about the country. The affair was known afterwards as 'the Pentland Rising'.

Briefly, for the period that came to be known as 'the Blink', the methods of terrorism adopted by Dalziel and others were eased, and in 1669 the Covenanting ministers were offered their charges once more on less stringent terms. Most refused, being unwilling to compromise their beliefs. As a consequence, a number were hanged and others were imprisoned.

Now field preaching became a capital offence. The 'outed' ministers were required to live at least twenty miles from their parishes. Thus they had an option: to desert their charges, or go into hiding and risk death by preaching secretly in the open air. Most deemed it advisable to remove until better times, and leave their earlier preaching to work in their absence. Some, however, lived for years a life of danger and hiding, conducting secret services, called 'conventicles', in cottages or sheltered places on the moors and wooded hillsides.* The danger, combining with the fervour of their spirit and worship in the open air, with the circling lapwings and calling curlews betraying their whereabouts to the troopers,† elevated these services to a pitch of such sharp and over-whelming intensity, that the Covenanters were more than fed. Their spirits were honed and stiffened to meet the sacrifices that lay ahead. News of the conventicles was passed from one parishioner to another across the countryside. Anyone the military authorities found guilty of involvement in these meetings was punished severely.

But there was retaliation. In many cases the people made the lives of the curates quite unbearable. Archbishop Sharp, once a Covenanted minister and at the restoration of Charles II the carrier of all the Church of Scotland's hopes, but latterly a persecutor very much aligned with the authorities, was dragged from his carriage and murdered before his daughter's eyes on St Magus Moor, near St Andrews. And on 1st June, 1679, at Drumclog in Ayrshire, a large conventicle elected to stand and fight a considerable force of dragoons, led by the notorious John Graham of Claverhouse, that was advancing upon them. The soldiers bogged down and were routed. It was the Covenanters' single victory under arms.

* The names of many of the hill-preachers are still popularly remembered: Welsh, Semple, Blackadder, Cameron, Peden, Cargill, Renwick.
† As a direct consequence of these birds' unwitting betrayal of the Covenanters, many countrymen coming upon a lapwing's or a curlew's nest, even today, will trample on it.

47

They marched to Glasgow, a force of several thousands. There was preaching and psalm singing.

> 'Now Israel may say, and that truly,
> If that the Lord had not our cause maintained;
> If that the Lord had not our right sustained,
> When cruel men against us furiously
> Rose up in wrath, to make of us their prey;
> Then certainly they had devoured us all ...'

But exactly three weeks after Drumclog they were confronted by a force of 10,000 well-armed troops at the early fifteenth-century Bothwell Bridge over the Clyde in Lanarkshire. Full revenge was exacted by the king's forces. Claverhouse and his men cut down the fleeing Covenanters without mercy. Twelve hundred prisoners were taken on the field. Some were executed immediately, many more after cursory examination in the weeks that followed. They were tortured. Bodies were left hanging in chains to rot and be seen. Hundreds were shipped from Leith to become slaves on the West Indian plantations, though many were released afterwards in London. In Greyfriar's Churchyard in Edinburgh they lay without shelter for months, fed with decaying food and water. More than 250, the last of those in Greyfriars, were battened down in a coffin ship which eventually drove on to the rocks of Orkney. The captain and crew, it is claimed, thrust those who made it to shore back into the waves to drown. Only a few survived.

The following year, on the anniversary of Bothwell Bridge, a group of about twenty Covenanters entered the town of Sanquhar in Dumfriesshire. After singing a psalm they read aloud a declaration, and then fixed it to the town cross. Since King Charles, they proclaimed, had never set foot in Scotland since his restoration, twenty years earlier, and had broken the National Covenant, which he previously espoused, they no longer recognised him as their king. And further, they pronounced him a tyrant and enemy of Christ against whom they declared war — twenty austere and passionate outlaws against one of the most powerful monarchs in Europe.

One of the signatories and leaders was a fiery and well-known young field-preacher by the name of Richard Cameron. From him this group of extremist Covenanters became known as the Cameronians. A price of five thousand merks was put upon his head; a regiment of foot and seven troops of horse were sent into the south-west to capture him. Their intent was again repressive. Dreadful punishment was inflicted upon any person even suspected of having had dealings with the Cameronians. And no matter how unjust, there was no-one to whom the Scottish farmers and cottars could appeal. They were victims of the law, and at the mercy of the troopers and their officers.

Richard Cameron was not on the run for very long. A month after the Sanquhar Declaration, at Airds Moss, near the source of the River Ayr, the Cameronians were surrounded by a force three times as great as their own, and defeated. Richard Cameron and his brother Michael, along with several others, were killed in the first charge. It was the first time the Cameronians had drawn arms. They had never trained or drilled, and pursued no military course. Their declaration of war was moral and spiritual, and it was the greater threat. Now those who fled were pursued and slain. Richard Cameron's hands and head were cut off for the bounty — and later identified by his stoical but grief-stricken father, a prisoner in the Tollbooth. His head was carried through the streets on a spike before the prisoners, and afterwards displayed. But his name lived on.

And other hill-preachers continued the work, though by this time many had been captured and executed, and others had fled into Holland. The great, inspiring Sandy Peden, outed minister of Glenluce, with a strange, almost Biblical conviction and fore-knowledge of events, for which he was nicknamed 'Prophet Peden', still wrapped himself in the heather and bogs, and slept in the wilds. For years he had lived like this, and he alone of all the field preachers survived to finish his work in the moors and return home to die.* But by this time he was growing old. Donald Cargill, too, had survived and was now aging. Many who had helped him and been his associates had gone to the gallows before him. A year after Cameron's death at Aird's Moss he was captured and executed after preaching to an almost recklessly huge conventicle in the Pentland Hills. He was seventy-one years old, tired but utterly convinced of God's love and understanding. "The Lord knows," he said, with the very rope around his neck, "I go up this ladder with less fear and perturbation than ever I entered the pulpit to preach."

Many, as Lauderdale laughingly described the hanging of the Covenanters, were 'sent to glorify God in the Grassmarket.' A number

* Knowing that his life was drawing to a close, Alexander Peden travelled to his brother's house. He was tracked there and the house was searched, but he was not found. Two days later he died and was buried in the Kirk of Auchinleck nearby. Forty days later dragoons dug up his body, and with crude and cruel jokes from their officers, carried him to the gallows of Cumnock, two miles away, and hung him up. Later he was buried at the gallows foot, in unconsecrated ground, with other martyrs alongside him.

first lost their hands; others were left hanging. Some of the executions were ghastly beyond credibility; in the case of poor, innocent David Hackston of Rathillet, who had been a witness to the murder of Archbishop Sharp, extending beyond hanging and gross mutilation to cutting his heart out while he was still alive. The Duke of York, soon to become James II, wanted to watch the tortures, which included the bone and joint-crushing 'boot'. Bishop Paterson of Galloway, a man of God, devised a double thumbscrew that was particularly agonising. Mostly, however, those who were sentenced to death for their Covenanting activities, were simply hanged.

In 1681 a Test Act was brought into force. This required everyone in public office to renounce openly the Sanquhar Declaration and acknowledge the king's total supremacy. Gradually, as lists were prepared, the act worked its way down to the common folk of every parish. By definition the Cameronians were excluded — at Lanark they had denounced both the Test and the proposed succession of Roman Catholic James — but almost everyone else subscribed to it, though frequently it was under pressure and in a sidelong fashion. There was little else to do, unless one wished to be a martyr, for to refuse the Test was to declare oneself a rebel. Several did refuse, however, and were executed.

Whilst the authorities expressed the view that Cameronian resistance was now negligible, and reduced to less than two hundred, the Cameronians themselves claimed perhaps as many as seven thousand supporters. They had organised themselves into a number of 'Societies', based throughout the south of Scotland. In December, 1681, they convened their first annual general meeting, and thereafter regular quarterly meetings were appointed and records were kept. As a result of these, and communications with Holland, where many Scots Presbyterian refugees had been made welcome and now lived, it was decided to send four young men for training. For only Sandy Peden still preached in the hills, and though the spirit was strong among the Cameronians, they lacked leaders. One of the four who was sent was a boy called James Renwick.

He returned to Scotland in September, 1683. He arrived like a fresh, young flame, only twenty-one years old and seeming younger, alight with the love of God. Immediately he was seized upon by the Cameronians as the leader or figurehead they had been lacking, and to some he seemed almost a second David. With equal promptitude he was denounced as an outlaw by the authorities, and a price was put on his head. Capture would have meant death or compromise. For four years he was on the run, hiding in caves and woods, his pursuers sometimes so close that he could watch them go by. During the summer he often went barefoot. His appearance was superficially so like any lad, his clothes so poor, that sometimes he walked right by his pursuers, who were looking for someone rather different. Several tales are told of his adventures.

In November, 1684, the hunt intensified, for in that month, very much against Renwick's wishes, the Cameronians published the famous 'Apologetical Declaration', proclaiming that those who 'make it their work to imbrue their hands in our blood . . . shall be punished by us according to our power and the degree of their offence.' Thus to their non-allegiance to the king was added the threat of guerrilla-type retaliation and even death to councillors, over-zealous curates, officers, troopers and informers. It was a dangerous document. Also, though in reality they abhorred violence and killing, they made the threat, and it stigmatised the Cameronians in the eyes of many as wild hill men and even monsters.

By test, an oath of renunciation could now be demanded against the Apologetical Declaration also. Those who refused to take it could by law receive summary punishment on the spot before re-examination, and even be executed. As Sir Walter Scott described the situation in *Redgauntlet*: 'It was just "Will ye tak' the Test?" If not, "Make ready — present — fire," and there lay the recusant.' And now not only preaching, but even attendance at a conventicle became a capital offence. It has gone down in history as 'the killing time'.

The officers entrusted with the work of investigation and suppression were not reluctant in carrying it out. John Graham of Claverhouse, Robert Grierson of Lagg*, Windram, Bruce, Douglas, and others — their names are still regarded with horror. Equally, however, the names of many martyrs live on in the history books and on the monuments across the hills, for their courage and faith.

---

* See 'Legends Concerning the Death of Grierson of Lagg'. Some notion of the hatred and moral repulsion with which he was regarded may be read into the description of young Grierson by a Covenanter: 'A great persecutor, swearer, whorer, blasphemer, drunkard, liar, cheat, and yet out of Hell.'

Though it is understandable and just that individuals should bear the accusations of cruelty, atrocity and even sadism, it must be remembered that they were the instruments of a calculated policy, approved by the king, to use brutality and terror to break down the Covenanters' fighting spirit. The officers were more than monsters: the hated Claverhouse, for example, was an outstanding soldier, passionately loyal to the king.

During the bare period 1684-85 at least seventy people — some claim considerably more — were put to death in the south-west for their faith, shot without trial in the open country or on the grass outside their cottages following a few summary questions. For every death there was a story. Two of the most famous incidents concerned the Wigtown Martyrs and the Martyrs of Kirkconnel: they are recounted elsewhere in this volume. Another concerned John Brown, only prevented from being a preacher by a slight stammer, whose brains were blown out as he stood by his lonely moorland cottage at Priesthill in Ayrshire. His

young wife stood nearby with three children, one unborn, one in her arms and one by her side. As she knelt to gather her husband's body together, and the soldiers reloaded, Claverhouse said to her: "What dost think of thy husband now, woman?" "I aye thocht meikle o' him," she replied with simple distress, "an' never mair than now." Hundreds were imprisoned, often in unspeakable conditions, or transported to the plantations as slaves. Many of them were branded: commonly men lost their left ear and women were burned with a mark on the cheek. But far from quenching the ardour and resolution of the Covenanters, the martyrdom of their friends and fellow sufferers only confirmed the moderate more firmly in their faith, even to the point of fanaticism.

In 1685 Charles II died, and was succeeded by his Roman Catholic brother James II. Throughout the nation there was a great wave of disaffection. Deeming the time right, the Protestant Duke of Monmouth, handsome and ambitious illegitimate son of Charles II, returned from exile in Holland to claim the crown. He was defeated at Sedgemoor, later captured, and beheaded on Tower Hill. The rebellion was followed by a ruthless purge, the most infamous figure in which was Judge Jefferies of the Bloody Assizes. In addition to countless other executions, 330 men were hanged, drawn and quartered.

Monmouth's rebellion was paralleled in Scotland by the landing of Archibald Campbell, ninth Duke of Argyll, who had fled to Holland in 1681, having escaped from prison after resisting the Test Act. But the Scottish rebellion in favour of Monmouth never really got off the ground. The leading Campbells were imprisoned. The Duke of Argyll, having been captured at Inchinnan, was taken to Edinburgh Castle and shortly afterwards beheaded on the 'maiden'. To make room for the arriving rebels, nearly two hundred Covenanters were ferried across the Forth and force-marched to Dunottar Castle on its stupendous sea-washed crag two miles from Stonehaven. Here, in the appalling 'Whig Vault', they were imprisoned in conditions of indescribable crowding and filth. A few who escaped were too weak to get far. Though emaciated, they were flogged and tortured. Several died.

In Galloway, as elsewhere, as a result of the two rebellions the persecution intensified. The Cameronians issued a second Sanquhar Declaration, this time disowning James as a 'murderer and idolater' who as a Catholic had no right to the throne.

Shortly after his accession James commenced a policy of establishing Roman Catholics in key government posts. It was the first step in a deliberate and unbelievably foolish attempt to turn Great Britain into a Roman Catholic nation. There were anti-Catholic riots. At the same time news began to arrive from France of the cruel persecution of the Huguenots by the king's cousin, Louis XIV. Naturally, Scotsmen were alarmed lest James should have similar ideas. The Scottish parliament was not willing to repeal the anti-Catholic laws, which in declaring that no Roman Catholic should hold public office, clearly pronounced the king's actions to be illegal. James, therefore, dismissed parliament and repealed the laws himself. Unwittingly he was paving the way for the re-establishment of the Scottish church.

In 1687, wishing to sweeten Scotland and gain a foothold for his own minority religion, James granted a Declaration of Indulgence allowing the Presbyterians once more the right to worship freely in their own churches. Though the extremist Cameronians refused to accept this partial recognition of their claims — they would consider nothing less than the Presbyterian nation of the Solemn League and Covenant — throughout the country the ministers returned to their parishes, exiles returned from Holland, the General Assembly once more convened in Edinburgh. The dissenters in England, however, also allowed the freedom to worship under the blanket of the king's indulgence, were less happy with his motives. And their mistrust was amply justified as James persisted in his rash scheme of filling more and more government posts with Catholics.

As the months passed, disaffection grew. William of Orange, married to James's daughter Mary, was invited by a number of Whig peers to deliver Britain from the Stuart misrule. On 5th November, 1688, he landed at Tor Bay in Devon. It was the signal for anti-Catholic rioting in Glasgow and Edinburgh. In the south-west, where the Cameronian sympathies were strongest, the troops were withdrawn. The curates who had been forced on unwilling congregations were driven out by riotous mobs, principally on Christmas Day. Some were maltreated. It was called 'rabbling the curates'.

James, by this time, had fled into France, where his Jacobite supporters gathered round him. In 1689 William and Mary were proclaimed king and queen.

That same year a parliament was constituted in Edinburgh by royal summons. Though William would have preferred to retain the bishops, their loyalties were questionable: most, indeed, supported James. This well suited the desires of the General Assembly. The bishops were deposed and Episcopacy was abolished, though in the more tenacious north-east a number of Episcopalian ministers continued in their parishes. The following year the Church of Scotland was established on the model of 1592, a century earlier, before the Episcopalian innovations of James VI, and the Union of the Crowns.

By this time Renwick was dead, captured in Edinburgh after more than four years on the run. He was taken to the Castle where the captain of the guard, Graham, 'seeing him of a little stature and comely youthful countenance, cried, "What! is this the boy Renwick that the nation hath been so much troubled with?" ' His moral and spiritual stature, however, were greater. During eighteen days in captivity he did not flinch for one moment from the fate that awaited him. Rather, as so many other Covenanters, he embraced it gladly, seeing death as his wedding, warming further and further towards transport of joy as the time approached. Throughout those days he was beseeched by friends and those of other persuasions to break his vows: "I would hardly be in this place if I was prepared to do so," he replied. He was hanged on 18th February, 1688, three days after his twenty-sixth birthday. Even on the scaffold one of the curates in attendance said to him: "Own our king, and we shall pray for you." Renwick answered with the frank disdain he had so often shown to them: "I will have none of your prayers. I am come here to bear testimony against you and such as you are."

His followers, a small but fervent band of Cameronians, remained true to their faith. They alone clung unshakably to the precise word and intent of the two covenants, and refused to join the re-established Presbyterian Church. Instead they formed their own sect. Many flocked to join them, especially in the early years, and their numbers increased rapidly. By 1690 they were several thousand strong and building their own churches.*

During the succeeding three centuries, of course, the Presbyterian Church has split time and again, and with the passage of years reunited once more. There have been many sects. The Reformed Presbyterian Church† is the oldest, however, the direct descendant of those in-transigent Cameronians, its history reaching straight back — along with the whole Church of Scotland, of course — into the heart of those troubled times.

* On 12th November, 1688, James II created John Graham of Claverhouse the 1st Viscount Dundee. The following month, in view of political developments, Dundee fled the country. In 1689, however, he returned to lead a Highland up-rising in support of James. At the Battle of Killiecrankie on 17th July, his Jacobite troops were completely victorious over William's army under the command of the veteran general Hugh Mackay. John Graham himself, however, was killed, shot under the arm as he was waving his troops on. He was forty years old. His death was a great blow to the Jacobite cause. Ironically, by a deft twist of national sentiment, 'Bloody Clavers' is also remembered as the brilliant 'Bonnie Dundee'.

Shortly afterwards, to help to suppress the Jacobite rebellion and restore order to the Highlands, the Cameronian Regiment was formed. It is said that 1200 men from the Societies volunteered in the course of a single day. Soon they were fight-ing overseas in the wars against Louis XIV. The Cameronians (Scottish Rifles), of course, became one of Scotland's most distinguished regiments, maintaining with pride the principles of its founders.

† The greater part of the Reformed Presbyterian Church united with the Free Church of Scotland in 1876. Only a few congregations now remain in Scotland, though the church is stronger in Ireland and the United States of America.

The Traveller and the Kelpie

It was a rough January night in those distant years when men made long journeys on foot across open country. The rain had stopped and the moon showed briefly between heavy clouds. The wind was high.

A traveller, descending later than he had intended from the moors, found his way barred by a swollen stream. For a while, in the darkness, he hunted up and down for a route across, but there seemed no way save by a stone in mid-stream. The current surged around it. Unhappily he stared at the racing, glinting water, then up through the tossing, winter-bare trees for a glimpse of moonlight to aid his passage. But the moon had vanished for the time being. Taking his courage in both hands, he retreated two or three paces, ran forward, and sprang for the rock.

He landed safely, catching hold of the wet stone for balance. Now he must leap for the further bank. The distance was greater but the landing was safe. For a moment he paused, however, and it was his undoing.

As the water surged past it seemed to him that the rock was floating, moving backwards up the river. He felt a little dizzy. Then it seemed that the rock was starting to spin. And was it inside his head, or was there a voice actually rising from the depths of the stream? It was a song, a kelpie song, which told him that by trampling on the stone he had woken the maiden from her dream among the weeds and sand at the bottom of the river. In consequence he would be her plaything until dawn lit the sky. At the hour of nine she would appear before him.

Even in his dizzied or bewitched state the traveller realised that it must be nearly that time as he stood there. He tried to pull himself together and make that saving spring to the riverbank. But before he could do so there was a gleam in the water nearby and a flash that illuminated the streaming rocks and racing surface of the river. For an instant he was dazzled, then beheld the kelpie and her train swimming easily in the current, glowing with light.

She was riding upon the back of an otter. He had heard that kelpies were dreadful creatures, but the maiden's face was fair, and as the rock ceased its spinning a glow of warmth stirred within him, for he was a young man. Her hair flowed to her feet, and he saw, with strange pleasure, that it was entwined with wriggling eels. Her slim body was decked in river weeds and iris leaves. A necklace of coral-hued newts was about her throat and shoulders. In her lap nestled two frogs, and around the otter and her trailing feet the water glistened with a myriad of minnows and sticklebacks.

His eyes glowed as he regarded her. And she was not unaware of his fascination, for quietly she glanced up at his young form on the rock.

She did not speak, and for a while he too was dumb. Then he remembered that kelpies — so it was said — were unable to speak to mortals in the air, only from beneath the water in their own element. His voice returned.

It was a bold, halting speech that he made, punctuated by periods of silence as his words and ideas ran dry, and the exquisite kelpie, rocking gently in the waves of the river, made no response. He admired her beauty and enquired of her home beneath the water: he told her a little about himself and sought personal details of her life in exchange. He wondered, even, whether he dare beg for a lock of her hair.

Perhaps in his ardour and enthusiasm he over-stepped himself, for suddenly the otter stopped paddling, webs spread athwart the stream. With a plunge and a dive the whole cavalcade vanished beneath the torrent. The light was extinguished.

His eyes now unaccustomed to the darkness, the young man stood lost on his stone in the middle of the stream. While the kelpie was there it seemed that warm airs had blown about him. Now the chill January winds returned from the moors. Slowly his vision began to return. He thought that she was gone.

Then from the bed of the stream the kelpie addressed him. He had been mistaken in the expression he thought he saw in her mouth and eyes, for his warmth and tenderness were not returned. His questions, she told him icily, would be answered when he reached the further bank of the stream, provided that he did so before the first light of dawn. Yet that would never be.

She spoke nonsense. The riverbank was only a long leap away. He prepared to jump, then found to his astonishment that he was unable to move a muscle. He grew impatient with himself, but it did no good. Still as a statue he remained rooted to the spot.

The rain came on again and drenched him to the skin. Slowly, imperceptibly, the ragged moon dragged westward across the sky. Ten o'clock came, and eleven, and midnight. By two he was sure it must soon be dawn. A thousand times he thought he perceived a faint brightening through the trees. For a time the rain became sleet. The darkness continued.

At length, however, deeply chilled and exhausted by the rigours of the night, he became aware that the eastern sky really was turning pale with the first light of the new day. The young man moved his feet, his legs so stiff that he nearly fell headlong into the torrent. He rubbed his muscles. In an agony the blood felt its way back along his limbs. A few minutes later he leaped clumsily from the rock, landed half in the water, and dragged himself to the bank.

For a moment he listened, and spoke to the kelpie, but there was no reply save the ripple and splash of the brimming river. Then he turned away, and as the light grew continued his journey down from the moors towards the lowland farms and small township that was his destination. The face and vision of the kelpie were to haunt him for the rest of his life.

FOOTNOTE

Traditionally a kelpie is a water-horse, haunting rivers rather than lochs or the sea. In the shape of a beautiful young stallion he tempts wayfarers on to his back and gallops directly to a deep pool, where striking the water with his tail he vanishes with a flash and sound of thunder, leaving the rider to drown. Occasionally he is said to devour the traveller. When the kelpie assumes human form it is as a shaggy man, who delights in springing on the back of a horse to crush the rider in his arms and frighten him almost to death. Before a storm or flood his wailing can be heard rising from the river. The kelpie in this story is more like a river nymph.

The Bad Bailiff of Rusko

Rusko Castle is situated three miles north of Gatehouse on the western slope of the Fleet valley. It stands on a raised riverbank backed with trees which shield it from the narrow road and the moors above. The small irregular windows face across level, sheep-dotted pastures to the winding Water of Fleet and the woods and hills of Castramont. At present all that remains is the trim stone tower, twelve yards by nine, which has recently been restored as a private residence. In the past, however, the castle was considerably more extensive, and the surrounding lands, now virtually empty, were built with many cottages.

Historically Rusko Castle was the home of the Gordons of Lochinvar.

'Of old the Lords of Lochinvar
Here dwelt in peace, but armed for war;
And Rusko Castle could declare
That valiant chief and lady fair
Had often wooed and wedded there.'

At the end of the sixteenth century it was occupied by Sir Hugh Gordon, a member of the younger branch of that family. He was a bluff, fair-minded, middle-aged man, and though living rather beyond his means, was well respected by his many servants and popular among the gentry of the neighbourhood.

One of his outdoor servants was a man by the name of Bell, whose daughter Barbara was a great beauty. Her hair hung in golden ringlets that were the envy of the ladies: her name was the toast of the district. Many young men from titled families far and near sought to win her favour. Barbara, however, was as sensible as she was beautiful, and knew what little hope of happiness lay in linking her fate to one of these young gentlemen. Instead she married a young workman of her own station by the name of Andrew Dennistoun, a quiet and steady fellow, a childhood sweetheart.

Many were disappointed, but one — significantly of lower rank than most — burned to think that she had chosen a common labourer in preference to himself. He was the bailiff of Sir Hugh's estate, and his name was Peter Carnochan.

Almost daily while her husband was working in the fields the bailiff called at their simple cottage on one pretext after another. In every way he could imagine, through little gifts and flattery, through offers of a better house and advancement for her husband, even through the expression of his own passion, he sought to seduce the radiant young wife. But his efforts were all in vain, for she was a virtuous girl and in love with her husband.

Unable to accomplish his design by this means, Peter Carnochan set himself out deliberately to destroy Andrew Dennistoun. Once she found herself in trouble and alone, he argued to himself, the young wife would be only too glad of the assistance he could offer her.

One night, therefore, armed with a knife and clad in an old gaberdine — an overgarment like a long smock, commonly worn by shepherds — the bailiff made his way secretly to the moor. It was his plan to slaughter a sheep and lay the blame on Andrew Dennistoun. The sheep scattered as he came close, but at length he managed to knot his fingers in the wool of a fine fat wether. Throwing the animal on its back he cut its throat. When the bleeding had stopped and the sheep lay dead, he opened its belly and carefully hid the innards beneath some long heather. Then he caught the legs together to bind them for carrying and reached to his pocket for the twine. With some irritation he realised that he had forgotten to bring it with him. A garter would do as well, however, and pulling one from his stocking he bound the legs tightly together. Then, slinging the dead sheep across his shoulders, he carried it quietly down the hill.

As he approached the labourer's darkened cottage his heart beat faster. Being careful not to disturb the couple within, he crept past and hid the sheep in a thicket a dozen yards away.

Then he returned home, his mind filled with what he had done, and thoughts of the golden-haired young wife. Throwing off the old gaberdine he pushed it into a chest, rinsed his hands free of blood, and went to bed.

The following morning the strong young wether was missed. Seemingly by chance, Peter Carnochan led the shepherds to the place where the heather and grass were trampled and stained with blood. With a cry a shepherd pulled aside a clump of heather to reveal the pile of offal. Aghast they gazed down, and the other searchers came running to see. The sheep had been slaughtered and stolen: this was a crime punishable by death.

A second search was now instigated, this time for the sheep's carcass. Sir Hugh Gordon was informed and he was very angry. All the cottages and outbuildings on the estate were ransacked, but nothing was found.

At length Peter Carnochan, with others, crossed to the brush thicket behind Andrew Dennistoun's cottage. There lay the gutted sheep, waiting to be skinned and jointed. In vain did the young labourer protest that he knew nothing about the animal. He had never stepped beyond the cottage garden after he returned from his work the previous evening. And what about the garter — he had never seen it before. Deeply distressed, his wife supported everything he said. But they were not believed. The presence of the garter only added to his guilt, for no-one else would have left it there. Though his astonishment and angry innocence were plain for all to see, his declarations were ignored and Andrew Dennistoun was seized.

The evidence seemed conclusive. His anger unbridled, Sir Hugh condemned him as a sheep stealer, to be hanged the following day, and ordered a gibbet to be set up on the back hill if no suitable tree presented itself. The young man's pleas of innocence and his request for a week's delay in the execution of the sentence were rejected. "What," cried Sir Hugh, "shall I bargain with a thieving rogue? I was mistaken in your character. You deceived me, Dennistoun! You shall be hanged!"

Everything had gone according to plan, thought Peter Carnochan. Give the beautiful young wife a few days to get over the wildest of her grief and let her sadness mature, then she would be ready to respond to his advances.

But Sir Hugh's wife, who normally did not take much notice of the servants so long as they carried out their duties to her satisfaction, was not happy that justice had been done. She knew the young man slightly. He was said to be of excellent character. The crime was alien to all she had heard of him. Accordingly she asked to be taken to the spot where the slaughter had taken place, and then to the Dennistouns' cottage to see the dead sheep.

In the heat of the events, no-one had been in a frame of mind to consider carefully the garter which bound the animal's legs together. It was a simple enough garter, but surely, thought Lady Gordon as she examined it, somewhat on the fine side for a mere workman on the estate. It was removed from the carcass and she carried it into the castle.

All the servants were summoned, but none recognised the garter. The pattern, however, seemed somewhat distinctive. Then Lady Gordon remembered that there was an old woman named Jeanie Livingstone on the estate, who wove such small articles on a hand loom in her cottage. A number of the more well-to-do servants had belts and garters made by her. She might be able to throw some light on the matter. Accordingly Lady Gordon called for her bonnet and set out for the old woman's cottage.

Jeanie Livingstone recognised the garter immediately. It belonged to Peter Carnochan, the bailiff. Lady Gordon was amazed. Surely the old lady was mistaken. But no, Jeanie Livingstone showed her how by

pulling the material a certain way the initials of the wearer were revealed. She did it for all of her customers, it was her speciality to weave them in quietly like that.

Holding the garter in her hand, Lady Gordon returned to Rusko. At once Sir Hugh was informed and the bailiff was summoned. Confronted with the evidence he blustered, and flung his own position of trust against the word of an old woman and the character of a lowly outdoor worker. But there were the initials, embroidered in the garter. Who else could it be? Then he changed his plea: he said that he must have lost the garter without knowing it, or it had been stolen by a servant girl. A search of the house, however, unearthed the blood-stained gaberdine from his trunk, and his knife, crusted with dried blood, still in the pocket. The evidence was incontrovertible: every word and gesture now proclaimed his guilt. Peter Carnochan was seized.

Orders were issued at once for the release of Andrew Dennistoun. That very afternoon Peter Carnochan was hanged from the high bough of a tree on the hillside behind the castle, the victim of his own ungovernable lust. Andrew was reunited with his loving wife, and as a reward for his sufferings and previous good work, was granted the now vacant position of bailiff on the Rusko estate.

Two Tales
of a Respected Minister

Samuel Rutherford, minister of Anwoth 1627-1638, was an eminent Scottish divine. Born in 1600 in Roxburghshire, he was a brilliant scholar at Edinburgh, and at the age of twenty-three was elected Professor of Latin at that University. Four years later, following some alleged indiscretion before his marriage, he was dismissed, and left the city for the little charge of Anwoth at the invitation of Lord Kenmure, who at that time was resident in the nearby Castle of Rusko.

These were the years of struggle between King Charles's Episcopalian Church, with its attendant bishops, Prayer Book and ritual, and the free Presbyterian ideals of Scotland. For his writings while at Anwoth, Rutherford was dismissed his charge in 1636 and confined in the city of Aberdeen, the centre of Scottish Episcopalianism. While there he missed Anwoth dreadfully and wrote, among his famous published letters of that time: 'When I think of the sparrows and swallows that build their nests in the Kirk of Anwoth, and of my dumb Sabbaths, my sorrowful bleared eyes look asquint upon Christ and present him as angry.' An English merchant who heard him speak shortly afterwards wrote: 'I heard a little fair man and he showed me the loveliness of Christ.'

Early in 1638, the year of the National Covenant, he ventured to return to Anwoth. Those ten years in Galloway he always considered the very heart of his Christian service. Despite his formidably strong ideals he was loved and respected. He knew his parishioners from the humblest cottar's wife and herd boy to Lord Kenmure, and filled every minute of his long day, which often commenced at 3am, with prayer and praise, writing, reading and pastoral care. He greatly loved the countryside also; his walks through the wooded fields and hills of the parish were a perpetual refreshment. A verse in his hymn 'Glory, glory dwelleth in Emmanuel's Land', which is commonly omitted from the hymn books, tells us:

'And if one soul from Anwoth
Meet me at God's right hand
My Heaven will be two Heavens
In Emmanuel's Land!'

By the time of his return to the little kirk and parish the Scottish church authorities had been made aware of his exceptional talents. It was believed that they should no longer be confined to the rustic vales of Anwoth, but would be of greater value in the wider world. A passionate and anxious petition signed by more than two hundred of his parishioners was resisted, and less than a year after he had been restored to his flock, with undying regret Rutherford was directed by the General Assembly in Glasgow to the post of Professor of Divinity at St Andrews.

For four years, 1643-1647, he was one of Scotland's eight commissioners at the Westminster Assembly of Divines, seeking to establish the freedom and structures of national worship. From 1647 until his death in 1661, he continued as Professor of Divinity and became Principal of St Mary's College in St Andrews.

With the published *Letters*, remarkable documents of love, humanity and piety, and his sermons, his most famous volume is *Lex Rex* (1644), the principal argument of which is the potential abuse and corrupting influence of power in the hands of an individual. 'Law is not the King's but is given to him on trust': 'Power is a birth-right of the people, borrowed from them: they may let it out for their good, and may resume it when a man is drunk with it.' For such opinions, when the monarchy was restored, the book was publically burnt by the hangman in London, Edinburgh and St Andrews.

That same year, 1661, he was deprived of his office and charged with high treason. The officer sent to arrest him, an arrest that may very well have ended in martyrdom, found Rutherford, now aged sixty, too ill to be moved. The officer was dismissed with the message: 'Tell the king, I have a prior summons to a higher court and judicature, where the judge is my friend: and where few kings or great ones ever come.' Deeming it unwise in view of public feeling to remove him forcibly, the authorities resorted to threatening gestures, one of which was to burn *Rex Lex* beneath his college windows.

During the illness of those last months he retained the simplicity that had so distinguished his life and ministry, and combined so remarkably with his spiritual love and depth of learning. Often at that time he 'broke out in a kind of sacred rapture, exalting and commending the Lord Jesus. ... Some days before his death he said, "I shall see him shine — I shall see him as he is — I shall see him reign, and all his fair company with him; and I shall have my large share. Mine eyes shall see my Redeemer: these very eyes of mine, and none other for me. This may seem a wide word; but it is no fancy or delusion; it is true. Let my Lord's name be exalted." '

On 20th March, 1661, he died, and was buried in the chapel of St Regulus at St Andrews.

Samuel Rutherford's name is still revered in Galloway. The ruin of his little church may be seen in the beautiful old cemetery at Anwoth, where in spring the wild snowdrops and daffodils grow, and the wooded surrounding hills are thick with bracken. On the summit of Boreland Hill less than half a mile away stands the Rutherford Monument, raised in 1842, a fifty-five foot obelisk of grey granite which can be seen for many miles around. As much as three centuries after his incumbency the following two wry, affectionate and half fanciful tales were still told of his ministry at Anwoth.

The Archbishop a Beggar

Archbishop Usher, a most distinguished and human prelate with ecumenical sympathies, had been on a visit to England and was returning home to Ireland through Galloway. On his journey he heard a great deal of Mr Rutherford's piety and devotion. It was said that the minister of Anwoth sometimes spent whole nights in prayer, particularly before his duties on the Sabbath. Archbishop Usher was anxious to witness such a great outpouring of the spirit, but was completely unable to think of a way in which this might be accomplished. To go in his own presence would be to change the whole circumstance of the minister's evening. For a long time he pondered, and at length hit upon what seemed a splendid idea.

Disguising himself as a pauper he called on the Saturday evening at Bush o' Bield, Mr Rutherford's house, and asked whether he could be given some place to sleep for the night, since it was growing late. The minister was fetched from his study and cheerfully agreed, sitting the man down in the kitchen and telling a servant girl to fetch him some food.

While he sat by the fire the archbishop was able to watch Mrs Rutherford examining her servants upon their faith. Turning to the wandering stranger she asked him how many commandments there were, to which the archbishop replied 'eleven'. Mrs Rutherford was shocked and rebuked him for his dreadful ignorance, lamenting his condition to the servants.

69

Afterwards Archbishop Usher was shown to a room in the attic, which by good fortune was situated immediately above Mr Rutherford's own chamber. It was exactly suited to his design. For a long time the archbishop sat up, listening and waiting. The servants and household retired to their beds. But from Mr Rutherford's room there came not a sound. Disappointed, the archbishop was compelled at length to conclude, correctly, that Mr Rutherford had gone to bed and was asleep. Though he had missed one man's devotions, however, this was only too good a reason and opportunity to offer up his own. Going upon his knees he presented himself to God and poured out his heart with fullness.

Soon he had forgotten his situation, so deeply was he engaged in prayer, and his voice woke Mr Rutherford sleeping below him. For a time the minister lay on his pillow and listened, then rose and pulled on a few clothes and climbed the stairs to the door of the archbishop's room. Quietly he listened and could distinguish some of the words. Clearly they were not those of a wandering beggar.

When the archbishop's devotions were concluded and Mr Rutherford heard him rise to his feet, he knocked modestly on the door and entered. From the tone of the prayer and the archbishop's accent Mr Rutherford was already half convinced of his guest's identity, extraordinary though it seemed. In some confusion Archbishop Usher confessed and tried to explain his strange disguise. Mr Rutherford laughed, and taking his hand, warmly invited the archbishop, whose sermons were celebrated, to preach for him the following day.

In a suit of borrowed clothes Archbishop Usher and the minister walked down the wooded lanes to Anwoth Church. Mr Rutherford introduced him as a passing preacher who would that morning be addressing the congregation. For his text Achbishop Usher took the words of John 13.34: 'A new commandment I give unto you, That ye love one another.' Its significance was not lost upon Mrs Rutherford who caught her husband's twinkling eye. The eleventh commandment — yet still she could not reconcile the beggar she had seen the evening before and at breakfast time, with this most eloquent and moving preacher.

As they returned to Bush o' Bield for lunch, Archbishop Usher extracted a promise that his identity and rather unclerical ruse should remain a secret. For the remainder of that day and a second night he was Mr Rutherford's guest. Then early on Monday morning, when the minister was the only man stirring in the house, Archbishop Usher clad himself once more in his beggar's garb and stole away. And for many years the prelate's visit to Anwoth remained a closely kept secret.

FOOTNOTE

Details in rather less well-known accounts add a certain ring of truth to this tale. In one, Archbishop Usher adopted the disguise of a beggar because he was apprehensive of his reception by a man of such Presbyterian convictions as Mr Rutherford. He was overheard early the following morning at private prayer in a wooded glade nearby. The footpath where Mr Rutherford walked that dawn, which ran through trees between the original Bush o' Bield and Anwoth Church, was until recent years still known as 'Rutherford's Walk'. In a third account the Archbishop adopted the disguise of a simple traveller, and was discovered on his knees in Anwoth Church. In all versions, however, the basic facts are the same: the disguise, the evening examination, the eleventh commandment, the discovery, the text from John. Somewhere between the second and the third account, it must be said, seems most likely. We must recognise, too, that Samuel Rutherford may have had his own reasons for keeping quiet about the Archbishop's visit, for to most Presbyterians the Episcopal clergy were anathema.

Three Stern Witnesses

Upon his appointment in 1627, Mr Rutherford's ministry covered three parishes, Anwoth, Kirkdale and Kirkmabreck. In the absence of a pastor the parish of Anwoth, at least, had been limited to one service every two weeks. Far from finding his parishioners the godly, virtuous people that a new minister might desire, they were described as 'a profane, irreligious set'. After morning service on the Sabbath, for example, it was the custom of many to retire to a pleasant meadow on the farm of Mossrobin, between the church and Skyre Burn, and there amuse themselves with games — caber tossing, football, putting the stone, even wrestling; and when other fields flooded and froze in winter there was curling.

Mr Rutherford disapproved strongly and remonstrated with them privately. This, however, did no good and the games continued. Then he spoke from the pulpit, but even such shame as this just rolled off their backs. Samuel Rutherford racked his brains for some scheme, for the practice must certainly stop.

At length he devised a plan. Choosing a Sunday on which the Sacrament had been administered, he joined the group of men gathered outside the little church at the end of the service. To their astonishment he asked if he might accompany them, and though doubtless some were very suspicious, he was warmly welcomed.

Arriving at the sheltered, grassy spot, Mr Rutherford announced that he had a new amusement he would like to show them. It required three large stones. They began searching, and being strong fellows soon produced three huge boulders which the minister pronounced as ideal for his purpose. Then he instructed the men to set them up firmly at regular intervals across the area where they played. Glad to use their muscles after the long sit in church, it was soon done, and Mr Rutherford called the assembly around him. Then in loud tones that all must hear he cried: "These stones that you have set up I pronounce emblems of the Holy Trinity: the Father, the Son and the Holy Ghost. Let them be witnesses against you on that awful day when you stand before your Creator, if you persist in these unholy and soul-destroying practices."

His words had the effect he desired. No more did the people assemble for joyful sports and games after morning service. And for many years the stones were held in peculiar veneration. They became part of the physical and spiritual landscape and were known as 'Rutherford's Three Witnesses'.

More than a century later a gang of men near the spot were erecting a stone dyke. It was early in the morning and they had not yet eaten. One, a jovial and rash fellow, deliberately flying in the face of the superstitious piety that surrounded the 'witnesses', announced that he would incorporate them into the dyke, for they would make a fine, strong base. His work-fellows tried with some warmth to dissuade him, at which he grew angry and proclaimed that he would shift one of them there and then, before he had a bite of his breakfast: even if the ghost of Rutherford himself were to rise from the ground, it should not prevent him.

True to his word, he knotted his back to the task and tumbled the huge rock across the level ground into the base of the wall. Then, with a satisfied grin, he seated himself upon it and took up his breakfast. But at once, even as he swallowed the first mouthful, the food stuck in his throat and choked him, so that he fell to the ground and nearly died.

The other two stones remained where they were.

Adam Forrester and Lucky Hair *

Adam Forrester was an eighteenth century farmer, proprietor of Knocksheen. His farm lay on the north bank of the Garroch Burn, a tributary of the Ken, four miles into the hills to the west of Dalry.

One evening he had been in the township drinking at Lucky Hair's, a notorious inn at Midtown Dalry. He often went there for the merry company, and more particularly because he had a fancy for the lively owner and barmaid, Lucky Hair herself. He liked to tease her that she had sold herself to the Devil to keep her youth, because in his eyes at least she looked bonnier with every year that passed. On this night, though he had managed to wind an arm about her waist early on, his hopes of a stolen good-night kiss were dashed, for without saying a word to anyone Lucky Hair had slipped away, leaving the bar in charge of a serving-man and pot-room drab. It was drawing towards midnight when Adam Forrester called his farewells, and mounting on his white horse, set off down the long hill towards the ford across the Ken.

The rough road led between the kirkyard and Dalry Mote a little above the river. Though the night was moonless the sky was clear and sparkling with stars and soon his eyes became accustomed to the dark. As he approached the kirk he was surprised to hear the dancing notes of a fiddle. Then, as he passed from behind some bushes and the building came into view, he was still more surprised to see that lights were burning within, illuminating the little windows and sending rays out into the night. He was filled with curiosity. Without dismounting he turned his horse in through the kirkyard gate and crossed between the gravestones to the east window. Then he climbed down, and holding the reins in his hand, crept close and peered through the slit in the heavy stone wall into the interior, where lanterns and flickering candles mingled brilliance and darkness and fleeting shadows.

* This is almost certainly the story that Robert Burns heard when he was tenant-farmer of Ellisland near Dumfries, probably from the well-known Dr Robert Trotter. In 1790 he turned it into the famous narrative poem 'Tam o' Shanter'. Since the relatives of some of the characters concerned in the story were still living and the district was not familiar to him, he transposed it to Ayrshire and Kirk Alloway, which he had known since boyhood.

He was astonished to see that the kirk was a scene of revelry. Up in the pulpit, the first person he saw, was an old man from the town, bedridden for twenty years and crooked like a gnome, playing the fiddle and jigging like one possessed, his face brilliant with toothless laughter. Beneath him — for the kirk had no pews in those days — the floor was thronged with whirling dancers, all going at it like twenty-year-olds at a harvest festival. But it was a long time since most of them had seen twenty. They were old folk, many of them the cripples and bedridden from miles around. And there too were the respectable good-living people that no-one would have suspected, figures from the manse and sober elders who read the Word and sat before the congregation every Sabbath with holy faces and clasped hands. But now their jackets were off, the women's skirts kilted high for the galloping reels. Their faces glistened with sweat and animal high spirits. Forrester knew most of them well, though sometimes it was hard to make out who they were in the swirl and dancing shadows.

One of the revellers was Old Nick himself, horns and black curls shining, having a wonderful time. He knew how to pick his partner, for of all the figures in the church he had got the only beauty. And how she danced, her waist and bosom turning, hair and ankles flying high. Adam Forrester could not take his eyes off her, but for a long time he could not get a glimpse of her face, for they were always in the thick of the dancing. When he did, however, he was stunned, and then delighted, for it was none other than his own favourite, Lucky Hair herself.

Wide-eyed and amazed he watched, until at length, half drunk, he could contain himself no longer. Lifting his whip he rapped loudly on the window, calling out: "Aye, are ye there, Lucky Hair? Ye'll no deny this the morn!"

Instantly the company broke up in wild confusion, with the most awesome swearing and cursing that ever dinned the sober grey walls of a church. Then the lights were extinguished and the kirk was plunged into darkness. Above the yells and fearful hubbub the cries rang out: "Catch him! Kill him! Drag him off to Hell!"

The kirk door flew open and the shrieking women and old men scrambled out into the night after him. Swiftly Adam Forrester sprang on to his horse's back, and kicking his heels in drove it through the gravestones, leaped the kirkyard wall, and galloped away down the road towards the ford by the Craiggubble Inn, hanging on drunkenly, his mind in a whirl. Down the rough road they flew in pursuit, filling the air with their cries.

Across the wide, splashing ford he went, and up the bridle path on the hillside opposite. The river did not check them for an instant: across they poured, some flying, some on the stepping stones, some wading and swimming — crooked limbs going like frogs, hair and clothes streaming in the water.

Long before he reached the summit of the hill Adam Forrester was being overtaken. Springing from his horse in a little meadow, he pulled the beast shuddering beside him, and drawing his sword described a circle in the turf around them, crying aloud: "I draw this circle in the name of God Almighty: let no evil thing cross over it!"

The witches flew at him with yells of triumph, then reached the line and suddenly started back in fear and alarm. With terrible threats and shining eyes they gathered around, but none, not the Devil himself, dared cross the mark. All through the dark hours they remained, stretching out their arms and cursing him, gathering into huddles, trying every wile in their power to get at him.

The horse was terrified and restless, showing the whites of its eyes. For an instant its white tail flew beyond the circle. In a flash the Devil seized it and pulled the tail right off. Lucky Hair managed to get her hand on the horse's rump, leaving a black, spread-fingered print which it bore for life.

The night seemed an eternity, but at long last the dawn showed in the east and the cock of The Cairnford crowed. With the cock-crow the power of the witches departed. Slowly, with many last threats, they turned from Adam Forrester's circle and made their way back down the hill. As they went their bones and joints stiffened, and by the time they passed from view they were hobbling and leaning on one another's shoulders for support. All around the circle, to a distance of three or four yards, the grass was blackened and scorched to the very earth beneath.

Adam Forrester, long sober, waited until the morning sun had lifted itself above the hills. Then, with a fervent prayer and still some apprehension, he ventured out of the circle and made his way slowly home to Knocksheen.

The mark of his sword — 'Adam Forrester's Circle' — remained in the turf of Waterside Hill for generations, and was visited by many thousands of sightseers. When in the course of years it grew faint, it was renewed annually by his descendants.

May of Livingstone

The slime of the Dee for his bridal couch,
For his pillow a cold, cold stone;
And heirless remains the wide domain,
Who would wed the May of Livingstone.

Loch Ken, with its wooded bays and islands, more than ten miles in length, lies in a shallow and beautiful valley to the north-west of Castle Douglas. Rather more than a mile to the east of the southern tip, in days gone by, stood the tower of Ernfillan surrounded by a fine estate. They belonged to a junior branch of the great Border family of Glendinning. In a raid by Southron and English marauders, the tower was destroyed, the estate laid waste, and the owner was murdered.

With the assistance of the border chieftain, Glendinning himself, the tower was partially rebuilt. There, with her four young sons — Edward, William, Thomas and David — the widow settled down and began the task of repairing the estate as well as she was able.

When Edward, her oldest son, was eight, he was taken east to the Border hall of Glendinning, where he was raised as the heir of the childless chieftain. On attaining manhood he engaged in many battles and skirmishes against the warlike Northumbrians, acquitting himself with great honour and becoming quite renowned.

The chieftain died and Edward Glendinning, still only twenty years old, succeeded to his fortune and great estates. Because of the old man's discipline he had not once, in those twelve Border years, returned to his former home. But now, as soon as his succession was firmly established, he put the estate in order for a lengthy absence. And one spring morning, with a retinue of lively young friends, he mounted his finest horse and set off west through the Borders to visit his mother and brothers at Ernfillan. His arrival, after so long an absence, was greeted with great joy and festivity.

A short while before this Edward had spent a month or two at court in Holyrood House, and while he was there he made the acquaintance of the Laird of Livingstone, whose estate lay on the west bank of Loch Ken, only three miles from Ernfillan. The laird's wooded lands were famous for their red deer, and he had invited the young chieftain to hunt them during his visit. Two days after his arrival, therefore, the hunt was arranged.

Early in the morning the excited band of young men assembled before the still partially ruined tower of Ernfillan, spirited horses prancing on the turf, harnesses jingling. Retainers had gone ahead of them to join the laird's keepers and drive a herd of stags to the hillside for their inspection. The hunting party set off and soon were splashing through the broad ford across the River Dee at the foot of Loch Ken.* Then they rode up the western bank of the loch through the river meadows and dappled woods to the place where the servants were waiting. A fine stag was picked out, young and well muscled, with a proud set of antlers. The huntsman raised the silver horn to his lips and the clear notes rang through the air.

The chase was on. Down the long slope swept the hunters, horse-hoofs thudding and sending up clods of earth, the air rushing past, manes flying, hair blown back from the eager young faces. Ahead the stag fled with long, graceful bounds through woodland and across the open, heather-covered hillside.

Meanwhile, from the house of Livingstone on the shores of Loch Ken a mile below them, the laird's daughter Helen departed on her morning walk. She was a simple and beautiful girl, with a great love of the countryside around her home. It was a fragile beauty, not unlike certain Renaissance portraits, and heightened perhaps by a blowing gown of green silk and trailing shawl of white lawn. It was her custom, also, to wear wild flowers in her little cap. Though her loveliness was well known she led a quiet life and had not met many young men. In the district, however, she was much spoken of, and was commonly referred to as the May, or maiden, of Livingstone.

That morning, as she proceeded along a quiet path by the loch, she heard the notes of the horns, and above her on the bracken-covered slopes of Livingstone Hill she saw the riders. Ahead of them, briefly, she glimpsed the wild, fleeting form of the deer. She rode to the deer hunting herself, but in her father's absence she wondered who the men could be. They passed from her sight.

An hour later, returning to the hall by a slightly different route, she heard them again, calling a little way off. Suddenly she stopped, hearing a crashing of branches in the wood ahead of her. The stag, obviously on its last legs, ran into the clearing. Its muzzle was lathered with foam.

* Loch Ken has been dammed and enlarged. It is still beautiful. The ford was below the present village of Crossmichael.

It came to a halt, mouth open, panting, brown eyes wild and rolling. Turning at bay by a dense thicket, it faced back the way it had come. The noise of baying hounds was in the wood. The stag lowered its head and made a tossing gesture with its antlers.

May was only a few yards away. She was frightened. The stag saw her and pawed the ground. The dogs came closer. Quickly she caught up her skirts and ran across the clearing. As the first dog, with a huntsman on its heels, bounded into the clearing, the stag charged at the girl's fleeting back.

On the instant the huntsman, who was Edward, slipped from his horse, flung himself at the stag's back legs, and with his hunting knife sliced through the hamstrings. The animal slithered to the ground. Edward sprang on its back, and hooking his arm beneath its head cut the white throat. The stag was dead instantly.

The girl's body lay senseless on the grass and twigs of the forest floor. His clothes smeared with earth and blood Edward knelt beside her. She was not hurt, she had only fainted, and a minute later began to stir.

A short distance away Edward's brother was calling his name. He replied, and the next moment William appeared through the trees. A tableau greeted his eyes: the stag slaughtered — as he said later, as if by a Kirkcudbright butcher — and his brother kneeling beside the most beautiful girl in the district. Water was fetched from a well nearby, ever since known as 'Helen's Well',* and soon she recovered. They escorted her home.

As they rode back to Ernfillan in the early afternoon Edward was unusually quiet. He had never been in love. Now the image of the girl's face would not leave his mind. William readily understood. He chaffed his brother, advising him to beware, for the man to wed May Livingstone would be drowned in the River Dee. Edward pulled himself together and asked his lively young brother what he meant. William, still half laughing, glanced at the circle of friends who had heard his words and drawn their horses closer.

He repeated the prophecy of Anaple Nabony, the Witch of Ernanity, a spae-wife from near their own home. She had prophesied that the man who sought to marry the lovely May of Livingstone would drown in the River Dee on his wedding day. All he should know for a bridal couch was the river slime, and for his pillow a cold stone. And more

* Unfortunately the location of this well is now unknown.

than that, his whole family would die, though not by the sword and not in their beds. Their lands should have no heir.

Edward exclaimed — there were four of them: surely they would not all die. Their young faces, glowing from the fresh air and exercise, grew momentarily solemn. Then William laughed gaily, and tugging at the reins of his horse urged it at full trot into the ford over the River Dee. The water splashed high, glittering and shining in the afternoon sunlight. The others spurred their horses after him.

Edward was truly in love. The long drawn out festivities of his homecoming, the athletic sports at which he excelled, interested him no more. He wandered alone, seeking sequestered hillsides and glades from which he could look across at Livingstone Hall. As soon as the laird returned he rode across to renew his acquaintance. It was plain from her shy manner and downcast eyes that his visit was welcome to May Livingstone. Soon, with the laird's blessing, he was calling more frequently; and sometimes in the evening the young pair would walk up the loch and watch the summer sun setting over the hills. The Livingstone woods turned gold with autumn and white with winter, then daffodils carpeted the ground and soon the trees once more were in summer leaf. At the end of a twelvemonth the wedding was announced.

They were to be married in the Abbey of St Michael at Glenlochar, three miles downstream from Livingstone Hall. Since the bride and her father needed to cross the river, it was natural for the wedding parties to meet at the ford.

Unfortunately the wedding was preceded by a spell of wet weather, and it was feared that the ceremonies would be dampened. However the day itself broke brilliantly fair, with warm sunshine and the last drops of rain shining on the twigs. In the late morning, downhill from Ernfillan and along the edge of the loch from Livingstone Hall, the joyful parties journeyed to the ford. But when they arrived, the bride and her friends on one bank, the groom on the other, they found that the river was still swollen. Grey and shining in the sunlight it swam down from Loch Ken, sixty yards wide, lapping high against the earth and gravel of the track. Though they rode horses, it was doubtful whether the bride's party would be able to cross.

But William, gay and light-hearted as ever, declared that he would himself escort the bride across the racing water. No-one should stop him.

Determined, his eyes dancing, holding his horse on a tight rein, he urged it into the flood. Voices called on him to be careful. The water rose to the horse's belly, and continued rising until it was more than half-way to the saddle. It was deeper than he had expected: impossible for the bride to cross. But he was in the middle, the water must now grow shallower. Even as the thought was in the minds of the onlookers, William's horse stumbled. It lurched, then seemed to recover, he was thrown forward over the pommel — then the pair were gone into the torrent. In an instant the water plucked William away. The horse plunged, and was swimming strongly. Reaching a pool fifty yards downstream where the rushing water slackened and turned, it drew towards the bank. But of its rider there was no sign.

Edward, already on the shore, flung off his jacket and plunged in after his brother. He was a strong swimmer. Thomas and David, the youngest brothers, waded in after him, and in a moment joined him in the swirling pool, wedding shirts clinging, hair sleek as seals. Taking a deep breath, Edward dived into the deepest part. They waited, with baited breath, but Edward did not reappear. Then David, the youngest, a boy of fourteen, was in trouble. Thomas, only two years older, caught him beneath the arms. In a spinning eddy they were sucked beneath the surface. Aghast the watchers regarded the turning, sunlit waters of the pool. The brown current surged against the bank and jutting rocks. It had happened so quickly, there was nothing they could do.

Boats were fetched and the pool was dragged. The four bodies were recovered, David still locked in Thomas's arms, Edward's hand fastened in the lapel of the fashionable jacket gay William had purchased for his brother's wedding.

Distressed beyond bearing, the bride's party returned to Livingstone Hall, and the widow accompanied the bodies of her sons to Ernfillan.

Two days later, wedding celebration replaced by funereal pomp, the four brothers were laid in the crypt of the Abbey of St Michael. The whole countryside attended their torchlit interrment.

The words of Anaple Nabony, the Witch of Ernanity, had come to pass: Edward and his brothers were drowned, their line came to an end, the fine estate of Ernfillan and the Border lands of Glendinning were left without an heir.

May Livingstone, the delicately beautiful and simple girl who loved the woods and hills of her home, for some time completely lost her reason with the shock. Though she recovered, she was never afterwards the same, and never married.

> Now the Livingstone bowers are green my love
> And green its birken shaw:
> And the wild rose blooms in Fininess dell,
> And the heath flower is red on Duchrae fell,
>   But joy is far awa, my love,
>   But joy is far awa!

Douglas Crosby and the Adder[*]

Newlaw Farm is situated half a mile from Dundrennan, inland from the coastal fields and the Abbey. The farmhouse, with the byres and sheds to one side, stands on a small tree-covered knoll, among open though rather rough and hilly pasture land.

In 1786 the tenant of Newlaw was Andrew Crosby, who lived in the present farmhouse with his wife Jane and three or four year old son Douglas.

For several days during a spell of perfect weather in that summer, Jane Crosby, a woman in her early forties, had heard her son speaking of meeting a 'beardie', who was his friend, in the garden.[†] She thought little of it: doubtless the boy was playing by some stream or pool, lying on the bank and trailing his little hands in beside the sticklebacks and minnows.

Every morning, however, in the early sunshine, he had taken to carrying his breakfast bowl of porridge out of the kitchen and eating it in the garden to the side of the house.

One day his mother chanced to be out there herself, and heard her young son say in his childish tones: "Keep yer ain side o' the plate, grey beardie." Wondering what he was about, she crossed to the knoll, and saw the boy sitting in the garden among the rocky flower beds, with the bowl of porridge lying on the grass beside him. To her horror, an adder was curled up right next to him, its head in the dish, feeding from the boy's breakfast in the most natural way. While she watched, frightened to make a sound, the little boy rapped the snake on the head with his spoon to send it round to its own side of the bowl. Then he proceeded with his breakfast, and the adder, having done as he wished, rested its throat afresh on the rim and resumed feeding from the same dish.

Quietly Mrs Crosby spoke to her son, telling him to get up softly and come to her. The little boy did as he was told, completely unafraid of

---

* This tale is the subject of the once popular poem 'The Boy and the Snake' by Charles or Mary Lamb, first published in their anthology *Poetry for Children* — 1809.

† A 'beardie', in this sense, is Scots for a stickleback or minnow, or even a small trout. It is the sort of error that a young child would make, accustomed to seeing and perhaps even handling the scaly, wriggling beardies in the Galloway burns.

the snake. Once he was well clear, his mother caught him away, alarming him with her fear and rough treatment.

At the commotion the adder slithered off into the rough grass and heather at the edge of the garden, only a few feet away. Mrs Crosby

called some of the men from the farm and told them what had happened. Cautiously, with sticks, they poked and thrashed through the clumps of heather and grass nearby. When the simple snake tried to slither away to safety, they clubbed it to death. The little boy was heartbroken at their cruelty.

Three years later, on the 1st December, 1789, Douglas Crosby died. He was seven years old. In later years, when the dates had been forgotten, it was said that he had died of grief. He was buried in the north-east corner of the graveyard which surrounds the beautiful ruin of the great Dundrennan Abbey. His gravestone is still there to be seen. Well beyond the middle of the last century the children of Dundrennan, knowing the story well, used to run down to visit the grave with handfuls of flowers.

Thou Shalt Not Suffer a Witch

In 1590 King James VI presided over the trial of John Fian and the North Berwick Witches, the most notorious witch trial in Scotland's history. Personally he authorised and watched the most depraved and agonising tortures that man can devise, and was amazed at the wild confessions that emerged. Seven years later he published *Daemonologie*, based upon his considerations following this trial, and his fascination and study of the subject. It was to set the pattern for the century of witch persecution that followed, during which, it is believed, well in excess of 4,000 witches were burned in Scotland.

The religious awareness, and even fanaticism, of Scotland, was never stronger than in those days following John Knox and his wild visions of Hell and the Anti-Christ. His teaching remained strong: the church must be vigilant! And concerning witches – apart from Satan himself – the Holy Book was specific. In the most famous of the Old Testament stories the people and ministers read of God's anger when King Saul went to the Witch of Endor to summon up the spirit of the dead Samuel; in the Book of Samuel they learned of 'the sin of witchcraft'; in Leviticus they were taught, 'A man also or woman that hath a familiar spirit, or that is a wizard, shall surely be put to death: they shall stone them with stones; their blood shall be upon them'; and most stark and unavoidable of all, Exodus counselled 'Thou shalt not suffer a witch to live'.

The law of the land, too, admitted witches, and laid down procedures of investigation and specific punishments for those found guilty. Repute was enough to convict, and for a century conviction, save in the slightest of cases, meant death.

The law, the church, the king – it is not surprising that the superstitious peasantry believed in witchcraft. It had always been the case, of course, in a simple, folklorish sort of way, but before the Reformation there was not a single case of burning for witchcraft in the country. The powers that be were to change all that.

'Scotland is second only to Germany in the barbarity of its witch trials,' wrote R. H. Robbins in his *Encyclopedia of Witchcraft and Demonology*. 'The Presbyterian clergy acted like inquisitors, and the church sessions often shared the prosecution with the secular law

courts. The Scottish laws were, if anything, more heavily loaded against the accused. Finally, the devilishness of the torture was limited only by Scotland's backward technology in the construction of mechanical devices. Suppression of any opposition to belief in witchcraft was complete.'

And in *The Hereditary Sheriffs of Galloway* Sir Andrew Agnew wrote: 'Presbyteries entertained ridiculous accusations against numberless old crones; having first egged on their kirk-sessions to ferret out witches, and then set the law in motion to bring them to the stake. The lists of these judicial murders are appalling; and, long as they are, probably are far from being complete. ... The presbytery records, which teem with evidence as to the virulence of the persecution, as conclusively prove the stupidity of the persecutors.'

The period of witch persecution in Scotland ran parallel to similar events throughout Europe. The 'Act Anentis Witchcraft' was introduced by Mary Queen of Scots in 1563. It was repealed in 1736 by George II. For the first three decades of this period — until the trial of the North Berwick Witches — there were only occasional trials and burnings for witchcraft. The last forty years were also comparatively quiet. The seventeenth century itself saw most of the witch hunts.

One of the first to be burned was Bessie Dunlop of Ayrshire, who in 1576 was convicted of being a member of a conclave of eight female and four male witches, and receiving herbal cures from the Queen of the Fairies. The last to suffer death was Janet Horn of Sutherland, who was prosecuted for turning her daughter into a pony, riding her through the air to attend a Sabbat, and having her shod by the Devil so that she was permanently lamed. For this she was tarred and feathered and burned alive at Dornoch in 1722.

In the minds of the people, however, witchcraft lingered on long after this. In Kirkcudbright as late as 1805 a woman named Jean Maxwell was brought to court for pretending witchcraft. Through charms and incantations she had completely taken over the common sense of a servant girl named Jean Davidson of Cocklick in Urr. Pretending to conjure up the Devil and place a young man in her power, Jean Maxwell had extorted considerable sums of money, food and clothing, which the servant girl had been in part compelled to steal. She was found guilty and imprisoned for one year, being shown in the pillory every quarter.

Earlier trials, however, ended in death. In 1644 five Wigtownshire women were tried and burned for witchcraft in Stranraer. On 5th April,

1669, nine Galloway women were executed at the Whitesands in Dumfries: as the sentence expressed it, 'there, between the hours of two and four in the afternoon to be stranglit at stakes till they be dead, and thereafter their bodies to be burnt to ashes.' This was the most common means of execution for witches, though some were drowned or hanged, and others were burned alive.

Witchcraft had been accepted in Scotland, as of course elsewhere, since time immemorial. In the context of superstitious rural life, hard work and poverty, the daily proximity of sickness and death, and ignorance combined with a fierce religious tradition, it is easy to understand. A young woman with a physical or mental blemish was an outsider: so was an old woman living alone, twisted with arthritis, drawn within herself through loneliness and pain. An intelligent woman living in this condition might well question the facile words of a visiting minister. What loving God did she know: who was to help her through the grey vista of days and long nights that stretched ahead? And in her beliefs she was not a woman apart, she was as superstitious as her neighbours. She had seen their looks. What were those strange moods and desires that sometimes came close to overwhelming her? Since God had elected to give her none of the comforts enjoyed by her neighbours, since she did not belong among them, then what harm could come from seeking elsewhere, through other means? And if accident seemed to provide an answer, then once she was descended to that level of desperation might it not be clung to as indeed some sign of powers beyond the normal? Probably she was confused and did not know. But even though she be as innocent as a baby, even of this foolishness, if in discomfort or irritation she had crossed words with a countryman and two days later his cow fell sick, then the reason was not hard to find. For in one way a witch was simply a scape-goat, someone present and among them for people to blame for misfortunes they did not understand.

It was not, in the minds of the country folk, a black and white situation. There were all shades of grey, and most of those nominated 'witch' lived lonely women to their natural deaths. Where there were no loved ones they lavished their affection on pets — the witch's cat. Their knowledge of simples and country lore was well known — they had plenty of time in which to learn, and the herbs and leaves supplemented their meagre rations. Some, being considered women beyond the normal, spaed fortunes: some were quietly placated with regular gifts of farm produce or cast-off clothing, which helped them along. They lived among yet apart from the community, an integral part of the natural and superstitious landscape.

They were the unfortunate who were brought to the attention of the church and secular authorities. Beyond the regularly constituted enquiries of church and state, the privy council appointed commissions of local gentlemen, specifically to investigate and seek out cases of alleged witchcraft within counties. Some were even granted power to pronounce the death sentence. Typical charges were 'addressing the Devil in the shape of a black beetle'; 'bewitching Goody Hannah by walking past the rowan tree at the corner of her garden'; 'muttering inaudible incantations in church'; 'changing herself into a bat to fly to some bewitched spot for carnal relations with a young man'. So unprovable and fantastic were the accusations that there could be no defence save denial, and the word of neighbours as to good character; and even kind neighbours were justly reticent about going forward, lest they should themselves be implicated in the accusation. What could an old woman with no friends say when she was accused by an upright villager, a pillar of the church, that he had seen her talking to the Devil before the altar, and every detail of the conversation and the Devil's appearance was recounted? – an actual case. Reputation convicted as readily as 'proof', and denial was soon overcome when a woman's nails were torn out and burning skewers were thrust through the resultant sores; when her head was thrown about roughly with a rope until she lost consciousness; when her leg and foot were reduced to pulp in 'the boot', or her thumb joint was crushed in 'the screw'; when needles were thrust into her head through the mouth; or she was made to lie naked on a cold slab without sleeping for days and weeks on end, always in the expectation of further torture. If the accused witch bore some blemish, such as a mole or a wart, then this was viewed as the Devil's mark and pierced deeply with a pin in an attempt to make the blood flow black and flush the Devil out. A larger flaw, such as a strawberry birth mark, was regarded with horror.

A witch, when viewed at this level, was a servant of Satan, and imbued with something of Satan's spirit. Non-confession, therefore, meant simply that the Devil was very strong in her and must be driven out more stringently; and confession, of course, meant death. Once an enquiry was started there was nothing a reputed witch could do to absolve herself from guilt. If the initial charges were not dropped, her only hope lay in the intervention of an influential well-wisher, or some incalculable change of heart among her accusers. She was hopelessly trapped by the evil thinking and false argument of the authorities. At the start of the more rigorous investigation, for example, if upon entering the ghastly torture chamber and being shown a cross or a Bible she showed any sign of fear or hysteria, then this was considered a clear initial indication of guilt.

It is cruelly ironic that the victim herself, if she possessed the money, was compelled to pay a fee for each of the tortures used against her, and ultimately for her own execution. There were two justifications for this. In driving the Devil out, the torturers, executioners and implacable clergy or other authority were performing a valuable service: also, since there were frequently a number of people on trial together, the considerable expenses did not thus fall upon the parish, which was often very poor. A condemned witch's estate was always forfeit to the crown. If she was well-to-do there was sometimes money to be made all round, even by the labourers who fetched the peats and faggots for the fire. On the other hand, if she was penniless, then the expenses were required of the church session or town council, or the owner of the estate upon which she resided.

All of those accused, of course, were not single women. Often country wives and girls, or men of a superstitious disposition, dabbled among the charms and elixirs, or tried their hands at spaeing fortunes. Harmless amusement as old as the hills, but not when it was brought to the attention of certain officials. Sometimes women of hysterical tendencies or emotional children — particularly around the age of puberty — pretended possession, and once the mischief was started were pressed deeper and deeper into webs of deceit and justification, to a point where only breakdown or death could release the accusers as well as the accused. And occasionally, of course, the unjust and inexorable law was used by a malevolent neighbour to pay off an old score.

The events are, save in the lighter of the church records, almost unrelievedly appalling, yet the civil and church authorities were not monsters, they simply reflected the times. Often they did not wish to proceed with prosecutions and they were dropped. Sometimes, however, they were pressed by members of their congregations or higher authority to take action which they did not wish or approve, and having learned little of courage from the story of Pontius Pilate, allowed people whom they considered innocent to be executed. No-one, at that time, could be seen to avoid punishing a witch with impunity, for there was the terrifying backlash to be avoided.

91

Twenty years after the publication of *Daemonologie* King James changed his opinion. He had investigated one or two alleged cases and found the claims fallacious. Principal among them, perhaps, was the thirteen year old Leicester boy, John Smith, because of whose mischie and deliberate physical tricks — which afterwards he would repeat several times in a day for the amusement of onlookers — nine women had been hanged and six more were awaiting trial. But by this time James was resident in far-away London and beset with political problems beside which the yearly torture and burning of a handful of innocent Scots was a comparative trifle. And so great was the swelling tide of witch persecution, not only in Scotland but throughout Europe, that it would have taken a considerable effort on his part to have checked it at all.

So the century of Scottish witch-hunts ran its course, from peak to peak of rigorous activity, through the Union of the Crowns, the Civil War, the Restoration, the Covenanting times, the ascension of the House of Hanover. But by the end of the seventeenth century opposition was mounting, and with the growing enlightenment of the early eighteenth century the death penalty was abolished.

The church followed in the wake of the law. As late as 1773 the ministers of the Associated Presbytery, which had always pressed for suppression and the greatest vigilance, passed a resolution declaring their continuing firm belief in witchcraft. And popular feeling lingered behind the church. Even in 1825 a suspected witch in Galloway took a number of people to court for assault. They had deeply torn the skin across her eyebrows, which was considered to render a witch impotent of her powers.

Generally from this time, however, belief in witchcraft declined from its being a real manifestation of Satan's evil, through folk belief and traditional superstition, to our present day dismissal. For most people now a witch is merely a hook-nosed fantasy from a child's fairy tale. How different was the truth.

FOOTNOTE

It is interesting that today, when man has been to the moon and we live in a world of scientific progress, education and hard-headed realism, films on modern witchcraft and demonology are repeatedly breaking box-office records. It is said, too, that the study and practice of witchcraft, though in a quasi-religious and more natural form, is on the increase. Almost every paperback stall has its rank of books on the occult. The fascination of King James, it seems, will always be with us.

The Witch of the Routin' Brig

The parish of Kirkpatrick-Irongray lies a few miles to the west of Dumfries. It is divided roughly in two, west from east, by the north-flowing Routin' Burn (Old Water of Cluden), a tributary of Cairn Water. Just before its confluence with the larger river, the Routin' (noisy, splashing) Burn drops thirty feet down a fine cascade between crags, to run into a deep dark pool. The crags are crossed by a bridge, the Routin' Brig, famous for its beautiful setting, with the white cascade on one side, the still, dramatic pool far below on the other, and the whole craggy, romantic spot overhung with oak trees.

In about 1625 an old woman lived nearby in a poor, mud-walled cottage, separated from the river by a field or two, and with a great forest behind. She had a few animals and a small plot of land, and supplemented what food she could produce with wild plants and berries from the countryside around. Her main work, however, was her weaving. She spun her own yarn on a pole and worked each day, sitting near the window with the clew of yarn hanging from her bead strings.

93

Mainly she wove stockings, but she wove other garments too, and lengths of household cloth.

Although she was a harmless and good-living woman, she was viewed with suspicion by her neighbours, who believed they had ample cause to call her a witch. With their minds heavily biased they found tell-tale signs everywhere. When girls visited her cottage for some little garment, they often emerged with their eyes stinging and watering from the wood-smoke that filtered about the room. Sometimes, feeling rather grubby, they stooped at the well nearby to bathe their faces or take a drink as they were leaving. A black letter Bible lay in the cottage window, unusually bound with polecat leather and fastened with ornate, gothic clasps. When she was in church her lips moved: either an old woman's mumbling or prayers beneath her breath. She was unusually acute in her observation of the weather, and predicted remarkably well. In the evening she liked to sit on a high rock above the river, where it was warm and sheltered by a bank of trees. Sometimes she took her work there and sang softly while she was busy, or even talked to keep herself company.

All this was woven into a fabric of sorcery by her neighbours, and the Bishop of Galloway was informed. Repeatedly he was urged to punish the witch. At length he came to investigate and the old woman was brought before' him in the open air, a little distance from the Routin' Brig. She knew what was being said and had to be dragged, terrified, from her cottage. The neighbours accused her of spaeing the fortunes of innocent girls so that they left her house in tears. Some, they said, needed to calm themselves by bathing their faces at her well, whilst others bowed their heads and even knelt by the water in continuation of the sorcery that had taken place within. A book of the black art lay in her window, plain for all to see — though with deep cunning she now made it seem like a Bible, showing how strong the Devil's power was in her. She invoked silent prayers to Satan in church. He informed her about the weather. Though there were plenty of places she might sit by the river, she had deliberately chosen a spot among the bewitching rowans. Often she talked to Satan there, they had seen her. And more than this, she practised tricks of glamoury by moonlight above the river and the Routin' Pool; she gathered rowan twigs for her fire; she walked widdershins about the well.

The Bishop of Galloway saw her only as a poor old woman, but was unable to discount the weight of evidence and the demands of the people for her punishment. Also he did not wish to seem laggardly in the eyes of his political superiors and other churchmen in punishing a witch. Almost reluctantly he pronounced that she should be put to death by drowning in the Routin' Pool. But this was not enough for the people gathered around. The witch must be burned, they cried. Only briefly did he hold out, then conceded to their demands.

In vain did the poor old woman plead her innocence and struggle. They dragged her to a flat place on a slope above the river and enclosed her in a tar barrel. Then they set fire to it. When it was blazing fiercely,

with wild whoops they bowled it down the hillside into a deep pool where, if any life remained in her, she drowned. (This was a variation of a more common practice, which was to bowl the witch down a hill in a barrel, and where the barrel stopped build a bonfire about it and burn her to death.)

For upwards of two centuries places in the vicinity remembered the incident in their names: the Bishop's Butt — the small piece of ground where the hearing took place; the Witch's Well — where the girls rinsed their faces; the Witch's Pool — where she was drowned; and the Bishop's Forest behind the old woman's cottage — through which the church-man rode away after his work was done.

Maggie Osborne — Fact Shrouded in Fantasy

Maggie Osborne was a witch in Glenluce. Many stories are told about her.* Younger and better looking than most of the old crones who were credited with witchcraft, she was understandably a great favourite of the Devil. Deep tracks in the heather between the northern Water of Luce and Carrick were well known as 'Maggie's Gate to Gallowa' '. The people of Glenluce hung bells about the necks of their cattle and water-holed stones above the stalls of their horses to protect them from her power. On one occasion, having impiously taken communion at the Moor Kirk of Luce, she carried the holy wafer in her mouth until she had passed the church door, where a sharp-eyed elder saw her spit it out in the direction of a large toad, the Devil in disguise, which instantly

gobbled it up. But such tales as these should perhaps be counted among the myths.

She was finally trapped by the evidence of a servant girl. At the time Maggie was keeping an inn at Ayr. Late one-evening she told the girl, a saucy creature who worked for her, to get on with some brewing. The girl claimed it was too late, and hot words were bandied between them. Maggie, however, was the mistress, and left the servant girl with red cheeks and her instructions.

The brew-house, a stone cellar or outbuilding, was lit by a dim

* See 'Crossing a Witch'.

lantern and full of steam. The girl was alone. At a little before midnight the door burst open and a number of large cats sprang into the room. She was very frightened. The largest of all crept forward as if it was stalking her, then suddenly yowled and leaped at her shoulders, clawing and biting, and nearly driving her head-first into the tub of boiling worts. With some difficulty the girl managed to throw the animal off. Seizing the big ladle to protect herself, she flung scoopful after scoopful of the scalding liquid all over them, particularly the largest cat, and drove them from the room.

The following morning, when her mistress did not appear as usual, the girl went to her bed chamber. Maggie was in some pain and discomfort. Pulling off the bedclothes, the servant girl saw her back and shoulders badly blistered, precisely where the boiling worts had hit the cat.

On the girl's evidence Maggie was summoned before the church session. She was examined and pronounced guilty, then handed over to the civil court which condemned her to death.

Even when bound to the stake among the faggots, however, she was not prepared to give up without a struggle. Offering to provide them with startling new facts, she required the magistrates to furnish her with two new pewter plates, which had never been wet. Quickly they dispatched the town sergeant. As he returned, however, he stumbled and let one fall into a puddle, but wiped it dry and continued back to the field of execution near the tolbooth. Instantly, as she received the plates, Maggie transformed them into wings and began to ascend from the pile of faggots. But the plate which had been wet drooped like a broken pinion, and before she could struggle to freedom the town sergeant hooked his halberd in her dress and pulled her back to the ground.

Much of this account, of course, is fantasy, and so are the earlier tales of her witchcraft, yet for fantasies no greater, people were burned to death. Certainly Maggie Osborne was burned as a witch, and as near as can be told, on some evidence very like that of the servant girl which has been given. Looking beyond this, however, it is suggested that she may have been the victim of jealousy. She was a pretty woman, attractive to men, and kept an inn that was famous for its good cheer. The impudent servant girl may well have been bribed to give the evidence she did. Jealousy and ill will could have taken a dozen directions against her.

Further tradition implicates a minister of Ayr, the Rev. William

Adair, a younger son of the Adairs of Kinhilt. For a long time he adored the pretty inn-keeper, and in desperate revenge at her refusal of his suit — possibly in favour of some other man — he prompted the prosecution against her, sat as one of the judges at her trial, and finally gloated over her sufferings. Whether or not this scandal is in any respect true, William Adair, along with other members of the church session, was certainly present at Maggie Osborne's dreadful end.

Elspeth McEwan

The most famous witch in Galloway and the last to be burned at the stake was Elspeth McEwan of Balmaclellan. She was an old woman who lived alone. Her solitary house was named 'Gubha', and was situated on the farm of Cubbox by the River Ken, a mile to the south-west of the village.

She was well known as a witch by the people of the district. Her neighbours claimed they were tormented by her. Every calamity that befel themselves or their livestock was attributed to her malicious tricks. Particularly, they said, she influenced the laying of their poultry. If the hens or ducks or geese stopped laying, if they took roup or the gapes and died, then she was at the bottom of it. On the other hand it paid to keep in with the old carlin, for if prices were high and more eggs were wanted for the market at New Galloway, then she could arrange that equally well.

Her greatest witchery, however, and the one they most resented, concerned a pin in her kipple foot — the bottom of a rafter in her smoky roof. During the hours of darkness, or when the rough meadows were unwatched, she issued forth and laid the pin against the udders of the cattle, sometimes creeping from one to the next through a whole herd. Thereafter, any time she wanted milk, all she had to do was to withdraw the pin from the rafter, and drain as much as she wanted from any cow she chose. This explained their sometimes poor milk yields.

For a long time the neighbours put up with it, but at length, in 1696, her supposed activities were brought to the attention of the church-session in Dalry, three miles away. She was summoned to appear before them on a charge of witchcraft, and on the appointed day the beadle, Mr McLambroch, was sent on the minister's mare to fetch her. When he arrived at the cottage door Elspeth expressed great wonder at his mission, but agreed to accompany him.

The return journey from Cubbox to Dalry was to furnish perhaps the most potent of the many 'proofs' of her guilt. As the old woman prepared to climb on its back, the mare trembled and showed signs of unmistakable terror. As it bore her across a ridge near the Dalry manse it was observed to let fall great drops of bloody sweat. From that time forward this stretch of the road was known as 'the Bluidy Brae'.

Elspeth McEwan was indicted on a number of charges. After undergoing an examination by the session, during which several witnesses gave testimony against her, she was proclaimed guilty, and sent for imprisonment to the Tolbooth in Kirkcudbright.

For two years she was held and tortured in the most appalling manner. Two gentlemen visiting the old woman at this time, apart from their very natural horror at her condition, found her to be a person of intelligence and superior education. At length, through the inhuman treatment, she was brought to such a condition of torment that she pleaded time and again with her persecutors to put her out of her pain.

In March, 1698, a commission sat to consider this request. To attain her desire, she was told, she must confess. Before her own minister, other churchmen, local dignitaries and her jailers, she declared herself guilty of a contract and regular commerce with the Devil, and of practising charms and other evil magical acts to the harm of the people.

The confession served its purpose and released her in the only way possible. On 24th August, 1698, Elspeth McEwan was taken from the Tolbooth to Silver Craig Park in Kirkcudbright, and burned to death at the stake.

William Kirk, her executioner, was 'an old, infirm man, without friends or relations', and one suspects of a drunken, indigent nature. For some weeks before the burning he had to be kept in jail to ensure that he would turn up at the appointed time. Within a year he was to become a penniless beggar, stoned away from villages, and whining to the Kirkcudbright magistrates for more money.

A treasurer's account of this time gives some indication of the mood and situation that prevailed. It details such expenses as regular drink for the executioner, even to the pint of ale he took while she was burning. The Provost, of course, preferred brandy — he took a gill — and the other dignitaries also enjoyed their drinks on expenses that day. The account lists the hay and peats for the fire; the carter's charge for delivering them; ropes and nooses; deliveries of candles for Elspeth McEwan's guards; various purchases of meal and legs of mutton for the executioner; his transport and accommodation; clothing for him, too, including new shoes, a new bonnet and a long muffler; a tar barrel; a gift for the Provost on the day of execution; a man to beat the drum at the appointed time; and various other items.

A lot may be pieced together, but here, as in all the witchcraft trials, the key piece is missing. What sort of woman, really, was Elspeth McEwan? Why was she the scape-goat?

Janet McRobert — A Little Enlightenment

Though the following events occurred near Kirkcudbright only three years after the dreadful persecution of Elspeth McEwan, one would like to think that a certain enlightenment was at last filtering down from the justiciary in Edinburgh.

Janet McRobert was a single woman of some learning who lived in the clachan of Milnburn. In 1701 she was arraigned before the Kirk Session of Kirkcudbright on charges of witchcraft. The evidence against her, compared with some investigations, was considerable.

One day the wife of Robert Crichton was winnowing in a barn owned by Bailie Dunbar, and seeing her there, Janet McRobert came and lent a hand. When they had finished Janet asked for some chaff for her pains, and was given a small quantity in her apron. She felt that it was not enough and the women crossed words. The following day Mrs Crichton's breast swelled dreadfully, as a result of which, we learn from the Minute Book of the Kirkcudbright Kirk Session, 'her young child who was sucking decayed and vanished away to a shadow'. Shortly afterwards their cow took a distemper which so tasted and discoloured the milk that for a considerable time no use could be made of it.

About the same time the child of John Bodden of Milnburn died. During the child's lyke-wake (the watch kept at night over his body), a dreadful noise was heard about the house of Janet McRobert, which so terrified a neighbour's son that he was afraid to go out of the door. John Bodden also heard it and was frightened. Janet declared that it was only her clocken (broody) hen, but John Bodden exclaimed that all the hens within twenty miles could not have made such a noise.

Three years afterwards young Elizabeth Lauchlon was being taught by Janet McRobert, and going to her door one morning the girl was surprised to see the spinning wheel turning and making the yarn by itself. For a while she watched, then going into the room she tried to stop it, but was beaten about the head and driven back to the door, though still the room remained empty. On another occasion Elizabeth Lauchlon was approached by a man in the house, whom she knew to be the Devil, and who told her to give herself to him 'from the crown of her head to the sole of her foot'. She replied that she would rather give herself to God Almighty, at which the Devil went away, and Janet, who was present, made her promise never to tell what had happened. On a second occasion, when she was alone, the Devil again came to her in the likeness of a gentleman, and desired her to go with him. When again she refused he disappeared, seeming not to go out of the door.

A certain Mr Howell had gone to Milnburn to buy two hens from John Robertson, but he had none to sell and suggested that Mr Howell should approach Janet McRobert. She declared that she had none to sell either. At this some old antagonism flared up and Mr Howell exclaimed that she had enough hens to steal the barley from his grandmother's field when it was sown. Perhaps, he said, his rough lad (his dog) would fetch some of her poultry to him. She replied that his rough lad certainly would not. Before he returned to the town his dog ran mad, and was seen by many people.

A friend in Rerrick Parish, who was in bed awaiting the birth of a child, sent her daughter to Janet McRobert to borrow some money. At first Janet refused, then reluctantly agreed, assuring the daughter that she would certainly lose it on the way home. The young woman was angered at her words, and carefully laid the money (two fourteens) beneath some turmeric in the bottom of her purse, and drew the neck tight. When she arrived home the money was gone, though the purse had no holes in it and she had not loosened the strings.

Agnes Kirk was the wife of John McGymper. Visiting her one day, Janet asked for a dead hare that had been caught by their dog and was hanging from a rafter, waiting to be skinned and cooked. Agnes Kirk refused, for they wanted it themselves. From that moment their dog was never able to run properly, or catch any more hares for them.

Finally, after Janet McRobert was imprisoned, John Linton — whose son had been so frightened by the noise about her house — saw a candle moving through the rooms at cock-crow, yet apparently there was no-one holding it.

Clearly the evidence as it stands is questionable, imaginative and circumstantial, yet many witches were tortured into false confessions and burned upon evidence no sounder, and accusations a great deal wilder. In 1701, however, the Kirkcudbright Kirk Session was denied permission to pursue Janet McRobert legally. The evidence, it was felt by the Edinburgh justiciary, was not sufficiently presumptive of guilt.

She was, however, banished from the parish, and went to live in Ireland.

The Simple Giant

There was great anxiety in the little township of Palnackie. For days there had been storms and the good ship 'Sark' was long overdue. At length their fears were laid to rest by the shouts of a boy, and running from their doors the townsfolk saw the vessel a mile downstream, sailing up the muddy, winding estuary through the green pastures. Soon it was drifting gently into harbour, the seamen on the rails laughing and waving to their families. After brief, bustling activity the ship was moored at the side of the estuary and the crew jumped ashore. A minute or two later the assembled townsfolk were amazed as Captain Ewart appeared at the ship's side holding the hand of a boy aged about three, with a foolish, simple expression on his face. While the 'Sark' was heaved to in the storm they had found him floating in a rowing boat, alone on the rough sea. One of the sailors lifted the boy ashore, and rather more stiffly than his young crew, Captain Ewart climbed down.

"Send him back," the townsfolk advised, looking askance at the sturdy child. "Give him back to the sea, or the sea will take several of us in revenge."

Captain Ewart said this was nonsense, and announced that he intended to adopt the boy himself, since his wife loved children and they had none of their own. His name, he said, was to be John A. Boe, since that was the name painted on the bows of the rowing boat in which they had found him floating.

The years passed, and John grew up. And grow he did — to an amazing size. At six he seemed more like twelve, and at twelve he had the build of a powerful man. But his brain was as weak as his body was strong. The schoolmaster despaired of him, and all his thrashings did nothing to drive a little learning into the young giant's head. Instead, John — who could have carried the schoolmaster under one arm and dumped him in the river had he wished — gave him a simple smile, showing his wish to please. But at length, in a fashion, he learned the most simple counts and reading and printing.

When he was twelve, alas, the good Captain Ewart was drowned at sea, and his wife pined away and died shortly afterwards. On the day she was put into her coffin people began asking what was to become of the huge, simple-minded boy. To the end of his life it was never known where he had come from or what he was doing in that rowing boat. Some of the townsfolk still believed he should be put back to the sea. Others were more charitable, but no-one really wanted him. At last a selfish farmer from the Boreland nearby, who saw how strong and biddable the boy was, offered to take him and make an odd-job man of him. Few of the townsfolk, who knew the farmer's reputation, were taken in by his declarations of charity.

For seven years John A. Boe remained with his employer, digging and hoeing and herding and fencing, all with the sweetest of goodwill, and for it he received not one farthing of wages beyond his keep. He had grown into a man seven feet tall, more powerful than a cart-horse but gentle and easily frightened, and so simple-minded that the children mocked him in the lanes and the townsfolk did not hide the fact that they considered him a fool.

One summer day he was going past a straggle of buildings in his rough working clothes — mostly other people's cast-offs and much too small for him — when he came upon a gang of young ruffians. They were stoning a large and rather sinister black cat which belonged to an old wrinkled woman of the town who lived alone and was generally considered to be a witch. Ignoring the boys' stones John hurried past them and gathered up the cat in his great arms. Then, glowering at the boys and sheltering the cat from further harm, stroking it tenderly, he carried it back to the old woman. She was very grateful, for she had received her full share of roughness and insult from the people of the district. He was the first one in a long while to do her a kindness, and in gratitude she offered to reward him with whatever was his dearest wish. The young giant knew exactly what he desired, but for a long time he could not get the words out, mouthing and gobbling and sighing, and staring at her like a bullock as if she should read his mind instead. It made the old woman impatient; in fact she grew quite angry. But at last he managed to tell her that he would like to do a great deed of valour, so that everyone would respect him in the town, instead of looking down on him as a great stot* and an idiot the way they did at present. She thought for a moment, then crossing to the table handed him an open pot of rich heather honey. He was to carry it just as it was along the road past the gallows on the way to Auchencairn the following day when the sun was high. Promising to do as she said, John returned to the farm.

* A young bull or ox: a stupid, clumsy fellow.

104

When he told his employer that he wanted the day off — his first free day in seven years — the Boreland farmer grumbled and complained, but so unshakably fixed upon it was John, that at length he had to give way.

At a little before midday, as he had been instructed, John set off along the rough stony road, baked with the summer heat. The steep bracken-covered slopes of Screel and Bengairn rose on his right, and the cool inlets of the Solway were on his left. He passed the empty gibbet and soon was walking above a morass where always the flies were thick in the summer. They buzzed in a fierce cloud about his head and swarmed around the mouth of the honey pot. The warm smell of the heather honey seemed to draw them from all the countryside around.

"Drat the wee devils!" John said to himself. "I'll never get a mouthful to myself. Go on, get away, shoo!"

Taking off his bonnet he struck at the flies above his head and beat at those buzzing in the mouth of the honey pot. Soon the surface of the thick honey was littered with their corpses. He stopped on the road and peered in. Now he would have to pick them all out with a twig. What on earth was the old woman about, telling him to carry the open pot along the road like that? She must have known there would be swarms of flies. Carefully he began to count the bodies — one, two, three — but it was so confusing, and he was never very good beyond twenty. Time and again he started, but soon was lost once more. A hundred seemed an enormous number. He settled for that and walked on, chewing a stem of heather. As he looked across the hot countryside through the dancing cloud of flies he thought of the great slaughter he had committed, and out of nowhere a little rhyme came into his head:

Here am I, great John A. Boe,
Who killed a hundred at one blow.

It pleased him, and he said it over and over to himself as his big bare feet sent up the clouds of dust from the road.

Then he thought it would be a good idea if he wrote it down in case he forgot it. Sitting on the grassy bank he reached into his purse and pulled out a stub of charcoal. With great concentration he printed the rhyme on the side of the honey pot. The letters were shapeless and the spelling was bad, but he thought it was quite wonderful. He was a real poet. Then, just worn out with the heat of the day and the unaccustomed mental exercise, he lay back in the grass and was soon fast asleep.

A while later a troop of young labourers and farmers from the district of Orchardton Tower came marching along the road led by Sir Peter Cairns. They were on their way to fight a force of English raiders who had crossed the Border and were camped by the Solway Moss. Seeing the young giant asleep by the roadside Sir Peter called a halt and dismounted. When the troop read the verse on the side of the honey pot — 'a hundred at one blow' — they knew that he had been sent by providence. Here was a man who definitely must join their ranks. Before he knew what was happening, John had been wakened up, put astride a great Clydesdale, and was being led along the road in the midst of the marching labourers. They stole a sheet from a farm-wife, and a tin of red paint for painting farm carts, and wrote out the rhyme in big letters. As they marched along they held it aloft as a banner.

Soon they were at the gallows. John was utterly bewildered: all he understood was that he did not wish to go along with them, and flung his arms about the gibbet. There was a great struggle, some of the labourers urging the Clydesdale forward, John refusing to loosen his grip. At length the whole wooden structure snapped off at the base, and the troop marched on.

Holding the great gallows clasped across his chest, John glowered around, wide-eyed with fear and sweating.

"That's a grand weapon for a man like yourself," the farmers said.

John's mouth worked furiously, but no words would come, only grunts and gasps and confused swallowings.

At last they stood face to face with the English raiders across the heathery moss. The farmers and Sir Peter urged John forward, but he was frightened out of his wits, and clung on to his horse. Sir Peter drew his sword and flourished it in the air.

"Go on, you gowk!" he cried furiously to John. "Tell them who you are!"

In total confusion and desperate to please him John roared aloud:

"Here am I, great John A. Boe,
Who killed a hundred at one blow!"

Just then a young labourer stuck his dagger in the horse's rump. With a wild leap the Clydesdale was away, John clinging on to its back in terror, screaming, the gallows flailing from his arms.

Totally appalled the English paused only long enough to be sure they were not dreaming, then turned and fled in wild disarray. By the time the Clydesdale reached their battle position, all that could be seen were a few last English backs and swirling horses' tails vanishing into the distance among the woods and heathery hills.

Sir Peter was delighted with the victory, and as they marched homeward John found himself a great hero. Still he did not know what had happened, his head was in a complete whirl, but as he rode at the head of the troop beside Sir Peter, he realised that something important had occurred, and he liked it. The red and white banner fluttered overhead. The people in the villages they passed through came running to see the great warrior-giant whose fame had gone ahead of him, and clapped him on the back and brought him flagons of ale to drink.

When they reached Palnackie the townsfolk could not make enough of him for the honour he had brought them. The schoolmaster reminded people how he had always said the boy would rise to great heights; those who had wished him given back to the sea remarked how often they had claimed he would bring them luck; the Boreland farmer anounced how hard he had worked to train the boy for this great day — but at heart he was bitter with disappointment, for he could see that he had lost his odd-job man, who had worked so hard and so long for no wages at all.

And still John did not know what had happened — indeed, to the end of his life he never quite understood.

When he went to see the old woman whose cat he had saved and who had given him the jar of honey, she only remarked: "Get the name of a good riser, and you may bide in your bed all day," — at which John laughed and nodded vigorously, saying "Yes, indeed," for he had no idea what she was talking about.

As for Sir Peter, he refused to be parted from the young giant, and settled him in a fine gate-house at the entrance to his splendid park. On a big board above the front door John's rhyme was boldly painted,

enough in itself, without sight of the great warrior, to keep the troublesome poachers and randy-beggars away from that estate.

He married a little milkmaid, who was very proud of her grand husband, and there, for the remainder of a long and happy life, John A. Boe lived simply and contentedly on the strength of his wild reputation.

Rowan Reek

Dan McKendrick and his wife, who lived in Sorbie village six miles to the south of Wigtown, were being driven nearly from their senses by the wicked and mischievous behaviour of their young son Tammie. No matter what they tried, they were completely unable to curb his wanton ways.

At last they were compelled to accept that the boy was not really their son, but a changeling the fairies had put in his place when he was a baby. So Dan went to see Lucky McRobert, a wise old woman of the nearby village of Kirkinner, to see if she could offer them any help. Indeed she could, and after warning him of the danger of meddling in supernatural affairs, told him to leave everything in her hands.

Having made previous arrangements with Dan and his wife, she arrived one evening at their cottage. Immediately she was greeted by threats and dreadful language from young Tammie. Their suspicions, she concluded, were well founded, and she locked the door to prevent the imp from escaping.

Her preparations were simple. The fire was already burning well on its raised flagstone in the middle of the floor. Taking two stools, Lucky McRobert set one on either side and instructed Dan and his wife to sit on them. Then she lit a candle in a tall candle-stick and set it at the edge of the fire between them, with an adder bead* fixed in the wax. A big riddle and some logs of rowan which Dan had cut specially stood at the side of the room. She carried them across and piled the fire high.

Seeing and understanding her preparations the boy panicked and tried wildly to escape, but the old woman captured him and dragged him back to his mother and father. Dan held him tightly while Lucky McRobert bound his hands and feet with some red cloths she had brought with her. Then lifting his wriggling body she laid him on the big riddle.

By this time the green rowan wood was smoking thickly, pouring up to the roof and only with difficulty making its way through the chimney hole. Taking up the riddle then, Lucky McRobert held it in the thick of the reek and riddled the boy to and fro until he must have

* A stone supposedly formed by adders: a particularly potent charm against witchcraft and fairies.

110

been choking, for they could scarcely see him. From out of the heart of the smoke came his curses and threats and dreadful shrieks of rage. When she drew him out, blackened and coughing, the curses did not cease, so she thrust him back into the thick of it, and riddled with re-doubled energy.

There was a knocking at the door, but they ignored it. The riddle jerked in the old woman's hands as the boy writhed and kicked in it, his cries and swearing rising to still greater heights.

At last the magical rowan smoke could be borne no longer. With a tremendous shriek the boy rose from the riddle, and whirling in a corkscrew like the smoke, flew away up the chimney and was gone.

The troubled candle flame steadied. The three people in the room were still and silent.

Then again from the door came the gentle knocking. Lucky McRobert went to answer it.

A plain, likable little boy stood at the entrance.

"I'm Tammy McKendrick," he whispered. "Can I come in?"

Alexander Murray

Alexander Murray, a shepherd's son from Palnure, near Clattering-shaws, was one of those few men to whom might rightly be ascribed the name of genius. Though largely self-educated, he rose to the position of Professor of Oriental Languages at the University of Edinburgh, and was the greatest linguist of his day.

He was born on Sunday, 22nd October, 1775, on the farm of Dunkitterick by Palnure Burn beneath the slopes of Craigneldar. They were an unusual family. His father, Robert, born in 1706, had married at about the age of twenty-four and had a family of one girl and four boys, all of whom, initially at least, became shepherds. Forty years later his wife died, and at the age of sixty-eight he married again, a shepherd's daughter named Mary Cochrane, who at thirty-five was several years younger than a number of his children. Nine months later her first child, Alexander, was born. He was to have one sister, Mary, two years younger. On Dunkitterick Robert Murray ran two or three score of sheep and four moorland cows. Though he had no money, equally he had no debts. He was, in his way, quite a clever man, perhaps somewhat irritable by nature, though not passionate. In private he was very religious, but in company merry, very fond of old stories and singing.

Dunkitterick was situated in a lonely spot in an open valley seven miles to the north-east of Minnigaff, at that time the largest market town in the Stewartry. The farm belonged to the tenant of Clattering-shaws, five miles further up the glen. When he was a man, Alexander Murray gave a brief sketch of the place himself. 'It is on the burn of the Palneur, on the south side about a quarter of a mile from the burn, and on a rivulet that flows from the high hills above on the south. The hills of Craigneildar, Milfore, and others quite overshadow the spot, and hide it from the sun for three of the winter and spring months. The cottage has now been in ruins for more than twenty years. ... This place, now laid open by a road, was, when my father lived there, in a completely wild glen, which was traversed by no strangers but smugglers.'*

Allowing for his father's advanced years, Alexander's early days were

* The reference to smugglers may be surprising, but the glen lay on a direct route

113

little different from those of any other shepherd's son. He played about the house and by the burn, learned about the natural life in the fields and on the hills around him, helped his father to herd the sheep, watched the clipping, sat quietly while his father read the Bible to them in the evenings, and slept behind curtains in a little box bed. Always the soft noise of the Palnure, flowing through gullies and boulders, rose on the mountain air.

About the time of his sixth birthday, since Alexander was eternally asking and wanting to learn, his father bought him a catechism, from which he began to teach the boy the alphabet. While he was away on the hills the catechism was locked up, for books were precious. Throughout the winter of 1781-82 the lessons continued. They drew the letters and words on the back of an old wool card with a stem of heather charred in the fire. In a poor kitchen, with the peat fire flaming in the grate, the oil lamp casting a pool of light over the table, and the west wind roaring about the cottage and in the crags across the glen, the white-haired old man, now aged seventy-five but seeming a great deal younger, spent part of each evening bent over the little book and bit of card with his intent young son. Soon Alexander learned to write as well as read, and became so immersed in what he was doing that for great periods of every day he practised with the card and heather stalk for his own amusement. Within a month or two he was able to read the easier parts of the catechism. In the spring Robert presented his son with a small psalm book, which was much more to the boy's taste. He tore the catechism in half and hid it from his father in a dyke.

Soon he had learned many of the psalms by heart, being able to read them easily, and was longing for new books, particularly the Bible. Though he was importunate his father always refused, considering Alexander too young. Also the Bible — down to the last dotted 'i' the word of God — was too precious a volume for reading lessons. At length, however, the boy managed to get a New Testament, and though still barely seven and never having been to school, 'read the historical parts with great curiosity and ardour', as he later wrote himself. Finally, discovering an old Bible from which the leaves were falling out, he carried it away a bit at a time to his own secret place and read it at his leisure, particularly loving the stories of Abraham and David.

from Wigtown Bay and some of the Solway coves through the hills to Edinburgh. The trade was very extensive, most of the country folk knowing something of it. A number of the smugglers were most respected men. It was, in fact, a smuggler who eventually was responsible for Alexander Murray getting his chance in Edinburgh.

Knowledge of the unusual boy spread through the glen, but there was just not the money for his father to afford lodgings away from home and school fees for the education he obviously deserved. In 1783, however, when Alexander was seven, his uncle, William Cochrane, returned from England, having made several hundred pounds as a travelling merchant. Money was made available, and the following Whitsunday Alexander was placed in the school at New Galloway, and lodged with his grandfather, a mile distant.

For a month he was an awkward figure, different from the other boys, laughed at for his pronunciation of words, and indeed his whole form of speech. Soon, however, he was standing Dux of the Bible class. But in November that same year he was seized with a bad eruption of the skin, and an illness which obliged his parents to take him away. He had attended school for fourteen weeks. He was to see it no more for four and a half years.

In the spring his health improved and he was put to assist the rest of the family as a shepherd boy. This work continued for two years. Every penny he could save went on ballads and penny histories. The eight and nine-year-old boy carried bundles of them with him to the hills when he went herding, reading huddled from the rain, or spread out in the heather with the sun shining and the grouse and curlews calling about him. Towards the end of this time it was discovered that he was short-sighted to such an extent that at no great distance he was unable to distinguish a sheep from a rock. Sometimes, when Alexander's account of the sheep differed from the obvious truth, his father was distressed, thinking that the boy had been idle and was telling lies. More important, however, it was realised that with sight so poor he could not possibly become a shepherd.

The constant reading, often in the cottage where the light was not good, did not help his eyes. There were not many books in the vicinity, and many of them, to our slight modern tastes, sound fusty and academic. Those he could get his hands on, however, he read. Some of them he milked dry. In later life he remembered particularly L'Estrange's *Josephus* and Salmon's *Geographical Grammar*, by his intimate private study of which he learned a great deal about history and geography. In the Salmon the section dealing with each country was prefaced by a copy of the Lord's Prayer in the language of that country. Though he was not yet ten, they fascinated him and he studied them closely, setting himself to memorise many. They represent a significant step in the path he was to follow.

115

One or two books he borrowed from Mr Kelly of Clatteringshaws, his father's employer. Others he received from a visitor to the house at that time, a certain Mr McHarg, a carrier of tea, a smuggler. Such a friendship, at that time, was perfectly acceptable. It was written of Mr McHarg: 'though smuggling was his profession, he was, in other respects, characterised by upright and honourable principles.' Later he was to play a most significant part in Alexander's fortunes. Meeting him as a young boy, however, Mr McHarg greatly admired his abilities, and brought books with him on his return from smuggling trips to the capital.

During the winter of 1787-88, when he was just twelve, Alexander was engaged as a teacher by two families in Kirkcowan parish, earning, for a winter's work, a total of fifteen or sixteen shillings. The money, of course, went on more books, two of which were a translation of Suetonius's *History of the Twelve Caesars* and Cocker's *Arithmetic*.

At Whitsunday, 1789, when he was thirteen, his father, now aged eighty-two, removed to Drigmorn, five miles from Minnigaff. Still Robert Murray was a vigorous, healthy man. He was to live to the age of ninety-one. The removal opened the possibility of Alexander's once more attending school. But his health was not good, and the distance from the school was too great, for Drigmorn was set in the hills on a little tributary of the Penkiln Burn. He did, however, attend for three days in the week, and not a minute of the time was wasted. He arrived an hour before the school started and worked while the other children played, using the books they had brought with them and he did not own himself. Unfortunately, after only six weeks he was again obliged to leave through ill-health.

At Martinmas he was engaged by three families in the moors of Kells and the district of Minnigaff to teach their children, arranging to stay with each family for about eight weeks, for they lived far apart. It was a mountainous area. In their houses, during that winter, he found books which to his great pleasure enabled him to proceed with his own education also. They ranged from Plutarch to Walker's *Arithmetic*, a history of England, and the recently published poems of Robert Burns.

An old woman at Drigmorn showed the boy her Psalter, in which the complete Hebrew alphabet was printed, letter by letter, throughout the long 119th Psalm. He made a copy and kept it for personal study.

The following Whitsunday Robert Murray removed once more, this time to Barncaughlaw, near the road and only two miles from Minnigaff. Thus Alexander was within easy reach of the school. He was fourteen.

116

The schoolmaster, recognising the boy's ability and the shortage of family money, remitted a large part of the fees. Also he encouraged Alexander, under his guidance, to pursue the course of his own studies.

It had become Alexander Murray's intention to go as a clerk to the West Indies, since at the time there was a great deal of trade between the islands and Great Britain. Only a little French was lacking from the qualifications that were necessary for the work. Consequently he set to, and within a fortnight, through great application, was reading the language.

Then, discovering that another boy at the school had once learned Latin, but not liked it, he borrowed the 'Rudiments' from him, and became fascinated by it. It was a private study and had nothing to do with his schooling. One day, however, absent-mindedly having put the Latin grammar instead of the French into his pocket for school, his dominie exclaimed: "Gad, Sandy; I'll try thee with Latin." It was the foundation, or perhaps more accurately the cementing, of what was to be a life-long love of the language and fascination for its authors. At the same time he was, on his own account, starting Greek, having managed to borrow a suitable volume. On this occasion he was at school for fourteen weeks, during which time in addition to the general lessons of his education he had learned French, become deeply immersed in Latin, and was rapidly absorbing the elements of Classical Greek.

At Martinmas he again took a tutoring post, in his spare time studying particularly an aged volume of Ainsworth's dictionary which he had managed to buy from an old man for eighteen pence. This gave all the Latin words, together with the Greek and Hebrew, side by side. Repeatedly he studied it from cover to cover. He read a number of the Latin authors in the original, particularly being delighted by 'the wild fictions of Ovid'. He discovered John Milton, reading *Paradise Lost* with an ardour and admiration that was almost overwhelming.

Two further periods of education were yet to come, both at Minnigaff, during which, so far as his linguistic education was concerned, he continued to study Latin, learned to write Greek, and by himself commenced a remarkable study of Hebrew. Entirely alone he mastered Hebrew grammar in a month, and at the age of sixteen read the Bible throughout in its original Hebrew. At the same time, while he was at Minnigaff, he commenced his solitary studies of Anglo Saxon and Welsh, and since he had got hold of a copy of the alphabet the year before, Ethiopian. Though these periods of education may sound considerable,

117

they amount in all, throughout his life, to sixty weeks, or by today's normal practice, one and a half years.*

During the winter of 1792-93 he worked as tutor to the miller of Minnigaff, for a total wage of thirty shillings, accepting the rate, low even for those times allowing for his age and ability, to enable him to attend an evening school at Newton Stewart. Around this time also he was writing poetry, including an epic in blank verse on the life of King Arthur — influenced, perhaps, by his admiration for *Paradise Lost*, and the Arthurian romance that Milton had reluctantly shelved. He had written several thousand stanzas before he had to admit that compared with the works of Ossian, Milton and Homer, his own verses were very inferior. He gave it up.

By this time, having earned very little money with his tutoring, and assisting the family as he could with the sheep when he was at home, he had reached the age of seventeen. What was to become of him? The scheme for working in the West Indies had been put aside. His health was still not of the best. By his nature and abilities as well as his short-sightedness, he was just not fitted to be a shepherd. And there was not the money to permit him to further his education.

* It is sad to relate that by the time Alexander finished his education at Minnigaff School, the lonely dominie who had been so kind to his talented pupil had become an alcoholic. Eventually he had to resign his post. Afterwards, as always, he remained considerate and helpful towards the boy.

Having spent the winter on the translation of a German professor's manuscript on the lives of the Roman authors, he set out with this and a number of poems, 'chiefly in the Scottish dialect', to Dumfries, hoping to have them accepted for publication. Neither of the two booksellers was interested in the translation, and Robert Burns, to whom he was introduced, advised him with kindness that he should, if possible, try to reach college without publishing his poems, since by his very age his writing was not yet formed, and later he might be ashamed of them. For this had been Murray's hope, of course; that through publication he might somehow make enough money to send himself to college. He took Burns's advice, and packing up his manuscripts and few belongings, returned to Minnigaff.

Fortune, however, was now with him. Mr McHarg was of a very different opinion concerning the worth of his poetry, particularly the ponderous Arthurian epic, and spoke of it in Edinburgh to James Kinnear, very likely one of his customers for tea or tobacco, a most respectable man of some position in the king's printing office. McHarg's desire was to see the verses printed, and bring the young shepherd some due recognition. Alexander was therefore instructed to send Mr Kinnear a letter detailing the progress of his studies and enclosing some of his verses. The style and content of the letter greatly impressed Mr Kinnear, and through his influence Alexander Murray was brought to the attention of Dr Baird, the Principal of Edinburgh University. Dr Baird agreed to see the young man if he could be brought to the city.

Shortly afterwards, in ribbed stockings, spun and knitted by his mother, with a sack of meal upon his shoulder — as was common with poor Scottish students well into the present century — Alexander Murray set out for the capital. He went in the company of Mr McHarg, whose own sack contained, beneath a covering of meal, his customary tea and some tobacco.

Seldom, if ever, can a student have arrived at a university having received so little formal education yet achieved so great a knowledge of languages. As well as his native tongue he had a firm grasp of German, French, Latin, Greek and Hebrew, was able to read Anglo Saxon, and knew something of Welsh, Ethiopic and Arabic. His examination by the Principal, together with Dr Finlayson and Dr Moodie (Professor of Oriental Languages whom later Murray was to succeed) was remarkable. Wherever they opened the book the young man in hodden grey was able to give them a ready translation, and honourably aquit himself under their detailed cross-examination. Even these mature academicians,

119

it is said, were astonished by his command of the four languages in which they examined him; and his private study extended far beyond their enquiry. From that day onwards the Principal became like a father to Murray. He approached the Provost of Edinburgh and without further examination obtained a Town Council Bursary for him — by no means the simple matter it is today. Also he obtained work for him as a private tutor, so that for the present at least, his financial worries were solved. After the minister of his home parish, the Rev. John Maitland of Minnigaff, had written a testimonial to Dr Baird, Alexander Murray was enrolled as a student of Edinburgh University.

His university career, it goes without saying, was distinguished. At nineteen he was considerably older than the majority — most students entering college then at the age of thirteen or fourteen. The majority, too, came from privileged backgrounds, with many years of schooling and private tutors behind them: not all, however, for the country dominies had often sent the highly talented sons of peasants to Edinburgh, those who were, as Murray, able to earn free places by their abilities. He was almost unique, however, in having received so little formal education. Also his knowledge of languages, particularly in scope, was remarkably ahead of his fellow students. Only once, apparently, did he receive reproof from his professors, and that was for reading Aristophanes and Plato in his first year, when it was considered that he must be unready. He continued reading them in private.

Murray, despite his shepherding days, was not a strong man, being of medium height with a slight stoop, rather fragile-looking. According to a sketch he looked quite like Schubert. His eyes were hazel and rather deep sunken beneath level brows, with a fine forehead rising to a thatch of black hair. He was short-sighted, peering through small-lensed spectacles on wire frames, though his eyes were said to sparkle unusually when he was stirred. On his right cheek there was a small dark birthmark. Lord Cockburn, a fellow student, remembered him at this time: 'a little, shivering creature, gentle, studious, timid, and reserved.' He was not a man to relish the rumbustious aspects of college life, and did not make a wide circle of friends. He was not lonely, however, greatly treasuring the friendship of one or two men, chief among whom was the brilliant John Leyden, born the same year the son of a Border shepherd, and also a classical scholar and outstanding linguist.

Qualifying from the Arts classes at the university, he passed into Divinity Hall. By now he was immersed in the dialects of various languages, Chaldee, Syriac, Ethiopic and Arabic. Privately he taught

120

Persian and Hindustani to young men heading for India. And about this time he finished *A New Hebrew Grammar, or Treatise on the Nature and Elements of the Hebrew Language.* His years in Divinity Hall ended with his being licenced as a preacher by the Presbytery of Edinburgh on 14th April, 1802. He was twenty-six years old.

During the following four years his interests were diverse. Under the editorship of Sydney Smith he worked for the *Edinburgh Review.* He saw a number of editions of the Greek and Latin classics through the press. For six months, following John Leyden, he was editor of the *Scots Magazine*, but left when the publisher, Archibald Constable, found him the job of editing a new edition of Bruce's *Travels to Abyssinia*, which required, through the journals and manuscripts, all his knowledge of the language and dialects of the region. It was a mammoth task, for the *Travels* extended to seven volumes, to which Murray prefaced a life of the author, and added copious footnotes and appendices detailing the history, philosophy and archaeology of the country, greatly extending the scope and academic interest of the work. Afterwards he wrote a more detailed life of Bruce, extending to more than 500 pages.*

In December, 1806, Murray returned to Galloway, having secured the appointment of assistant and successor to Dr Muirhead, the minister of Urr. Less than two years later Dr Muirhead died, leaving Alexander Murray in full charge of this sequestered rural parish.† Six months afterwards, in December, 1808, he married the daughter of one of his parishioners, Henrietta Affleck. They lived close to the four-square Reformation church at Haugh of Urr, and were very happy. Within the next three or four years Henrietta was delivered of two children, Agnes and James.

The situation suited Murray perfectly. He performed his pastoral duties with the concern and thoroughness that were natural to him, and he became much loved, though he was a retiring man and the quiet

* Concerning this editorial work an amusing incident occurred some years later. A Mr Salt, who had been on a mission to Abyssinia, returned with a letter to George III from the Ras of Tigré. No-one, however, was able to read it. They were at a loss. Then Mr Salt, who had used the new edition of Bruce's *Travels* on his journey and found it invaluable, said that the one man in the country who could read it was Alexander Murray. The letter, accordingly, was sent to him at Urr, in the depths of the Galloway countryside. Murray returned it at once, with a translation, giving so much satisfaction that when he died, two years after this incident, his widow was awarded a government pension of eighty pounds a year.
† Urr is a long and rather narrow parish, extending through rolling farming country from Kirkpatrick Durham to Dalbeattie and south to Colvend.

reason and erudition of his sermons in the old galleried church, placed them considerably above the heads of most of his parishioners.

The study of language was his recreation. The range of his knowledge was now phenomenal. To those that have already been mentioned can be added Phoenician, Samaritan, Slavonic, Hungarian, Finnish and Lappish, Scandinavian, Dutch, Gothic, Alamannic, Chinese, Sanskrit, and so on, with other dialects. In 1808 he drew up the long prospectus of the work that should have established him as a major figure in the history of philology. Anxious to have the manuscript ready for publication by 1810, he pressed himself onwards without due regard for his always uncertain health, and before it was finished he fell ill. In addition he was troubled by a winter cough that would not leave him. By the time he left the parish of Urr, however, in 1812, the work, *A History of the European Languages*, was complete.*

In that year Dr Moodie, Professor of Oriental Languages in Edinburgh, died, and Alexander Murray, one of three scholars considered for the vacant chair, was elected by the town council, who had the appointment in their charge. Leaving his wife and family at Haugh of Urr — for he was until his election still the minister, and did not have a house in the city — he travelled once more to Edinburgh. Immediately the senate of the university conferred upon him the degree of Doctor of Divinity. At the end of October he commenced his work with the students. For them, at once, he published a small book entitled *Outlines of Oriental Philology*. So popularly esteemed were his lectures that even those from without the classes came to listen.

True to his nature he laboured constantly, but alas was not even to complete his first session. The winter was exceptionally bad, the unremitting work had been too much for his fragile health. His illness, pulmonary consumption, came to a crisis, so that he was confined to his room. It was a very different picture from that of the boy who went herding on the hills and whose intellect burned so brightly in the little shepherd's cottage at Dunkitterick. Not realising that he was dying, Murray hoped to join his wife and children in Urr to recuperate. At length, however, he had to accept that he could not make the journey, and wrote to his wife requesting her to join him on 16th April. Prompted

* Within the year Murray was dead. His history remained unpublished until 1823. During those eleven lost years other works appeared, and though Murray's was greater in scope and vision, it was denied the honour of being the first. The laurels went, instead, to Franz Bopp and Jacob Grimm. But as much as twenty years after its publication, nothing was being written that had not first been projected by Alexander Murray in his little country manse at Haugh of Urr.

by his friends she set out before his letter arrived and reached Edinburgh three days earlier than he had requested.

She found him busy working in his room, in a chair by the fire, and interested in all the family news. He slept well, and the following day ate well also. But he was weaker. Realising at last the concern of the doctors and those about him, he gave his wife directions concerning his private affairs. His night was disturbed, and he spent much of it in prayer. He was particularly pleased when having left off the recitation of a psalm, his wife continued. At six o'clock in the morning, to the last in full possession of his faculties, he passed away peacefully. It was 15th April, 1813. He was thirty-seven years old.

Alexander Murray was buried in the churchyard of Greyfriars in Edinburgh, close to the church wall at the north-west corner. In 1877 a fine obelisk of Dalbeattie granite was raised above his grave.

On the north bank of the Palnure Burn, less than a mile down the glen from Dunkitterick, a seventy foot obelisk was erected in his honour on the summit of Duncraig Hill. It is a magnificent monument, set against the sky and high mountain slopes, with a spectacular outlook up and down the rough glen. On a grey June day in 1834, somewhere in the region of three thousand people gathered in that lonely spot for the laying of the foundation stone.

In 1975, to commemorate the bi-centenary of his birth, the fallen dry-stone walls of the cottage at Dunkitterick were raised to lintel level and gable-end. There they now stand, stone-floored, with the crags dark across the glen, and the crystal-clear stream splashing nearby, foaming white down the hillside after rain. Save for the forestry plantations and his own monument, the scene remains just as Murray must have known it when he was a boy, going out with the sheep to read his books on the hillside.

His family, alas, did not thrive. Agnes inherited her father's weak constitution and did not long survive him. Henrietta died ten or twelve years later, still a comparatively young woman. James, a gifted boy with a talent for singing and painting and a great love of poetry, became a doctor. Newly qualified, he took a post as ship's surgeon on the merchant vessel 'Elizabeth', trading as far afield as Quebec and China. On his first voyage the vessel was shipwrecked and he was drowned.

Alexander, however, we still remember. Standing on the summit of Duncraig Hill beneath the beautiful granite spire, and looking across the rough valley and winding silver river to the tiny cottage snuggled beneath the slopes of Craignelder, one feels a strong sense of his achievement and the pride with which he is remembered throughout the Stewartry.

The Murder Hole

One dark November night a young pedlar, little more than a boy, was making his way up the lonely mountain road that runs north by the Water of Minnoch to the west of the Merrick. He was frightened, and not just by the blackness of the night and the emptiness of the moors that rose about him. A lot of travellers had vanished in that part of the countryside, so many that nearly all of the inhabitants had departed for other, more kindly districts. Indeed only one family remained, an old widow and her two sons by the name of Mackillop, who sadly proclaimed that they were too poor to make the removal, and clung to their cottage and tiny parcel of land. There had been reports of loud cries of fear. A shepherd who lost his way had descended from the mist to see three men struggling violently at a distance, then one had inexplicably vanished and the other two walked away together.

The young pedlar, with his pack on his back, was altogether regretting the bravado which had made him push on in the darkness. He passed the Black Burn and the invisible, lapping shore of Loch Moan, where the wind sang across the water. Briefly, between storm clouds, the rising moon showed over the hunched shoulders of the Merrick, and he glimpsed the river beneath him, glinting and twisting down the broad glen. Then the moon was gone, the darkness returned. Scarcely able to distinguish the rutted road, he walked on.

Two miles passed. The mountains rose on his left hand also. His fear rose with them. It came on to rain, a fierce mountain squall.

Suddenly, a little distance ahead, he spotted a twinkling light. As he drew closer he recognised it as the window of the Rowantree Cottage, where he had called with some other packmen and travellers a few months previously. It was the home of the old widow and her two sons, the only habitation in the district. It was a cheering sight, for on that earlier occasion he had been made welcome; indeed the old woman had pressed him to stay on for a while as the others were departing, but he had gone with them for company on the road. Sure of a kind reception, he walked the last quarter of a mile, and arriving at the roadside cottage rapped with considerable relief on the wet door.

The house had been silent, but at his knock a hubbub broke out within. He waited, then knocked again, but still the door was not opened. At this he walked a few steps to the lighted window and peered through the partially drawn rags of curtain. The old woman was sprinkling dry sand on the floor, while her two sons were cramming something bulky into a large black sea-chest that stood against the wall. A bloody butcher's knife lay on the table. Wondering if they had been poaching a deer or a calf, he tapped on the glass.

Swiftly they turned and stared at him, then in an instant the door was flung wide and one of the sons had him by the arm. Before he could think he was hustled into the cottage, and the door shut with a bang behind him.

"What do you want here?" said the old woman, pulling the shawl more closely about her shoulders.

"I'm . . . I'm a pedlar. I was here two or three months ago," the youth replied. "I was hoping you might give me shelter for the night." His clothes dripped on the sanded floor, his face was red and beaten with the rain.

"What did you see through the window?" demanded one of the sons, a black-haired ruffian with a thick belt.

"Nothing. You were busy, that's all."

"Who's with you?"

"I'm travelling alone. That's why I want the shelter, more than for the rain. People are telling stories about the moors here."

The mother grinned, a thick-set woman with ropes of grey hair.

"Ah, well. Yes, I remember you fine. You're welcome, young pedlar," she said.

He removed his wet clothes and for a while joined them at the fire. When he was warmed through, the mother ladled him a full dish of stew from the pot that stood at the side of the fire. Clearly, he saw from the chunks of lean meat, they were not short of mutton. When he had finished and laid the plate aside, the second son, only a strip of coarse face showing between his red beard and rough hair, lit a candle and led him into a small room where he was to sleep. It was in disarray. A little table and chair lay tumbled on the floor, the curtains about the box bed had been torn down, the blankets were strewn wildly about the rough pallet. Quickly the heavy son tidied up, then left him alone with the candle, which fortunately was almost new.

Tired and ill at ease, for his reception had certainly not been what he anticipated, the young pedlar dumped his pack against the wall. The door stood ajar. He saw that the bolt was splintered, and pushed the chair beneath the handle to hold the door shut. Then pulling off his jacket and jersey he lay down on the bed. Occasionally the low murmur of voices drifted through to him. After a while he dozed.

Suddenly he was awakened by a loud cry and commotion from the next room. He sat up, breaking into an instant cold sweat and the back of his neck prickling with fear. The commotion subsided. Gazing towards the door he was appalled to see a dark tide slowly ooze beneath. Taking up the candle, still with an inch or two to burn, he held it close. The tide was scarlet and thick, undoubtedly blood. Horrified, he put his eye to a crack in the door. The two men were bending over something on the floor. The dark one had the butcher's knife in his hand. The young pedlar squinted to see lower. To his inexpressible relief he saw a goat that they had newly slaughtered. Neck gaping wide it lay on the earth floor of the cottage.

"That's that, then," said the slaughterer, straightening.

"I wish all the throats were cut that easy," said his brother.

"Aye, you're right." The man laughed.

The young pedlar could hardly prevent himself from crying out.

"What about yon laddie in there?" The coarse ginger fellow nodded towards the door.

The other drew the knife across his black neck. "I'll give him it when we're ready."

His brother shook his head. "Why not straight to the hole? It's cleaner and done with. A crack, a splash, and that's that."

"We'll see. Anyway, he's got a tidy bit goods in that sack if I'm not mistaken."

"Aye."

Their mother said something from elsewhere in the room and they bent once more to the goat.

Hearing the fate that so cruelly awaited him, the young pedlar backed from the door in horror. Desperately he looked about the little room. The window was small, but large enough for him to squeeze through. Very cautiously he loosened the catch and slid it down. Then, kneeling on the recessed window sill, he pushed his head and shoulders out into the chill night air. For a moment he hung, half in and half out, then writhed his waist and slithered through. But as his legs flew up in the bedroom they caught an old ewer and sent it toppling to the floor.

The loud smash was heard by the widow and her murderous sons. Instantly the two men rushed to the bedroom door, but for a moment it was held against them by the chair. Then they burst through. The

127

window stood open, the young pedlar was gone. They ran outside, but the youth had vanished. They listened, but nothing was to be heard save the night noises of the moor.

"Loose the bloodhound!" cried one.

"Mother, fetch me the knife!" called the other.

Barely a hundred yards away the pedlar heard them. The fearful words gave added speed to his desperate flight. Half clad and bootless he ran across the boggy moorland, falling blindly into open peat banks. Clambering across the rocky hillsides he wrenched his ankles and gashed his stockinged feet on invisible rocks. Behind him he heard the bay of the bloodhound.

He had run perhaps a mile when suddenly the ground fell away below him, and staggering into mid air he dropped four or five feet full length across some ragged boulders. The breath was knocked from his body, the sharp corners of rock struck his ribs and raked painfully across his stomach and side. For a full minute he was unable to move. He felt the blood trickling down his skin. Forcing himself to his feet again, he struggled on.

Only moments later the bloodhound reached the spot where he had fallen. One brother held it on a rope, the other was not far behind. The young man's blood was upon the rocks. Considering its job done, the dog gave up the chase. All its masters' threats and blows could stir it no further.

During the night there were sweeping showers of rain and sleet that made the young pedlar's shirt and trousers cling about him and plastered the hair to his head. He was chilled to the bone. His chest pained him at every breath, his feet received wicked punishment from the rough hillsides. Dawn was not far off when at last, in a desperate condition, he staggered into a village.

Most of the inhabitants were still asleep, but at his account they were quickly roused by neighbours. The men knew well enough the family he meant. They were more than angry, for several had lost friends and relatives out there on the moors. Now it seemed plain enough what had become of them. At once a great gang of men, almost the entire male population, set out to seize the old woman and her murderous sons. With a borrowed coat pulled about his shoulders, too fatigued to walk, the young pedlar accompanied them on horseback.

When they arrived at Rowantree Cottage the widow and her two sons protested and tried to bluff their way out of the monstrous accusations. The villagers, however, were so incensed that it seemed not unlikely they would tear the murderers limb from limb. In the end they confessed to the deaths of nearly fifty travellers. Some had been knifed first, and all had been sunk in an exceptionally deep pool, a little way across the moors.

Three rough gibbets were erected. The mother and her two powerful sons received sentence and punishment on the spot. For a time their legs danced in the air, but at length they hung still.

When the villagers looked through the cottage and outbuildings they found the valuables and best clothes of the victims stored away in boxes, and a considerable sum of money hidden in the back of a drawer. Some of the items they recognised as having belonged to missing friends. In the large black sea-chest in the living room they discovered the bloody body of a man who apparently only minutes prior to the young pedlar's arrival had occupied the bed where he had lain. The youth recalled the scene he had witnessed through the window, and the turbulent state of the bedroom from the man's struggles. Some of the villagers took shovels from the shed and buried the murdered man decently out on the moor. But the widow and her two sons they left hanging from the gibbets.

A short distance from the cottage they found the 'murder hole'. It was a dark moorland pool, long and narrow, almost hidden by tall grasses. It was deathly cold and seemed bottomless. The young pedlar gazed at the black water with horror. Only the dying bleat of a goat and later a painful fall, he realised, had saved him from joining those fifty bodies far down there in the heart of the moor.

FOOTNOTE

This is a well-known tale of Galloway. The events are said to have occurred about four centuries ago. There is, however, some disagreement as to where the hole and cottage are located. Here we have taken the Rowantree Toll (Inn), as it later became, just west of Shalloch on Minnoch on the road north from Glentrool. This is supported by Malcolm Harper in *Rambles in Galloway*, Andrew McCormick in *Galloway*, and *Nicholson's Tales*. The Rev. C. H. Dick in *Highways and Byways in Galloway and Carrick* places the story at Rowantree in the Ness Glen, by the north-west corner of Loch Doon. Other accounts are divided between these two locations. The best known version of the story is by S. R. Crockett in his novel *The Raiders*. For the convenience of the action he transfers the cottage to Craignaimie, just to the south-east of Loch Enoch in the wilds below the Merrick, and the 'Murder Hole' to the western arm of Loch Neldricken, a mile further south. Though indeed there is a very deep hole in this loch, which can be seen like a black eye fringed with a circle of reeds, and it is named 'Murder Hole' on the Ordnance Survey maps, it would be difficult if not impossible to reach save by a boat, for the surrounding bottom is composed of a deep quagmire of peat.

A famous and very different 'Murder Hole' is to be found in Cardoness Castle. This is a removable grid above the castle entrance through which, it is said, boiling pitch was poured down on the heads of enemies. It was also used as a trapdoor through which goods were raised to an upper floor.

The Rope of Sand

Tam Campbell, who had fought the Devil for the plague of Glenluce,* was left on his own. His long-suffering wife, troubled at last beyond bearing by his feckless ways, had taken the children and left him. It had the effect she desired, for to his dismay he discovered that when he dropped his shirt and trousers on the floor they did not turn up miraculously washed and clean in a drawer the next time he wanted them, but lay there and mouldered until he did something about it. After several months of living in a condition little better than a pig, he realised that he would have to pull himself together. Making a great effort he cut down his drinking, put in longer hours at his work in the smithy, and with the extra money he earned, started to put his house to rights. It was not a very big house, situated in a quiet, beautiful spot just above the shore at Crow's Nest Bay. In a few weeks, had she returned, his wife would hardly have recognised the old place, with the fresh paint and new thatch and smart chimney-piece, and all the saucepans glinting on the shelf.

Now although the Devil had been captivated by Tam's bagpipe playing, he had never forgiven the young smith for getting the better of him — though it was never admitted — in the business of the wrestling and the poke of plague. Seeing Tam so reformed a character, it seemed a grand opportunity to make mischief and possibly drive him back to his evil ways. So from his legions of wicked spirits he chose a young demon and sent him to Tam's house, with instructions to cause as much trouble as he possibly could. He was never to give up, whatever happened.

That very evening, when Tam returned home tired from a hard day's work at the smithy, he found his immaculate house turned into a shambles. Half the new thatch was pulled from the roof, soot was tumbled down the chimney and flung about the rooms, and a small cauldron of stew, his dinner for several days to come, lay spilled across the floor. A mischievous imp-like demon sat on the window-sill, hands black from the work, kicking his heels against the newly whitewashed walls.

The mess was so great that Tam was beyond anger. "Oh," he said calmly. "I wondered when I would be hearing from him again."

* See 'The Devil and the Highlandman'.

131

Weary and hungry, he set about cleaning up the house. Afterwards, when some semblance of decency and order had been restored, he pulled a turnip from the field and ate it raw. Grinning, more trouble-some than evil, the demon pulled the clothes from his bed and threw them about the room, then blew the candle out.

The pattern was set for the weeks to come. When Tam returned from his work some new mischief would be done; and in time, as the demon ran out of ideas, the old tricks were repeated. He was not so bad a demon, all things considered, and as the days went by Tam began to have an inkling of his restless character. Sometimes, for something to

do and a change, he would even help the young blacksmith to clear up the mess.

One evening Tam, who despite his wastrel ways had taught himself to read a little, was sitting by the fire with a book, while the demon performed various monkey-like feats up and down the curtains. Suddenly recalling his instructions the demon jumped down, and rushing across the room tore out the page that Tam was reading, ripped it to shreds, and threw over the lantern. Patiently, for the twentieth time, Tam laid his book aside, set the lantern upright and re-lit it from the glowing fire.

"You must get very bored, doing the same thing over and over again," he observed.

The demon, who by this time was sitting on the back of a chair, rolled backwards to the floor, pulling the cushions with him. He looked up mischievously and shrugged. "I've got used to it," he said. "Anyway, it's what I was sent for."

"Yes, I know, but it's so childish and dull — always doing the same thing. Is there nothing else you could try that would be more interesting?"

The demon looked puzzled and a little forlorn. "Do you not think I'm doing very well?" he asked.

"Oh, you're doing fine," Tam reassured him, not wishing to hurt his feelings. "You're driving me mad. But there must be other things, that you haven't thought of. I mean, I'm still young, and you've only been at it for a few weeks so far. What's it going to be like by the time I'm old? You'll be bored to death. What kind of a life is that, spending all your time for forty years tipping out bowls of broth and scraping soot down the chimney?"

By now quite sad the demon looked at him anxiously. "I can't think of anything else," he said.

"Well, I don't know your instructions," Tam said innocently. "Have you got to stay with me for the rest of my life, doing the same tricks over and over again?"

The demon wrinkled his brow thoughtfully. "Well, there is one way out," he confided. "If you can set me a task that I can't do, then I've got to keep at it for ever." He shook his head sadly. "But I can do everything."

"Are you sure?" Tam asked him. "I'll tell you what! We'll make a game of it. I'll set you a task, and you see if you can do it. It will make things more interesting for you."

"All right!" said the demon, throwing the ornaments off the mantlepiece as he brightened up considerably. "What shall I do?"

Tam gazed down at the fragments of china in the hearth. "Well, you can get me some more ornaments for a start. Something really beautiful."

For a moment the demon paused, then laughed with inspiration and scattered the peats from the fire. A minute later Tam saw him far away across the sands of Luce Bay, digging furiously. The sand flew in the air. Hither and thither he raced, every now and then crying with triumph. Within fifteen minutes he was back, his arms loaded with lovely archaeological pots and ornaments of gold, dripping from their rinsing in the sea.

Tam was very impressed and set them up on the mantleshelf, where they glowed in the lamplight. He thought. There was only one possession for which he really longed, a neat little yawl. A boat and peace from the demon, and his life would be perfect.

"What shall I do now?" cried the demon. "What next?"

"Yes," said Tam, "I could do with a boat. I fancy a nice clinker-built ..."

But before he could finish the demon was away. Tam waited and watched, and suddenly, though he had not seen it drawing in from the sea, a beautiful green-painted yawl was gliding in to the sands below the house. The demon sprang ashore with a mooring pin, thrust it deeply into the sand, and raced up to the door where Tam was standing open-mouthed with delight.

"There," said the demon, pushing past him into the house and leaping high to tear down some bunches of herbs that hung drying from the rafters. "You see, I can do anything." He was pleased as Punch with himself.

Hardly able to tear his eyes away from the boat, Tam was terrified that it might with equal ease be taken away from him. He gave an exaggerated sigh of admiration and despondency. "You're too much for me," he admitted. "I did have one more thing in my mind that I thought really might fox you, but ... well, now I've seen how clever you are there isn't any point."

"Yes, what is it?" cried the young demon, revelling in the flattery. "Tell me."

"Ach, it's just a little thing." Tam shook his head. "You wouldn't be interested."

"Yes, tell me, tell me," cried the demon, dancing with excitement.

134

"Well, I wanted you to go down to Luce Bay and make me a rope of sand long enough to draw my boat from low water to the dunes. But it's not worth it. It's just wasting your time."

"Yes, yes, I'll do it," the demon shouted. "From low water to the dunes! I'll do it!"

Pausing only long enough to pull all the cabbages from Tam's garden, the demon raced down the field and dunes to the shore.

He did not return. For a time, as the light faded, Tam saw him far down the sands, a small bent figure. Then darkness hid him from view.

In an hour Tam retired to his bed, and from the open window, against the roar of the sea, he thought he could distinguish a faint, distant cry of distress, though it could have been a seagull a long way off. Then he fell asleep, and for the first time since the demon came to his house, he enjoyed a good night's rest and dreamed of the green yawl.

While he slept the Devil, hearing his demon's cries, came to the shore to see what ailed him. Learning the trick that Tam had played he called up his grotesque legions and charged them that though they might work until the day of doom they must accomplish Tam's task. But every time the tide crept in over the sands their work was washed away. Their wailing mingled with the noise of the wind and the waves and the flooding tide.

The demon never returned, and within a few days Tam was able to repair the last of the damage.

Hearing such good reports of her husband, and missing him, for despite his feckless ways he was a good man, his wife returned with the children. Soon they were a merry family, and through his Solway fishing in the yawl Tam earned enough to open a forge of his own.

From the start, when the children returned, they said that the noise of the sea was different. And once, as Tam was wending his way home from the inn in the early hours of the morning — for he allowed himself the occasional relapse — he was sure that he saw the beach at low water thick with strange figures, all screwing at the sand. Passing the place where in earlier times he had wrestled with the Devil, he thought he detected a faint whiff of sulphur and a familiar shadow, but the moonlight was patchy and his footsteps were uncertain. He was not sure.

In any case, the Devil troubled him no more, and they all lived happily ever after.

The Earl the Tutor
and the King

The Douglas family was powerful, great among the great. Traditionally, until the murder of the young 6th Earl in 1440, the chief took the titles of Earl of Douglas, Earl of Wigton, Lord of Galloway, Lord of Bothwell, Lord of Annandale, Lord of Eskdale, Lord of Longueville, Duke of Touraine and Marshal of France. William, the 8th Earl, was particularly rebellious to the king, and when he formed a league with the Earl of Crawford and the Earl of Ross, commanded a potential power greater than King James himself. It was said that if necessary they could between them have fielded an army of 40,000 men. Enmity existed between them and most of the nobles at court. The league constituted, as everyone realised, an ever-present threat to the crown and state.

Secure in the knowledge of his strength, William in the south-west began to oppose the execution of the king's laws, and pursue still futher the aggrandizement of his own power. He did not love the king. He did not have to look back many years to seventeen-year-old William the 6th Earl, who with his brother David was beguiled to court by subtle and hated Crichton (the Lord Chancellor) and the king's guardians, to be presented and dine with the ten-year-old monarch. At the arrival of a bull's head on the table — a prearranged signal — the two youths were seized, given a swift mock trial, and instantly executed in the yard of Edinburgh Castle. With this death the power of the Douglases was disseminated. But four years later, in 1444, by his marriage to his second cousin Margaret — the Fair Maid of Galloway, a child-bride — a great part of that earlier power was brought together once more in the person of William Douglas, soon to become the 8th Earl. Those who supported the king, William Douglas considered enemies to his house, and if they were unfortunate enough to live in the south-west could well expect to feel the weight of his powerful and often ruthless arm.

One such was Sir John Herries of Terregles. Douglas's supporters had commited robberies on his land. Without success Herries sought restitution, then gathering a small force marched into the earl's territory for revenge and to claim at least some compensation by plunder. They were routed with almost disdainful ease and Herries was captured. King

James sent a firm letter insisting that his loyal supporter was not to be harmed. With total disregard William Douglas clapped Herries in irons, then still further to demonstrate his contempt and independence of royal command, put him to death.

Another passionately loyal supporter of the king, and a kinsman of Herries, was Sir Patrick McClellan, the Tutor of Bombie, a powerful figure himself. His coastal lands were bordered inland by Douglas's domain and liable to be overrun or pillaged at any time. Repeatedly Douglas tried to persuade McClellan to join his confederacy, but without any success. On the principle, justified in this case, that those who were not for him were against him, Douglas was very angry, and for safety McClellan retired to Raeberry Castle, his principal stronghold, a seemingly impregnable fortress built on the brink of a precipitous cliff above the sea, five miles south of Kirkcudbright. He was wise to do so, for under pretext of reprisal at a dubious tale that McClellan had killed one of the Douglas servants, the earl laid seige to the castle in 1452.

It is uncertain how the castle was taken. One account claims that it fell by sheer siege and force of arms. Another states that Douglas talked his way in with gentle words and false promises, and once there either overpowered the guards, or made the Tutor of Bombie his prisoner and compelled the guards to open the castle gates. The most popular version, however, is that McClellan was betrayed by one of his followers whom Douglas had bribed. When the man sought payment, Douglas had such contempt for his treacherous action that the money was heated in a crucible and poured molten down his throat: thus he was both paid and punished at the same time. However it was, Patrick McClellan was made prisoner and conveyed to the Castle of Threave, Douglas's massive tower-house and fortress on an island in the River Dee, two miles west of the present market town of Castle Douglas. There he was kept in close confinement, possibly in the dreadful dungeon.

McClellan's uncle on his mother's side was Sir Patrick Gray, commander of the royal guard. Holding this position and naturally being much at the palace, Sir Patrick possessed both the confidence and favour of King James II, at that time a young man of twenty-one. The king was disturbed to hear of the desperate situation of his loyal subject, and furnished Sir Patrick with a letter for the Earl of Douglas, couched this time in more gentle terms, requesting as a favour that he would deliver McClellan into the hands of Sir Patrick Gray, who would bring him to Edinburgh where he would stand trial for the death of Douglas's servant. Sir Patrick himself carried the letter south and presented it to Douglas at the Castle of Threave.

He arrived and was ushered up the winding staircase into the earl's presence just as he was rising from dinner in the great hall. Appreciating at once, even before Sir Patrick had time to present the letter, what his errand must be and what the king's message contained, the earl replied in apparent courtesy: "It's ill speaking between a full man and a fasting one." Servants therefore brought food and Sir Patrick had no option but to sit to a substantial dinner.

While he was eating, Earl William gave orders that the Tutor of Bombie should at once be taken to the outer courtyard of the castle and beheaded. His head was to be removed from sight, and his body covered with a white cloth.

Having finished the meal as swiftly as good manners and his own hunger permitted, Sir Patrick presented the king's letter. The Earl of Douglas received it, broke the royal seal, and perused the contents with great respect and humility. With seriousness and counterfeited gratitude he thanked Sir Patrick for bringing him so friendly and gracious a letter from his sovereign. At once they would go and see the Tutor of Bombie. Taking Sir Patrick by the hand the earl led him from the chamber and out over the drawbridge to the green court by the river where the dead tutor lay. Servants drew back the white cloth to reveal Sir Patrick's beheaded nephew.*

"Alas, we have come too late," said Earl William. "Here is your sister's son — though he lacks a head. His body, however, is at your disposal."

With difficulty suppressing his distress and anger, Sir Patrick Gray replied: "My lord, since you have taken his head, you may take his body also."

Calling for his horse Sir Patrick mounted immediately and was escorted as far as the drawbridge by the Earl of Douglas. Then he rode away. He had not gone many yards, however, before his feelings overcame him, and wheeling his horse he loudly upbraided Douglas before the listening servants and his followers as a bloodthirsty coward and a disgrace to knighthood. Shaking his mailed glove he cried: "If I live, you shall pay dearly for this day's work!" Then he put spur to his horse and galloped to the foot of the island, splashed across the ford, and rode away up the wooded riverbank.

* Written accounts do not correspond with the structure of Threave Castle. It is possible that the Tutor of Bombie was beheaded in the gloomy flagged cellar-courtyard beneath the kitchens, next to the dungeon.

The Earl of Douglas watched him go. He was not accustomed to receiving language of this nature and was greatly angered. Turning on his followers he exclaimed: "To horse and pursue him!"

Fortunately Sir Patrick, as commander of the king's guard, had a strong fleet horse, and was able to avoid his pursuers. The chase, however, was kept up for eighty miles, and ceased only when they came in sight of Edinburgh.

Such flagrant breach of the king's express and personal desire was not to be tolerated: further, indeed, it demonstrated a complete breakdown of law and sovereignty. What was King James to do? To challenge and contend openly with the powerful earl and his confederates would be more than hazardous for the crown, and reduce Scotland to a state of civil war. After many doubts and fears he decided on a policy of persuasion, backed by artifice and if necessary bloody violence. It was by no means the first time that a king of Scotland had resorted to such measures. However, the crown and stability of the kingdom were at stake. King James invited Douglas to meet him to discuss matters.

The earl was justifiably suspicious, even though the king promised to remove Crichton — author of many devious and treacherous schemes — from the court. The king furnished Douglas with letters of pardon and protection bearing his personal seal and signature. Some of the loyal nobles, it is said, backed the king's assurances with letters of their own, promising support if James were to break his word. The Earl of Douglas at last felt assured that on this occasion, if ever, he would be safe at court, if honour meant anything.

The king was at Stirling and there the Earl of Douglas rode on 19th February, 1452, with a large retinue of armed followers and supported by a number of lesser nobles. He was received at the palace with every demonstration of friendship and invited to dine with the king the following day.

As the earl entered the gateway of Stirling Castle a little before dusk on that fateful February evening, his friends and supporters were denied access. Sir James Hamilton was thrust back and even struck upon the face by the king's old guardian Livingstone, who was a relative, and when he rushed forward with drawn sword he was repulsed by a lance and the gates were shut against him. Only later did he realise that this was a kindly gesture.

Though the Earl of Douglas must have been alarmed by these proceedings, he was received most cordially by the young king, and at seven o'clock they dined amicably and were entertained. Afterwards the earl and the king retired to a private apartment, and there, in a window recess, they at last entered into discussion of affairs of state.

The king spoke mildly of recent events, the earl replied, and gradually they warmed to the subject of Douglas's league with the Earls of Crawford and Ross. The king urged that it was an evil thing, dangerous to the country: not only was it contrary to the earl's personal allegiance, but demonstrated to the peasantry that Scotland was a nation without law. The earl replied haughtily, accusing the king of mal-administration and mis-government, citing many instances of corruption and dishonour at court. The king, controlling himself with some difficulty, told Douglas that if he persisted in his actions, then he deserved what inevitably must follow — loss of life, lands and goods, his titles abolished, ancestors and family honour disgraced. The earl observed, with growing contempt, that abolition of the league was not in his hands alone, and in any case he cared little about those who named him traitor: he owed allegiance to worthy friends, and was man enough to disregard the 'boyish caprices' of his enemies.

Stung into sudden, impetuous rage, the king drew his dagger and struck at the earl's throat, crying: "By heaven, my lord, if you will not break the bond this shall." A second, less mortal blow, struck the Earl of Douglas in the lower part of the body. Already dying, he fell to the floor of the royal chamber.

Sir Patrick Gray, with some others, had listened to the altercation, either within the chamber or at the door. As the earl fell they came rushing forwards. Sir Patrick was already prepared for revenge, with a pole-axe in his hands, and striking the mighty earl a great blow in the head, laid him instantly lifeless on the floor. Others showed their zeal by further blows, stabbing him with daggers even after he was obviously dead.

Thus William, the 8th Earl of Douglas and Lord of Galloway, was slain. Such power as his, as he realised well enough, could not run parallel with the crown. Either the king or he himself must bend or be broken at some stage.

His bloody corpse was thrown from the window where they had talked into a piece of ground on the north side of the castle called the Nether Bailey. It seems probable that he was buried where he fell, in unconsecrated ground. No other grave is known, and early in the nineteenth century the skeleton of a man was discovered buried beneath the fatal window, which was believed to be that of the turbulent earl. The room where he died is still known as 'The Douglas Room'.

The Tutor of Bombie was taken from Threave to the great Abbey of Dundrennan for burial, and a freestone monument bearing a life-sized statue was raised above his grave.*

* For associated history see 'Mons Meg' and 'The Death of Black Morrow'.

Stranraer Bugs

Two young fellows, little more than boys, set out from Kirkmaiden for the great Stranraer Fair. They had never been away from home before. It was a long, hot walk and the lanes were stony. Soon their stiff new jackets were over their arms and they were glad to hitch an occasional lift on a rattling farm cart.

They were country lads and knew little of the world and its ways. When they arrived at Stranraer the fair was magic to them and for a time they wandered wide-eyed through the tents and booths and jostling crowds. Before giving themselves up to its pleasures completely, however, they thought they had better find themselves lodgings for the night.

They had been warned about bugs, especially in the poorer quarter of the town, for where they lived, in open country far down the Mull of Galloway, they had never met with them. They were fierce beasts, their friends had told them, so blood-thirsty that at night they lifted the slates of the houses and grinned down at the people who passed beneath, especially folk fresh from the country with good red blood. So when the boys, unable to afford lodgings in the better part of the town, were compelled to seek them in the shabby quarter most commonly frequented by sailors, they were anxious that the house should be bug free.

A brisk, business-like wife opened the door to them and showed them a room. When they asked about bugs she was insulted and angry, but soon smiled, realising that they came from the country, and assured them she was certain that her house was as free as any lodgings in the town. Not a bug dared cross the threshold. Only partially reassured, for they had also been warned that Stranraer was full of tricksters, they took the room and returned to the great fair.

It was late when they wandered back. They were unaccustomed to drink, and for a while, as they lay awake talking about the wonders of the evening, it fumed in their brains. First one, then the other, took the lantern and looked about the floor, in all the dark corners, to see whether any bugs were present, just to be on the safe side. Then tiredness and beer took their toll and they fell asleep.

The moon shone in the window and moved across the room.

Suddenly one of the lads woke. Something was scuttling about the floor. He clutched his friend's arm, and together they stared down at the wooden boards and thin rug. First one then another shadowy little beast ran along the edge of the wall. Bugs! So much for the landlady's reassurance! They must kill them or their blood would be sucked. Pulling on boots to protect their bare feet and ankles, and clutching the shirts about their knees, they seized their sticks and began striking out at the horrors, which scuttled from sight beneath the cupboard and bed, and led them a terrible chase. At last the boys got them cornered, and gave them several rattling good thumps to ensure that those bugs, at least, would never suck anyone's blood again. Quite pleased with them-

selves and feeling that they had coped well with the emergency, they examined the remains, retired to their bed once more and were soon sound asleep.

The landlady heard their terrible row, but she was accustomed to sailors on shore leave, and as it soon stopped she did not interfere.

In the morning, when the two lads came downstairs, somewhat sorry for their excesses of the evening, she greeted them with a smile. Well, had they been troubled with the bugs? No, they assured her, they had coped with them fine. There had been a couple, sure enough, but they had flattened them and everything was all right. She was appalled. Bugs in her clean house! She demanded that the boys should show them to her. Readily the two lads led her to their room. There, beside the wall, battered almost beyond recognition, were the two guinea pigs her sailor son had brought home from abroad.

"Oh!" she cried. "My poor guinea pigs! They got out again!"

Realising that something had gone wrong, but not quite sure what, the two lads looked down.

"Guinea pigs!" one of them exclaimed. "A guinea for one of them? I could buy better pigs in Kirkmaiden for a shilling the pair!"

143

Signals from the Other Side

On a January Afternoon

An old shepherd lived alone in a cottage a little distance from the road a mile or two above Gatehouse. He did not see many people, especially during the winter when the roads were bad. Once a week or so he walked into the small town for provisions. Then, for a little companionship, he visited the inn and drank half a pint of beer, which was all he could afford.

Late one afternoon in January, as he looked out of his window past the peat stack, he was amazed to see a nearby stand of half a dozen oak trees blazing like torches. He went out to look more closely and saw the flames leaping into the sky, though there was no heat. Later, when the fire had gone out and he returned to the trees, they were unharmed.

The same day the following year, when the ground was covered with snow, on looking out of the same window he saw the clear, freezing, late afternoon sky darken with a strangely moving cloud. It drew close and descended on his garden and the surrounding trees and fields. The cloud turned out to be a tremendous flock of owls. They stood shifting their feet in the snow, rustling feathers, blinking, clicking, and hooting conversationally. He went among them. Shortly afterwards, when he looked from the window by the peat stack, they had gone. The snow was unmarked.

The third year, when that date came round, he was half expecting some apparition. What he saw at first seemed nothing strange. A man was approaching across the wintry fields. He entered the garden and stood in the falling snow a little distance from the house. He was a negro, tall and majestic, with a strange flail over his shoulder. His eyes, dark and direct, regarded the old shepherd through the window. When the shepherd stepped outside the negro's face lightened in greeting, though he did not speak. Like the owls, his feet had made no track in the snow.

The fourth January the shepherd brought his nearest neighbour, an old lady whose cottage was half a mile away, to witness whatever might appear. In the late afternoon the fire was dying down and he went out to bring in some peats. She watched him through the window. Only

144

three or four yards from her he stopped, the bucket in his hand, and raising his head looked all around the sky. She saw a strange look, almost of wonder, in his face. Then he fell to the ground. He was dead when she reached him.

Wraith Light

A widow and her daughter, a girl of twelve, lived in a small cottage a hundred yards along the road from the graveyard in Glenluce. One night, when she supposed her daughter to be asleep, the woman was surprised to hear three sharp knocks from the girl's bedroom. Immediately afterwards she heard her daughter's voice raised in alarm, calling her to come through. Quickly she caught up the lantern and carried it into the bedroom. The girl was frightened. She had heard a loud knocking at the window.

The widow set down the lantern and drew back the blinds. All was dark outside, and then she saw a light going down the path from the

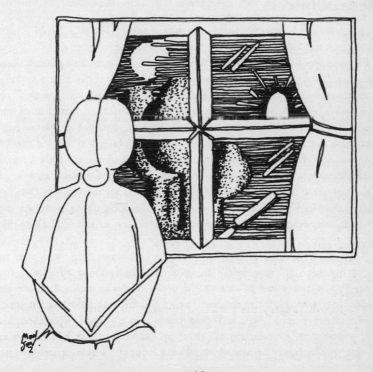

door to the gate. She thought it must be some boys playing pranks and rapped on the window-pane. But the light did not waver from its steady path. Through the gate it went, and away down the road. Soon she could see it no more and hurried to the cottage door for a better view. The light continued steadily down the rutted road, then turned in at the graveyard gates. For a few moments she saw it glimmering among the gravestones, and then it was gone. Looking back to her own front gate she saw that it was shut and chained as normal.

Truly frightened, the widow returned into the house and her daughter's bedroom. She asked the girl how she was feeling and was told that she felt fine. Nevertheless she made her drink a health-giving mixture of meat essence and herbs before she settled down again for the night.

It did no good, the girl's fate was already written. Three days later she died. Inevitably her coffin was carried down the track her mother had seen taken by the 'deid licht' to the graveyard.

The Grandfather

A man of reliability and unquestionable honesty, told John Mactaggart the following story about his boyhood.

He was spending the summer holidays with his aunt and grandfather. Early on a fine morning he was working at the end of the house making a 'grinwan' — a willow rod with a hair noose for catching trout — to take down to a deep pool in the burn. His grandfather came out of the house and stood for a moment watching him, but the boy was concentrating on tying the noose to the rod with a length of waxed thread and did not speak. The old man turned away and pursued his normal track across the side of the hill to look at the cattle and a couple of foals that were in the field. When he had gone it struck the boy that his grandfather had been unusually silent, and looking up he watched the old man wending his way along, the customary crooked stick in his hand.

Soon the grinwan was finished and the boy went into the house to beg a measure of 'sowens' — steeped and boiled oat siftings — for scattering in the water to attract the trout. He was stunned to see his grandfather sitting on the settle-stone at the fireside smoking his pipe. "Lord preserve me!" he cried, and could say no more. Surprised, his aunt asked what was wrong and the boy led her outside, but there was no sign of the figure he had seen walking from the house. There was no doubt that it had been his grandfather, he even remembered a particular pair of fingerless mittens in the old man's hands as he stood beside him.

That same evening his grandfather, always so upright and ruddy with health, took ill. It was a Saturday. On the Monday morning at six o'clock he died.

Three Merry Boys

On a warm autumn morning two old friends went into an inn to share a bottle of beer. They sat at their usual table and poured the ale, foaming, into two glasses. Regretfully they spoke of a friend, who normally made a threesome with them at the inn, but now was ill. The conversation moved on. Suddenly they were struck dumb as the table between them was rapped sharply three times, as if with a light stick, though there was no-one within several feet. Alarmed, they pushed back their chairs, then leaving their drinks unfinished were soon outside the inn in the late morning sunshine.

Shortly afterwards they learned that their good friend had died, as nearly as they could tell at the same moment as they had heard the knocking on the table. Further, they remembered that normally he carried a light willow wand with him, and frequently as they sat at the inn, he blithely sang a verse that began: 'Here are we met, three merry boys.'

The Seafaring Son

It was a late autumn morning. On the hillside above his cottage at Buittle an aging cottar was lifting potatoes. Looking across to the rough

main road he was surprised to see the figure of his son walk down the track towards the cottage and pass out of sight behind the gable wall. He was surprised because his son was working on a timber-carrying vessel several miles along the coast, and was not expected home before the weekend.

Taking the potatoes he had already lifted, he carried them down the hillside to the cottage. His daughter was preparing the midday meal in the kitchen. He asked her where her brother had gone, and why he had come home so unexpectedly. She was astonished at his words, and then alarmed, for her brother had certainly not entered the house. He looked around outside for the young man, but he was nowhere to be found. Unable to believe it, for he had seen him so plainly from the hill, the old man sat down in his wooden armchair beside the fire. The hands of the clock stood at twelve.

In the late afternoon a messenger brought them tragic news that the young man was dead. In the course of his work he had fallen between the sloop and the wall of the quay. He was crushed, and his body sank almost immediately. The time was a few minutes before midday.

Handless Sammy

His name was Samuel Hannay, which had a dignified, south-western ring about it, but everyone called him 'Handless Sammy'. He was a labourer — when he was in work. There was nothing bad about him exactly, his mind just wandered. He went off with the cart for a load of gravel, and an hour later, when all the masons were standing idle waiting for his return, the foreman found him sitting on the bank of the stream, a grass between his teeth, gazing into space. The horse, as content as himself, stood cropping the clover at the edge of the track. When the foreman roused him and Sammy realised how long he had been sitting, he jumped to his feet in distress and rushed at the gravel pit like a man demented, but really it was no good and soon he was out of a job again.

It was a great worry to his wife, for she had a family of five to care for, and another on the way. His father, a thrifty, hard-working man, had given up his only son as hopeless a long time before.

One September evening when things were very bad, Sammy was sitting on the shore watching the tide flow in across the mudbanks. The sun set over the open sea, and as the colours spread and daylight faded

148

into the comfortable gloom of evening, the worried lines smoothed from his brow. Peace settled on his shoulders like the dew.

Suddenly, when the tide was nearly full, Sammy saw a light dancing in the water just off shore, a merry light that twinkled and came in on the splashing waves. He was filled with wonder, and an unusual sense of joy. Beneath him the light sparkled in the foam at the very brink, and then, still dancing, moved up the beach to the dunes and rough stones and autumn bracken. Soon it was gone from sight. Curiously, Sammy clambered down the hillside to look more closely, but the light had vanished, there was no sign of it anywhere.

Soon he returned to his vantage point and settled himself once more, this time beneath a tree, where the thinning boughs sheltered the earth from the evening damp. The light faded and the moon gained strength above the Cumbrian hills far across the water. The tide passed the flood and began, almost unnoticeably at first, to ebb.

Then from the tangled undergrowth below a light appeared. It was not the same light, for this was dim, pale and so translucent as sometimes to be almost invisible. Slowly and quietly it floated down the shore to the lapping waves, filling Sammy with a great sense of sadness, which he could not explain. Then the light was on the water, rocking gently and slowly moving out from the shore. Soon he could see it only briefly as it rose on the crest of a wave, and then it was gone.

Not long afterwards Sammy rose and made his way home along the cliffs and up the moonlit lanes to his poor cottage. As he went he was filled with a mixture of emotions, joy mingled with sadness, and though he had neither a job nor money, a strange sense of peace.

Three days later, early in the morning, his wife was delivered of a beautiful baby daughter. And that same evening a neighbour of his father brought news that the old man, who had been ailing for some time, had died.

Sammy went at once to the house. His father had left a letter for him. Among other, private matters, it instructed him to look for a canvas bag beneath the rafters. Sammy found it, and when he pulled open the strings found that the bag was full of gold sovereigns, his father's life's savings.

In following years his wife had two or three more children, and they all lived frugally, but happily, ever after.

The Pentland Rising*

In the autumn of 1665 Sir James Turner M.A. was sent into Galloway with a force of one hundred and forty horse and foot guards. His task was to seek out those who opposed the Episcopalian dictates of the king; assist the troubled curates who had been sent to replace the 'outed' ministers; curb civil disorder; and ensure that the fines levied against non-attenders at church were paid. He established himself in Dumfries. The work was carried out efficiently, with ruthless disregard for the feelings of the people. By order, troops of soldiers were billeted upon families in the manner of an occupying force: their demands and depredations reduced many to a state of poverty. It was oppression rather than rule. It was only to be expected that at length the bitter resentment of the people would express itself in action and revolt.

On 13th November, 1666, a bleak, sodden day, four men who had been hiding in the hills came down early to seek food in St John's Town of Dalry. They were hiding because they would not betray their consciences by attending the curates' services, and were unwilling to face the fines and rough treatment of the dragoons. As they descended the rough road they encountered three soldiers under the command of Corporal George Deanes, who were driving a number of peasants before them. They were on their way to the steading of a poor old farmer named Grier, to thresh and seize his corn in payment of fines he had incurred by non-attendance at church. The fugitives – Robert MacLellan, laird of Barscobe Castle, a mile north of Balmaclellan, and three other men – were angry but passed by, not wishing to draw attention to themselves, and feeling, as everyone always did, that there was little they could do.

In a while they were sitting in the little clachan ale-house at Midtown, Dalry, having breakfast, when news was brought that the soldiers had seized Grier. They had bound the old man hand and foot 'like a beast', and in his own house were threatening to strip him naked and set him on a red-hot gridiron, along with other tortures, to see whether he had any hidden savings, for he was maintaining that he had no money at all to pay the fines. Burning with anger the four ran from the inn and caught Corporal Deanes and his men red-handed. Robert

* See 'The Covenanters'.

150

MacLellan cried, "He is an honest farmer. Why do you treat him so?" Others shouted, "How dare you bind the old man like this?" The soldiers replied arrogantly, "How dare you challenge what we do?" Hot words were exchanged and two soldiers came running from an inner room with their swords drawn. Falling upon the four fugitives they wounded two of them. Robert MacLellan answered by firing his pistol, which in the absence of proper shot he had loaded with pieces of tobacco pipe. Corporal Deanes was wounded and fell to the ground. Seeing their leader fallen the soldiers surrendered.

But what was to happen now? There would certainly be reprisals. The militia could not afford to let such an attack go unavenged. Robert MacLellan and the others were undecided. But events moved swiftly, almost like a moorland fire, and in the sudden upsurge of feeling decision was virtually taken out of their hands.

Three miles away in Balmaclellan a conventicle was in progress when news of the affair was brought hot-foot from the farmhouse; and immediately after the affray they were joined by some of the principals involved. Realising that they would all be implicated through knowledge of their covenanting sympathies, they took matters into their own hands. For the first time in their dealings with the militia they took the initiative. Boldly they sought defence in attack and launched themselves against a local garrison of sixteen soldiers. One dragoon was killed in the skirmish, and the others were made prisoner.

Now the die was cast. Reprisals following such an action, as they knew full well from previous dealings with the king's forces, would be terrible. A meeting was held and it was decided, in an atmosphere of wild excitement and apprehension, to march upon Dumfries and take Sir James Turner hostage. With him in their power, they felt, they would be in a position to bargain, both for their own safety and for religious tolerance. Already men were coming forward to join them: they were sure they could count on others. News was sent ahead and through nearby parishes that supporters should meet them at Irongray Church, four miles to the west of Dumfries, a little before dawn.

During that night Corporal Deanes, though wounded, managed to escape, and made his way to Dumfries ahead of them. He showed his wounds to his commanding officer and informed him of the insurrection and the plan to take him hostage. It was too much for Sir James's military spirit. Summoning his guards, he retired indisposed.

The weather was dreadful and the torrential rain hindered the Covenanters' progress. It was already dawn when Robert MacLellan with a force of fifty-four sodden cloaked riders, and John Neilson of Corsock leading a hundred and fifty tired men on foot, arrived at the rendezvous. Here, strangely, command was assumed by a man of whom little is known, save that he was called Mr (or Captain) Andrew Gray, rode a little pony, and vanished irrevocably into the Carsphairn mist a couple of days later.

Riding at the head of the bedraggled troop of insurgents, Andrew Gray led the way over Dervorgilla's Bridge to the house of Bailie Finnie, where Sir James 'Bloody-Bite-the-Sheep' Turner was living in some comfort. It was eight o'clock in the morning. Though they were expected they were a large force and the guards offered little resistance. Assembling before the house, they called on Sir James to surrender.

No bold leader in fine uniform strode out to answer their challenge, but at the window appeared a vision attired in night-cap, night-gown, drawers and socks, and a tremulous, scholarly voice was heard calling for quarter. John Neilson, a true country gentleman, promised it, but when Sir James appeared before them, Andrew Gray prepared to shoot him. Neilson intervened, and Sir James was spared.

Now Andrew Gray ransacked a chest in Turner's house, taking papers and more than six thousand merks. After it had been safely stowed in bags, the Covenanters marched to the town cross, where they pledged a health to the king — which at this time was still their practice — swore their allegiance to the Covenant, and reviled the hated bishops. Then, leading Sir James on horseback — still in his night-attire and by this time rather damp and cold — they gathered on the bank of the Nith, opposite to the church of John Blackadder,* and held a council of war. They were not well armed and made a search of the district, during which there was a scuffle which resulted in the death of a second soldier.

---

* John Blackadder was one of the great field preachers. Shortly before this uprising he had taken his family to a lonely hill farm about fifteen miles to the north-west. While he was absent redcoats arrived and ransacked the house, stabbing swords through the beds in which children were cowering, threatening to set fire to the place and kill them all, breaking the furniture, strangling all the hens. Blackadder took his family to Edinburgh and hid them in the warren of the Cowgate, right beneath the Castle. From here he issued out on circuits of field preaching. On one occasion he gave communion to three thousand souls. Eventually he was captured and sent to prison on the Bass Rock, where he spent the last five years of his life. The cold and climate were such that he developed very bad rheumatism and would have been sent ashore. Since he resolutely refused to adjust his principles in the slightest degree, however, he was held on the rock and died there. He was seventy years old. His family of five sons and two daughters, who had such a strange childhood, were outstandingly successful.

Still having no settled plan, they decided to return to Dalry, and after allowing Sir James time to get dressed, marched the sixteen miles back up the Rivers Cluden and Cairn to Glencairn Church by Moniaive. After a rest they continued, and marching all through a second night also, were back in Dalry by the morning.

For that day they had rest, but in the evening alarm came, at which they set off once more, for the higher wilds of Carsphairn. Here, in the dark and the rain, after committing Sir James to the care of sixteen horsemen, Andrew Gray quietly vanished with the goods and money he had annexed in Dumfries, and was never heard of again by the men he was leading.

Quickly news of the insurrection was taken to Edinburgh by Bailie Stephen Irving of Dumfries. Lieutenant-General Thomas Dalziel was issued with very definite instructions to march with a large body of soldiers and suppress the uprising. He was a remarkable figure, dramatic and conspicuous in unfashionable clothes, his own head bald in days of periwigs, with long hair and a beard that had not been cut since the execution of Charles I seventeen years earlier. He embarrassed the king when he went to court. A harsh man, who had seen service in Russia, Dalziel was referred to by some as 'the Muscovite Beast'. He was to carry out his orders on this occasion with expected thoroughness.

Meanwhile the Covenanters were marching for Edinburgh, gathering supporters on the way. They took a north-western route, by Dalmellington to Ayr, where they arrived on 20th February. By this time they numbered seven hundred men. They were joined by Colonel James Wallace of Auchans in Ayrshire, who now officially took command, and trained his wet, tired troops in basic drill, marching and rifle fire, though they had few arms. They continued by Cumnock, Muirkirk and Douglas to Lanark. Here, on Sunday, 25th February, having now swelled to an army of approximately two thousand, they held two tremendous services, one for horsemen at the townhead, and one for foot soldiers at the tolbooth, where afterwards they issued their pacific 'Declaration of Those in Arms for the Covenant'.

The weather was still appalling. For two weeks the rain had not ceased, and it was through further torrents that they marched out of town in the middle of the day. Bedraggled and half-fed they were a pathetic army — gentry, farmers, shepherds, ploughmen and tradesmen, and thirty-two 'outed' ministers — with a poor assortment of weapons. Their physical discomfort was added to by the discovery that Dalziel, who rattled through Lanark on the Sunday afternoon, was at their heels with a vastly superior force — 500 horse and 2500 foot soldiers, well-armed and well-equipped — which now began firing into their rear in a desultory manner.

Manfully they struggled on along roads that were little better than quagmires, bogged above the ankles in mud, sodden to the skin. As they moved north, fewer and fewer supporters had joined their ranks. Now, as they marched towards Bathgate, the support was little more than verbal, merely admiration for the plucky underdog. Wretched, anticipating defeat and cruel reprisals, and not knowing what they could do once they reached the well-defended capital, men began deserting.

From Bathgate they marched on, yet again through the night, to Newbridge and turned aside over broken, boggy ground, to arrive on Tuesday at Colinton, on the very edge of the city. Some were so tired that they roped themselves to comrades to keep going. For the rest of that day and the night they lay in the church and churchyard. The weather grew colder. During the night snow fell, and when dawn came on Wednesday, 28th February, the Pentland Hills were white. But more important, they discovered as a count was made, that more than a thousand men had deserted: their numbers were down to nine hundred.

One who had left them the day before, though not by deserting, was Hugh McKail, the young, consumptive preacher, who had come out of hiding to join them. Since the age of twenty-two, when at the church of St Giles in Edinburgh the last sermon of his trials had by implication been much too outspoken, he had been on the run, in Holland and quiet places in Scotland. The conditions of the march had so weakened him that he could not stay on his horse, and though he pleaded with men to hold him there, they were exhausted themselves and it was not to be. He was left behind at Cramond Water. Seeking to make his way home to Liberton, he was captured in the Braid Hills.

Messages had been dispatched ahead into Edinburgh and behind to General Dalziel. Messengers tried to break into the city to force a hearing. But the capital refused to listen to their case. Dalziel maintained an ominous silence. Within the city Archbishop Sharp, once a covenanted minister and at the Restoration a messenger bearing all the Covenanters' hopes, now wrote to Dalziel wishing him a speedy victory over the 'deluded rabble'.

The rebels were in a desperate situation: no recognition, no support, exhausted, poorly armed, outnumbered in the enemy's stronghold, and a long way from home. The prospect of surrender was even more appalling than conflict. Their only hope was to retreat and pray that once their intentions were apparent they would not be too cruelly harried by Dalziel. On the Wednesday afternoon they mustered for the last time, and with weary feet began to march south, away from the city.

From the ruthless repression that the king, military and other authorities had almost always shown towards them, the Covenanters should perhaps have realised that their hopes were naive. They had gone little more than a couple of miles, surprising and arousing pity in the local people by their ragged and distressed condition, when battle was forced upon them by Dalziel at Rullion Green, a market village in the lower Pentland Hills. The spot was well known to the shepherds of Ayrshire and Galloway in those droving days. With coolness and courage as the afternoon light dimmed, Colonel Wallace marshalled his men on the well-selected south-eastern slope of Turnhouse Hill. Mr Neilson of Corsock took command of the advance guard. Sir James Turner, who was still with them, was sent down to Dalziel to speak on their behalf, but the General would not treat with them. He would consider nothing but unconditional surrender. Battle was inevitable.

Their bravery was not enough. Nine hundred men could not withstand the assault of Dalziel's three thousand trained troops. Wet, tired countrymen, clad in workaday clothes, half numb with the cold, they formed their line of defence. For weapons they had flails, ploughshares, spades, scythes, staves, clubs: only the better equipped carried swords and rifles. The fresh, irresistible horse of Dalziel swept through them like scythes through a cornfield.* In vain the warlike ministers cried their ecstatic slogans: "The God of Jacob! The God of Jacob! See the Lord of Hosts fighting for us!" The brave and ragged rebels fell back. The line broke. Soon it became a rout. In the darkness which fell while they were fighting, the Covenanters were hunted and cut down. The dead, as always, were stripped of their few possessions. By clear moonlight, across the hillsides and through the copses of the Pentlands, the pursuit continued.

Royalist losses were slight, but Dalziel's men were harsh, and were ordered to be. Fifty or a hundred of the Covenanters were killed — the accounts vary — often cut down when they were defenceless and even had surrendered. Many more were slain in flight. At least one hundred and fifty were taken prisoner.

* The story was told afterwards that the bullets hopped off Dalziel like hailstones, proving how strong the Devil was in him. The idea is fanciful and typical of the times, but it does suggest, perhaps, that while they were fighting there was a rattling shower of hail.

They were treated cruelly, for from the start, as the Covenanters had anticipated in Dalry, it was intended that by firm repression further uprisings would be discouraged. Some, including the fresh-faced young preacher Hugh McKail, and 'that meek and generous gentleman' John Neilson of Corsock, were tortured with the 'boot', to try to discover whether the uprising was part of a greater plot being hatched in Holland. Poor Neilson's cries could be heard far out over the city. Hugh McKail withstood the pain with almost unbelievable fortitude until his knee was crushed and he was carried off unconscious. For four days he managed to maintain a feverish gaiety, until he was hanged, so weak and damaged that he was quite unable to stand at the gallows. His behaviour had a stunning effect upon those who saw him. Numbers were hanged in the Edinburgh Grassmarket, and at Glasgow, Ayr, Dumfries, Kirkcudbright and elsewhere. Their heads were displayed on public pikes as warnings. Those who had signed or subscribed to the Covenant at Lanark had their right hands cut off. Many were dispatched to slavery in the plantations of the West Indies. Some died in jail. And all because they wished to be free to worship Christ in a Christian country.

Sir William Bannatyne, with four hundred foot soldiers and a troop of horse, was dispatched to Galloway to ensure that any last vestiges of the revolt were stamped out, and those who had been at Rullion Green were hunted down and brought to justice. They were billeted at Holm in Balmaclellan and Earlstoun House, from where they issued out with carte-blanche to any treatment and acts they might consider necessary, and terrorised the countryside. Families were molested and threatened, and occasionally even tortured when it was believed they had helped their husbands and fathers to escape. The wife of David McGill, for example, from the parish of Balmaclellan, was seized and bound and had lighted matches placed between her fingers, the pain of which made her distracted. As a result she lost one of her hands, and died a few days later.

And thus, with many men made fugitive and military vigilance and absolute authority settled like a blanket over the countryside, the Pentland Rising slid backwards into the past. But as Archbishop Sharp had predicted long before, the oppression and terrorism, coupled with the martyrdom of their comrades — intensified thirteen years later following the Battle of Bothwell Bridge and most of all during the 'Killing Times' of 1684-85 — only strengthened the moderate Covenanters more firmly in their resistance.

It is interesting to note what became of one or two of the principals in the Pentland Rising.

Robert MacLellan of Barscobe survived Rullion Green and was declared an outlaw, exempted from the 'King's Indemnity'. He survived Bothwell Bridge also, but was captured three years afterwards by Cornet David Graham, the brother of Claverhouse. Sentenced to be hanged for treason and rebellion, he took the Test acknowledging the king's total supremacy, and was set free to return home to Barscobe. Since he was a leader, it was viewed with an especial sense of betrayal by the Covenanters, and stories have come down the years that in reprisal he was strangled or smothered in his bed. It was claimed that at his death the banshees screamed about the house to take his soul away to Hell, where it belonged. The truth is very different. Himself a gentleman of moderate appetites and manners, he became involved in a scuffle at an inn over the honour of a lady. During this he fell into the fire, almost certainly, it seems, due to an epileptic fit, and died from the shock almost immediately afterwards.

Sir James Turner was called to account for his behaviour and capture in Dumfries. It was an impossible task. He was deprived of his commissions in 1668, totally appalled at the vision of himself as 'ane absolute beggar' and the 'ruine of a poor gentleman'. For fifteen years he lived in the shade, but in 1683 was recalled to his command in the south-west of Scotland.

Archbishop Sharp, the ambitious turncoat, as he was seen by the Covenanters, was waylaid in his coach on St Magus Moor near St Andrews in May, 1679. Ironically it was a chance encounter. Though he pleaded and screamed for mercy, before the eyes of his terrified daughter he was dragged from the coach and murdered. His death was to have appalling repercussions.

General Dalziel was rewarded with the forfeited estates of some of those he had pursued. In a highly congratulatory letter, praising his great zeal in so efficiently quelling the uprising, the King to whom the Covenanters had vowed allegiance subscribed himself to Dalziel, 'Your very loving friend . . .'

Colonel Wallace, who had with such manliness and ability taken over the leadership of the Covenanting force at Ayr, and done all that any man could do at Rullion Green, escaped to Holland, and died there in 1678.

Heather Ale

From the bonny bells of heather
They brewed a drink long-syne,
Was sweeter far than honey,
Was stronger far than wine.
They brewed it and they drank it,
And lay in a blessed swound
For days and days together
In their dwellings underground.

R. L. Stevenson

The secret of heather ale died with the last of the Picts on the Mull of Galloway.

Sixteen hundred years ago Niall of the Nine Hostages was the Ardrigh (king in chief) of Ireland. So stable was the situation in his country that he was able to leave commanders in charge and lead the army himself in foreign campaigns. He attacked the Roman legions in Gaul and Britain, and so far as the present story is concerned, he made an expedition against the Picts of Galloway.

The campaign was a great success. The Picts fell back before his fierce Scots warriors: the land was plundered. In six days of merciless slaughter the Picts were virtually annihilated. Following this massacre only one Pictish clan remained, far down the long southern horn of the Rhinns of Galloway. Having vowed that no Pict should remain alive in the whole of that countryside, Niall made preparations for his final advance.

Now there was with Niall a Pictish spy and traitor by the name of Sionach the fox, who had been his adviser throughout the campaign. Although he had been useful, Niall heartily disliked the man for his treacherous, ambitious ways. Sionach now approached the warrior king and told him that this particular clan, since time immemorial, had been hereditary holders of the secret of making heather ale. For centuries others had fought and schemed to wrest it from them, but even unto death the secret had been maintained with passion and pride. Surely Niall's people in Ireland would be glad of such a recipe, for they were known to be a thirsty race.

158

Niall contemplated his vow, balancing it against the benefits to be wrought from the recipe. At length a messenger was dispatched bearing favourable terms for the safety and reprieve of the clan, the last of the Pictish race, in exchange for their secret. His overture was haughtily rejected, and Niall attacked, angered by the rebuff.

The Picts fought cleverly and boldly, but little by little they were driven back towards the southern tip of the long peninsula. Men, women and children, all died. The heather was stained red.

At length only four Picts remained alive, a father and his three sons. They retreated across the isthmus that separates the great final headland, the Mull itself, from the rest of the peninsula. Just beyond this isthmus was a great defensive trench and embankment, and the four Pictish warriors ranged themselves along it to repel the Scots' attack.*

For seven days they kept Niall's forces at bay. Their strength was maintained by the supply of 'Biadh-nan-treun', the food of the heroes, which they had carried with them. But at length the supply of food ran out and they began to weaken. Starvation, it seemed, must accomplish what the Scots of Erin could not.

At length the aged father agreed to receive another messenger from Niall, who offered them their lives in exchange for the secret of how to make ale from the heather that bloomed about them as far as the eye could see. The old man agreed, but only upon certain terms. He could not live to witness the disgrace of his clan. Therefore he and his two younger sons must honourably be slain. Then his oldest son, whose name was Trost, would whisper the secret to Sionach the fox. Never would his clan permit the secret to pass from their people. Let that dishonour be Sionach's. In return Trost, in whom rested the future of the Picts, must go free.

The king agreed. The old man and his two brave sons re-crossed the deep ditch and were butchered by the swords of the Scots.

Then Sionach, the coward and traitor, descended into the ditch and climbed apprehensively to the headland. He approached the powerful young Pict, who according to the treaty was unarmed. Trost gestured for Sionach to follow him to the furthest and highest crest of the Mull. The sword gripped tightly but still trembling in his hand, Sionach

* This long entrenchment, which can still clearly be seen and is known as 'The Double-Dykes', is probably of Viking origin. Disregarding this historical inconsistency, its defence by the four Picts was a mighty achievement. (The isthmus, from West to East Tarbet, was used until the last century by fishermen, who dragged their boats across it in rough weather to avoid the turbulent water and fierce currents that flow about the Mull itself.)

climbed the rough slope behind him. At last they reached the summit. Trost beckoned Sionach closer. He would whisper the words in his ear, no-one must hear even the breath from his lips. Sionach hesitated, looking back to the assembled ranks of Niall's men. He wanted to flee, but now, he realised, his own life rested in gaining the secret from Trost. Raising his sword he crept close. Trost's direct eyes stared straight into his own. Then in a flash, before Sionach could move, the young Pict bound his arms about the traitor's body, pinioning his sword arm, and sprang to the edge of the great precipice. Crying then, "The secret is saved!" he leaped from the grassy brink. Together, hero and coward, they fell and fell through space and circling sea-birds to the rocks and blue waters of the Mull of Galloway far below.

Another, more fanciful, version of the story, describes the Picts as small men with red hair and feet so broad that when it rained they could lie on their backs and turn them up over their heads like umbrellas.

Robert Louis Stevenson reminds us that they lived underground. In his account the Scottish king who was hunting the Picts was angry to discover that apparently they had all been slain before they could be forced to give up their secret. By chance, however, his servants discovered two survivors, a father and son, hiding beneath a stone on the moors. The king offered the swarthy, dwarfish pair their freedom in return for the secret of the drink. The father replied that in youth honour was high and death of lesser consequence, whilst at his advanced age the reverse was the truth. Consequently the king should kill his son to save him the dishonour of his father's betrayal. The young man was bound 'neck and heels in a thong' and flung from the high pale precipice. Then facing the fierce king the Pict cried that unyielding courage could not be demanded from a beardless youth, but now, though the king might torture him with fire, the secret should never be revealed.

Stevenson says no more, but two other versions round the story off. In one the Pict is freed by the king because of his great bravery. In the second, after his son has been slain by the sword, the father bursts from his captors and flings himself from the cliff, and thus, as in every account, the secret dies with him.

Since those ancient times, in century after century, men have tried to rediscover the secret of the heather ale, but though the hills of Galloway and Scotland remain purple with heather, they have never succeeded.

The Wedding Plate

It was a delightful summer day in Glenluce. The air was warm, butterflies danced in the hedgerows, the morning sun glittered on the water of Luce Bay. From all the district round about guests made their way along the country lanes to a wedding. The beautiful daughter of the miller was marrying her childhood sweetheart, a former apprentice of her father, who now had a mill of his own three miles away at Crow's Nest.

The family did not have a great deal of money, but everyone had lent a helping hand, for the miller was well known and popular. The scoured trestle tables, decorated with flowers, were set out on the grass near the river and the mill. Glenluce Abbey had lent fine plate and goblets for the meal, and donated the best of its kitchen gardens. The women had been baking and roasting. There were barrels of ale and a few firkins of contraband wine and spirit to which the excise officers turned a blind eye. It promised to be a perfect day.

The ceremonies were concluded, the feast was enjoyed, fiddlers and pipers played for the dancing which followed in the afternoon sunshine. The hours raced by, and all too soon it was time for the young couple to take their leave. But their departure was no sign for the festivities to draw to a close. They continued in full swing. Everyone was merry.

Then a rumour started among the crowd. A silver plate of great value, which had been lent by the Abbey, was missing. The miller confirmed it.

A blacksmith was one of the guests, a great burly fellow with a reputation for violence. He had been drinking. "Ah, my friend," he cried, trailing a massive arm around the miller's shoulders. "What an outrage! Ill befall the man that took the plate and disgraced you. May the villain die by cold steel this very day! He deserves no better!"

Despite the shadow which the theft and the blacksmith's words had cast over the celebration, it continued.

A young gentleman by the name of Hay, from the nearby Castle of Park, well known for his wildness of spirit and rebellion, was among the guests. The blacksmith approached him, and soon was repeating his curse. The young man nodded in agreement and tried to humour him.

161

Then the blacksmith recalled that Hay owed him some money for a recent shoeing.

"I will pay you tomorrow," young Hay assured him. "Send to the house, and you will be fully paid."

Somewhat disgruntled, the blacksmith gave him a dark look and went off. But he could not let the business drop like that, and soon returned to the young man's side.

"What are you doing here, in any case?" he demanded. "This is for our people, not the likes of you, from the big house."

Growing angry, for he had long been a friend of the newly married couple, young Hay tried to turn aside. But the blacksmith restrained him.

"Damn the man who stole the Abbey plate!" he cried, so loudly that everyone in the vicinity turned to look at him. "And you, too. Knew the miller's daughter, didn't you? I wouldn't be sure but you knew her too well. I know the likes of you. I wouldn't be surprised if you knew more about the plate than you're saying, as well. Do you, eh?"

He gave the young laird a push.

"Do you?"

Struggling to contain his temper Hay tried again to turn aside, but the blacksmith would not let him be, and struck him across the side of the head with his fist.

Before he could stop himself young Hay had drawn his sword, and with a rapier-quick thrust, run the blacksmith straight through.

The guests cried aloud.

But then, as the blacksmith stumbled and fell, the Abbey plate slipped from beneath his jerkin and rolled across the grass, shining and winking in the late afternoon sunshine.

The crowd gazed with dismay from the plate to the glinting sword and the body of the drunken, dead blacksmith. With awful poetic justice his curse was fulfilled.

A strange fate thereafter followed young Hay. He retired unhindered from the ruined party, but soon the authorities were on his trail. Having been involved in a number of scrapes he thought it best to make himself scarce, and fled the country. He was away for several years and what happened during that time is unknown. He returned as an idiot tramp, which astonished and shocked the countryside. Wandering through the villages he blew a long horn and recited strings of jingling, doggerel verse, for which some people out of pity gave him a bite of food or a penny. He was well known throughout the district and in many parts of

Galloway as 'Jock o' the Horn'. Particularly he liked his old haunts, and sometimes even went to the door of Castle of Park, his old home high above the river. He was not commonly admitted, though it was whispered in the neighbourhood that his madness was only a disguise, and when the Hays dined alone and the servants were absent, he threw off his rags and once more resumed his place at the family table.

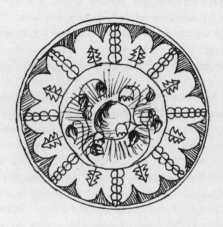

The Rerrick Poltergeist

On top of the hill on Collin Farm stand the three gaunt 'Ghost Trees', all that remain of the wood on the ancient 'Ringcroft of Stocking'. One beech is dead and stripped of bark, the other is dying, and in the middle, blown all one way by the wind, is a tougher oak. They stand in a high pasture surrounded by grey boulders. To the west, beneath a younger wood, lies Bengairn Loch with hills rising beyond. To the east is a magnificent view above the village of Auchencairn to the bay and Heston Island, and the mountains of Cumbria far off across the Solway.

Just below this crest of hill stood the house of Andrew Mackie, a mason and small farmer. Here, during the months of February, March and April of the year 1695, a most remarkable series of events is claimed to have occurred. It is perhaps uncharitable to use the phrase 'is claimed', for a detailed and thorough account of the whole affair was written that same year by the minister of the parish, the Rev. Alexander Telfair, and attested to by many other ministers of the area, and farmers and crofters of the surrounding district: eminent and respectable citizens. Mr Telfair was witness to many of the events that occurred, and familiar with all the people concerned. Finding that exaggerated tales were already springing up, he wrote his account to quell them and reduce the events to their proper perspective. So extraordinary were they, however, that today it is difficult to accept the account as fact. Mr Telfair entitled his report 'The True Account of the Rerwick Apparition', but since no figure repeatedly materialised — though indeed there were apparitions — and the events partially, at least, involved objects flying about of their own volition, the word 'poltergeist' now seems more appropriate. The events at Ringcroft of Stocking were used for many years by the Encyclopedia Britannica as a particularly well documented account of a poltergeist's activity. But even this definition is not really satisfactory, for the generally mischievous events commonly associated with these spirits are much slighter than the continuing period of violence, with disembodied voices and apparitions, that occurred at Andrew Mackie's House. Also it seems fairly conclusive that poltergeists are in some way connected with young people, often around or just beyond the age of puberty, as if some unconscious inner violence was being expressed externally. In Mr Telfair's account there is insufficient evidence to relate the events particularly to Andrew Mackie's children, though at least one, and possibly more were of an appropriate age. In the superstitious and strongly religious times in which the events occurred — covenanters and witch persecution — the weird occurrences were ascribed to 'a spirit which infested the house', and this seems about the best definition to which we can adhere today.

Three possible reasons for the infestation are offered by Mr Telfair, though as he admits, none seems adequate. First, it was claimed that Andrew Mackie had, upon taking the mason word, devoted his first child to the Devil. This was completely denied and difficult to believe, for he was a good-living man. Secondly, it was claimed that certain garments belonging to a woman of ill repute, which had been left in the house, had upon her death been misappropriated. Andrew Mackie, however, swore that this was not so. All her clothes had been contained in a bundle which was never unfastened, and at the appropriate time was handed over to her friends. No possession of hers remained in the house. The third suggestion is more complicated. Some years previously the house had been occupied by a man named McNaught, whose health was poor and whose personal circumstances were always at a low ebb, no matter how he struggled. As things declined from bad to worse he wondered whether there might be some unnatural influence at work against him, and accordingly sent his oldest son to a noted spae-wife, nearer to a witch, who lived by the Routing Bridge in the parish of Irongray. The young man's home circumstances cannot have been very happy, for encountering a troop of soldiers as he returned, he enlisted with them on the spot, and soon found himself in Flanders. There, some time afterwards, he met another young man from the parish of Rerrick, named John Redick. Learning that Redick was soon to go home, young McNaught asked him to deliver the spae-wife's message to his father. He was to raise the stone slab at the threshold of the house, and beneath he would find a tooth which must be burned. Until this was done none would flourish in the house. When Redick returned, however, he found that McNaught was dead and the house had passed to a man named Thomas Telfair (no relation of the minister). John Redick informed the minister, but since McNaught was dead the matter was left alone. News of the witch-wife's words came to the ears of Thomas Telfair, however, and he raised the slab. Beneath he found something which indeed did resemble a tooth, though whether human

165

or of some animal he could not tell. He cast it into the fire, as were the instructions, and saw it burn like tallow, or a candle. But neither before nor after this did Thomas Telfair have any trouble whatsoever while he lived in that house. When he left, some years later, the next occupant was Andrew Mackie.

The trouble started in a small way. During the month of February, Andrew Mackie discovered that the bindings of some young beasts which he had tethered for the night were broken and they were running loose. Attributing this to the unruliness of the animals he made the tethers stronger, but the following morning they were broken again. He made them stronger yet, of willow withes and osier, but still they were broken. Realising that the strength and restlessness of the animals could not fully account for it, he removed them from the place. The following morning he found one beast bound to the back of the house with a a hair tedder,* so tightly that its feet barely touched the ground, though it was not hurt.

Shortly afterwards, while the family slept, a full back-creel† of peats was stacked up in the middle of the house and set on fire. The smoke wakened them and they were able to put the fire out. Had they been much later, the house would have burned down.

On the 7th March the stone throwing commenced. It was to continue for nearly two months. The beginning was naturally alarming but not too violent. Small stones were flung about the house, in all parts of it both inside and out, but they could never see from where they had come. While they slept they were disturbed by stones rattling about their beds.

It is reasonable to wonder why the Mackies did not leave the house, even at this stage. Eventually they did, but that was much later. These events were only the beginning.

One morning when everyone was working outside and the house was known to be empty, the children saw what they thought to be a person sitting by the fire, covered with a blanket. They were frightened until the youngest, a boy of nine or ten, saw that the blanket was his. Saining° themselves, the children advanced into the room. Then the youngest ran forward and pulled his blanket away, at which it was discovered that only an up-ended four-legged stool lay beneath it.

* A tether of hair, commonly associated with witchcraft.
† A large back-basket for carrying peats or fish.
° Blessing: shielding from the evil influence of devils, fairies, witches, and other spirits.

The following day, a Sunday, the pot-hooks disappeared, and though the family searched for hours they were not to be found. Four days later two neighbours discovered them in a loft, a place which had been searched several times before. While they were about the house these neighbours were subjected to attacks of stones, though as yet their size was quite small and they did not hurt. Already it had been noticed that

the stone throwing was worse when the family was at prayer. On the Sabbath it was worst of all.

After church that day Andrew Mackie told the minister, Mr Telfair, about their trouble, and on the following Tuesday he visited them in Ringcroft of Stocking. They prayed together and nothing strange occurred. But as they stood outside afterwards, Mr Telfair saw two small stones drop down on the croft, then from within the house some-one cried that it was as bad as ever. They returned indoors where the minister himself was struck by one or two of the small stones.

For a week there was calm, then on the Sabbath the stone throwing recommenced. The stones were larger and began to hurt. For three days it continued, then the minister returned to the house and spent a great part of the night there. During this time he was struck several times on the sides and shoulders with a great staff, so hard that those in adjoining rooms heard the strokes. Other objects were flung about and directly at people. The side of the box bed was torn off. On chests and boards there was a knocking like someone wishing to come in. Neighbours also were witnesses to much of this — Charles Maclellan of Collin, William McMinn and John Tait of Torr.

Still nothing had been seen. That night, however, Mr Telfair, leaning on a bedside at prayer, felt something pressing on his arm, and looking down saw a little white spectral forearm with the hand on his sleeve. Presently it vanished. Nothing else of human form was ever seen, save by a friend of Andrew Mackie, who said he saw a boy of about fourteen years, in grey clothes and with a bonnet on his head, who shortly disappeared. And of course there was the apparition the children believed they had seen at the fireside.

The trouble increased. Neighbours who called were beaten with staves, and bombarded with stones from the yard both on arrival and departure. Thomas Telfair, the late owner of the house, was one of these. Andrew Mackie's brow was cut, his shoulder pushed several times, and at last he was caught by the hair and felt what seemed like fingernails scratching his skin. Some were dragged about the house by their clothes. A man named Keige, the miller in Auchencairn, was caught by the side, and screamed that he thought his side would be torn away.

The bedclothes were pulled off the children, and what seemed to be a hand beat them about their hips so soundly that all in the house heard it. The bar of the door, and other objects, went through the house as though someone invisible was carrying them. Repeatedly a stave rattled loudly on the sides of the beds and on chests. At the close of prayer a voice cried "Whist, whist!" at every sentence. So clearly and distinctly did the spirit whistle that it brought the dog running across the yard to the door, barking as though they were going hunting. Apparently it was not frightened, a fact not mentioned by Mr Telfair three centuries ago.

And so the spirit continued until the beginning of April, whistling, 'whisting', rattling, throwing stones and pursuing people with staves.

Early in the month a number of ministers convened at Buittle, near Dalbeattie, six or seven miles away. Andrew Mackie with his landlord, Charles Maclellan of Collin, gave them an account of the matter. In consequence two ministers, Andrew Ewart of Kells and John Murdo of Crossmichael, went to the house and spent the night in prayer and fasting. Rocks of up to half a stone in weight were flung at them. Mr Ewart was twice wounded in the head and bled profusely. His wig was pulled off and the napkin was flung from his hands with a stone in it. Mr Murdo was bruised and wounded with a beating. That night the attacks were furious and everyone was punished. A flaming peat was thrown from the fire. At the conclusion of morning prayers stones poured down on all who were within the house. Later in the morning some thatch straw in the barnyard was set on fire.

Shortly afterwards, carrying peats into the house, Andrew Mackie's wife felt a broad stone by the doorway shake beneath her foot, though it had never been loose before. The next day, following a night when many visiting neighbours were stoned, she lifted the slab. Beneath it she found a scrap of filthy and bloodstained paper. Wrapped within it were seven small bones and some flesh. The blood was fresh and bright. She was frightened and ran to Collin, quarter of a mile away. While she was gone the disturbances in the house were worse than ever before. Stones flew about wildly and fire balls appeared, bowling from place to place but vanishing before they did any damage. Later, when the children were sleeping, a stone landed in the bed between them, so hot that it burned through the bedclothes. It was removed by their eldest brother, and even more than an hour and a half later, lying on the floor, it was still too hot to hold in the hand. The spirit thrust a staff through the wall above the sleeping children and shook it over them and groaned. Charles Maclellan, who had returned with Mrs Mackie, was attacked cruelly when he fell to prayer, but when he picked up the bones once more the trouble ceased. The bloody bones and paper were sent to Mr Telfair, who came at once to the house and offered up more prayers, at which he received the same treatment as Charles Maclellan. When he had finished, however, all became quiet and remained so for the rest of the night.

This was a Saturday. On the Sabbath the stone-throwing recommenced, and William McMinn, a blacksmith, was cut on the head. Also a ploughshare and heavy stone trough were cast at him, the trough landing on his back, but he was not harmed. The house was twice set on fire. Returning home at dusk Andrew Mackie's oldest son was bathed in an extraordinary light, which then moved swiftly ahead of him to the door, and the trouble continued as before.

Going down the rural close by his house the following morning, Andrew Mackie found a letter both written and sealed with blood. On the back was written: '3 years thou shall have to repent a nett it well.' Within the message read: 'Wo be to thee Scotland Repent and tak warning for the doors of haven ar all Redy bart against thee, I am sent for a warning to thee to flee to God yet troublt shall this man be for twenty days repent repent repent Scotland or else thou shall.'

The house was twenty-eight years old, and now it was wondered whether some murder had been committed there. Accordingly at noon on the day when Andrew Mackie found the letter, all the people who had ever lived in the house were summoned by the civil magistrates to appear before an examining body, consisting of Mr Telfair, Charles Maclellan and others, but no new information was forthcoming. All were required to touch the bones, but nothing happened.

The next day the bones and letter were sent to an assembly of ministers in Kirkcudbright. Several were dispatched to Ringcroft of Stocking to spend as much time in prayer and fasting as they were able. Their presence galvanised the spirit into activity. Stones flew at them and the whole house shook. A hole was broken through the timber and thatch through which big stones poured down upon them. Other rocks were flung about the house. The barn door was broken down. Several of the ministers felt their legs gripped, as if by a hand. The feet of others were hoisted into the air so that they were raised and then fell. And for the following three days the violence continued, while those within the house strove with prayer.

At this time a neighbour arrived with his dog, which on the way had killed a polecat. The polecat was shown to the assembly and then dropped in a corner. Three visitors to the house shortly afterwards were soundly beaten about their bodies and heads with the stinking animal, which was then flung down before them. One of the three was a pedlar, who had not heard of the trouble. He was greatly frightened. As he stood there he was caught by the clothes and what seemed a hand was thrust beneath them, at which he was taken sick.

These events continued more or less unabated until the following Sabbath. Seeing a sieve raised on that day Andrew Mackie grasped the rim and in a struggle the rim was torn off. Then the mesh was rolled up and hurled at a man named Thomas Robertson of Airds. Boulders large enough to break men's legs were bowled at them. William Anderson's head was severely gashed so that he lost a great deal of blood. The whistles, groans and sighs continued, and the spirit cried "Bo, bo," and "Kick, cuck." It shook men backwards and forwards and hoisted them as if to lift them off their knees when at prayer.

Long overdue, the family left the house and five neighbours went to stay there. No harm was done to them and the trouble stopped.

Outside, however, the cattle were thrown to the ground and their tethers were broken.

All being so quiet indoors the family returned. For a day there was no mischief save that the sheep were tied in pairs at the neck with ropes made from a bottle of straw taken from a stable loft three or four bow-shots distant. Additional rope which the spirit had twisted was left lying in the sheep-house.

During the next two days, however, a change occurred. The spirit turned to words and said as it struck people: "Take you that!" or if the blow was to be repeated: "Take you that till you get more!" And so it continued for three days, the only development being the flinging of peat mud along with the stones and pebbles.

To combat the evil spirit, as it was considered, April 24th was appointed a day of humiliation in the parish, when the people should deny themselves and seek the Lord with particular humility and fervour. On that day the trouble recommenced in all its violence, the family and neighbours fearing lest they should be killed.

Two evenings later the speech was reinforced. The spirit began to denounce all within the house as witches and rooks, claiming it would send them to hell. At the time Andrew Mackie, being very tired, was sleeping. Realising that perhaps this was an opportunity to converse with the spirit he was woken by one of the family. Hearing the spirit say, "Thou shalt be troubled till Tuesday," he asked, "Who gave thee a commission?" To this the spirit replied that it was sent by God, and repeated what had been written in the letter of blood, only in rather more detail. It claimed to be caught inextricably between the worlds of God and the Devil, one minute calling all people to repent and the next longing to be adored. "Praise me and I will whistle to you; worship me and I will trouble you no more." In the name of God, Andrew Mackie required that that night he and his family should be delivered out of the hand of Satan. To this the spirit replied: "You might as well have said, Shadrach, Mesach, Abednego." The conversation, which was listened to by a number of witnesses, reached no satisfactory conclusion.

The following day seven fires were started about the house, and the day after that, Sunday, April 28th, from sunrise until sunset the house was perpetually being set on fire, first in one place then another. In the evening, when it became apparent to the spirit that the house would not be burned to the ground, the whole gable end was pulled down. It was impossible to remain in the house any longer and the family removed to the adjoining barn. While they tried to rest the spirit

171

hoisted a log as big as a plough-head into the air above the children, crying, "If I had a commission I would brain them!"

The following day, since the fire-raising continued, Andrew Mackie extinguished the fire they had for cooking and warming themselves and poured water in the hearth. But still the little fires continued breaking out all over the house and barn, though there was no flame within quarter of a mile.

In the middle of the day the spirit whispered to Andrew Mackie, who was threshing in the barn: "Andrew, Andrew." He did not reply. Though it tried to prompt him to speak he would not. Then it said to him: "Be not troubled, you shall have no more trouble, except some casting of stones upon Tuesday to fulfil the promise. Take away your straw."

At eleven o'clock that evening Mr Telfair with some others went to the house once more. He stayed until three or four o'clock in the morning, during which time all was quiet save for two little stones which fell down the chimney on their arrival. After he had gone, however, a few stones were thrown as formerly, and were seen by Charles Maclellan and John Tait, who had remained after the minister departed. It was nearly dawn.

That evening, Tuesday April 30th, several people were gathered with the family in the barn. As they were at prayer Charles Maclellan seems to have been the first to notice 'a black thing' in the corner, and drew it to the attention of the others. While they watched it increased in size like a black cloud, almost as if it would fill the whole barn. From it barley chaff and mud were thrown in their faces. They were all very frightened. Several were gripped by their middles or arms, and other parts of their bodies, so fiercely that for days afterwards they could still feel the grip upon them. Then the blackness faded, and for the rest of the evening and the whole night the house and barn were at peace.

It was the end. On Wednesday night, May 1st, a little sheep house was set on fire, but from then onwards it was as if the whole affair had been no more than a bad dream.

Mr Telfair's account, of which this is a shortened version, is attested to by fourteen named witnesses, none of whom is a member of the family concerned, and several of whom are ministers. Many more people signed the original document, the list of names has simply been curtailed in the published version. Also many people are referred to by both name and abode throughout the account, which was, as has been said, written within months of the events taking place.

Undoubtedly something extraordinary occurred at Ringcroft of Stocking, but whether it was a poltergeist, the visitation of one of the Devil's spirits, or some strange illusionary experience, we will never know.

FOOTNOTE

In 1654 an almost equally well documented and possibly more famous poltergeist manifested itself in Glenluce. It was known as 'The Devil of Glenluce' and related to a young adolescent. This presence, however, has not been so widely accepted as the Rerrick poltergeist.

The Tinkler's Tale

An old tinkler and his wife had for many years set up their camp on a rich estate. The laird made them welcome to a site by the river, and bought tins and hornware and baskets when they called at the house.

The first morning after their arrival one summer the old man left the tent to fetch sticks for his wife's fire. Looking for driftwood along the edge of the river he was surprised to see a little raft-like basket floating down towards him. He pulled it ashore with a branch and was astonished to discover that the basket contained a baby. A note was pinned to the child's wrapping. It read: 'Whoever takes this baby in shall never want.'

The old man took the child in his arms and carried it to his wife, who pronounced it a little girl. They had no children of their own and adopted her. She was called Nan Gordon, and brought up not knowing that she had been found in the river.

Sixteen years passed, and again the tinkler family were camping on the rich estate. The laird's young son and heir, whose name was Peter Maxwell, was out hunting when he heard a sweet voice singing behind a knoll. Creeping close he found himself looking down on the little encampment. The father was tapping at his tins, the daughter plaiting willow baskets, the old mother baking on an open fire. The scene of freedom enchanted him: the beautiful Nan, singing to herself as she worked, filled him with love. He descended from the knoll and told the old man that he would like to join them and follow the gipsy life, leaving his house and the cares of estate behind him. Also he wished to take the tinkler's daughter for a wife.

The old man protested. At length he agreed to go the following day to the finest inn of the neighbouring town and wait until Peter Maxwell joined them.

The day after their arrival he rode up on a fine horse. He and Nan were married. Afterwards the tinkler went off to buy all the young man would need to take up the wandering life.

Three years passed, and again they were camping on the fine estate. The young husband had become most proficient in the tinklers' arts, and the travelling life had greatly changed his appearance. Their young baby was playing in the grass. Looking up from his work Peter Maxwell

saw his father and mother approaching. He pulled the bonnet over his face. His mother admired the baby, never dreaming that this was her grandchild. It was arranged that the following morning he should take a whole collection of their baskets and tins to the kitchen.

With his arms full of wares Peter was invited into the house. Being left alone briefly, he could not resist sitting at the end of the big table where he often ate his meals as a boy. The cook discovered him there and thought she recognised him. Looking closely she spotted a dark mole on his jaw. She raised a loud cry and soon the laird and his wife came running into the kitchen.

They could not believe that the brown-faced tinkler was their dear son. He told them that he would not exchange his free life for all his father's riches and fine estate. His father asked that he would not disgrace them by going about the country as a gipsy. He would buy him a great inn if he would consent to become an inn-keeper. The young tinkler agreed.

The inn was near the coast. Soon Nan had three children, two girls and a boy. As the inn-keeper's pretty young wife she was very popular.

One day a group of sailors was eating and drinking there and Nan caught the eye of the captain. He invited the young couple aboard his ship. They went, leaving the children to be looked after by Nan's parents. The captain took them for a sail.

175

When they were far at sea and it was time to return home he said to Peter Maxwell, "What way does the wind blow?"

He replied, "It blows south."

"Then will you walk the plank into the sea, or hang by your neck from the mast like a dog?" the captain asked.

Nan pleaded for her husband's life. The captain filled a small boat with provisions and he was cast adrift. The ship sailed away with Nan to a distant country.

For weeks the young tinkler drifted on the currents of the sea until all his provisions were gone. He was starving. For drink he licked the dew that formed on the wood and canvas. One night he was woken from his sleep by the knock of the boat landing on a sandy shore.

There was no habitation, nothing but woods and glades. For a long time he wandered, making a shelter for himself at night, living on figs and lemons and animals he trapped.

One day, at last, he saw an old man ahead of him, a traveller weaving baskets out of wands. They went down to his camp where his wife made them a meal. When Peter showed them the baskets he could make they were delighted and invited him to stay with them.

For many months they wandered the strange land.

In time they came to the foreign port where Nan was living. One morning the old woman went to the door of a house with baskets and Nan came to examine them. Seizing one that had been made by her husband she examined the work and told the old woman to bring the man who made it to the house.

So Nan and her husband were reunited.

It was exactly one year and a day from the time he had been cast adrift in the boat. The captain had vouchsafed to honour her for that period. The following day they were to be married.

Nan told her husband to go to the harbour where that afternoon a ship was to be sold. Whatever the captain bid he must bid more.

He did so. After the deal was settled Peter invited the captain with his young lady to come aboard for a sail and some wine in the way of friendship. When they were far out at sea he took the captain on deck.

"What way does the wind blow?" he asked.

"From the south."

"Whatever way the wind blows you deserve to die. You would not spare my life, but cast me adrift in the middle of the ocean. Now you will walk the plank."

The ship sailed on, and at last came to port where they had joined the captain's boat so long before.

When they reached the inn they were greeted by Nan's mother and father. For a time they hid their identity from their children, but could not keep up the pretence and caught them in their arms.

The old mother and father, Nan Gordon and Peter Maxwell, and their seven children, remained faithful to their gipsy ways and lived happily to the end of their lives.

The Fairy Who Hated the Irish

In 1798, at last, the Catholic ferment in Ireland exploded into rebellion. In Wicklow and Wexford the uprising assumed the proportions of a civil war. It its wake the Catholic peasants in other counties also rose against their Protestant landlords. The government felt it had been tried beyond endurance and struck back so ruthlessly that, as a modest encyclopedia expresses it, 'the rebellion was at last quenched in blood'. The irregular and ill-disciplined troops exacted appalling retribution, repressive measures of which the government largely approved. Catholic violence was answered with violence and sometimes atrocity. Even in quiet areas the Protestant soldiers did not enquire too closely into the circumstances of a supposed traitor, and hundreds were arbitrarily executed. To be seized or suspected was but a short step from being hanged. Many sought safety by fleeing the country.

From County Down to Galloway across the North Channel is only twenty-two miles. It was one of the major escape routes. Having made their way north to Down or Antrim, a night's row found the refugees safely ashore on the lonely western coast of the Rhinns. Many crossed in hastily-made coracles of wattled willow covered with skins, vessels so frail it was a miracle they survived. The government soon learned what was happening and dispatched militia to patrol the Scottish cliffs and headlands, to keep watch and intercept or track down the fleeing 'rebels'. More than forty miles of irregular coast, however, was too great a distance for the numbers who were sent to police efficiently in those days of poor roads and rough country. So the local fishermen were recruited, and hundreds of pairs of fetters were distributed among them, with locks attached, to hold the rebels until the soldiers came to mete out justice with rifle and rope. The Irish bodies were flung into hastily scratched graves, and that was that. The fishermen were paid a bounty of five shillings a head — a shilling more if they were willing to do the burying — enough to get drunk two or three times. Some were sympathetic to the Irishmen's plight, and the fetters grew rusty on the wall of the barn. Others were not.

At this time a young woman by the name of Margaret McCutcheon lived in the little farm of Muldaddie, set on a slope above the village of

Port Logan, seven miles north of the Mull of Galloway. From the farm-house, on fine days, she could clearly see the hills of Ireland across the North Channel.

One day she was walking along the cliffs by Cairnywellan Head, near her home, when she saw a little girl about twelve years old, prettily dressed, dancing and singing to herself on top of a rock. Margaret walked closer. The little girl ignored her, indeed seemed totally oblivious of her presence. She was a remarkably fair-skinned child, with glowing cheeks and long yellow hair that flew as she danced. She wore a white dress bound at the waist with a blue ribbon, white stockings and

scarlet shoes. As she whirled the short skirt flared out, and with each turn she cried aloud in Gaelic: "Aon dha tri: aon dha tri!" She was laughing, and seemed wonderfully pleased about something. Her whole body radiated delight.

One of the goats on a knoll nearby bleated loudly and for a moment Margaret was distracted. When she looked back at the little girl — she had vanished. There was the rock — known as Carrick-a-sheean — but it was empty, the hillside was deserted. Frightened and greatly wondering, Margaret returned to the farm.

The following morning at Slocknavata, about four miles to the south, three Irish rebels were discovered hiding in the rocks. The Galloway fishermen made them captive and informed the militia, stood by as the rebels were shot, said they would bury the bodies, and duly received their eighteen shillings.

That afternoon, about the same time, Margaret returned to Carrick-a-sheean, but the little girl was not there. In the morning no rebels were taken.

But later that day Margaret saw the yellow-haired girl a second time. Her happiness was even greater than on the previous occasion. There was an element of wildness about it. As she whirled, her red shoes tapping on the rock, she sang: "Aon dha tri, ceithir coig sia: aon dha tri, ceithir coig sia!" Her eyes danced with merriment.

Six pairs of shackles were used that night, four at Portencorkrie and two at Carrick-a-mickie. The soldiers were along later in the day.

The third time that Margaret McCutcheon saw the fairy she was quite wistful. Still she danced and her skirts flew, but the joy was subdued. Sadly and sweetly she sang: "Aon dha: aon dha."

And as Margaret now anticipated, only two poor Irishmen were discovered that night. But in the afternoon the little girl's spirits were quite recovered, and she sang: "Aon dha, tri ceithir coig: aon dha, tri ceithir coig!"

It had often been said that when Margaret McCutcheon was born the midwife had omitted to put salt in her mouth. In consequence the fairies had got in there, and she was ever afterwards touched with strange fancies and the second sight. So for a time she did not mention the little girl. But at length, so distinct was the child and so audible her song, that she told her friends. The word spread and many people accompanied her to the rock on Cairnywellan Head. The fairy danced and Margaret pointed, but her companions could see nothing. Their eyes opened wide, however, as the merry laughter and 'aon dha tri' rang clear as crystal through the afternoon air. It was a great wonder.

The fairy continued her dancing until the rebellion was finally brought to order beneath the military heel, and the refugees ceased their pathetic flight.

For more than forty years, so far as this story is concerned, she was heard of no more. But then, at the time of the dreadful potato famine in 1846 and 1847, she was seen again in Ireland, singing and dancing day and night long, counting and counting into the thousands, hair and white dress flying, eyes dancing with wild delight.

180

Robert Bruce in Galloway

On 10th February, 1306, Robert Bruce met John Comyn (the Red Comyn) in the chapel of Greyfriars Monastery at Dumfries to discuss their troubled and contentious relationship, and rival claims to the throne of an independent Scotland. Comyn had already revealed secret arrangements and discussed the situation with Edward I in London. In a passionate fit of anger before the high altar, Robert Bruce flew at him with a dagger. Comyn was seriously wounded. Realising the implication of his action, Bruce rushed from the church and informed his friends and supporters outside what had happened: "I doubt I've killed the Comyn." Roger Kirkpatrick, one of Bruce's followers, seized upon his words. "You doubt! Then I'll mak' siccar!" Going directly into Greyfriars Chapel himself he found that the wounded Comyn had been taken into the vestry by friars. There he finished him off. When he returned to Bruce, Comyn lay dead upon the chapel floor.

By this one rash act Robert Bruce, then aged thirty-one, denied himself support from the people of Galloway, the church, and half the greatest families in the land. For Comyn was a Balliol, a nephew of King John Balliol, and heir of that much-loved family with such strong Galloway connections — one of the greatest families in Britain. Also he had committed a great sacrilege — that sin and crime most abhorred in the Middle Ages — and a local sacrilege, for Greyfriars Monastery had been founded by Comyn's grandmother, the famous Dervorgilla.*

---

* Dervorgilla, wife of John Balliol, was one of the greatest ladies of the thirteenth century. She was born at Kenmure Castle near New Galloway, and though she possessed great estates all over England, her favourite residence was said to be at Buittle, near Dalbeattie, now sadly reduced to a neglected and overgrown mound. Following her husband's lead she built New Balliol Hall, now Balliol College, Oxford. She founded many churches and religious centres, and built the magnificent old bridge across the River Nith at Dumfries. Upon her husband's death in 1269, twenty years before her own, she had his heart embalmed in a beautiful casket of enamelled ivory bound with silver, which accompanied her everywhere. At the table, it is said, the heart was deferred to and served food, which afterwards was given to the poor. For its final resting place she built the beautiful red sandstone Sweetheart Abbey beneath Criffel, just inland from the Solway. There, by the high altar, she was buried, with her husband's heart resting upon her own.
'A bettyr lady than scho wes nane
In all the yle off Mare Bretane.'
                                                            Andrew Wyntoun.

Rather than flee, submit to Edward I, or wait for reprisals, Bruce and his men instantly took the initiative. Mounting Comyn's horse, Bruce led an attack on Dumfries Castle, threequarters of a mile away, even before news of the murder had reached there.* Then, leaving the castle garrisoned, he marched directly to Glasgow to receive the church's endorsement, and on to Scone, where on 25th March, 1306, with maimed rites, he was crowned King of Scotland.

In the English court the whole affair was treated as a great joke. Laughingly they dubbed him 'King Hob'. But Edward's reprisals were swift and terrible. To be caught was to be executed, and to have been involved in the affair at Greyfriars Church was to suffer the same fate as Wallace — hanged, cut down alive, emasculated, disembowelled — entrails and genitals being flung on a fire — then finally beheaded and quartered and shown about the country.

In June Bruce met the English forces at Methven, a few miles from Perth. The Scots were routed, and Bruce for a time took to the hills of Perthshire and Argyll. In September he was forced to withdraw from Scotland, and spent the winter on Rathlin Island off the Antrim coast, fifteen miles west of the Mull of Kintyre.

In February, 1307, Bruce joined an advance party in the west of Arran, establishing himself briefly in the King's Cave, two miles north of Blackwaterfoot — which among other places claims for itself the famous spider.

On the ninth of that month two of his brothers, having landed at Loch Ryan in Wigtownshire, were captured and sent to Edward in Carlisle 'for his special brand of execution'. Within a year of his coronation Bruce had lost three of his four brothers, and his womenfolk were seized and confined — some in cages of iron and wood, exposed to the elements and the gaze of the curious, hanging from the battlements of Berwick and Roxburgh Castles.

A spy was sent from Arran across the Firth of Clyde to the Ayrshire coast, with instructions to light a fire on Turnberry Head fifteen miles away, if it was safe to make a landing. The spy discovered that Turnberry Castle was held by Percy's men, and the area was swarming with English. By ill chance, however, someone else lit a fire on the headland — prob-

* Greyfriars Monastery was situated in the middle of the present town: in that part of Castle Street which is in the square at the top of Friars Vennel. At present the site is occupied by a supermarket. Dumfries Castle, of which only traces now remain, was situated in Castledykes Park. Each year at the splendid Riding of the Marches, the Scottish Royal Standard is unfurled at the spot to commemorate this decisive moment in Scotland's history.

ably a farmer or shepherd burning the heather — and seeing it Bruce concluded that the coast was clear and made the crossing. It did not take him long to discover the truth of the situation. Still angry at the capture of his brothers, he made a swift raid on the village of Turnberry, and slew the sleeping soldiers who were garrisoned there.

It was already known that Bruce was somewhere in the vicinity. Now his enemies — the English and the supporters of Comyn — knew precisely where. Bruce took to the hills once more. Though there was a certain amount of support in Carrick, there was not nearly enough for him to consider making his challenge through set-piece battles. Instead he resorted to a form of hit and run guerrilla tactics — the strike out of the blue, then vanishing once more into the hills. His enemies were unaccustomed to this, but through it Bruce was able, with only about three hundred men, to create a certain air of panic, and in a most dramatic way foster an intense awareness of his presence.

He was in Galloway and on its borders for no more than three months. All of that time he was on the run, from Scots as well as the English. In a very real way it was civil war. Nevertheless it was here that the tide turned, here that he won his first victories against Edward I, 'the Hammer of the Scots'.

The area has been called 'the cradle of Scotland's independence'. The maps still retain many references to his presence — Bruce's Wa's, the King's Ford, the King's Stone, Bruce's Well — and so on. A number of stories also remain from that time.

Carlin's Cairn

Polmaddie Burn runs east from Corserine, the highest peak in the beautiful Rhinns of Kells. In the middle of the magnificent two-mile crag that runs north from Corserine, stands the lesser but equally well-known peak of Carlin's Cairn. Some say that this unusual name commemorates the burning of a witch; others that it recalls the execution of an aged covenanting martyr by Sir Robert Grierson of Lagg, who was a laird of that district. The truth, however, leads us back three hundred years before the witch-hunts and covenanting times, to Robert Bruce on the run in the Galloway hills.

Wandering alone in the wilds one chill March evening, he was weary and hungry when he came upon Polmaddie Mill, near the confluence of

Polmaddie Burn and the Water of Ken beneath Dundeuch Hill.* Wearing at the time rather finer clothes than were customary, Bruce drew his cloak about him and called to ask for shelter and food. The miller, it soon transpired, was a supporter of the slain Comyn. His wife, on the other hand, confessed herself a secret champion of the king in the heather.

For the night Bruce accepted their shelter. The following morning, while he was from the house, four men-at-arms called, enquiring whether they had heard anything of King Robert the Bruce, who was known to be in the vicinity. The miller, though not suspecting the truth, was about to tell them of the stranger who had stayed the night. His wife, however, quicker in surmise, interrupted him with quick words that no-one calling himself by that name had ever visited their humble mill, nor had anyone brought news of him. The men-at-arms were satisfied and departed.

Fearing then that her husband would call on neighbours and mention the stranger and the soldiers' visit to them, she packed him off to his work, and soon Robert Bruce returned.

At first he was cautious at the woman's questions, but at length confessed that indeed he was the king. The woman declared her loyalty, but with real anxiety spoke of her husband's support for the Comyns.

When he returned she introduced Bruce as a blood-relative of the king, and a relation of the Earl of Carrick. The latter condition, allied to the fact that the miller could never have betrayed any Scotsman to the despised English, secured his confidence.

Later in the day a second party from the nearby English garrison called at the house, this time demanding to search the premises. Bruce and the miller were in an inner room. Quickly the miller led him from the house into the mill and pushed him into the space behind the hopper — the inverted cone or funnel through which the grain passed into the mill itself. Bruce struggled down among the tumbled sacks, all thick with dust and dirt from the mill floor. The miller pulled them roughly over the king's back, and jammed a big sackful of dust on top.

The miller's wife held the soldiers back for as long as she could, but a minute or two later they were swarming over the house. Harrassed and exclaiming, running from room to room in case they stole anything, she tried to distract their attention. They searched the mill, even

* The ruined medieval village of Polmaddie, including the mill, stands on the hillside half a mile up Polmaddie Burn from the Dalry-Carsphairn hill road. More precisely, it is situated on the northern bank, above a fine semi-circular sweep of the river.

184

behind the hopper. One trooper, with his sword drawn, smote at the fat sack of corn dust, causing a great cloud to rise in the air, which got in his eyes and made him cough and sneeze.

Soon, with warm instructions that the miller was to inform the garrison if he discovered anything, the soldiers were on their way. As soon as the coast was clear Bruce was rescued from his hiding place, his nose and mouth filled with dust and chaff.

All the fortresses in the vicinity were held by the English and their supporters. News came, however, that the king's brother Edward Bruce and Sir James Douglas had assembled a band of Carrickmen, and were waiting for him near the head of Loch Trool. Promising that their loyalty would be rewarded when he came into his kingdom, Bruce left the astonished miller and his wife and rode off to join his troops.

He was as good as his word. As king of a united Scotland he made a visit to his maternal castle in Loch Doon and sent for the miller and his wife. In recognition of their bravery and assistance he awarded them land, freehold of the mill, and a sum of money.

In return she wished to raise some monument to his memory. Gathering her kinsfolk and neighbours she caused them to erect the fine cairn on a summit to the north of Corserine — two miles south of the King's Well — where she could see it far off against the western sky from the door of the mill. There it has remained for more than six and a half centuries, visible for many miles around, and famous in the whole south-west.

The Battle of Glen Trool

While Bruce lingered in the wilds of upper Galloway the English forces, backed by an army of Highlanders and supporters of Comyn, began to close in. At length he was trapped, ringed from the south-west around by the north to the south-east, outnumbered by more than ten to one. With an army at this time of about two hundred he waited, uncertain what to do, passing his days in hunting deer for provisions. At length scouts brought news that a force of fifteen hundred or two thousand men, sent by the Earl of Pembroke to ferret Bruce out of the mountains, was advancing up the River Cree — as the crow flies six or eight miles south-west of where they were encamped in the wild hills above Loch Trool.

By this time Bruce was growing accustomed to the mountainous terrain. He called his advisers and worked out the most likely route for the army to advance to meet them at the eastern end of Loch Trool. Then he sent all his men, bearded and brown with their days in the hills, to gather boulders on the crags and steep slopes of Mulldonach above the south-east corner of the loch. By the morning a rampart of huge granite rocks, looking almost like a broken wall, was strung across the hillside.

The news that came was good. The English troops had left their horses by the farm of Borgan, where the River Minnoch meets the River Cree, and were advancing on foot. They were heading up the Water of Trool towards the south side of the loch, which is concave like a boomerang. Leaving about a third of his men on the hillside, Bruce positioned the remainder out of sight at the end of the loch a few hundred yards distant. Then he himself retired to the mountain slope opposite, half a mile away, from which vantage point he would be able to see and control the battle.

The English came on, led by Aymer de Valence, unaccustomed to mountain warfare. On the rough, broken ground they were unable to maintain military formation. As the long slopes of Mulldonach steepened they were reduced to several ragged columns of single file. Beneath the crags, where in places the hillside was almost precipitous, was a projection known as the Steps of Trool — swept away in a landslide during the nineteenth century — beneath which was a drop of about twenty feet to deep water. When the English were strung out across this slope, already in some disarray, with the rugged hillsides rearing above them, the king's bugler blew three clear blasts, ringing across the water. Previously hidden among the rocky outcrops, Bruce's men sent the great boulders rolling and bounding down upon the English troops. With cries they scattered, and the massive rocks kept coming. Some were struck into the loch and drowned, others were killed.

Then Bruce's men in hiding near the head of the loch poured a rain of arrows and bolts from cross-bows upon them, and advanced with swords, spears and clubs, all kinds of weapons. Some of the English vanguard were driven back into the loch; others, who retreated, were scattered still further as a second wave of boulders crashed down upon them.

It was a rout. The helmeted English soldiers, swords flapping, boots slipping, were pursued across the rough hillsides by the fierce Carrick-men. Those who were killed were buried on a strip of greensward at the end of the loch. To this day it is known as the Soldiers' Holm.

The Battle of Glen Trool was the first victory of Robert Bruce against the English, and it had far-reaching consequences. A number of Scots, who previously had held back, now came forward to join the Scottish army.

In 1929, on the six hundredth anniversary of Bruce's death, a memorial in the significant form of a huge granite boulder, was unveiled on an eminence above the north-eastern shore to commemorate this victory, which within a few years was to lead Bruce to the unquestioned throne of an independent Scotland.

The Battling King

From the heights of Loch Enoch, beneath the Merrick, Robert Bruce looked down on Sir Aymer de Valence, who with twenty-two men at arms and eight hundred Highlanders on foot, was advancing from the hills of Carrick to the north. With fewer than three hundred men under his command the king did not wish to engage in battle and fell back. In doing so he did not have sufficient regard for what lay behind, and nearly retreated straight into the arms of John of Lorn, who at the same time was advancing with a great force from Glentrool to the south-west.

In an attempt to confuse the pursuit which must be expected, Bruce divided his men into three groups, instructing them to make their escape by different routes through the mountains and great oak forests. They were to join him again at Craigencallie, beneath the steep slopes of Cairngarroch to the east of Loch Dee.

John of Lorn, however, had with him a fine and very large blood-hound, which had once belonged to Bruce. It had been given his scent, and when they came to the dividing of the ways the snuffling, dewlapped animal soon set off on the track of the group among which the king was travelling. Dropping east down the steep and dramatic hillside known as the Nick of the Dungeon — between the crags of Dungeon Hill and the crags of Craignaw — Bruce saw the soldiers on the crest of the slope high above, and gave his men the order to disperse. Accompanied by only a single follower, a foster-brother, Bruce continued his flight. But still the nose of the bloodhound led it unerringly on his trail.

Soon they were far down the slopes in shrouding forest. Feeling that they were coming close, John of Lorn sent five lusty Highlanders on ahead to try to overtake the king and hold him back while the force came on more slowly with the dog. Having spent all their lives in the hills, the Highlanders swiftly caught up with Bruce and his companion, and compelled them to stop and give battle. Three turned on the king and two on the soldier. Bruce was a wild and brilliant fighter.* Instantly he slew one of his assailants and the other two drew back momentarily. At this Bruce flew at one of the men who were setting upon his young foster-brother, and soon this man too lay dead in the forest. Then the others returned to the attack and in a fierce skirmish with sword and targe Bruce dispatched them both, whilst his companion killed the other.

They continued their flight downhill, and on their heels came John of Lorn and his hundreds of soldiers, led by the remorseless bloodhound. Bruce had fought like a man possessed and spent his energy so that he ran in a daze. He was so fatigued that his foster-brother had constantly to urge and encourage him.

At length they came to a broad, gravel-bedded stream, probably the Cooran Lane that runs through the great flat glen beneath the slopes of Craignaw. On either side lay the treacherous area of boggy ground know as the Silver Flow, overgrown with bushes and thickets. Immediately they waded in, knowing that the water would wash away their scent. For hours then they crawled and waded downstream in the icy April current, never daring to put a foot on dry land, even when they had to negotiate deep pools. At last, when they had gone so far that it seemed certain the bloodhound would never find their trail again, they stepped out on the opposite bank and lay back exhausted in a spinney of young oak trees, still winter-bare. †

* Perhaps the most famous example of Bruce's fighting skill was at Bannockburn itself, when in a preliminary skirmish on horseback he electrified his troops by his speed and strength in cleaving the helmet and skull of Henry de Bohun to the chin, shattering the axe handle with the power of the blow. By this time, seven years later, he was commonly acknowledged the finest knight in Christendom.
† In a different conclusion to the bloodhound chase, Bruce was for a time unable to continue after the ferocity of the battle. His foster-brother doubled back up their tracks, and from a dense thicket set well back, put an arrow through the dog as it passed.
Also, according to a third version of this tale, the fleeing Scots were not tracked by a bloodhound, but by two stag-hounds which had previously belonged to Bruce: they had been captured, as he nearly was himself, when Doon Castle was taken by English forces. The king's foster-brother sent him up a tree to hide, and continued on foot himself with a band of Bruce's followers. The staghounds, as he had anticipated, recognised his scent also, and the chase continued. Alas the brave young man was overtaken and slain. Bruce escaped, and made his way alone to Craigencallie.

But the hardships of the day were not over. A little while after they had resumed their journey, stiff from the rest and uncomfortable in sodden clothes, they came upon three men carrying a live wether, trussed up so that it could not struggle. Bruce asked where they were heading. They replied that they were seeking the king, since they wished to join his party. The manner of their reply and well-armed appearance made Bruce suspect that they were more likely keen to capture him and claim the reward that was upon his head. Possibly, from his clothes and manner, they suspected his identity already. Playing for safety, Bruce replied that he was himself going to meet the king, and if their intentions were honest they might accompany him. They seemed somewhat confused by his words, then agreed, and the five proceeded together.

In time they came to a ruined cottage where the men killed the sheep and made a fire beyond the gable wall on which to cook it. Bruce insisted that he and his companion would cook their own portion on a second fire, at the opposite end of the house. They were given a leg of mutton, roasted it, and ate their fill. Then Bruce lay down to rest, while his foster-brother kept watch. But the man was tired from the hard travelling, and soon fell asleep in the warmth of the fire.

Bruce was wakened in the early dusk by the stealthy sound of the men's feet, and the metallic whisper as they drew the swords from their sheaths. Instantly wide awake he sprang back and drew his own sword, calling aloud and kicking his foster-brother to wake him. Startled and dazed with sleep the young man was slain before he could rise to his feet. Single-handed, for the second time that day, the king faced three armed assailants. Not with the sword and targe alone, but with axe, dagger and bow, Robert Bruce was a superb fighter. Perhaps, also, the three were ruffians chancing their fortune, rather than true warriors. One after the other, by that ruined cottage and the fading fire, Bruce killed them.

Then, having with sadness made some sort of grave for his foster-brother, the king continued on his way to Craigencallie to join up once more with his forces.*

* The second part of this account is similar to another story. Robert Bruce, travelling alone with a page, was set upon by a father and his two sons, who had been bribed by de Valence to murder the king. Bruce seized his page's bow, and firing as he turned, put an arrow straight through the head of one, then fought and killed the others. This happened on 'a quiet pathway' claimed to be the track up the west of Loch Doon.

Craigencallie and the Battle of Raploch Moss

After the death of his kinsman, Bruce journeyed downstream beyond the place where the Cooran Lane joins the Black Water of Dee. His clothes were still sodden, his legs, cross-gartered, were smeared with mud to the knees. He was alone in the forested mountains when darkness fell, and he spent the night beneath Darrou under the trees.

The following morning another mile or two brought him to Craigencallie, a little to the south of the river, midway between Clatteringshaws and Loch Dee.* He was hungry, and took the chance of calling at the little house, snuggling under the craggy and steep eastern slope of Cairngarroch. It was owned by a widow, a plain, forthright countrywoman, who invited him inside.† At the time, of course, Bruce was all the news in the district, and observing something about his bearing and certain details of his clothing, she asked directly whether he was the king in hiding. Bruce confessed that he was, and judging the widow's support to be warm, enquired whether she had any menfolk who might join his forces. She replied that she had three sons living, to three separate husbands. If indeed he was the king, then they would join him with her blessing.

Considering his hunger then, she prepared a breakfast of goatsmilk and meal, which was all she had in the house. His cape and plain woven tunic steamed at the fire.

While she was busy her three sons returned, strong lusty fellows carrying crooks and harness, who had been seeing to the animals. Learning the stranger's identity, all declared themselves willing and glad to join his guerrilla army in the mountains and forests they knew so well. Bruce asked what arms and weapons they possessed. They told him that apart from fighting with staves for amusement, they were used only to the bow and arrow. When he had finished eating Bruce accompanied them outside so that they could demonstrate their prowess. The eldest, whose name was McKie, drew an arrow upon two ravens that perched upon a high grey crag above the house, and with a superb shot pierced

* The sturdy old stone farm of Craigencallie is now a base for outdoor pursuits — hillwalking, orienteering, canoeing, fishing — and used by schools, scouts and guides. The original house where Bruce stayed, and which in fact he may have used as a shelter for some time, lies somewhat over a hundred yards further on. Though still known as 'Bruce's Wa's', it fell many years ago, and is now reduced to a pattern of grassy mounds and hollows, hard to distinguish.

† There is some uncertainty as to the widow's character. In one account she is said to have been shy, which is understandable, but in view of her three husbands, three lusty sons and canny request for land, it seems unlikely.

them both through the head with a single arrow. Bruce was impressed and observed wryly that he would not wish the young man to shoot at him. Then the second son, named Murdoch, took aim at another raven, which was flying high overhead. His arrow picked it out of the sky with a little puff of feathers, straight through the body. The youngest son, whose name was McLurg, then drew his bow, but his shot was not so good.

Shortly afterwards the three led the king to a vantage point high on the slope of Darnaw, a mile from the house. From here they gazed down on a great body of English soldiers which had been pursuing him, now encamped on the opposite north-eastern side of Black Water of Dee, in a low and rather boggy area known as Raploch Moss.* By this time the first bands of Bruce's men were arriving, but even when they had all gathered they would total less than three hundred. The English, as always, hopelessly outnumbered them.

Once more King Robert was at a loss. Then the widow's three sons suggested a plan, which after a little thought he adopted. As his men continued arriving throughout the day, they left off their heavy arms and plaids and joined the others, rounding up all the goats and horses — wild and tame — in the vicinity, and driving them into a great river pasture. At dusk, as the light grew too poor for any English spies making reconnaissance to see what was happening, they disturbed the animals and kept them circling round and round the pasture, so that their neighing and bleating sounded like a great army assembling. The men spoke loudly and continuously, their voices mingling with the noise of the animals. For a while after darkness the sounds continued. English morale fell.

A little before dawn, while the English camp was still asleep, from the opposite direction Bruce and his combined men made a wild and fierce attack. A mile away beneath Darnaw, calling aloud and occasionally blowing horns, the widow's sons kept the cattle and horses swirling in the pasture. The English thought they were caught between opposing forces and panicked. They floundered in the boggy ground. Many were killed and the remainder fled. †

* Most of this area is now flooded by Clatteringshaws Loch. The district boundary follows the old course of the river.

† In another version of this tale, spears and stuffed sacks were tied to the backs of horses and cattle, and the whole assembly was kept circling in the last of the daylight and dawn so that they seemed a great force. Shortly before the battle Bruce was joined by the Earl of Douglas with reinforcements. Curving around

It was Bruce's second victory against King Edward's army. While he leaned back against a great stone, flushed with the heat of the battle and victory, his men gathered up their spoils.* This same boulder, known as 'The King's Stone' or 'Bruce's Stone', stands today ringed with trees beside Clatteringshaws Loch.

Afterwards Robert Bruce asked the widow whether there was any reward he could offer her for the inestimable help of her three sons. She replied: "If your majesty could just give me the wee bit hassock o' land atween Palnure and Penkiln," — two large streams in the district, bordering an area approximately five miles long and three miles broad. Gladly Bruce awarded it to her, and when he came into his full kingdom ensured that the gift was truly ratified.†

His victory on Raploch Moor enabled Robert Bruce to break through the surrounding ring of English troops and drive towards the north, now gathering supporters as he went. On about the 10th May he clashed with the Earl of Pembroke's main force at Loudon Hill, about twenty miles inland from Ayr. Bruce's tactics, based as previously and at Bannockburn upon a close attention to the terrain, gained him another resounding victory. A relief force too was routed. News of his repeated success spread like wildfire.

By the following summer Bruce had won over the greater part of Scotland, but still Galloway held out for the English king. In May Robert sent his remaining brother, Edward Bruce, to tackle the English soldiers and subdue the troublesome south-west. Many place-names remain to mark the progress of his splendid and victorious campaign. In recognition of his great services King Robert I awarded his brother the Lordship of Galloway, which Edward had desired since first he stood on that splendid height above Loch Ken, which is still known as Cairn Edward Hill, and looking down over the lovely rivers and glens, and across to the Galloway hills had cried aloud: "This beautiful country must be mine!"

* Well into the nineteenth century, and perhaps afterwards, farmers digging peats in the vicinity were recovering broken swords and pike heads from the moss.
† The widow's three sons became the founders of the well-known Galloway families McKie of Larg, Murdoch of Cumloden, and McLurg of Kirrouchtrie. In time their land extended considerably beyond the boundaries of Penkiln and Palnure. For their armorial bearings McKie took two black ravens on a silver field, their heads pierced by an arrow; and Murdoch a flying raven, pierced by an arrow, on a red field.

through the hills at night, they caught the English, hampered by the bog, in a pincer-movement.

Bruce and a Bowl of Porridge

For much of his life, of course, Robert Bruce had been a popular knight at the court of King Edward. The story is renowned of how, when his life was in danger, a friend sent him spurs and a sum of money to indicate that he must flee. During those years with Edward, Robert Bruce was a knight among knights. Between them, ideally at least, courteous behaviour and respect ranked very high. Even between enemies formal courtesy was expected.

Early one morning, wandering a long way south of his mountain fastnesses — probably at the time of his attack on Buittle Castle, stronghold of the Balliols — Robert Bruce came to the Mote of Urr, a magnificent green mound islanded by the river, two miles north of Dalbeattie. He had no eyes for the old fort, however, for he was being challenged by a famous English knight, Sir Walter Selby, in fine formal style. Bruce was extremely tired, and more than that, he liked Sir Walter. He had no wish to engage in conflict, and tried to avoid the challenge. Viewing it as a matter of honour, however, Sir Walter would not be gainsaid, and compelled him to battle. With drawn swords and spiked, studded shields, the two knights faced each other across the bright morning grass on the brink of the river.

Now it happened that in a nearby cottage at the time, the wife of a certain Mark Sprotte was stirring a pot of porridge for her husband's breakfast. Looking from her doorway she saw the two knights preparing. From the words they exchanged and the bearded, warriorlike appearance of Bruce, she recognised him as the king about whom everyone was talking. A moment later the air resounded with the thud of shields and the dint of their massive swords. Leaving her pot of porridge, Dame Sprotte ran across the mote and watched.

The swords were heavy and the two men grunted with the effort of swinging them. Through their panting, occasionally one cried out a challenge as he lunged forward. Dame Sprotte's fighting blood mounted with the conflict, yielding to a great access of patriotic fervour. Seeing an opening, before she knew what she was doing she flung herself at the Englishman's knees, and brought him to the ground with a crash.

Bruce, of course, was unable to take advantage of the situation. Laying his sword aside he helped Sir Walter Selby, who was considerably shaken, to his feet. The battle was resigned. Honour was satisfied. Together they retired to the good woman's cottage to rest and recover in knightly companionship. Gladly Dame Sprotte presented a dish of porridge to King Robert, but refused haughtily to have anything to do with an Englishman, turning her nose in the air and looking aside when Sir Walter addressed her.

Partly to reward her for the goodness of her heart, but perhaps more accurately to avoid embarrassment, Robert Bruce promised that as soon as the Scottish crown was firmly on his head he would grant her as much land as she could run round there and then, while he ate his bowl

of porridge. She did not need a second invitation. Picking up her skirts Dame Sprotte made off across the dewy grass like a stag.

According to one tradition, Bruce then helped Sir Walter to a plateful of good salt porridge; and according to another he and the English knight shared the dish that the goodwife had given him, taking sup and sup about with the same spoon.

However it was, in due time Mark Sprotte was presented with the twenty or so Scots acres that his wife had managed to encompass. Locally, from this time onwards, the Mote of Urr was called 'the King's Mote'.* The family — the Sprottes of the Mount — held the land with pride for five hundred years.

* This explanation is not satisfactory. The Mote of Urr, nearly eighty feet high, with a series of defensive trenches, is the most notable monument of its kind in

As late as the eighteenth century the River Urr, dividing two or three hundred yards upstream, ran on both sides of the mote. The main, western channel — which has been dammed and ploughed over — was crossed by a line of stepping stones. Near the foot of the mote, at the end of this crossing, was a cluster of small dwellings known as 'Step-End'. Their ruins can still be seen.

In a second, more colourful version of the above story, it was to this spot that Robert Bruce came, early one spring morning, accompanied by his brother Edward, the Earl of Douglas, and one or two other gentlemen. They had spent a cold night and were tired and hungry. Calling at the cottage in the hope of a warm fire and some refreshment, they found the goodwife in the process of making a large pan of porridge that would provide her husband with several good meals. When she recognised the king, at once she set the party to the fire and flung a spotless white cloth over the table. They must have breakfast. In gratitude Bruce promised her as much land as she could cover from the time she set the food before them until their plates were empty. Such an offer was too much for the woman's good heart to cope with. Vainly loyalty struggled with avarice.

Pushing the pot of porridge into the heart of the glowing fire, she brought it to a furious boil. In another pan she boiled the milk as well, and set the porridge bowls in the hearth, where soon they grew so hot that they scorched the cloth as she lifted them clear. The spoons she thrust among the blazing peats until they glowed white hot. Then, swiftly flinging the boiling, sizzling meal on the table, she left them to eat it as they might, and fled from the door.

Greatly amazed, Bruce and his companions watched her flit across the stepping stones and race through the meadows, cap and skirts flying, gaining an extra yard or two with every second the meal was cooling. But they were hungrier than she had anticipated. Before she had gone quarter of a mile, their loud cries from the door of the cottage brought her to a halt. In any case she could hardly have run any further. Weak at the knees and gasping for breath, she leaned against the trunk of an ancient oak tree.

But the land was won, and as always, Bruce honoured his promise. Only one condition was attached. On any future occasion when a king

Scotland. If the name is that old, it probably goes back a little further, to the eleventh or twelfth century, when the mote was crowned with a Norman fort or castle — and possibly long before that.

visited the Vale of Urr, she or her descendants must offer him a dish of porridge. It is not known whether they did so, but 'King Robert's Bowl' was treasured in the family for many generations.

The End of a Curling Match

One dark and freezing winter's night, around the middle of the eighteenth century, a man named John Gordon was sitting in Lucky Hair's notorious inn at St John's Town of Dalry. He lived in Balmaclellan, three miles distant. The hours slipped by in good fellowship, and all too soon it was time for him to think of returning home. To his consternation he realised that there was no man from Balmaclellan in the company: he would need to face the dark walk over the fairy hill of Moloch and the old haunted bridge of Garple by himself. He visualised the long hill out of the village with its rocky outcrops and copses, and the rushing water beneath the grey stone bridge. It was a daunting prospect. However he recalled that the same day a bonspiel (a curling match) had been played between the parishes of Dalry and Balmaclellan on the Boatweel — the deep pool in the Water of Ken below the township. The prize was to be a dinner at McNaught's Inn. He would find plenty of company there for the walk home.

McNaught's Inn was a riot of noise and laughter and deep drinking. The tankard went round swiftly, with long draughts and spillage. John Gordon joined in the high spirits and fine companionship. Soon the terrors of the return journey were forgotten.

There had been in the district a great deal of talk about witches.

Sights had been seen.* A gentleman from Balmaclellan who held the tankard raised it high.

"Damnation to the witches!" he cried.

Suddenly the lights were violently extinguished, as by a great wind. The man choked: an invisible hand clutched him by the throat. In a moment he had tumbled from his chair to the floor. He lay there still in the firelight, his face dreadfully distorted.

Everyone thought that he was dead. Every means was used to bring about his revival, and to the relief of the company he slowly pulled around. Somewhat recovered he took his seat once more at the table.

Immediately, a second time, the lights were blown out.

They were re-lit, and a third time extinguished. At the same instant burning peats came flying from the fire, directed chiefly against the gentleman who had spoken, but scattering everyone in the bar-room, and a shrill, piercing voice cried out: "If I canna hit the boot, I'll hit the boot heel!"

The room was in an uproar. A man called upon God to protect him, a second roared for his horse, a third gabbled the Lord's Prayer. The gentleman against whom the invisible attacker vented its malice escaped through the door, fighting off those who pleaded with him for his own sake to stay among friends when such an evil presence was abroad. Seizing his horse from the ostler he rode madly away from the place into the darkness that shrouded the hill of Moloch.

No-one, after the spirit's fearful demonstration, was willing to accompany or pursue a man who seemed so wantonly bent on self-destruction. Though he might hope to reach the house of a good friend in Balmaclellan, and there shut himself away from the forces of the night, no man in the company felt confident of his safe arrival. The hill of Moloch and the haunted bridge across the Garple Burn — it was too much to expect.

They stayed at the inn. The candles remained lit — suggesting fearfully that the spirit was now elsewhere. The tankard was filled to the brim, a steadying bumper was passed around. A few Dalry men ventured home but most remained, either drinking or sleeping it off in one of the many beds, until daylight. Among them — and wild horses would not have dragged him out while the darkness lasted — was John Gordon of Balmaclellan.

Shortly after dawn a party issued forth to discover whether the

* See 'Adam Forrester and Lucky Hair'.

horseman had reached his friend's house safely. They found him less than a mile from the township, on the hill of Moloch, mangled and long dead in the marshy ground near Moss Roddock Loch.

And so ended the great bonspiel dinner.

The Death of Black Morrow

In the reign of King James II a bloodthirsty ruffian named Black Morrow jumped ship from a pirate barque that was moored in Manxman's Lake below Kirkcudbright, and hid in the thick woods of St Mary's Isle until the vessel had set sail for the open sea. For some time he roamed the district, robbing and putting the country folk in mortal fear, until at length he settled down in a rough shack on the eastern shore of Manxman's Lake beneath a great wood. From this base, in a stolen boat, he rowed across to Senwick on the further shore of Kirkcudbright Bay, and there committed his acts of terrorism and plunder. Often he stole liquor, and the nuns on St Mary's Isle heard his drunken roars and songs rolling across the water in the night.

At length news of his activities was brought to the ear of the king, who promised the fair lands of Bombie, fine coastal estates near Kirkcudbright, to the man who brought the murderous outlaw to him, dead or alive.

A young man by the name of William McClellan, who lived in that part, decided that he would claim the magnificent reward. Arming himself with a barrel of rum and a sword, he went by day while Black Morrow was absent, to his shack on the shore. A stream trickled through the wood and formed a small well in a hollowed-out stone. Diverting the water from the well, McClellan poured in his barrel of spirits. Then he retreated to an ash thicket nearby to await the robber's arrival. Drawing his sword, he laid it beside him, ready for instant use.

The day was far gone when Black Morrow returned from his expedition, big boots trailing, broad shoulders thrusting aside the branches. Pausing only to chew some half-cooked lumps of mutton, he threw himself on a rough straw pallet in the shack and fell asleep. His fearful snores issued through the broken doorway to the ears of young McClellan. His plan had misfired. For a long time he lingered in the ash thicket wondering whether it would be safe to approach, for rumour had it that despite his snoring Black Morrow slept like a cat.

The ruffian's own nature threw him into McClellan's hands. Dreams of demons and enemies rampaged in his brain, his sleep grew troubled. Suddenly with a loud cry he woke. His eyes stared wildly about into the darkness. Seizing his great sword he charged out of the door into the shadowy moonlight, calling on the fiends and devils to come out and face him. Ferociously his sword slashed and cleft the air about him. Only slowly did he calm down, and panting sat on a rock and took his head in his hands. The stream trickled by, cool and refreshing. Crossing to the well he kneeled and bathed his hands and face, then scooped the water to his lips. But it was heavy with rum. Puzzled he paused, and again looked about him. The night was quiet, he had no light. At such a time anything was possible. In any case, it was an opportunity too good to miss, a whole well full of rum. He scooped his hands again and sucked the spirit from his palms. He drank again — and again.

He had taken enough. Relaxing, he felt the warm lethargy creep down into his legs, and lay back against a rock. The noise of the tide rose from the shore. The demons left him. He sang a little. Slowly and gratefully he sank into a drunken oblivion.

Then, when once again his snores rose upon the air, young McClellan crept from his cover and slew Black Morrow with his sword, then cut

off his head. Carrying it by the hair, he walked up from the shore and along the dark lanes to the cottage where he lived with his parents. For the want of somewhere better he left the head in the cool pantry, where his mother was greatly surprised to find it a little after dawn.

The following morning, riding bareback, William McClellan made his way to the king, who at the time was residing only a day's ride distant in Edinburgh. Though an unseemly visitor to the court, so remarkable was the young man's story and appearance that the king granted him an audience. With the head of Black Morrow impaled on the point of his sword, William McClellan entered the chamber and told his monarch that he had come to claim his reward. But the king had forgotten, whereupon McClellan reminded his majesty to 'Think on.' The king recollected. True to his word the lands of Bombie were granted to young William McClellan and remained in his family for many generations.

There are other verions of this legend. By some the rover is named 'Black Murray'. He is called 'black' because of his black-hearted nature, as well as his dark complexion. He is described as a Saracen, interpreted generally as a gipsy. Some, however, claim that the name 'Black Morrow's Wood' is a corruption of 'Blackamoor's Wood', and that the ruffian was a true black-faced Moor. The Ordnance Survey map names it 'Black Moray Plantation'. The wood was felled and replanted a number of years ago. The well, now hidden beneath a wild rhododendron and neglected, stands in the dyke at the side of the road.

The history behind the legend takes us back to the murder of Patrick McClellan, the Tutor of Bombie, by William, 8th Earl of Douglas, in 1452.* The murder, at Threave Castle, was so deeply resented by Patrick McClellan's relatives that they made many retaliatory raids upon Douglas's territory in Galloway. Despite the provocation and the fact that the McClellans were loyal to James II — whilst the Black Douglases were a perpetual threat — such lawless revenge was not to be tolerated, and in the end the Barony of Bombie, together with the lands of some of the laird's supporters, was forfeited to the crown. Shortly afterwards it chanced that a band of wild gipsies or reivers from Ireland settled in the district and greatly disturbed the whole countryside by their raids and pillaging. King James offered the lands of Bombie to whoever would disperse these raiders and bring before him their leader, known as Black Morrow — dead or alive. William McClellan, the son of the murdered tutor, determined to win back his inheritance. With a band of armed followers he laid an ambush for the raiders in a wood near Kirkcudbright where they commonly assembled. The well in the wood may have been drugged, spirits may have been left nearby, or conceiveably even poured into the well as the legend has it. However it

* See 'The Earl the Tutor and the King'.

was, the gipsy band was dispersed and Black Morrow was slain. Young William McClellan carried the head to Edinburgh and presented it to his sovereign — dramatically, it is claimed, on the point of his sword. The king had forgotten his pledge, whereupon the spirited young man advised him to "Think on!" King James remembered, the lands were restored, and McClellan was knighted.

In 1455 two crests were assumed by William McClellan, the new Laird and Tutor of Bombie. One bears allusion to the battering down of Threave Castle that same year by a great cannon, claimed to be 'Mons Meg'.* A strong force of McClellans had supported King James throughout the siege. The more famous crest, however, depicts a Moor's head on the point of a sword and bears the motto 'Think On'.

* See 'Mons Meg'.

The Murder
of Young McDowall

It is often difficult today, when one sees a tidy country road and cleared acreage of farmland, to imagine the wooded or scrubby wilderness traversed by a rough track that must have existed there in days gone by. On the lawn behind the present lodge gates of Ardwell House, just to the south of Ringvanachan Point on the eastern shore of the Rhinns of Galloway, lies an irregular block of whinstone. It is approximately three feet long and eighteen inches wide, and stands more than a foot above the neatly trimmed grass. Deeply inscribed in this stone is the word MURDER. The Lodge Wood, twenty or thirty yards away, covers part of a once more extensive area of woodland that traditionally was known as the 'Murder Plantin'. The story behind these names takes us back to the early years of the seventeenth century, when that long southern peninsula, as indeed the whole of Galloway, was an altogether wilder place than we know today.

The Laird of Portcorkerie, whose name was McKinna, had a single child, a daughter who was as desirable for her beauty as her inheritance. She was wooed particularly by two suitors, the heir of McDowall of Logan, and young Gordon of Castle Clanyard — a branch of the noble house of Kenmure. Their three houses were situated within a few miles of each other in the southern Rhinns of Galloway.*

One day news came to McDowall that Gordon had thrown love to the winds, and seizing the beautiful young heiress from her home had carried her off to Cardoness Castle, fifty miles away, the home of another branch of the Gordons. In anger and outrage young McDowall called for his horse and rode directly to Cardoness.

When he arrived beneath the castle walls, on that rocky wooded promontory above the River Fleet, he demanded to see the young lady; insisted that she must be released to return with him to her father's

---

* Castle Clanyard stands a mile west of Kirkmaiden. Portcorkerie (now called Barncorkrie) is situated a mile south-west of Clanyard. Logan lies four miles north of Clanyard, just inland from the Mull of Logan. Ardwell House stands two miles further north again, set back in beautiful woodland off the east coast road. Cardoness Castle lies many miles to the east, close to Gatehouse of Fleet.

house. Hot words were exchanged, his demands were refused, and he was compelled to ride empty-handed away.

There may have been some insupportable insult, or a history of bad feeling, or perhaps young McDowall constituted a real threat to Gordon's plan. However it was, the young man was either passed on the road or overtaken inland on the long journey back to Logan. A few miles short of home, as he passed the spot where the Murder Stone now lies, he was set upon by a band of armed followers and servants of the Gordons, dragged from his horse, and slain.

The horse bolted at the struggle and made its way home to the stable at Logan. The clattering of its hoofs in the yard roused the sleeping servants. Peering through the curtains into the darkness they saw that the horse was loose, and grumbling went out to stable it. But there was no sign of the young master. The saddled horse was restless, and evading them turned back up the road. Uneasily they dressed, took up clubs and followed it into the night. Rough bushes and wild acres of woodland formed black pools of shadow on either side of the stony track. Two miles from home they came upon the lifeless body of young McDowall. His assailants had vanished.

In view of the flighty nature of some girls it naturally seems possible that McKinna's daughter had chosen to run away with the lively young blade. This was not the case, however, it was a genuine abduction, for as time went by Gordon made little progress towards winning her hand. They returned to Castle Clanyard, but the splendid residence and lands did nothing to lessen her contempt and resolve. At length, in a desperation of unrequited love, he rode on Portcorkerie with a band of armed followers and made her father, too, his prisoner.

The old man refused his consent to every proposal that was made. But Gordon was not to be denied. Turning at last from threat and persuasion, he resorted to violent and extreme measures. One afternoon McKinna was taken from the castle to the western cliffs, tied by the thumbs with an end of line, and flung over the highest, wildest precipice in the vicinity. With the terrifying drop beneath his swinging heels, and the young villain's sword chafing the edge of the taut cord, the old gentleman was compelled to repeat after him the following rhyme, still remembered in the district:

> From me and from mine,
> To thee and to thine,
> The lands of Portcorkerie I for ever resign.

Thus, though he did not win the lady, young Gordon acquired her lands, which were at least part of what he so passionately desired.

There is a justice, however, for in time, as the fortunes of the Gordons faded, the star of the McDowalls was in the ascendant. Castle Clanyard, once the largest residence in the district, fell into ruin. Their lands and heritage became the property of the McDowalls, as also did the estate of Portcorkerie, so ruthlessly annexed those many years before.

There is no record that the murder of young McDowall was brought to law, but it did not go unavenged in the family. Shortly afterwards Uthred McDowall, the young laird of Garthland, was arraigned with others for the 'crewal slauchter' of James, the son of John Gordon of Barskeoch.

Crossing a Witch

It never pays to cross a witch. The countryside of Galloway is black with the tales of dreadful punishment meted out to those who have done so.

The Snow Wreath

Maggie Osborne, the witch of Glenluce, was some way from her home one morning when she encountered a funeral procession coming down the hilly track towards her. Not wishing to be seen, she changed

herself instantly into a black-beetle. But before she could crawl from the path she was trodden upon by a shepherd, who was one of the carrying party. Had it not been for a dry rut that partly protected her, she would have been crushed and killed. As it was she was merely bruised and hurt. As soon as the procession had passed and the coast was clear she turned herself back into a woman, and stood staring down the track after them, nursing her aching body. She vowed vengeance on the innocent shepherd, but since he was a good-living man it was a long time before she could bring her powers to bear. One snowy day, however, when he had been out late in the hills and was very tired, he omitted to say grace before his meal. It was the very opportunity she had been seeking. Using her magic she caused a great snow wreath to gather on the steep mountain slope above his cottage. In the middle of the wild and snowy night she hurled it down, and the shepherd and his wife were suffocated in the avalanche.*

A Nice Hot Bath

The servants of a well-to-do farmer were having to placate a local witch of great power. Almost every day they had to take her a pound of butter or a bag of flour, a piglet or a bucket of corn for her hens.

One morning the farmer decided that things had gone far enough, and issued his servants with firm instructions that they were to let her have no more. She was to do her worst.

Later that same day the farmer was out hunting on horseback, and passing near the witch's cottage saw her in the window, watching. She was there again on his return. He saw her cross her little yard to the well and draw a bucket of water.

It was a cold afternoon, and when he arrived home he was chilled, tired and dirty. The servant girl and his wife had pots of water heating on the stove. Soon the steam was rising from a deep, warm bath. Pulling the door to, the farmer stepped from his clothes and subsided into his tub with sighs of pleasure.

For a while he just soaked, enjoying the soothing heat of the water. Then it was time to soap himself, but to his great alarm he found that he was unable to move. He tried to call to his wife to come and help him, but he was unable to speak also. It was a dreadful situation. And then it became worse, for minute by minute, he discovered, the water was growing hotter. Clouds of steam obscured the further wall of the room. His skin was lobster-red.

It was only by the greatest good fortune that his wife, thinking he was taking rather longer than usual, pushed open the door and popped her head in. At first she could not see her husband, and advanced into the steam. When she discovered the situation she cried aloud for the servant girl, but she was out of the house for a moment. They were alone. Then she tried to lift her husband from the bath, but she was a little woman and he was a fat man. The water was starting to burn even her arms. Screaming for help she ran from the house and into the fields. They were deserted.

The brother of the servant girl, one of the men who had refused the

* See 'Maggie Osborne' in 'Thou Shalt Not Suffer a Witch'.

209

witch her dues that day, was ploughing near the witch's cottage. Hearing the loud cries he left the plough and crossed to the gate. The farmer's wife ran towards him calling out what had happened. At once the young man realised that this was the witch's work. It would take longer to return to the farm than go directly to her cottage. Quickly he unharnessed one of the horses, sprang on its back, and galloped across the fields to the witch's door.

She did not answer his knock. He peeped in through the window and saw her crouched by the fire, holding her sides and rocking with pleasure. Greatly daring he pushed open the door and went into the dark room. She did not need to ask him what he wanted. And when he offered her all the flitches of bacon and crowdie and corn she wanted in future, she refused, and said that the farmer must be taught his lesson.

In the little cauldron that was heating on the fire, the young ploughman could see a mannikin, with its legs and arms bound, and a chip of potato plugged deeply into its mouth.

Desperate to release his master from her spell, he started forward, but a single glance from her eyes was enough to drive him back and frighten him from the house.

Outside he was more brave. For a moment he thought, then seized a bucket from the side of the door and filled it at the well. With great difficulty he managed to carry it on to the sod and broom roof of the cottage. Very quietly he clambered up to the chimney and peeped down through the peat smoke. There was the witch, still chuckling over the steaming cauldron. With a quick prayer he lifted the bucket and sent the entire contents gushing down the chimney into the fire. Instantly the glowing logs were doused, the cauldron was flooded and spilled over the witch's feet, and the little mannikin fell out on to the floor and broke.

At the same instant back in the farmhouse the farmer was released from his torture and flung from his bath clear across the room, scarlet and boiled, and so suddenly that his wife screamed again and fled.

As for the poor young ploughman, I do not know what happened to him.

Three Sailor Lads

For a few days, while their boat lay at the Abbey Burnfoot, below Dundrennan, three young sailors spent every penny of their wages enjoying themselves at the howff — a popular tavern or drinking parlour — in a little clachan a couple of miles away. Each day they returned briefly to the lugger, just to keep an eye on things, and on these journeys they took a roundabout route to avoid passing the cottage of a crabbed old woman with the local reputation of a witch. Their brief leave over, however, with a last drink swimming in their heads, they decided to brave her and take the direct road back to the shore. She was waiting outside her house as they drew close.

"So you've come at last," she cried. "At last you'll pass the poor croft of an old body, and maybe give her a word or two on your way back to the sea. It's well seen that I can't tempt you as well as Peggy up at the howff yonder. I'll wager you haven't a brass farthing left among the three of you — now have you?"

The youngest sailor flew up at her uncivil speech, and called her all manner of witch and impudent old woman. Seeing how angry she became, his two companions could not resist joining in. When they left she was speechless with rage; but as they descended towards the shore her voice came back and she screamed dreadful threats and curses after their diminishing backs.

Two days later they sailed for Cumberland. Roughish weather was blowing the waves up on the shore, but as darkness fell the lugger was setting well out to sea. There was no reason why they should run into difficulties. The following morning, however, the boat was washed up a wreck on the Galloway sands. The bodies of the young sailors followed, a day or two afterwards.

The Moonlit Meeting

Sometimes the power of the witches extended beyond the grave.

One evening the wife of a labourer from Glenluce, a sensible, decent woman, was returning home late — so late, in fact, that it was drawing near the witching hour. Thinking nothing of it and enjoying the moonlit night, she made her way along the rough road by the edge of the wood. In time she came to the place known as the Clay Slap, where she was surprised to find the way blocked by a gathering of women. Sensing her approach they turned and waited for her, and as she came close she recognised some. In a moment, indeed, as she joined them and saw their faces, even in the deceptive moonlight she discovered that she knew them all. Several were ladies from the manor, and two from the nearby manse.

Then one of the women stepped forward. Glancing down, the labourer's wife was appalled to discover that where she should have worn fine shoes, instead her feet were bare, and cloven. There was no doubt of it. Then she saw that the legs of the others ended in shining hoofs also. In dismay she called aloud to a neighbour and friend, who was one of the gathering, to help her, for she did not know what to do. Enraged at being recognised, her friend cried out and raised a clawed hand in the air. Then all the party were screaming aloud that she must be killed since she had seen and recognised them. The labourer's wife pleaded for mercy, and swore that she would never betray their secret for as long as any of them lived. Though she was a good neighbour to them all, it was with great reluctance that they agreed. With many hisses and threats of terrible revenge if she were to break her word, they stood aside and she continued on her way along the moonlit track.

For many years she never breathed a word of their secret. As news came of the death of now one and then another of the witches, she would nod her head slowly and say mysteriously, "Ah, there's another of them away." And at last every single member of the coven had

passed on. She alone, now an old woman, remained to bear witness of that moonlit meeting.

And one afternoon, considering that she had kept her word to the letter, she told the story to her oldest daughter and a neighbour. That night, having climbed alone into her widow's bed, she lay in a burning agony. It was as if, she said, the flames of a fire on either side were roasting her between them. The fires that should have burned the witches they turned back upon her from the other side of the grave. She survived, however, and lived long into a contented old age, surrounded by her family and grandchildren.

The Nosy Witch

A little old lady of Whinnieliggate was a witch and lived on a lonely stretch of the road, three miles to the east of Kirkcudbright. She looked the part, and was described as having straggling grey hair covered with a black kerchief, strange whitish-green eyes, ugly teeth and a hooked nose. Commonly she wore a saffron shawl embroidered with toads, snakes, spiders and jackdaws. Her house contained dried kail stalks, and leg and arm bones gathered from the graveyard, arranged into the form of a star. Above her bed was a crude drawing of the zodiac. Instead of curtains, in some of her windows at least, the whitened skulls of animals and birds dangled from thin ropes and clicked and swung in the wind.

It was the little old lady's custom to stop everyone who passed and enquire their business.

One day a farmer and his labourer passed with a cart piled high with hay. They determined to ignore her, partly through impatience and partly in devilment. But when she addressed them the labourer could not resist commenting, "What the deil business is it of yours?" to which the farmer added, "Aye, John, just that; you speak the truth." She was speechless, and they passed on, feeling rather pleased with themselves.

Shortly afterwards their way took them through a wood by the Buckland Burn. Suddenly a hare sprang from the trees at the side of the track, right before the horses' eyes. The horses shied. Time and again the hare crossed and recrossed the path. The horses shied again and backed with the load of hay. The farmer could not control them. Then the cart went right off the track into the wood, tumbling down a steep bank into the burn. The horses were dragged with it and would have been severely hurt had not the harness broken. The farmer and labourer jumped for safety and were unharmed, but the entire load of hay fell into the water and was ruined.

On a later occasion this same John was driving a cart full of seed potatoes to the harbour at Kirkcudbright for shipment to Liverpool. The little old lady was standing at the side of the road as he passed, and called out demanding a few of the potatoes for herself. He neither stopped nor answered, just rattled on along the rough road. Upon his arrival at the quay the horse straight away backed the cart over the edge into the high tide. Both rider and horse were only with great difficulty saved from drowning.

The Bedridden Son

A young man of Kirkmaiden had returned home, having been absent for many months. Late one clear, wintry afternoon he took his gun and went out shooting. A little distance from the house he came upon a hare sitting in the track. It did not run away. Raising his gun he aimed and shot at the animal, but missed. Still it did not run. Twice more he fired, from ridiculously close range, but he just could not hit it. Clearly something supernatural was afoot. Slipping a small silver coin from his pocket, he dropped it into the barrel. At this the hare addressed him, saying, "Would you shoot your own mother?" He was astonished and returned home, where he discovered that indeed this had been the truth. His mother confessed it — she was a witch.

He did not know what to do — but very soon the matter was taken out of his hands. That very evening his strength deserted him. He felt it draining from his limbs like water. He could not stand, he could not walk. With his mother's help he retired to his bed. Though he felt well and ate his food, and in every other respect was fit enough, he was tied to the house, a complete prisoner. No-one called, he never had a visitor. There was no chance of giving away his mother's secret. For five years of his young manhood he lay there.

Then his mother died. As the last breath left her body and her eyes closed, he felt the strength flowing back into his arms and legs. He rose from the bed and dressed. Two days later, in a smart new suit bought from her savings and with a flower in his buttonhole, he walked down the road behind his mother's coffin.

The Shepherd Fiddler

Sometimes an amulet, in the form of a hare's foot or an adder-bead or some religious relic, will ward off a witch's power. But woe-betide the man who takes advantage of its protection and then is caught without the charm in his possession.

An unmarried shepherd who lived in a lonely part of the country a mile or so from Gatehouse of Fleet, was a noted fiddler. He lived for his music. His only neighbour was a witch, and her cottage was so close to his own that she could hear every note when the shepherd practised in the evening. She hated the merry music, and did all she could to put a stop to it — but he was impervious to her strongest witchcraft through a particularly potent adder bead, which had been passed down through his family for generations.

One fine summer day there was a big wedding in Gatehouse, and the shepherd had been asked to play for the dancing which was to follow on the green afterwards.

The sunshine was hot, they had eaten well and the festive wine was making his head spin a little. But it was said in the town that he played best of all when he had a little drink in him, so tucking the old fiddle beneath his chin he struck up into a spirited, dancing jig. The young men cast off their jackets and soon the couples were swirling on the cropped grass to the gayest of his dance tunes. Without giving it a thought the shepherd too flung off his jacket, for he was perspiring, and threw himself into the fiddling in real earnest.

No-one saw the witch peeping from behind the corner of a barn nearby. When she saw the shepherd in his shirt-sleeves, with his jacket hanging from the twig of a tree many yards away, she was delighted, for by the power in it she could tell that the famous adder bead was still in his jacket pocket. He was unprotected. In an instant she had made and cast her spell, then sat back in the shade to watch the consequences.

Soon the joyful dancers were tired, and waited for the music to stop. But it did not stop: the fiddler played on. Then some of the young men called out 'enough', and tried to walk from the circle of dancers. But to their astonishment they were not able. So long as he played they had to dance. And from the house nearby the older couples came running to join in. Soon everybody, from the youngest child to the oldest grandfather, was dancing and leaping on the wedding green, kilts and dresses swirling, heels and hair flying.

The poor shepherd tried his hardest to bring the music to an end, but some power kept him playing: just as he drew his bow across the end of a fiery jig, the fiddle struck out into a galloping reel, as if it had a life of its own.

Soon everyone was sweating and feeling faint and calling out to him for pity's sake to stop. The girls' dresses split with their exertions, the young men's buttons popped and their shirt tails climbed out of their trousers and kilts. Totally exhausted the older members fell to the grass; but as soon as they had recovered a little they sprang to their feet once more and danced on.

The wedding afternoon passed, and the warm summer evening. The sun was sinking behind the trees when at last the shepherd, his arm still bowing, toppled to the earth with fatigue and his fiddle tumbled across the grass. Only two or three dancers still remained on their feet: when the music stopped they collapsed where they stood.

For a long time they all lay there. The sun set, the sky reddened, their clothes grew damp with the dew. At last the bridegroom found the energy to crawl across to where the shepherd was lying. Pulling himself to his feet, he jumped on the fiddle, again and again, until it was no more than splintered matchwood.

Still no-one had seen the witch. Delighted with the success of her scheme, she crept away into the evening.

Though he still had the adder-bead — its power was far too great for the witch to dream of stealing it — the shepherd never had the heart to buy another fiddle. For him the joy had gone out of music. He never played again. And no-one ever asked him.

A Simple Girl's Revenge

Laura and Eppie were twins, and they lived with their father and mother in a little croft cottage on a fine estate on the western shore of Wigtown Bay. Although they were poor, they were a happy loving family. The two girls, however, were very different. Laura was beautiful, and as she grew up was greatly admired by all the boys and young men of the district. Eppie was more plain, and a deaf-mute. She had been away to school in a large town, where she had distinguished herself as a clever girl. Particularly she was excellent in the art of handwriting, and had become a most skilful needle-woman and milliner.

Many of the local boys sought to find favour with Laura, who was as kind as she was beautiful, but none of them was able to win her affection. At length, however, her attractions aroused the feelings of the factor of the estate upon which her father worked. He was an unscrupulous man and strikingly handsome. With no thought but for himself he sought to win the love of the crofter's daughter. He called repeatedly at the house under the pretext of discussing work with her father. He made himself agreeable to the girls and their mother, he granted little kindnesses. Eppie suspected his motives, for his attitude towards the family had changed. She did not like him from the start. Laura, however, innocent and knowing little of the world, soon fell for his good looks, soft words and small attentions. In a little while she was meeting him secretly, and he became her lover.

The truth could not be withheld. But soon, wearied by her love and submission, he began to tire of her. Her reputation was ruined in the district, it was impossible for her to remain at home. She took a menial job many miles away, and all were in tears as Eppie and her parents saw the girl off in a little post-chaise, her few belongings packed about her feet.

Meanwhile the factor, unashamed and even proud of his conquest, rode about the estate on his horse, handsome and a fine figure of a man.

Eppie, who due to her misfortune did not have any admirers, loved her twin sister with a passionate devotion. She was stunned by the deliberate cruelty with which the factor had disgraced her sister, ruined her future and removed her from the bosom of their family. Increasingly she began to spend time alone. Her normally cheerful and loving

217

disposition deserted her. Her brain turned and she began to grow strange.

In a while a governess, a young woman, was appointed to the manor house to commence the education of the laird's children. It was not long before she attracted the attention of the factor. She, however, was not a simple country girl, she was a lady. Her position was very suited for her to become the factor's wife. His genteel attentions were received with favour and a few months later they became engaged.

For years Eppie's skill as a needle-woman and milliner had been well-known in the district. She received quite a number of commissions from ladies who found her both inexpensive and excellent — and often tried to cover up their meanness with protestations of how they helped the poor thing out by giving her a bit of extra work.

One day the governess, a more kindly and pretty young woman in a dress of sprigged muslin, called at the cottage with a straw bonnet. It was of the style fashionable in those days, shaped like a flour scoop and projecting at the sides — called 'kiss me if you can'. Writing on the pad that Eppie kept by her, she explained that she wanted the bonnet re-trimming with a pretty new ribbon. She would call to collect it the following morning.

When she had gone Eppie sat for a long while, her hands gathered tightly in her lap, staring into space. Since her sister's departure her face had worn an expression that was strange and withdrawn, as if she was living within herself. Now it was intense.

With the governess's handwriting before her as example, she forged a note to the factor, pleading with him to meet her at nightfall in a quiet gully a little distance away by the edge of the sea. Having sealed and addressed the envelope, she laid the letter aside to be dispatched later. Then she went into the kitchen where scraps of her father's stake nets hung on the wall. Cutting out a strong fragment a few feet square she fashioned it into a bag, and stitched the opening firmly to the tapes of the governess's bonnet. Finally she went out to the peat shed where one or two crabs from her father's creels still moved slowly in the bottom of a chest. Taking the largest, a huge creature, she dropped it into a bucket and filled the bucket with sea water. Soon it began to revive.

As darkness approached she called a local boy and instructed him to deliver the letter to the factor. Then, taking the bonnet, the net and the crab with her, she slipped secretly away along the shore to keep her assignation.

It was almost dark as the factor, curious and perhaps warm with anticipation, descended the rocky slope to the sea-washed inlet. All was silent. He peered around into the gloom. Then suddenly there was a strange cry, a loud splash and a commotion in the water. Several yards away, not far from a small cave, a bonnet floated on the waves. He scrambled closer as quickly as he could move on the rocks and saw that it was the straw bonnet of his fiancee: there was no doubt, there was none other like it in the neighbourhood. The bonnet moved and jerked in the water, there was an agitation beneath it. The factor was not a strong swimmer, but he knew he must rescue her. Flinging off his jacket he plunged into the water and struggled the few yards to where he believed she was drowning. Desperately he cast about below the surface, and feeling something plunged lower.

The girl's stratagem was so foolish as to be almost ridiculous, but either because of some higher justice or its very hopelessness, it worked. The factor thrust his hand deeply into the bag, straight into the powerful claw of the crab which immediately, like a vice, closed on his thumb and crushed it. He screamed, he tried to pull the crab off. His arm was entangled in the net. He struggled. He was swallowing water. In little more than a minute he was gone.

The facts are known because it chanced that at that moment a game-keeper was returning to his cottage on the estate and heard the commotion. Peering into the gully in the half darkness he saw the factor struggling in the water. Though he scrambled down the rocks as quickly as he was able, when he arrived at the spot all signs had vanished. The water rippled in from Wigtown Bay.

The tide was ebbing. Rather than run to the nearest cottage for help he remained, lest there should be something he could do. While he waited the last glimmers of daylight faded from the sky. The water slowly fell.

At length he saw something washing in the black, glinting water at the edge of the rocks. He climbed down. It was a sodden straw bonnet, torn by the man's struggles. The ribbons were fastened to a twisted bag of fish netting. The man's arm was still tangled in the mesh. As he pulled at it the game-keeper saw that the man's hand was gripped by the crushing claw of a great crab, still imprisoned in the net. Appalled by this he drew his strong pocket knife and thrust it through the crab's head. The crab died, its hold on the factor's hand was released.

The game-keeper pulled the body clear of the water, then made his way out of the gully to run to the nearest house and get help. As he reached the rim and looked down, he was astonished to see the almost indistinguishable figure of a woman emerge from the cave. He went back and hid, to see who she was, but the woman did not pass his way. He tried to follow her, but she moved silently and swiftly, and in the darkness eluded him.

But circumstances pointed unwaveringly at Eppie — the bonnet, the stitching, the net, the sodden forged letter in the drowned man's pocket, the motive, her strangeness. Though popular opinion was in no doubt of her guilt, and may have been sympathetic to a degree, Eppie's sad fate was sealed within herself. From the time she returned home from the gully she began to show unmistakable signs of real mental derangement. As the days went by these grew worse, and at length it became necessary to remove her to an asylum for the insane.

What became of Laura is unknown: her father and mother too, and the last days of Eppie are hidden in the past. The game-keeper, however, who was a man of great spirit, became a soldier. He lost a leg in the Crimea and was pensioned off by the army. Because of a tremendous admiration for Lord Raglan, his great hero, he was commonly given the by-name of 'Raggie'. He was a great story-teller. This tale of his, remembered from young manhood, was one of his favourites, and vouched for by his later associates in Wigtownshire as being entirely true — 'as true as the fourteen' chapter o' John.'

Mons Meg

For centuries there has been a tradition in Galloway that Mons Meg, the great cannon that stands so splendidly on the ramparts of Edinburgh Castle, was manufactured in a small blacksmith's forge at the Buchan, by Carlingwark Loch, quarter of a mile from the present-day market town of Castle Douglas. A number of historians and even the Statistical Account of Scotland have maintained the local tradition as historical fact. Today, still, there are many who accept this account of Mons Meg's origin rather than that now conclusively supported by documentary evidence, which is that the great bombard was made, as its name suggests, at Mons in Flanders.

In February, 1452, the young King James II, in an impulsive fit of anger, had stabbed to death William, 8th Earl of Douglas, at Stirling Castle. The principal reason was that Douglas refused to break a league he had formed with the Earls of Crawford and Ross, a league which made them, potentially at least, a greater power than the throne itself.* William's brother James, who became 9th Earl of Douglas, with three younger brothers, rose in rebellion against the king. James applied for a papal dispensation to marry his brother's young widow Margaret, the Fair Maid of Galloway. Through this union, since William had no children, James sought to acquire her large, unentailed estates: indeed as his second cousin she was a powerful landowner in her own right. Amazingly the king supported the application, the dispensation was granted, the marriage took place. Thus the Douglas power was united once more, and increasingly, as time went by, it became a threat to the state. So great was the danger that the king even contemplated abdication and flight from the country. Finally, however, he determined to fight, and hopefully to end once and for all the power and authority of the Black Douglases.

Laying sudden siege to the Earl's Castle of Inveravon near Linlithgow, King James captured and dismantled the stronghold. His troops then overran the Earl's estates in Annandale, Douglasdale and the Ettrick Forest, and besieged the Castle of Abercorn near South Queensferry. Though James Douglas rode to the relief of Abercorn, he was deserted on the eve of this major battle by almost all of his

* See 'The Earl the Tutor and the King'.

supporters. Left with only two or three thousand troops to face the royal army his position was hopeless, and the Earl had no option but to withdraw. Throughout the winter he lurked in Annandale and Galloway. The following May, 1455, a rising by his three brothers was crushed by the Red Douglases, Earls of Angus, at the battle of Arkinholm at Langholm. James Douglas escaped through a wood and fled for safety to his ally the Earl of Ross. Later, with no more than a few attendants, he crossed the border into England where he stood in high favour with Henry VI.

A month after Arkinholm, James Douglas was condemned by act of parliament. His estates and honours were forfeited — and later divided between the king's second son, Alexander, Duke of Albany, and loyal supporters. In the end, only the Castle of Threave held out.

The castle, the very core of the Douglases' power in Galloway, stands on an island in the River Dee, a mile and a half due west of Castle Douglas. It was built by Archibald the Grim,* 3rd Earl of Douglas and Lord of Galloway, towards the end of the fourteenth century, a massive five-storey tower-house intended to withstand any attack known at that time.† The river was too wide to bridge and, save at the foot of the island, too deep to ford. The island itself, twenty acres of flooding but fertile ground, provided ample food in time of siege. The castle walls were eight feet thick. From the top, seventy feet above the ground, the defensive outlook over the flat valley and surrounding country was magnificent. Because of the wild reputation of the Black Douglases, the castle was often referred to locally as 'the Lion's Den'.

So important did King James consider the total and final overthrow of the Earl of Douglas, that later in 1455 he himself marched into Galloway at the head of a large army to conduct the siege of the castle. It was to last a month. The king's forces camped in wooded pastures a mile away, at the Three Thorns of Carlingwark, close to the western shore of the loch as it lies today.

It is at this point that the local tradition really begins. The royal artillery, which had followed the king from Linlithgow, was not powerful enough to cause significant damage to the thick walls of the castle, and the multitude which thronged from the surrounding country to

* So named because of his fierce, warrior-like expression in battle.
† A twelfth-century fortalice built by Fergus, 1st Lord of Galloway, had previously existed on the site. The great outer wall, with its towers three storeys high, was not built until the sixteenth century, following the battle of Flodden.

witness the bombardment saw cannonball after cannonball bounce from the stonework with little more than a crumble of dust.

A blacksmith by the name of McKim — better remembered as 'Brawny Kim' — from the nearby Buchan,* was one of the watchers. Turning to an officer he remarked that they needed much heavier ordnance. The officer replied that they had none. At this the black-smith closely inspected a cannon which was nearby, and offered to construct what they wanted if they would furnish him with the raw materials and necessary equipment. The king was informed and readi-ly agreed to the suggestion. The leading inhabitants of Kirkcudbright each furnished the blacksmith with a gaud (bar) of iron, for they were anxious to rid themselves of the Douglases' tyranny, and wished to avenge the bloody murder of the Tutor of Bombie.

The blacksmith and his seven sons set to work, and in a short time had constructed the great cannon. It was fashioned from a series of iron bars welded together longitudinally and bound by a series of strong hoops shrunk over the top down the entire length, so that it formed a sort of cask. The breech was either forged or cast in a single piece.† Mounted on a strong carriage, the huge weapon was with considerable difficulty hauled to the top of a small hill opposite to Threave Castle, which from that time forward was known as 'Knockcannon'.

While McKim was busy with the gun, masons on the summit of the Bennan Hill, many miles away on the west shore of north Loch Ken, were fashioning huge cannonballs of Galloway granite to fit its 19½ inch calibre. As each was finished the masons bowled it down the steep hillside to the loch road with a fine smashing of branches. Carts transported them to Knockcannon.

Forty feet above the gateway of Threave Castle projected a stone, traditionally known as the 'gallows-knob'. It was Douglas's boast that for fifty years it had 'never wanted a tassel' — perpetual reminder to

* In 1455 Buchan's Croft, as it was then called, was the principal clachan in the district, and situated very close to the Three Thorns where the king's troops were encamped. All around was farming land and rough countryside. Cause-wayend, the first village on the site of Castle Douglas, was not to be established for two hundred and fifty years.

† There is astonishing disagreement in the basic statistics of Mons Meg. The following figures are taken from the Catalogue of the Armouries, H.M. Tower of London: original overall length 15'0"; weight 6·9 tons; calibre 19½"; weight of charge 105 lb; range at 45° — 1408 yards with iron ball weighing 1125 lb — 2867 yards with stone ball weighing 549 lb (a 19½" sphere of pure granite weighs 380 lb). For firing the gun was removed from its carriage and secured to a timber bed on the ground.

friend and foe alike of his power. From windows in the west wall above the river, the last supporters of the Black Douglas watched the preparations, feeling for the present, at least, secure within their great stronghold. When the first shot was fired and the ball struck, the heavy walls shook to their foundations. From the forces of King James and the assembled country folk there came a great cheer. The supporters of Douglas within were thrown into confusion, for they had believed the fortress to be impregnable.

A tradition that the Earl of Douglas was present, tells how at this time, realising that the castle would be taken and not wishing his treasure to fall into the king's hands, he carried it into subterranean chambers beneath the level of the river, and opened a sluice gate. The water flooded in, the riches were submerged and saved. Later, he hoped, he would return and recover them for himself. A similar tradition claims that there was an escape tunnel which led from the cellar of Threave Castle beneath the river to a hidden bolt hole.

The cannon was loaded for the second shot. Traditionally it took a whole peck (two gallons) of gunpowder, and the cannonball weighed 'as much as a Carsphairn cow'.* The assembly stood back and the powder was ignited. With a shattering explosion that stunned the air and made the ground heave, the cannon fired. The cannonball tore straight through the wall of the castle. Within, in the dining hall, Douglas's wife, the Fair Maid of Galloway, who had refused to surrender, was endeavouring to maintain some semblance of order and control by sitting to her dinner. The cannonball took her right hand clean off as she was raising a glass of wine to her lips. When this news reached the countryside it was said to be divine punishment, for that same hand had been given to two brothers in wedlock, and that while the wife of the first was still alive.†

* Carsphairn is a hill village: thus a hill cow, lighter than a lowland beast.
† Margaret, the Fair Maid of Galloway, had barely completed her twelfth year when she was married to her second cousin, William Douglas, a political match in which, of course, she had no say. He was already married and had to obtain a papal dispensation to divorce his wife. The Fair Maid was twenty when she married his brother James, greatly against her wishes. By neither did she have any children. After the forfeiture of James, while he was still alive, she married John Stewart, Earl of Athol, uterine brother of James II. She was apparently an exceptionally lovely woman.

Various historians give five accounts of her fate during the siege of Threave: she lost her hand; she was unharmed and went on her knees to the king, who forgave her; she was held in Threave as a prisoner by her husband's supporters; she fled

The garrison immediately surrendered. The last stronghold of the Black Douglas was taken. Their power was finally broken.

In recognition and gratitude the king presented to McKim the forfeited lands of Mollance, two miles to the south-west. In the district, as indeed throughout Scotland, it was frequently the practice to designate people according to the names or locations of their houses. McKim's family were thus known by the sobriquet 'Mollance'. Now his wife, whose name was Margaret, was well known for her loud voice, a real 'muckle-mou' Meg'. It was said that her mouth was as wide and loud as her husband's great cannon. And so it was, jestingly at first, that her name was given to the huge bombard — Meg from Mollance, or Mollance Meg, which in time was corrupted to Mons Meg.

Other traditions support the legend. The cannonballs which were used in the siege, and those which now stand by the cannon in Edinburgh Castle, are claimed to be of Galloway granite. Only two balls were fired at Threave. The first was taken from the wall at the end of the eighteenth century and given to a Mr Gordon of nearby Greenlaw. The second, which pierced the wall, was discovered in 1841, in the process of clearing work in the castle, at the bottom of a hidden well, in direct line with Knockcannon and the place where the wall had been breached.*

During the Napoleonic wars the castle was used as a barracks for French prisoners, and during the work of preparation 'a massive gold ring', inscribed on the inside with the words 'Margaret de Douglas', was found by the workmen.† The ring was said to have been on the finger of the Fair Maid when her hand was blown off, and some claim that when it was found it still encircled her finger, attached to 'a straggle o' banes' that had once been her hand. Later, possibly in 1822, the ring was stolen at a hotel in Edinburgh.

* Unfortunately Edinburgh Castle is unable to corroborate this claim regarding the cannonballs which stand by the great bombard. Still more unfortunately, the Department of the Environment's official pamphlet on Threave Castle suggests that no cannon was ever fired. From payments made by the royal exchequer, it seems probable that the officers of the garrison, finding themselves alone and without hope of assistance, were simply bought off by the king.

† Following the siege of Threave the castle was repaired. After the Battle of Flodden in 1513 it was strengthened. In 1640, garrisoned with a hundred royalist troops, the old fortress withstood a thirteen week siege and heavy bombardment by the Covenanters. Finally, by order of the king, it volunteered an honourable surrender, and shortly afterwards was dismantled.

before the bombardment and sought refuge in Whithorn Priory; and she had been absent in England for a year.

When the great military road was being laid at Carlingwark more than three centuries later, the men engaged in its construction came upon a large mound, which proved to be of the cinders left from a forge. This was at the precise spot where Mons Meg was reputed to have been built, though there had not been a forge there for as long as anyone could remember. As recently as 1950, however, repairs to a very old house at the Buchan revealed in the gable wall a chimney way six feet four inches wide, which evidently had once been a blacksmith's forge.

King James, in 1455, was so pleased with the successful outcome to the siege and the final overthrow of the Black Douglases, that he elevated the town of Kirkcudbright into a Royal Burgh, which proud title it has held to the present day.

It is a miserable thing, following such a splendid and ancient tradition, to present the bare facts. Though one would wish to, it is surely a little naive to believe that a rural smithy could within the short time and pressure of a siege construct this enormous cannon, when at the time Scotland had no means of artillery manufacture whatever, and according to Holinshed the first cast-iron pieces were not made in England until 1543, eighty-eight years later.

Mons Meg was made in the town of Mons by Jehan Cambier in 1449. He was a distinguished master-gunner and merchant, one of the very first in the long line of great weapon dealers and manufacturers in Western Europe. The huge bombard – by no means the largest, 'Mad Margaret' had a bore of thirty-six inches – was commissioned by the Duke of Burgundy, and sent in 1457, two years after the siege of Threave, as a gift to James II to help him against the English. It was accompanied by sixty-one granite cannonballs – more than it ever fired – also from Belgium; three thousand pounds of gunpowder; and a second bombard, weighing four tons. Though all arrived safely, the great cannon proved to be so weighty and unwieldy that it was not used for many years: indeed, its usefulness on any occasion is very questionable. Its value lay in the threat, rather than the performance. From the very start, in a manner that was customary, the weapon was called 'Mons' after the place of its manufacture. The 'Meg' was added later, possibly about 1486 in reference to Margaret of Denmark, the Queen of James III.

Since Mons Meg arrived in Scotland after the siege of Threave, we wonder where the local tradition came from. Long before the siege of

Threave the Stuart kings were importing large guns from Flanders,* and in 1441 the boy James I took possession of the great cannon known as the 'Magna Bombarda'. State records detail the considerable expenses incurred in transporting this weapon from Linlithgow to the siege of Threave Castle: sturdy carts were built, bridges strengthened, teams of horses hired, inn charges referred to the royal treasury. The cannon was accompanied by William, Earl of Orkney. It was not, however, Mons Meg.†

* In 1430, for example, James I imported the beautiful brass cannon known as the 'Lion' from Flanders. This was the weapon which blew up and killed James II at the siege of Roxburgh Castle in 1460.

In October 1680 the barrel of Mons Meg was split when firing a salute in honour of a royal visit to Edinburgh by James, Duke of York. The reason seems to have been that early gunpowder was comparatively weak, but two centuries after the cannon's construction it was much more powerful, and due regard to this was not taken by a cock-sure English cannoneer. It was never fired again. Despite the damage, however, Mons Meg was still viewed as the most powerful weapon the Scots had ever possessed, and in 1754, in the wake of the Jacobite rebellion, it was taken to London — where, it is claimed, a woman was got with child inside the barrel. In 1829, in deference to national sentiment, the cannon was restored to Edinburgh Castle.

† This journey and theory are closely examined by 'Reviresco' in his article 'Mons Meg: its Traditions and History' to be found in *The Gallovidian Annual* of 1921. 'Reviresco', however, did not have the advantages of recent scholarship and discoveries, and claimed that the Magna Bombarda and Mons Meg were the same weapon.

Local historians speak easily of dragging the great weapon to the summit of Knockcannon, which occupied 'a commanding position . . . right in front of the castle'. Unfortunately the nearest 'Knockcannon' to Threave is by Camp Douglas, two miles to the north. Even allowing the amazing range of 2,800 yards, Mons Meg would never have been able to reach, let alone score a direct hit twice in a row. Behind the farm of Threave Mains, however, less than half a mile from the fortress, a small tree-covered hill rises from the flat valley floor. On a detailed and very large-scale estate map, this is significantly named the 'Kennan Hill'. Beyond bow-shot and within range, the hill fits the tradition very well. Assuming that the great cannon was brought down from Linlithgow and used in the siege, this may well be the spot from which it was fired.

The Ghost of Galdenoch

Galdenoch Tower lies a mile inland from the great North Channel of the Irish Sea, due west of the village of Leswalt. The original tower was built by the Agnews of nearby Lochnaw Castle about 1560, but by the time of the present story a century later, the property had passed from them and the building was being used as a farmhouse.

They were covenanting years and a son of the house had thrown in his lot with the Presbyterian forces. Journeys and marches had taken him many miles from home, and in the end he was with the ragged covenanting army when it was routed by royalist troops — it is not certain in which battle. The survivors scattered for their lives and were hunted down by dragoons, who showed scant mercy to those they captured.

The farmer's son from Galdenoch was one of those on the run, and like hundreds of others was making his way home secretly through the woods and moors and quiet lanes. When evening came he was weary and hungry and the weather was rough. Hoping for a kind reception, but easing his pistol in its holster, he knocked at the door of a lonely house and requested food and shelter for the night. The owner was a coarse, blustering fellow. None the less the young man was made welcome, a meal was provided, and not too many questions were asked. When the night came he was given a bed by the side of the fire.

Early the following morning the covenanting soldier was up and preparing to make a good start when he was accosted by the owner of the house. Previously the man had been most courteous in his own way, but during the night he had changed. Possibly he saw some chance of gain in handing the young man over to the authorities, or perhaps certain royalist leanings had resurrected themselves. However it was, heated words were exchanged and the angry owner laid threatening hands on the covenanter's sleeve, barring his way to the door. Being convinced that the man meant to detain him, which in the circumstances would almost certainly have meant death, the young soldier drew his pistol and shot the man dead. Quickly then he saddled a horse from the stable and set off to the westward.

His return home was greeted with great joy. A feast was prepared and he recounted his experiences.

229

At last it was time for bed. But no sooner had the young man laid his head upon the pillow than he was disturbed by something moving about the room. He rose in his bed and peered about in the moonlight that filtered through the little tower window. There was nothing to see. He heard a malicious chuckle and then recognised the gravelly voice of the man he had killed two days before. There was no doubt of it. He tried to sleep, but the spirit made it quite impossible by knocking on the furniture, tossing objects to the floor and suddenly shrieking when all was quiet. The young covenanter moved to another room and the ghost followed him. Though he was exhausted, all night he had no rest.

The other members of the family, too, were disturbed by the ghost's mischief. That night and in subsequent days and months they were tormented. Though they went to the minister and tried every ruse they could think of, nothing would exorcise the troublesome spirit. At length, utterly exhausted, they were compelled to move away from the tower and live elsewhere.

When new owners moved into Galdenoch Tower they found the ghost firmly established. Life, however, they found to be tolerable, though some of its tricks were dangerous and savage.

One evening as they sat at the fire playing a game which involved passing a burning stick from hand to hand,* one of the family remarked how brilliantly the peats were burning. The hearth was a glowing bank of white and orange. "I wouldn't fancy taking one of them in my hand," he said. No sooner were the words out of his mouth than a big glowing peat rose up from the very heart of the fire and disappeared, leaving a white-hot hole in its place. They were astonished and appalled. A minute or two later there was a loud cry of "Fire!" from outside, and rushing into the night they found the thatch of the farm steading ablaze. Edging close with buckets of water, everyone saw the white-hot peat in the middle of the blazing roof. It was only with a struggle that they were able to save the farm buildings from total loss.

On another occasion the ghost removed granny from the midst of the family. The old lady was sitting alone at her spinning wheel with a fresh dyeing of wool, when suddenly she found herself lifted bodily into the air and borne swiftly along above the ground for several hundred yards. There was nothing to see, it was like flying, but all the

---

* The stick was passed from hand to hand while the players chanted:

'About wi' that; about wi' that;
Keep alive the priest-cat!'

Whoever held the stick when the flame or spark died was required to pay a forfeit.

231

time a voice mumbled in her ears: "I'll dip thee, I'll draw thee!" Soon she came to the Mill-Isle Burn — a tributary of the Galdenoch — and was abruptly flung into the middle by the power which carried her. Then the cruel ghost dipped and possed the old lady up and down in the water like a bundle of wool or an old pair of breeks until she lost consciousness. At dinner time she was missed and the family were astonished. Where could she have wandered? They searched everywhere, but she was not to be found. Then the gritty voice they had heard so often spoke laughingly out of the air: "I've washed granny in the burn, and laid her on the dyke to dry!" Together the whole family ran to the place and found the old woman hanging naked over the field dyke, terrified and half dead with the cold.

Several times they approached the church authorities, and a number of ministers came to the tower. By psalm singing they attempted to drive the spirit away. It was, however, possessed of a particularly lusty voice and sang them all down with profane and bawdy songs. One minister, more than the others, was dreadfully affronted. He had travelled from a considerable distance, and was somewhat puffed up with his own reputation. No ghost in the kingdom, it was said, was proof against his spiritual power, wonderful singing and brilliant disputation. The Ghost of Galdenoch, however, drowned his singing with ease, then interrupted his harangue and answered his solemn debate with such wit and impudence that the congregation could not keep their faces straight, and were brought at last to outright mirth, rolling in their seats with laughter. The minister was fearfully insulted and stormed from the tower, vowing never to return. He had gone only a few yards beyond the gate, however, when the ghost called after him, promising to whisper in his ear something that nobody else knew. The minister could not resist the temptation and returned to the doorway, only to be greeted by the ghost's mischievous and delighted cry: "Ha ha! I hae gotten the minister to tell a lee!"

Following these attempts at exorcism the ghost redoubled its efforts. Almost every day the family were subjected to its noisy interference and malicious tricks. Peat lumps were flung into the porridge; unsavoury materials were dropped in the kail pot; the spinners' threads were broken short; a smuggled keg of spirits was filled with cow sharn; during the night all the buttons in the house were torn off their clothes and flung into the sea.

At length a new minister, the Rev. Mr Marshall, a well-known persecutor of witches, was appointed to the parish of Kirkcolm, immediately north of Leswalt. He was a man possessed of unshakable confidence, and one of those splendid stentorian voices that made the church rafters ring and the backsliders cower and tremble in their pews. On a calm day when he preached out of doors, his voice could clearly be heard on the opposite shore of Loch Ryan. He had not been long in his parish when it became plain that a battle royal between Mr Marshall and the Ghost of Galdenoch must soon be waged. A large company gladly volunteered to assist. They came expecting verbal fireworks, and they were not disappointed. It was a tremendous night, the minister and his congregation making the very walls of the strong tower shake with the volume of their psalmody; the considerably less sacred verses of the ghost, not one whit abashed, resounding and redoubling above it, making their hair stand on end. The hours passed. Midnight came and went. The voices of the company grew weaker and croakier and at last left them altogether. But still Mr Marshall and the ghost kept at it. It seemed, to those whose hearing remained unimpaired, that a certain note of desperation had come into the ghost's voice. But the longer the minister sang, the greater and more sublime grew his tones, until at length, as dawn touched the shattered eastern windows of the tower, it became clear to all that the ghost was faltering. Not many minutes afterwards, as Mr Marshall turned the page to start yet again on Psalm 119, there was a strangled cry of horror. For a moment the minister paused, and in the silence the company heard a croaking, wheezing breath. Then a weak, laryngitic voice whispered: "On ye go, Marshall. Roar awa'. I can sing nae mair."

At that moment the ghost left Galdenoch Tower, and was never heard of again.

FOOTNOTE

In the late eighteenth century the grand old tower-house of Galdenoch became a haunt of pirates, and some say that the ghost story was invented and reinforced by them to keep away the superstitious peasantry. If so, then they did not make the ghost very fearsome. Whether or not this is true, however, it is a famous and very detailed haunting, spoken of in the district for more than two centuries.

The Martyrs of Kirkconnel[*]

Early on the morning of 20th February, 1685, Sir Robert Grierson of Lagg, who had been in the far south-west levying fines and rooting out Covenanters, left Wigtown for Dumfries. He was accompanied by Colonel Douglas in command of detachments of Claverhouse's troop of horse and Strachan's dragoons. After a ride of about twenty-five miles, they arrived in the afternoon at the lonely inn of Gatehouse of Fleet, where they paused for refreshments. By the time they departed daylight was fading, and in the gloom of evening, thickened by a bank of fog rolling up from the Borgue shore, they lost their way on Irelandton Moor. For a time, with patience wearing thin, they cast about, and at length a trooper rode up to Lagg with the news that he had seen a light.

It proved to be a farmhouse called 'Gordon Cairn', belonging to an elderly couple. The farmer, Gabriel Rain, informed them that they were well off the road for Dumfries, but offered to point them in the right direction. It was not enough for Lagg, who demanded that the old man should go with them, there and then, and ordered one of the troopers to take him on the back of his horse. The farmer resisted, however, and told them that he would take them as far as the small thatched cottage of Calfarran, where they would find someone younger and stronger than himself, who would guide them back to the road.

Arriving at Calfarran the officers marched straight in, and found Thomas Clinton sitting among his family. He was a man of Covenanting sympathies, but not so strongly that he would consider martyrdom for them. Realising something of the situation from Clinton's ill-considered remarks, Lagg temporarily suspended his interest in the Dumfries road, and began enquiring about local families. Particularly his questions turned towards the family at Mayfield, a little distance away.† Realising

---

* See 'The Covenanters'.

† Although referred to as 'Mayfield' in old accounts and on the martyrs' monument, this farm at Glengap is now called 'Miefield'. It was, in the seventeenth century, suitably remote and a popular spot for conventicles. In fair weather they were held near the summit of Dow Craig Hill (Miefield Hill), immediately behind the house. From here there was a spectacular outlook over the surrounding countryside, so that advancing dragoons could be spotted far away. A nick forming a natural seat in the grey rock on the southern side of the hill, is deeply inscribed 'Martyrs Chair'. Traditionally it was here that the field preacher sat, with the Covenanters gathered before him.

which way the wind was blowing, Thomas Clinton exaggerated the difficulties of a journey to Mayfield in the dark of such a night. Lagg saw through his stratagem, however, and challenging Clinton with Covenanting sympathies himself, ordered him to accompany them to Mayfield immediately.

Thomas Clinton had no alternative, since already Lagg had drawn and brandished his pistol in a threatening fashion. Pulling on a coat, he led the party out into the wilderness of rough moor, horses and men stumbling in the darkness. As they proceeded the troopers taunted him to sing: an officer supported them, demanding that he sang the anti-Whig and anti-Covenanting song 'Awa, Whigs, Awa'.

As they drew towards Mayfield, the hills rising dark on all sides, Thomas Clinton raised his voice high, so that those within the house would hear it and take warning. His ruse succeeded. As the soldiers and officers burst into the house, they found it deserted, but showing every sign of a recent rushed departure. A large peat fire burned in the hearth, steaming bowls of brose lay on the table, sticks and caps and overturned chairs were strewn about the room. Immediately they rushed outside, but there was no chance of catching those who had fled in the foggy February night. Lagg decided to remain where they were, and begin a search at daybreak. One of the troopers threatened to run Thomas Clinton through with his sword for having given the warning, but was told to refrain, for he had been ordered to sing.

While they settled down for the night, Clinton made himself very useful, directing troopers to stabling for their horses, finding hay and blankets and peats. By the time they tumbled to his ruse, he was gone, vanished himself into the darkness.

The following day Lagg issued his instructions. Though the general direction of their travel was still towards Dumfries, the dragoons were instructed to spread out and search all the moors and glens in the vicinity.

On Kirkconnel Moor, only a mile to the east of Mayfield, five men were discovered hiding in the heather, just above a boggy hollow in a cleft of the hills. They were the men who had fled the previous evening: Andrew McRobert, James Clemet, Robert Lennox of Irelandton, David Halliday of Mayfield, and John Bell of Whiteside in Anwoth — the stepson of Lord Kenmure.

Grierson of Lagg behaved with even more than his customary ferocity. They had offered no real resistance, but their submission only seems to have fed his anger. When John Bell asked for fifteen minutes before they were put to death, Lagg replied: "Pray! What the devil! You wish to shrive yourselves now? Have you not had time enough to prepare since Bothwell Brig?" Drawing his pistol then, he shot John Bell in the chest, at which signal the other four were murdered on the spot.*

At Lagg's orders the bodies were not buried, but left where they lay, beneath the sky on the open moor.

Later they were carried down by friends. Andrew McRobert was buried in the churchyard at Twynholm; Robert Lennox at Girthon; David Halliday at Balmaghie; and John Bell at Anwoth. James Clemet (or Clement), a traveller and stranger, was buried on Kirkconnel Moor at the spot where they were killed.

Shortly after this Lord Kenmure encountered Lagg, in the company of Claverhouse, in the streets of Kirkcudbright, opposite the door of an inn. Kenmure accosted Lagg, bitterly reproaching him for his barbarity — not even allowing his kinsman decent burial, since apparently at that time orders had been issued that the bodies must rest where they lay. Lagg retorted brutally and with contempt: "Oh, take him yourself, if you please, and salt him in your beef barrel." Kenmure was so incensed that he drew his sword, and would have run Lagg through on the spot, had not Claverhouse drawn his own sword and promptly interposed himself between the two.

The flat, raised stone of Bell's grave in Anwoth Kirkyard is covered to the edges with a long verse recounting the events of his death. It begins:

> 'This monument shall tell posterity
> That blessed Bell of Whitesyde here doth ly,
> Who at command of bloody Lag was shot,
> A murther strange which should not be forgot.
> Douglas of Morton did him quarters give,
> Yet cruel Lag would not let him survive.'

It is a beautiful and famous setting, by Rutherford's ruined church,

* Lagg had often met Bell in society on equal terms, and apparently been friendly with him. Yet when Bell came before him as a Covenanter he was quite pitiless.

There are varying accounts of these events. In one, though Lagg gave the order to shoot and leave the bodies, he did not kill Bell with his own hand. In another the five were refugees hunted down following a disturbed conventicle in the moors nearby — possibly at Mayfield. Douglas of Morton promised them quarter, at which they surrendered. When they refused the Test, however, Lagg over-ruled him and they were shot.

with dark yew trees, daffodils and snowdrops growing wild in the spring, and the wooded and bracken-covered slopes rising nearby.

Today, threequarters of a mile up the moorland track from Kirk-connel Farm above Ringford, the grave of James Clemet may still be seen in the hollow, marked with a white stone two feet square, greened with lichen. Above the inscription the stone is embossed with a skull and crossed bones. Six feet away stands a fine granite obelisk, twenty feet high, inscribed with a tablet on each face. One tablet reads: 'Sacred to the memory of — their names and homes — who suffered martyrdom on this spot A.D. 1685 for their adherence to the Covenants and true Presbyterian Principles by that wicked persecutor Grier of Lagg'. On 11th September, 1831 — for nineteenth century romanticism was great-ly moved by the story of the Covenanters — ten thousand people gathered at this remote spot for an open air service at the unveiling of the memorial.* The area is walled on three sides, thirty yards square, with a lower fence fallen. The grave and monument are situated at the bottom of the slope, above a little bog, backed today by a jungle of wild rhododendrons and overshadowed by spruce and pine, with oak, lime, sycamore, rowan and tall larch growing nearby on the otherwise treeless hillside.

* The nineteenth century, more than a hundred years afterwards, interpreted the Covenanters in the light of its own romantic attitudes. The Covenanting move-ment was so apt, it might have been a fiction specifically created for the Victorians. Sir Walter Scott wrote of them considerably. One of his best-known characters was 'Old Mortality', a stone engraver, who went about the south-west visiting the graves of the martyrs, chiselling their inscriptions very deeply and erecting new monuments. He was a real character, Robert Paterson of Balmaclellan, whose wife looked after their family by teaching a school, while he roamed the countryside on a white pony, caring for the memorials. These and many other monuments, most of them nineteenth-century, are to be seen all over the south-west — Steven-son's 'Standing-stones on the vacant wine-red moors'. The very first piece of Stevenson's to be published, in fact, was a teenage account of the Pentland Rising. Our attitudes today are very much coloured by the strength of the Victorians' feelings, and the stories they resurrected.

Lammas Night[*]

It was Lammas night in Kirkmaiden and the harvesters were drinking late. Outside a summer storm flattened the uncut barley and tumbled the stooks on the stubble. The gusty showers rattled on the inn windows.

Talk was of witches and the Devil, and all that occurred on Lammas night when the hour reached twelve and the forces of darkness took over the land.

"Pity the man who is out in the storm this night," said a reaper.

"Aye," said another, "I wouldn't walk past the haunted hawthorn by the gate of the Maiden's Kirk† for a thousand pound."

"Ach, you're a lot of old women," cried young McCulloch, a spirited lad who had taken his fill of the drink. "I'll go to the old kirk for you, and be back within the hour — with the big kirk Bible for proof."

"No, no." A dozen heads shook at his headstrong notion. An old man put out a hand to pull him back to his seat. The youth pulled himself free of his grip and took another mouthful of the strong liquor.

"Within the hour!" he cried recklessly.

In the company that night there was a stranger, sitting in a nook just out of the circle of lamplight. He was listening to the talk with eager interest, laughing with the harvesters, his black eyes burning bright.

"I'll wager a golden guinea you are not back within the hour," he said.

Every head turned towards him.

"You're on," cried the young man. "A golden guinea it is." He reached out his arm and clasped the stranger's hand. The bargain was sealed. Flinging the plaid about his shoulders he seized his heavy stick and tossed off the last of his drink. The wind whirled through the room as he pulled open the door, then it shut with a bang and he was gone into the wild Lammas night.

A weight seemed to settle over the assembly with his departure. The laughter died, conversation became desultory. All minds were on the foolhardy youth running through the storm: all eyes kept turning to

* The first of August and traditionally the start of harvesting: formerly observed as a festival.
† The Old Kirk was three miles to the south, just above the eastern shore by the Mull of Galloway: half a mile north of St Medan's famous Chapel, Cave and Well.

the ancient wag at the wa', ticking out the seconds and minutes like the strokes of doom.

Then from the night, above the roar of the wind and the spattering of raindrops, came a sombre sound, the deep tolling notes of the wraith bell that rang for departing souls from the depths of Luce Bay. A man cried aloud, another spilled his ale: all shivered, wrapped in their knowledge of McCulloch's fate.

The fire crackled in the still parlour. The hour passed and the minute hand of the clock drew on. Their precognition became fact.

At last the stranger spoke again. "Who will venture with me into the storm? We must see what has become of him."

No man volunteered.

The stranger's eyes burned and caught a beam of the lamplight. "Will none come with me?"

They shook their heads doggedly and kept their eyes averted towards the fire.

Suddenly a blue flash and hiss of flame flared in the room and the stranger was there no more. Sulphurous coils of smoke curled from the nook where he had been sitting. In awful dread the harvesters remained rooted to the spot.

By morning the storm had passed, and in the early sunlight they ventured from the inn. Staying close together they walked down the muddy, puddled lanes towards the Maiden's Kirk. As they reached a bend and the kirk came into sight beyond the glistening hedges, the man in front stopped and gave a cry. They followed his pointing finger. There, caught in the branches of the haunted hawthorn by the church gate, was the body of young McCulloch. The branches curled about him like brambles. The heart had been torn from his breast.

On the wall by the gate they found the huge church Bible which he had laid down to pull the heavy gate shut behind him. In that unprotected moment the devils of the Lammas night had seized him, and after wreaking their dreadful pleasure, had wrapped his body, in place of a winding sheet, in the piercing thorns of the old haunted hawthorn by the church.

> 'An' certes, there are nane, I trow,
> That by Kirkmaiden bide,
> Will, when they hear the wraith-bell jow,
> Gae oot at Lammas tide!'

FOOTNOTE

A few hundred yards north of the Point of Lag, on the opposite, eastern shore of Luce Bay, stood the church of Kirkmaiden in Fernes, dedicated to St Martin. Here was the ancient burial ground of the McCullochs of Myrton. When this parish was united with Glasserton, the pulpit and bell were removed. The aim was to place them in the new church of Kirkmaiden (1638) which had been built in the village itself, near the Mull of Galloway. They were to be transported by water. As the boat carrying them was in the middle of Luce Bay, a strange storm blew up out of nowhere. The boat foundered, taking with it the pulpit and bell. As soon as they were gone the storm passed and the survivors were easily rescued. The reason for the storm was not hard to fathom. The bell had been consecrated by a bishop: clearly it could never ring in the bell-tower of a Presbyterian church. Yet ring it did. On the approaching death of any descendant of the McCullochs of Myrton, the wraith-bell (ghostly passing-bell) rang solemnly from the watery depths of Luce Bay.

(Clearly, since young McCulloch went to the old kirk and the bell was being brought to the new, in the union of these two legends there was some inconsistency, but it does not detract from the story.)

In awful commemoration of young McCulloch's fate, that ancient, twisted hawthorn was nicknamed 'Man-Wrap' by the people of the neighbourhood. For hundreds of years it was known by that name, even to the turn of the present century.

The concluding verse is taken from 'A Legend of Kirkmaiden' by David McKie.

The Troublesome Son

The proprietor of Park Place, Glenluce — now called Castle of Park — was having trouble with his son. There was little wrong with the boy, he was just high spirited and lacking proper respect for his father, the baronet. His mother, too, was having her problems with him.

One day the baronet gave his park keepers the order to cut down a stand of trees. A fine spreading oak, however, of which he was particularly fond and stood on a point of vantage, they were instructed to leave standing. The men carried out their task to the letter.

Shortly afterwards, however, the baronet's son, being as usual rather hard up, sold the tree to a timber merchant in the town. Before the baronet knew anything about it the sawyers had the tree felled, cut up, and transported away. When he found out he was furious, and not knowing who was responsible cried out that he wished the thief might never rest easy in his grave.

At the same time the boy's mother was driven nearly from her mind by his carrying on with her pretty cook. She did not know what to do. Finally, her warnings having been completely disregarded by the headstrong young man, and the saucy cook being too clever to be found out, she put poison in the young woman's beer and left it for her to drink on a shelf in the kitchen. Her son was out hunting at the time, and coming into the kitchen for a quick kiss and a cuddle, was gasping for a drink. Seeing the beer he swallowed it off at a long draught. In no more than a minute or two he was dead.

Shortly afterwards, during the night, the baronet was disturbed by a loud knocking at the heavily studded front door. He went to answer it. There stood the ghost of his dear, reckless son, with the ghostly trunk of the great oak tree across his shoulder.

Within a short time the boy's spectre, as troublesome in death as he had been in life, disturbed their nights so much that the baronet had to call on the help of the church. A young minister named Campbell, the son of a weaver from Campbell's Croft nearby, came and laid the young man's spirit to rest.

The Levellers

Against the poor the lairds prevail
With all their wicked works,
Who will enclose both moor and dale
And turn cornfields to parks.
The lords and lairds they drive us out
From mailings where we dwell;
The poor man cries, "Where shall we go?"
The rich say, "Go to hell."

From: 'The Levellers' Lines' — a ballad.

In the early years of the eighteenth century the landowners of Galloway began to see that all was far from ideal in their agricultural management. The agrarian revolution was gathering momentum: on progressive estates in England the enclosures were well under way. The proprietors of Galloway, many of whom had estates in other parts of the country, did not wish to lag behind the times. Here, as in most of rural Britain, the old feudal ways prevailed. Most of the estates were covered by a patchwork of small farms and crofts. The borders were vague, one estate mingling with another in an area of hundreds or thousands of acres of common grazing. Suddenly, in the light of the new thinking and projected profits, it was seen that even though tenants were desperately poor, their rents were disproportionately low. The profits being made from cattle were far beneath what they could be, with careful breeding and import from Ireland, fattening, and shipment to richer markets north and more particularly south.

It was not difficult, in physical terms, to adapt to these new and sensible ideas. Indeed they could be encompassed by two basic changes: a proper demarkation of private land; and larger farm units.

So labourers were engaged by the improving landlords — soon known as 'parking lairds' — to erect earth and stone dykes. Each estate was separated from its neighbours. Within the estates, on a much larger scale than formerly, arable fields were divided from pasture, and on the hill each proprietor enclosed his own rough grazing.

This had two crucial effects upon the cottars, crofters and small

243

farmers of Galloway. The common grazing, which immemorially had been a right, albeit unwritten, was at best split and at worst taken away from them: and the new farm units required fewer men. Families were evicted wholesale from their cottages and the small patches of arable land adjoining their homes, which for centuries had been carefully farmed and tended by their forefathers. Five, ten, as many as sixteen families were removed from a single estate. Where were they to go? Many emigrated, being among the first in the great exodus of the dispossessed, which was to swell to a flood by the middle of the following century. In Scotland the parallel cannot be avoided with what happened a hundred years later, as great landowners with similar ideals emptied the glens of the Highlands.

Understandably feelings ran high, and they were at a pitch in the early days of 1723, for on Whitsunday of that year many of the eviction orders were brought into force. Great hardship followed. There was no grazing for the animals. Many families had nowhere to go. They were hungry.

Six weeks or so afterwards, a number of the most forceful spirits and rebels gathered at the great Keltonhill Fair, two miles from the present market town of Castle Douglas — at that time only a little village called Causewayend. The fair was a famous gathering point for the south of Scotland. At a number of secret meetings in Rhonehouse, the nearby village, plans were drawn up to resist the landowners' selfish schemes, and particularly the building of more dykes to keep the tenant farmers and peasants from the common grazing. It was not to be a haphazard affair, but was organized with great care. Committees were formed, which met secretly to arrange matters and take decisions. The already dispossessed, those threatened with eviction, and their supporters, were divided into districts, mainly by parishes. Leaders, termed 'captains', were elected. In the drinking tents of Keltonhill Fair and the taverns of Rhonehouse, and later across the whole of the Stewartry, change-house orators stirred to anger the feelings of injustice. They sang such songs as 'The Levellers' Lines' — not great verse, but enought to inflame a poor man in an ale-house. And at their backs the cooler heads of the organisers shaped these feelings into action. They called themselves 'the Levellers'. They had much in common with their industrial brothers the Luddites, who ninety years later gathered in gangs to smash the machines of the new wool and cotton barons.

The captains were often men who had seen military service, and they prepared their forces with skill; assembling and drilling the crofters and farm boys, teaching them the rudiments of defence and attack, even engaging in rifle practice by moonlight on the hillsides.

Since it had been organised at Rhonehouse, it was in this district that the landowners of the Stewartry first felt the Levellers' power. More than a thousand men from the parishes of Kelton, Crossmichael, Tongland and Twynholm issued forth, sometimes together, sometimes in parties of fifty. The dykes fell. They smashed gates, and destroyed the carts and tools used by the dyke-builders. So accurately did they express the feelings of injustice and frustration throughout the country-

side that wherever they went they gathered followers. Parishes further afield — already involved through the Keltonhill Fair meetings — formed action committees, and the movement swelled. Soon they had cleared all the new dykes along the Solway coast from Kirkcudbright Bay to the mouth of the River Nith.

As they proceeded they developed the style and pattern of dyke destruction that was to become famous. It was — so far as the landowners were concerned, who had been to great expense to have the dykes erected — horribly effective. The men furnished themselves with strong poles, from six to eight feet in length, known as 'kents'. Stringing themselves along a length of wall, equal distances apart, they inserted the kents through the dyke a little distance from the ground. Then, at the loud cry of the captain, "Ower wi't, boys!" they heaved on the sticks, and with a crash, and a jubilant cry of triumph that might be heard for miles, the wall tumbled to the ground.

Having cleared dykes as far as Kirkcudbright, the local force marched on Kelton estate, which was then owned by a Captain Johnstone, whose high wall from the public road was one of their key objectives. Captain Johnstone was not an unjust man, and had built this unusually high and solid wall purely in the interests of improving his estate. Whether or not it had been his intention to remove certain families from the land, his hand was forced in the matter. Learning that the Levellers were marching upon him, he sought the advice and assistance of the minister of Kelton Kirk at that time, the Rev. William Falconer. At the advice of Mr Falconer, who read the men's hearts with a somewhat cynical accuracy, Captain Johnstone ordered great quantities of beer, bread and cheese to be brought to the Gallows Slot, near Lochbank, where the dyke began and where they planned to meet the Levellers.*

When the rebels had arrived and assembled, kents in hand, the minister addressed the gathering, assuring them that Captain Johnstone had not erected the great dyke for the purpose of subdividing his estate, but purely as a march-dyke from the main road. Further he promised them that Captain Johnstone had no intention of removing any family from its house or yard, and that they should continue to grow as much corn as formerly. Then the beer, bread and cheese were delivered to the hungry men. The wall was not thrown down, and before they departed

* The Gallows Slot was a corner of land below Furbar House, by the main road. Here, in unconsecrated ground, the people who had been hanged in Castle Douglas — often at the Three Thorns of Carlingwark — were buried.

Captain Johnstone was loudly cheered for his kindness. Mr Falconer, however, accompanied the Levellers to the end of the long dyke to be on the safe side.

Among the gangs and mobs of Levellers there was a certain robust cheerfulness, a reckless, even merry air. Behind them, however, came the 'Houghers', with a more vicious and cruel response to the same problem. They maimed and mutilated the landowners' animals, particularly the Irish cattle that had been imported. The Levellers did not seek to hide their presence: even though they might have marched to an objective silently, their ringing cheer as the dykes tumbled woke everyone in the district. The Houghers, however, with their axes, knives and clubs, worked quietly in the dark. Many landowners, having been undisturbed during the night and imagining that all was well, would find when daylight came that the Houghers had been at work, and their beasts lay maimed and dead in the fields. Most of the Levellers, of course, worked with animals, and their job entailed caring for them. They did not like the nocturnal butcheries of the Houghers, which spoiled the popular support they had in many quarters.

In Wigtownshire the movement commenced rather earlier than in the Stewartry, and on the very first night more than three miles of stone dyke were thrown down on the estate of Sir Alexander Maxwell of Monreith, who had erected a ring fence around the Fell of Barullion. In the Shire the method of toppling the wall was different. The Levellers used an instrument similar to a battering ram, which could overturn more than five yards at a stroke. There were, here as elsewhere, many skirmishes. During one fray, when the Levellers were attempting to overthrow the fences of a certain farmer for the third time, one of the rebels was killed. Several of those concerned in this affair were taken to court and imprisoned, and following it the authorities decided upon some sort of concerted action. The ministers of the district, upholding as customarily the rights of the landowners, threatened 'Death and Damnation' to all those who persisted in the destruction of gentlemen's property. Combined with civil powers it had the desired effect, and the activity of the Levellers, in that district at least, seems to have stopped.

In the Stewartry of Kirkcudbright, however, the Levellers became more and more bold, and their numbers increased. Troops of horse and dragoons were dispatched from Edinburgh and other parts to contain the uprising. In reply the Levellers carried weapons: clubs, scythes, pick-handles, swords, pistols, whatever they could lay their hands upon.

Indeed the tools of their nightly work — kents, pitchforks, gavelocks and spades — were weapons enough in themselves.

One of the leaders was Billy Marshall, King of the Gypsies,* an ex-soldier who commanded a troop of farmers, crofters and cottars, as well as his own tinklers. He it was who first took his men to practise the use of firearms on the hills by moonlight. He was a remarkable man. Here, as elsewhere on countless occasions, his genius allowed him to take personal advantage of the situation. While overthrowing the dykes for the benefit of all those assembled, he contrived to line his own pockets into the bargain. On Cairnsmore of Fleet, a great common grazing, where formerly only the Deil's Dyke† had run, the landlords were busy erecting many walls, and the labourers lived in bothies in sheltered corries on the mountain. Billy's tinkler followers, mainly at the cave known as McClave's pantry‡ and in shielings on the Stell Brae, were distilling raw spirit to sell to these men. With his Levellers he had to strike a fine balance, knocking down enough dyke to prevent them from enclosing the land, yet leaving enough standing so that the proprietors did not give in and dismiss the labourers, thus removing the market for his appalling whisky. At length, however, the landowners had had enough and the men were taken away. Shortly afterwards Billy was arrested and held captive by the dragoons, but through the assistance of a great friend, a private soldier in the regiment of Black Horse named Andrew Gemmels,° he was able to escape.

At Culquha, near Ringford, in the parish of Tongland, a great gathering of Levellers — the numbers are disputed, but there were certainly many hundreds — faced dragoons under the leadership of Captain O'Neil across the Tarff Burn. The soldiers were gathered a mile away at Barcaple. Considerable pressure was exerted that the dragoons should attack, and rout the illegal gathering. It was pointed out, however, that the Levellers were armed and arrayed very properly in military lines; that they were desperate, and were led by experienced soldiers. To attack must be to cause much bloodshed and greatly aggravate the

* See 'Billy Marshall — King of the Galloway Tinklers'.
† Also called the Roman Dyke or the Picts' Dyke. A great territorial wall, generally eight feet high, built in the time of Hadrian by the Niduarian Picts, and wandering through the hills and countryside from Loch Ryan to Annan.
‡ Named after a Covenanter who had hidden there from the dragoons forty years earlier.
° This soldier, in later life, was the man from whom Sir Walter Scott drew the character of Edie Ochiltree in his novel *The Antiquary*. In one of several skirmishes with the Levellers, he cut a man's ear clean off with his sword.

situation — not only in the surrounding district. Accordingly, several gentlemen and ministers, carrying a flag of truce, crossed the Tarff Burn to Culquha. They were correctly received, and after a number of fair promises had been made, the bulk of the Levellers dispersed.

The more extreme, however, refused to do so, and joining with groups from other parishes, confronted the dragoons again, at Duchrae, by Black Water of Dee, to the north-west of Loch Ken. This time battle was engaged, and the Levellers were soundly defeated by the dragoons. Although Captain O'Neil had instructed his men to use their swords, so far as possible, only for self defence, so fierce was the fighting that a number of the Levellers were killed. Throughout this whole period Captain O'Neil distinguished himself by his attitude of humanity and leniency towards the dispossessed men. For it he was much criticised by many landowners, who wanted them severely dealt with; but by his actions he seems certain to have avoided shameful bloodshed and contained the uprising exceptionally well. At Duchrae more than two hundred prisoners were taken, but on the return march to Kircudbright the sympathetic officers and dragoons rather pointedly looked the other way and a good number of them escaped. Those who reached the Tolbooth and were tried — the leaders among them — received only the sentences they must have expected: some were fined, others imprisoned, and some were transported to the plantations.

The end, or at least the beginning of the end, came in May, 1724, when a mob of perhaps two thousand attacked the fences of Galtways, on Bombie Moor, two miles south-east of Kirkcudbright. The ringleaders were captured by the dragoons and taken to the Tolbooth, where eight months later they were brought to trial and found guilty of having, 'in a most ryotous, tumultuous, and illegal way assembled and convened themselves with several hundred of other ryoters, mostly all armed with gunns, swords, pistolls, clubs, battons, pitchforks, and other offensive weapons'. That night on Bombie Moor they had thrown down nearly two miles of earth dykes, each rood of which cost eight shillings Scots to build. They were ordered, in reparation, to pay Lady Mary Hamilton, the proprietor, nearly eight hundred pounds Scots, and the ringleaders were sent to jail.

The severity of the fine and the imprisonment of these leaders finally quelled the spirit of rebellion that for more than a year had burned like a fire throughout the Stewartry. The work of enclosure and agricultural improvement continued with little further hindrance. The dispossessed — moving to other parts of the country, emigrating,

occasionally finding a vacancy on another estate, taking to the road —
managed as well as they were able.

Lucky Grier

Lucky Grier was a noted Galloway witch, from Hannaston in the Kells, a mile west of the Earlstoun Loch. Her powers were great: she drowned men by sinking a snail shell in the ale barrel in her kitchen, terrified people by appearing to them as a little naked boy in the night, sucked the cows in the shape of a white hare, turned herself into a cat walking on its hind legs, and many other such glamorous cantrips.

One evening, seeing that the cow of a neighbouring farmer had given birth to a fine calf, she thought to benefit herself from the rich dairy produce that must soon follow. So early the following morning she walked across to the farm and begged a burning peat from the fire to light her own hearth. The farmer's wife, anxious to keep on good terms with the witch, obliged her, and holding the smoking peat in an old pair of tongs, Lucky Grier hurried back to her cottage.

It happened that a travelling shoemaker who had stayed the night was busy in the barn that morning, and heard Lucky chuckling to herself as she hobbled along. Realising that something mischievous was in the air, he left his work and crossed to the farmhouse. He knew a little about witchcraft and immediately asked about the cow. Learning that she had calved a couple of days before, and seeing the churn full of rich creamy milk, at once he guessed what Lucky was about. Quickly he looked around the kitchen. His cobbler's wax was melting in a small pot on the fire and a tin basin stood in the hearth to take the balls of resin. He pushed the wax out of the way.

"Hurry," he said to the farmer's wife, "the old carlin's up to her tricks again. Fill the basin with spring water and I'll run out to the byre and shove a handful of sharn into the cow's mouth. Quick!"*

In little more than a minute they were back in the kitchen. The shoemaker took up the tongs from the hearth, and reaching into the fire pulled out a glowing peat. Standing back he plunged it into the basin of water. The clear water hissed and boiled and sizzled and the steam rose. Then great lumps of golden butter came rising to the surface, mouth-watering and creamy. Amazed and considerably frightened, the farmer's wife stared down.

"Just in time!" The shoemaker chuckled. "We'll have some rare fun now. Come on, follow me."

Picking up her skirts, the farmer's plump wife ran after him across the field.

Lucky Grier's cottage was built into the side of a hill. Softly the shoemaker pushed a strong stick through the latch so that it was jammed, then climbed up the hill and stepped gingerly out on to the sod roof. The farmer's wife followed him. Together they peered down the wide chimney through the fragrant peat smoke.

Lucky Grier was on her knees by the fire, muttering strange incantations over a battered and not very clean basin of water that stood beside her. The long strings of her greasy flannel cap trailed in the hearth. Reaching into the fire with a pair of tongs she lifted out the

* It is interesting to note that for centuries it was a common practice to put sharn (dung) into the mouth of a newly born calf to ward off the evil eye.

very peat she had carried from the farmhouse and plunged it into the basin of water. For a moment all was hidden in the clouds of steam. Then dreadful Gaelic curses and swears came raging up the chimney, and when the clouds had cleared they saw that instead of the butter which Lucky Grier had invoked, the water in the bowl was speckled with great lumps of cow dung, and even while they watched still more came bouncing to the surface.

The watchers on the roof shook with silent laughter.

"Eh, Lucky," the shoemaker called down the chimney, "it'll be grand on your sowens* the night. If I'm passing this way maybe I'll drop in for a crack and you'll gi'e me a dish."

For answer the witch shrieked and flew across the room, but the door was wedged shut. Her screams of anger and threats rose on the morning air as they retraced their steps across the fields to the farm.

Lucky did not forget, and that weekend when the shoemaker returned home, his wife greeted him with the news that their cow was desperately sick. At first he did not associate it with the witch, but when an old man most skilful with cattle could find nothing wrong with her, he realised in a sudden flash of intuition that Lucky Grier was at the bottom of it.

Very angry he went into his house and set a saucepan of water in the heat of the fire. When it was boiling hard he flung in a handful of pins.

"You keep that boiling," he said to his wife. "I'll teach yon old witch to meddle with me. When the pan boils dry, fill it up again, I'll not be that long."

Pausing only to light a lantern he left the house and made his way directly to Lucky Grier's, only a few miles distant. With little ceremony he knocked on the cottage door and let himself straight in.

"Well, Lucky," he cried cheerfully. "How are you the night? I just thought I'd look in for a crack on the way home. Have a plate of sowens, maybe."

The witch was clawing at herself feverishly with long dirty fingernails, every now and then screeching and twisting to pluck at some place newly stabbed by the boiling pins.

"Good gracious, Lucky," he said innocently. "What's this? Have you been down to England and got yourself the itch?"

So sharp was the pain that she could hardly piece her words together,

---

* A dish made by steeping and fermenting the husks, 'seeds', or siftings of oats in water, and then boiling.

but the threats she uttered were truly terrible. Suddenly, with a fearful scream, she writhed and fell to the floor in convulsions. At the same instant her bristling cat, squalling even more loudly, turned into a red-hot coal, then vanished in a flash of lightning, leaving a dark pall of smoke and smell of brimstone in its wake.

Not realising the violence of the spell he had made, the shoemaker ran away in terror. Lucky Grier's curses pursued him into the night. Before he had gone a mile he caught his foot in a branch on the road, fell headlong, and broke his arm. And when he reached home his wife greeted him with the news that half an hour earlier the saucepan had vanished up the chimney with a clap of thunder. A minute later the old man who had returned to look at the cow came running into the cottage in wild alarm. Suddenly, as if it had been pole-axed, the beast had dropped to the ground at his feet, stone-dead.

The shoemaker was furious with himself. So anxious was he to be revenged on the witch that he had forgotten to take the curse off his cow.

But things had gone far enough — too far. The following day, managing with one arm, he made a fine pair of soft slippers and presented them to Lucky Grier. Mollified by his beautiful gift the witch renounced her threats of revenge, and the feud was brought to an end.

The Coach with Blue Lamps

The cow-herd and his wife were very happy, for early that morning she had given birth to a beautiful baby son. In their little cottage at Auchneight, two or three miles to the north-west of the Mull of Galloway, she lay in bed and he busied himself about the house, looking after them and doing all the little tasks that normally fell to his wife. It was a joyful and even idyllic time. During the afternoon, alas, their peace was disturbed by a summons from his master, Sir Godfrey McCulloch. The herd was to go at once to Cardoness Castle, fifty miles away near Gatehouse of Fleet. By the time he had made all the necessary arrangements within the house and for his journey, darkness had fallen. Reluctantly he said goodbye to his wife and baby son.

It was Hallowe'en, but as he made his way through Kirkmaiden and up the lonely road by the eastern shore, his thoughts were not with the spirits of the night but the two he had left behind him. Soon he was at the crossing of the Grennan Burn, with the small gully beneath it, descending to the dunes and shingly beach of the bay. Looking out to sea he was surprised to see a blue light moving swiftly over the waves some distance from shore. He halted, watching. Soon he could make out that it was not a boat at all, but a tiny carriage drawn by six white

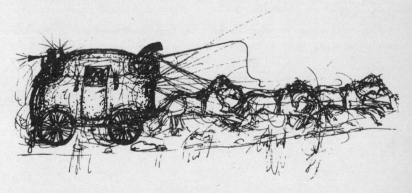

horses. Remembering the night and the fairy reputation of the spot where he found himself, he was frightened, yet stayed where he was to see more. The carriage came in to the shore and up the tumbling water of the burn towards him. Reaching the earth road it swung on to it and swept right past.

Within, he could see, the coach was crowded with elfin figures. The driver floated his whip over the backs of the fresh, snorting horses: blue coach lamps illuminated the road ahead with a pale and mysterious light. To either side outriders galloped past the young herd, so close that he could have reached out and touched them. There was the sound of laughter and high spirits, and a clear fairy horn rang out across the moors. The coach passed and soon was far down the road. Rounding a bend it was gone, and the laughter faded into the noise of the burn and the waves washing on the shore of Luce Bay.

Some time later the farmer of Barncorkrie, a mile and a half north of the herd's cottage, was astonished to see the troop of tiny horsemen riding in hot haste through the meadows a bow-shot from his door.

At a little before midnight the young mother was woken from her sweet sleep by the jingle of harness and trampling of horses outside. The sounds were accompanied by the chatter of clear voices. Terrified in the darkness, with only the moonlight on her curtains, she sat up in bed and took her baby in her arms. The door flew open and a throng of tiny figures dressed in green, with lanterns in their hands, poured through the entrance and gathered towards her bed. They were excited and did not for a moment cease in their pointing and chattering and laughter. Then one taller than the others and more richly clad, made his way to the front and held up his hand for silence.

Her hair falling loosely about her shoulders, the mother drew back to the wall.

"We have come for your child," the fairy addressed her in bell-like tones. "It is All Hallows Eve and we are riding. Come, let me have the boy."

He reached his arms towards her.

"No! Oh, no!" the young mother cried, distracted. "God forbid!"

Even as she spoke God's name the lights vanished, the room was deserted. All was quiet. A patch of moonlight fell through the open door.

St Ninian

According to tradition St Ninian, founder of the first Christian settlement in Scotland, was a Galloway boy. His father, chief of a tribe of the Novantes, was one of the first to be converted to the new beliefs — brought from Rome by the Roman soldiers garrisoned in the district, and wandering missionaries who in the first three or four centuries following the death of Christ had penetrated as far as Scotland. Roman influence in Galloway was generally very slight. Tertullian, however, observed that 'areas inaccessible to Romans are subject to Christ', indicating that from the first, in Britain as elsewhere, the missionaries were doughty travellers and messengers.

Ninian was born about 362 AD. He is reputed to have been a lively and intelligent boy, quick at the lessons which he took with some of the important local citizens and officers from a Roman tutor. By the age of ten he was reading both Gaelic and Latin fluently. More and more, as he grew to manhood, he was influenced by the teaching of Jesus Christ, and at about the age of twenty-three he left Galloway for Rome, armed with military passes and letters of introduction to help him on his way. Travelling by foot the journey took him six months.

He remained in Rome for ten years, first as novice and then as priest. In about 395 AD, being deemed ready, he was consecrated bishop by Pope Siricius, and shortly afterwards set out on his mission to Scotland to convert the southern Picts. For a year, on the return journey to his homeland, he remained in Tours with St Martin the great evangelist, whose belief it was that monasteries should be houses of light dedicated to spreading the word of God, rather than merely retreats for contemplation and study by the monks and priests themselves.

In 397 AD, he arrived back in Scotland, disembarking from his ship in what is now the harbour at the Isle of Whithorn in south Wigtownshire. There, on the headland overlooking the sea, assisted by continental masons who had accompanied him, he built his church, the first stone-built church in Scotland. While it was under construction, news arrived of the death of St Martin, and in memory Ninian named the church after his greatly admired friend and master. More commonly, however, the church was known as Candida Casa — the White House. The partially restored thirteenth century St Ninian's Chapel stands upon the same site, though no remains save those of an earlier twelfth century church have been discovered.*

The wild, windswept headland, however, was completely unsuitable for Ninian to establish his Celtic monastery. A spot was found three miles away, where now the country town of Whithorn stands. The fields were good for agriculture, the site was comparatively sheltered for that exposed part of the country. Here the great monastery was begun, a group of small, scattered buildings enclosed within a bank of earth or stones: a Christian settlement in a pagan land. The buildings were dry-stone, turf or wattled, and roofed with thatch or sod. Some were little bee-hive huts with corbelled roofs of stone. Among the monks' dwellings, guest-houses and barns, were a number of small wood or stone churches, some crosses, a library and a scriptorium, all built higgledy-piggledy as the years went by and the monastery was more firmly established and extended.

From the start the centre was a place of worship, learning, education — and evangelism. The monks and Ninian himself ventured forth on missionary journeys, dangerous in that wild countryside. He travelled not only throughout Galloway, but as far as the Central Lowlands and the east coast. To a remarkable degree he was successful. Bede reports that the southern Picts renounced idolatry and turned to the faith of Ninian. In later years missionaries from Whithorn were to travel to the ends of the country. Many churches were named after him. As far away as Shetland a Celtic church bearing his name was established in the sixth century.†

Occasionally Ninian, and the priests of the community, needed a

* There is considerable disagreement concerning the site of Candida Casa. One body takes the opinion that it was built upon the windswept headland, and in this they are supported by the writings of Ailred, Bishop of Rievaulx, who visited Whithorn as missionary in 1164. Others believe that there is no connection at all between the Isle and St Ninian himself, except the old pre-Roman fort where he may have lived for a short while. Candida Casa, they insist, was built within the walls of the great monastery at Whithorn — which is supported to a considerable degree by Bede's Ecclesiastical History of the early eighth century. A small dry-stone oratory excavated in recent years, which was found to be daubed with white plaster externally, ties in well with Bede's description, and may be the Candida Casa itself. According to those who take this view, it is most likely that St Ninian's Chapel was built on the headland eight centuries later, to provide a light for vessels at sea and those entering the Isle of Whithorn harbour, which by that time was quite important.

† Here it was, in the ruined church on St Ninian's Isle, that the beautiful silver treasure was discovered in 1958, hidden in haste from marauding Norsemen more than eleven centuries earlier.

retreat, and this they found in a cave four miles to the west of St Ninian's Isle, on the other side of Burrow Head. To this hermitage — twenty-five feet above a pebble and boulder beach, set in a cliff crowned with grass, and with a view along the sea-swept shore to further cliffs and hills — for centuries the monks went for solitude and contemplation and refreshment.* Also, perhaps for as much as a thousand years, the cave was used by pilgrims from all over Europe, right up until the late sixteenth century when such pilgrimages were banned. Many votive crosses were carved in the walls, not rediscovered, strangely, until a century ago. A sea-worn boulder was set below a trickle of water and carved into a washbasin, with a drainage channel. And a low wall was built across the entrance, with four steps descending to flagged floors: but these are later additions, possibly connected with the smuggling in Luce Bay a mere two centuries ago.

Though the cave is understandably renowned, most travellers were sheltered in the small guest cells and huts of the monastery itself. As the centuries passed, of course, accommodation improved, and many of the pilgrims were people of eminence. Robert Bruce, possibly then a leper, travelled to Whithorn shortly before he died. James IV made the pilgrimage frequently, twice or even three times in a year; and once on foot, when following the death of her first child his wife was not expected to live — she recovered. And of course Mary Queen of Scots was there in 1563.

When at the age of five, in August 1546, Queen Mary made the crossing from Scotland to France to join the Dauphin, her four-year-old husband designate, the blessing of St Ninian was invoked to protect her journey. And when after a shocking six day crossing — which the young queen alone seems to have enjoyed — her vessel finally put into Roscoff, a tiny chapel was built to St Ninian in thanksgiving for her deliverance. The old stone walls still defy the gales on that rocky coast of Brittany. Significantly, in view of Mary's marriage ten years later and the Auld Alliance, the chapel became known corruptly as the Chapelle de Saint Union. Until the present century the fishermen's wives of that part called upon St Union to protect their menfolk on the sea. They may do so even yet.

He became known as a guardian saint of Scotland also, under the names of Trinian (Treignan in France) and Ringan, as well as the more

* It is strange to note that it was near this cave that the Lindisfarne Gospels, oldest surviving English prose translation of any part of the Bible, were washed ashore towards the end of the ninth century.

familiar Ninian or Nynia. In the south-west, where many churches bear his name and his memory is revered, he became the patron saint to whom people appealed when they had lost things — private possessions or animals, and particularly sheep. It was a natural progression from his days of pastoral care.

As the word spread, St Ninian, growing old but still a vigorous evangelist, saw other churches springing up in the wilds of southern Scotland. When he died, traditionally on the 12th or 16th September, 432 AD, his body was laid to rest in his own Candida Casa.

For a time afterwards the remarkable missionary zeal slackened and faltered, and paganism flourished anew. Still at Whithorn, however, and in many of the churches, the Christian message glowed and lived.

A hundred and thirty one years after Ninian's death, in 563 AD, St Columba settled on Iona as a self-inflicted penance, and the missionary work was renewed with a drive and conviction that even the ruthless Viking raids could not crush. The great work of Ninian has been to a large extent eclipsed by the Iona community, and that is a pity. It is well to remember how magnificently St Ninian paved the way for St Columba — some of Columba's own tutors had been trained in Whithorn — and that without Whithorn there may well have been no Iona.

For twelve centuries the Whithorn community withstood the disruption of invasions, feuds and political change. Somehow, always, the work went on, the monastery continued. It took religious change to destroy the religious community: the Reformation reduced the living Priory of Whithorn to a relic. The pilgrimages were banned, the Latin service was banned, the number of monks declined, ideals were watered down to accommodate the new regime. The priory was gifted, with some dissent, to first one then another branch of the royal family. The last of the canons, increasingly aware of his income and the comforts of life, died shortly after 1590. And in 1605, along with its revenues, the priory was united with the bishopric of Galloway.

It was swamped in the floods of religious change that were sweeping Britain. Neglected, the priory buildings fell into decay. But by that time the great work was done.

Today, visiting the ruins of the priory at Whithorn, and the chapel on the bleak headland at the Isle, we can, in our minds' eyes at least, look back all those years to the dedicated missionary Ninian, who arriving in a largely heathen country, established his church and led Scotland forward into the light of Christianity.

The Yule Beggar

There is a tradition that St Ninian, in the name of Ringan, returns to Galloway every Christmas Eve. He reveals himself, however, only to simple, God-fearing shepherds, as the shepherds in the gospels, and as he himself sought to follow in the footsteps of Jesus.

It was Christmas Eve. The shepherd of a flock in a rural wilderness had gone away to a yule fair and left a young herd-boy in charge of the ewes. Alone in a wattled clay hut the boy looked out from the fire and saw that the short afternoon light was already fading. His master had left strict instructions that all the sheep must be in before dusk, for in those days they easily got lost, and wild animals sometimes killed them in the darkness. Also it was wintry weather and the snow might come. Pulling on a ragged jacket the boy went out into the cold afternoon to bring in the flock.

Soon he had them rounded up and safely penned for the night — all but one ewe. He searched and searched, remembering the shepherd's parting words, but he could not find the animal anywhere. The light faded, the last dark fires sank in the west. In the faint light that fell

from the evening sky through gaps in the cloud he searched on, fearing to let down his master.

At length, after hours of wandering in the darkness, filling his boots with icy bog water, scratching his face and hands on briars and the twigs of thickets, he stood once more by the little clay hut. Dejectedly he went in and sat by the side of the dying fire. His little crusie lamp flickered in the draught, throwing shadows on the rough walls.

After a while he stirred the embers into life and threw on a few twigs and some broken ends of peat. Smoke rose and filtered in the air before finding its way through the chimney and chinks in the roof. He pushed off the hard, broken boots and nursed his bare feet in the warmth. Soon the moon would rise. He would wait until then and go out again, but he had little hope of finding the lost sheep.

Then suddenly he thought of St Ringan's Well, which lay a little distance away. People often went there in time of trouble to enlist the saint's aid — sometimes people who had lost things. More than that, it was Christmas Eve: everyone said that Saint Ringan came back to Galloway every Christmas Eve. He paused — but a saint only helped proper folk, he wouldn't be interested in a ragged herd-boy like himself. And they always took him a gift. The boy looked around. He had nothing. All he possessed in the world were his few poor clothes and the bowl of kail brose he was to eat for his supper. It was hardly enough to offer a saint. Besides, he was hungry. Regretfully he realised that hungry or not, he must offer the brose to Saint Ringan. He just had to find the ewe, and he needed help.

The herd-boy warmed the bowl of brose at the fire, and carried it carefully through the darkness to the well. He set it down on the stone edge. Then he knelt, and fervently, though with an eye half open in case anything creepy happened, he begged Saint Ringan to help him find the lost sheep. When he had finished he stood up. Nothing had changed. He waited, looking around into the dark bushes. No bleat came to his ears. Through clear, widening gaps between the clouds, like tracks of water, the stars glittered frostily. A bitter breeze chilled his face and felt through his jacket. With a last, longing look at the dish of brose, the boy turned away and began to walk back to the hut.

He had not gone very far when he heard a little noise behind him. Turning, he saw a thin, ragged man sitting on the edge of the well, supping at his brose. The herd boy began to protest — he had left his supper for a saint, not this tattered beggar. Then charitably he thought that since Saint Ringan had not turned up, the poor hungry man might as well have it.

The beggar waved his spoon at the boy. "It's a grand night, laddie," he called cheerfully.

"I wish it was," the herd-boy replied dejectedly, coming back. "I've lost one of my master's ewes. Some wild animal will kill it during the night, or it will stray so that I'll never find it."

"Don't worry yourself," the beggar cried. "It's not so far away. You'll find it caught in a bramble bush — in the deep ditch beneath yon saugh trees that always bloom first in the spring."

The boy shook his head. "I won't. I've been along that ditch a dozen times, and it's not there."

"Well, that's where you'll find her."

The boy sighed. He could have done with more helpful advice than that.

In a while the beggar finished the dish of brose, and together they walked to the place he had described.

To the shepherd boy's astonishment there was the ewe, caught in the thorns near the bottom of the ditch, its wool screwed up so tightly in the brambles that it could not move. He scrambled down through the tangled vegetation until the verge was high above his head. His boots went through the cat-ice into the water and mud. But no matter how he tugged and tore his fingers on the thorns, the boy could not release it.

The thin beggar joined him deep down in the cold ditch, and somehow together they pulled the wool apart, broke off the bramble stems, and hauled the animal up to the grassy brink. But the sheep was so far gone with exhaustion and cold that it could not stand, and slumped to the ground when they released it.

The boy was not yet strong enough to carry it, and looked down at the forlorn beast. "I doubt it will die here, anyway," he said, not far from tears. "I don't know how to get it home."

For answer the beggar bent, and catching the sheep by the legs slung it around his shoulders. Side by side they returned to the little clay hut and set the tattered animal down by the still glowing fire.

"Will you not stay here the night?" the boy said. "It's cold outside. I have nothing more to eat, but you're welcome to the fire."

"Thank you, laddie," the beggar replied. "It's a kind offer. But I must be on my way, or I'll be late."

"Late?" exclaimed the boy. "But where are you going at this time of night? It's nearly midnight."

263

"Where? Why, Bethlehem, of course! Where else would I be on Christmas night?"

The herd-boy was bending for a handful of sticks for the fire. When he looked up in surprise at the words, the beggar was nowhere to be seen. Quickly he crossed to the entrance and stared out into the cold night. The beggar had gone. But there, by the rising moon, was a glittering pathway that led from the poor doorway of the little clay hut, straight to the east.

This story was originally told by an old lady named Janet Tait, born in 1827, a field worker, latterly crippled with age and confined to her tumbledown cottage, a mile from Castle Douglas. She was a lively, good-living woman, with bright blue eyes, and a great fund of tales from the old days. The events in this story would have occurred some time around 1580. The shepherd lad, as an old, old man, had told the story to a boy who was Janet Tait's ancestor — her grandmother's father's grandfather, to be precise. The story was passed down through her family for something in excess of two and a half centuries.

In 1580 Castle Douglas did not exist. The first village was not established on the site for over another century. All was wild country. The nearest clachan was at Buchan's Croft, half a mile from the present market town along the shore of beautiful Carlingwark Loch.

The shepherd boy's hut stood somewhere near the west of today's small town. St Ringan's Well, I believe — there are several in the southwest — stood very close to the entrance to Castle Douglas Golf Club. It may be the well which is still to be seen in the club practice ground. The ditch where the saugh trees bloomed first in spring lies two hundred yards further on. Until the First World War it was steep-sided, wild and overgrown, ten feet deep. It has since been drained and half filled with earth, and is now a dry bunker running across the middle of the third and fourth fairways.

Ninian's Pasture

Though the early monks of Whithorn were given a certain amount of food, for the most part they had to grow their own. They tilled the earth to produce corn and vegetables, they herded cattle and sheep and goats. Most of the land was unfenced and unhedged. Often they grazed the animals several miles from the monastery, where the grass was richer. To guard them from thieves and wild creatures, and prevent them from straying, the herdsmen had to stay with their animals all night.

One evening Ninian walked to the grazing ground, some distance from Whithorn, where he knew the flocks and herds were pastured. He summoned the monks to bring all the cows, sheep and goats about him. When they were settled, cropping the grass and bushes, occasionally lowing or bleating, he raised his hand and blessed them all, beasts and men. Then, with his staff, he traced in the turf the outline of a large pasture in which the animals should be penned for the night. His monks were tired and needed a rest. God, he assured them, would see that the beasts remained within the boundaries he had drawn. They would be safe.

Gladly the monks accompanied him to the house of a good woman not far distant, who had offered them food and shelter for the night.

By moonlight, while the monks slept, robbers found the cattle, sheep and goats untended, and crossed Ninian's boundary to drive them away. No sooner had they done so, however, than the bull of the herd, normally a peaceable animal, snorted and stamped with its hoofs on the ground, so hard that deep prints were made in the solid rock.* Then it attacked them angrily and fiercely, and catching the leader gored him to death.

In the morning, as usual, Ninian and the monks rose early. When they reached the herds they found the robbers running wildly about within the boundary marks as if they were insane. At the sight of the saint they cried out as though they were possessed, and fell at his feet, trembling in supplication and fear.

A little way off lay the body of their leader, his entrails torn out and the grass about him red with blood. Ninian was distressed to have been, even though unwittingly, the cause of the robber's death, and prayed fervently that he might be restored once more to life. For a time God was obdurate but at length he relented. The man was healed and sat up in the grass, wondering what had happened.

Ninian gently reproved them all, showing the punishment that awaited a robber. Then he dismissed them with a blessing. The man who had been gored to death underwent a complete conversion, and became God's faithful servant to the end of his days.

* For many years this place was remembered in the Saxon as 'Farres Last' — the Bull's Mark. Unfortunately the location of St Ninian's Pasture and Farres Last is now unknown.

The Groom of Arbigland

Arbigland, the fine estate on the Solway coast by Kirkbean, is famous principally because John Paul Jones, naval hero of the American Revolution, was born in the gardener's cottage in 1747. About the same time, however, a daughter was born to William Craik, the owner of the estate, and some years later a romantic and tragic story attached itself to this young lady.

The Craiks were a wealthy and landed family of Dumfries and Cumberland merchants, who in 1679 had bought the estate of Arbigland. Quite the most prominent of the line from then onwards was William (1703-1798). In common with other members of his family he was a great agricultural improver: among other projects, for example, his estate workers transformed four hundred acres of barren water-logged clay into good fertile land, a task that took forty years. He built the new Church of Scotland at Kirkbean; he engaged Robert Adam, the most distinguished architect of the age, to build the fine mansion house that still graces the gentle Arbigland slope; it is a fair assumption that he was profitably engaged in the smuggling trade during its most lucrative years; he was a distinguished figure in Dumfries and Galloway society; and he lived, lord of all he surveyed, to the age of ninety-five.

It was not to be tolerated, therefore, when his daughter Helen, possessed of all the advantages of her station, fell in love with one of the Arbigland grooms.

He was a young man by the name of Dunn, pleasant and attractive, of fine physique and good manners, but in those days, of course, hopelessly beneath his mistress in social position. Though the details are unknown, it is believed that she was some years the older.

There could have been no happy outcome to the attachment. Even if he had been sympathetic, William Craik could not have given his blessing for the sake of family honour. The mores of society were completely against it. If they had run away together, the young man would have found it impossible to obtain a suitable position without references, and Helen Craik would have been regarded almost universally as a fallen woman. The situation was hopeless.

During the days and months before her family knew, the poor woman's love must have been woven with great anxiety and distress. By its very admittance it must have been overwhelming, a complete fixation on the young groom.

For him the situation was quite different. He may have loved her, he may have taken advantage of her, he may foolishly have hoped to gain advancement through her, or he may innocently have found himself caught up in something beyond his control. However it was, his situation and livelihood were in daily jeopardy.

When the Craiks found out — William the figurehead, his hot-blooded sons, and the thoroughbred women of the household — what scenes there must have been. So dramatic an outcome, however, can hardly have been expected.

One day a single shot was heard, a little distance from the house. It was investigated and the lifeless body of the young groom was discovered lying at a place known as the Three Cross Roads, a wooded spot a few yards from the gates of Arbigland. He carried a brace of pistols — possibly because he was engaged in carrying valuable mails to Dumfries, for William Craik, of course, was a wealthy merchant. One of the pistols lay beside him.

The sheriff investigated the affair, and after what seems the most cursory enquiry, confirmed what William Craik and his sons had claimed from the beginning, that Dunn had died as the result of a shot from his own pistol when he was thrown from his horse at the cross-roads. Popular local opinion, however, had it otherwise. It was claimed that the young man's pistols were still loaded when he was found. Undoubtedly, it was believed, Dunn had been shot by Helen's brothers: in revenge, to eradicate the blot on their family honour, and to end the affair. William Craik himself attempted to laugh the whole thing off, and it seems likely that the sheriff did not press beyond the bounds of what the influential landowner told him and wished him to believe.* There are no family records (these vanished when the last of the Craiks left Arbigland for Holland in 1852, where it is believed they died of fever), and certainly the affair never came to court.

Local memory, however, remained strong: and popular conviction of the Craiks' guilt was reinforced when almost immediately afterwards Helen Craik left Arbigland and went to live with relatives on the family's older estate at Flimby, due south across the Solway on the Cumberland shore.

* In another version of the tragedy there is no mention of horses or an accident. The young groom is said to have been shot by a single brother who left the discharged pistol on the ground beside him. The law was encouraged to the view that he had committed suicide due to the hopelessness of his passion.

The young groom, alas, found no such escape from the scene of his murder. His ghost is said to have haunted the Three Cross Roads, just beyond the fine curving gates of Arbigland, for many years afterwards.* The figure of the handsome young servant was a well-known local apparition.

* It is interesting to note that the gates of Arbigland were built by Allan Cunningham, a Dumfriesshire stone-mason, at the age of twenty-one. Cunningham, later a distinguished poet and author, is probably best remembered for 'A wet sheet and a flowing sea' and his collections of Scottish song.

Legends Surrounding the Death of Grierson of Lagg

Sir Robert Grierson of Lagg is notorious in the annals of Galloway for his ruthless hunting down and persecution of the Covenanters during 'the killing time' of the 1680s. So hated was he that a number of unnatural and diabolic stories have grown up surrounding his death.

The latter part of his life was spent in Dumfries, in a house known as the Turnpike, which was distinguished by a remarkable spiral staircase. It stood facing the High Street at the head of the Turnpike Close, about two hundred yards from the River Nith.

Sir Robert had lived well, and as he drew towards his last days he was tormented by the gout. So acute was his distress, it was said, that relays of servants were posted to pass buckets of water from one to the other from the Nith, up the streets, and up the spiral staircase to his room. And as he lowered his feet into bucket after bucket, the water began to hiss and boil.

On the 31st December, 1733, he died. So corpulent had he grown during his last illness that his body could not decently be carried down the winding staircase, and a portion of the wall had to be removed to accommodate it. But at length he was laid in his ample coffin.

The funeral procession prepared to leave his house, but as the coffin was laid on the hearse a corbie flew down and perched upon it, black as night, and as saucy and as confident as could be. Bystanders were appalled and even the funeral party were not too happy about it. Attendants waved at the bird to fly away, but it would not, and ambled up and down the polished wood. Only after extreme measures were taken could they make it quit the coffin. Even then, however, the bird did not depart, and accompanied the black funeral procession all the way to the graveyard at Dunscore, eight miles to the north-west.

But the journey was not completed without further difficulty. The horses that were drawing the hearse had little more than started when their progress became slower and slower, as if the coffin had become an impossible weight. On the banks of the Nith, not a quarter of a mile from home, they came to a dead stop. Though they were thrashed to struggle and foam, they could not move the hearse any further. At this

Sir Thomas Kirkpatrick, a relative and comrade of Grierson who was said to have moved deeply among the black arts, grew angry and took charge. With a great oath he swore that he would drive the hearse with his own hands and get it to Dunscore even though the Devil himself was in it. Then he ordered a magnificent team of Spanish horses to be fetched from his own stables at Closeburn, a dozen miles away to the north. The townspeople of Dumfries gathered with curiosity. The funeral party waited while grooms fetched the horses and harnessed them to the hearse. Mounting into the driver's seat, Sir Thomas whipped them forward. Instantly the beautiful team broke away in a mad, head-long gallop that he was completely unable to control. Behind them the hearse leaped and bucketed over the potholes until the coffin sprang right in the air. As if they knew the way without his guidance the gleaming chestnuts fled hell-for-leather through the town, then out along the country roads, mile upon mile to Dunscore. Reaching the graveyard gates they slithered to a sudden halt, lathered in sweat. Then, still in the traces, one after the other they fell to the earth dead.

That same day a small lugger at the mouth of the Solway was fighting its way towards the Galloway shore against a wild north-easterly wind. Darkness fell and the moon showed through black ragged clouds, hurrying across the sky. Far astern one of the seamen saw another vessel, as he thought, making up-channel after them. But where they were tacking to and fro and making heavy weather of it, this vessel came rushing on, racing across the wild waves. The moon went behind a cloud and for a while it was lost from sight. When the moon re-appeared the crew of the lugger found themselves staring at the strangest vessel that ever took to the water. For it was not a ship at all, but a great state-coach, midnight black, drawn by a team of six splendid jet black horses. The driver lashed them forward, coachmen rode behind, with outriders, torch-bearers, footmen and a great company of followers, all driving furiously through the foaming waves. Soon it was abeam and drawing past them at a rattling rate. One of the seamen, gathering his courage, put his hands to his mouth and called, in sailor fashion, through the storm: "Where bound; where from?" Clear and distinct across the wild night waters came the reply: "Dumfries from Hell — to tryst with Lagg!"

Smuggling in the Solway

Good healthy smuggling, like poaching, is an occupation almost universally smiled upon by those not engaged in the upkeep of the law. There is an air of breezy adventure about it, a reckless challenge of the individual against the oppressive and ever-increasing demands of the state. Never was the practice more universally engaged in than during the eighteenth century along the lonely and rugged northern shore of the Solway.

There were several reasons for the sudden mushrooming around that time. Principal among these in 1725 was the imposition of a tax of six-pence a bushel on malt, construed by the ale-drinking and very poor population as a great injustice. This led to a decline in the consumption of malt-based drinks, and a wild counter-swing towards other, more potent liquors. These too were heavily taxed, but it was found not too difficult to bring them into the country illegally from the Isle of Man, which of course was not subject to the same laws as the rest of the British Isles, and at its nearest point only twenty miles south of the Wigtownshire coast. There were rich markets for duty-free goods in Edinburgh and Ayrshire and the towns of the Clyde valley. It was not to be wondered, therefore, that the poor crofters and farm workers of Galloway turned enthusiastically to this new means of earning a living, and a much better living than they had hitherto enjoyed.

At the height of the trade it is true to say that almost the entire population was involved somewhere along the line, even if it was just an old woman who turned a blind eye to the borrowing of her horse, but knew well enough where to find the half dozen bottles of brandy pushed into the bottom of a haystack; or the boy who declared that his father had been repairing a harness by the fire the previous night, when in fact he was absent. Ministers, even, were sometimes up to the neck in it. It is said that Mr Carson, minister of Anwoth, was dismissed his charge on account of his involvement, though the very opposite is the more telling truth. Mr Carson was one of the few who disapproved of the smuggling and seems actively to have interfered, for two trumped-up charges of seduction and immodest language were brought against him. Thus, for a time at least, the smugglers removed him from their midst.

The principal commodities were those items in great demand which bore a heavy tax. Among them were tea, tobacco, lace and salt (which at that time carried an almost prohibitively heavy duty), and of course brandy, gin, rum and wines. They were brought from the Americas and the continent to the Isle of Man and there discharged. Then, when arrangements had been made, they were transhipped to the mainland either in small open sailing boats known as 'scouts', or certain other vessels up to heavy luggers armed with as many as twenty-two guns and carrying crews of around fifty. Some ships sailed directly from continental ports, though these more likely landed their cargoes further south. Often the luggers were swifter than the revenue cutters which sought to restrain and capture them, and the smuggling skippers better seamen than the naval officers.

News of a vessel's landing place and cargo travelled ahead, but it was often impossible to say when it would arrive. A watch was kept on the shore, sometimes for weeks, by men and boys posted in quiet lookout spots. When the vessel was sighted a series of prearranged signals was exchanged — to verify the vessel's identity, ensure that the coast was clear, pass on the need for more horses since the cargo was greater than anticipated, and other such important information. The signals from the shore were of many kinds. In place of the customary showing and flashing of a lantern, there might be a small straw fire beside a barn, a man repeatedly striking a light for his pipe, a blacksmith releasing a shower of sparks from his chimney in a certain succession — signs that would be construed as innocent by any lurking militia.

Having received the all-clear, the smuggling vessel pulled in to the appointed cove. All along the Solway shore, from the Mull of Galloway to Annan, the names coined in those days still remain: Crow's Nest, Dirk Hatteraick's Cave, Manxman's Lake, Frenchman's Rock, Adam's Chair; and the names of spots that will ever be associated with the smugglers: Pan Bay, Luce Bay, Abbey Head, Heston Island, Raeberry Castle, the Bay of Fleet, and so on, for mile upon mile. Sometimes, if the vessel was a small scout, only a couple of men were there to greet it as it drew up the muddy creek. At other times crowds assembled on the sands or barnacled rocks, and for hours the shore was a scene of bustling activity.

Usually the goods were hidden, waiting for full arrangements to be made before they were taken inland. The shore is indented with count-less caves, some of which can only be entered by boat or at low tide, while others are hidden among thickets and half-way up steep rock

faces. Dirk Hatteraick's Cave on the Ravenshall shore is a famous example, a narrow crack dropping, it seems, into nothingness, yet there inside is a floor of dry sand, with racks of square pigeonholes rising above to take the contraband bottles. Hundreds of these caves were used at one time or another. The cargoes were also stored in cellars, with concealed and more important cellars directly beneath. They were hidden in haystacks, sunk in the sea, buried on the moors, left in the middle of barley fields, secreted in thickets and woods, even on one occasion whisked into bed by a farmer's daughter who pretended to be very ill. Every *Whisky Galore* device and ingenuity was adopted. Some of the larger smuggling concerns took coastal farms, on which it might be observed that the crops were not particularly good considering the number of men who were always about the place. Great Solway land-owners with their cellars full and ships drawing up below the house, entertained customs officers with dinner and excellent contraband brandy, and if there was a gaffe the guests turned their attention more closely to the woodcock, for they were not fools.

The military were the principal enforcers of the law, for at that time the preventive officers were very few, due to the shortage of both men and money. There were so many miles of remote and wild coast, how-ever, so many hidden bays and creeks, that it was impossible to police them more than sketchily. Add to that the universal support that the smugglers enjoyed, and their job was in the long run hopeless. Those they did capture, and there were many, were commonly taken to Edinburgh for trial, since in Wigtownshire, at any rate, it was almost impossible to obtain a conviction.

The quantity of contraband discovered in a hiding place was often considerable. Six tuns of Jamaica at Garlieston, five casks and a dozen hogsheads at Port Mary, a hundred quarter hogsheads of brandy at Fleet Bay, were quite common entries in the excise reports. In a subterranean cellar on the Wigtownshire farm of Clone, a revenue party discovered 200 bales of tobacco, nearly 1200 gallons of brandy, 80 chests of tea, and other goods. It paid the officers to be vigilant, for the prize money was good. For this haul at Clone the officer in charge received £269, the sergeant £42, the corporal £28, and even the private soldier £14, a worthy sum of money in those days. The excise officials enjoyed an even greater share. And at the other end of the legal rope, of course, they received bribes from the smugglers to turn their heads the other way, delay a search, or overlook an inadvertent discovery.

Sometimes, feeling unjustly treated by a small seizure and fully aware how vulnerable the authorities really were, the smugglers struck back. In Ruthwell a hundred women broke open a storeroom and carried off their precious cask of brandy: in Glencaple the revenue officers were given a beating: in Annan a crowd of smugglers and their friends mobbed the magistrates and collectors to seize back four casks of brandy.

The goods were transported to their markets in as many ways as there were means of transport. A farm girl was sent across the hillside in the early morning with a couple of buckets on a yoke to buy some salt; a carter carried barrels through the town beneath a load of straw or grain; packmen set off walking through the quiet hills to Edinburgh with their packs full of tea and covered with a little oatmeal for sustenance on the way; a string of twenty ponies, slung with bales or barrels, wended its way along little frequented tracks in the dark of the night; a great chain of a hundred, and even two hundred horses, accompanied by an army of lawless tinklers, rattled and whinnied in broad daylight through the glens and hills, too powerful a force for the redcoats and excisemen even to think of challenging. In 1777 a smuggling train of 210 laden horses, accompanied by half that number of lingtowmen, passed openly within one mile of Wigtown, defying the revenue officers and more than thirty soldiers. A boy who watched them pass, and may have followed them for some distance, remembered that four horses dropped dead in the road through the exceptional heat of the summer day, combined, it was said, with the heady fumes of the tobacco they were carrying.

The 'lingtowmen' were the smugglers who accompanied these strings of horses, so named because of the 'lingtow', or rope, which they used to tie up the burdens and at other times wore bound about their waists or shoulders. Often they were tinklers and their clans ruled the hills and moors that lie above the coastal farmland.*

There are countless stories of sea chases and pursuits along the shore, of excisemen outwitted and taken captive, of adventurous death and lighthearted roguery. A number of these, telling of individual escapades, follow this account.

Socially, however, there is a different tale to tell. Naturally the poor people were glad to supplement their incomes, but so hard was the work upon the land for a bare subsistence, and comparatively so easy the money to be obtained by joining the smugglers, that it demoralised those who had hitherto worked steadily and somehow got along — an

* See 'Billy Marshall — King of the Galloway Tinklers'.

275

interesting parallel to the effect of the big money that is to be made in certain industries today. The small farmers and labourers lost respect for their work and neglected it. There was a marked change in many districts from a community which of necessity had always been industrious and law abiding, to a lesser community which survived by breaking the law and substituted long periods of idleness for days of steady labour. The story is told of a traveller who seeing so many men lounging about a village asked what they all did: "We smuggle a little," he was told. In addition there was always plenty of drink around, not the harmless ale which their forefathers had brewed or bought and drunk since time immemorial, but wines and fiery spirits. The combination of the two, idleness and alcohol, naturally led to an enormous increase in drunkenness and dissipation.

Also it must be remembered that human nature is not always sunny. Some of the smugglers were villains and desperadoes; others became so. There were those who had known jail, and many had lost cargoes. Among them resentment smouldered: they did not intend it to happen again. None wanted to be caught.

Thus there were two sides to those smuggling days: the daring spirit of risk and adventure with its attendant generosity and good humour; and the darker desperate aspect of violent resistance to the law, bloody reprisals and moral degeneration.

As early as 1670 a number of Liverpool venturers settled at Douglas in the Isle of Man, with the set intention of starting up a trade in contraband with the British mainland. Their offers were so tempting that soon ships were discharging there in preference to their home ports of London or Bristol. In 1725, as we have seen, the activities of the smugglers, by now firmly established through any number of contraband agents, were greatly assisted by the imposition of the malt tax. The trade continued to flourish: while desirable goods were heavily taxed there was a ready market. In the 1770's smuggling was given a further boost by the levying of still heavier duties, to pay the costs of fighting the American War of Independence. During the last quarter of the century the trade was at its height. Smuggling companies were established in which otherwise respectable gentlemen were able to purchase very profitable shares. They were the golden years.

The end, or the beginning of the end, came in 1806 when William Pitt the younger greatly reduced the tax on many smuggled goods. This meant that prices fell and smuggling became generally unprofitable, since legitimate traders could challenge contraband goods in fair competition. At the same time much more stringent laws were passed against the smugglers. Their boats were confiscated. Signalling from the shore was made a penal offence. The military force was strengthened. Lookout and signalling stations, customs posts and substantial barracks were established along the coast. Much of the smugglers' success had been due to the remoteness and wildness of the region. The road was a potholed morass with fords impassable in wet weather. In 1760 the 'old' military road was started, driving through from Dumfries to Portpatrick with a hard surface and fine bridges, opening up the Stewartry and the Shire. Faster, more powerful revenue cutters known as 'preventive boats', capable of overtaking and capturing the armed luggers, were stationed in strategic harbours. And when the smugglers were captured there were more severe penalties — three years hard labour, or for the strong young men five years compulsory service in one of the king's men of war. Taken in hand, most of them made fine seamen.

By 1830, save for a few small luggers that continued trading up and down the west coast well into the reign of Queen Victoria, the days of the smugglers were over.

Captain Yawkins

Captain Yawkins, the prototype of Dirk Hatteraick in Sir Walter Scott's *Guy Mannering*, was undoubtedly the most famous smuggling skipper of them all. His seamanship was superb — he was admired even by the naval officers and British seamen whom he so often outsailed and out-manoeuvred. It was said that he had sold his soul to the Devil in exchange for the safety of his vessel, which was called the 'Black Prince' in honour of the deal. So often was he in scrapes that led to bloodshed that some claimed the Devil's dues were not Yawkins' soul but the tithe of his crew every trip. He was a business associate of Billy Marshall, King of the Galloway Tinklers, and often, it was said, they sat yarning on boxes or kegs on the dry sandy floor of what is now known as 'Dirk Hatteraick's Cave', near Ravenshall Point, and shared a few glasses broached from a cask of Yawkins' best quality brandy.

On one occasion, while discharging a cargo in Manxman's Lake, three miles up the narrow Kirkcudbright Bay, he was surprised by two revenue cutters, strangely named the 'Dwarf' and the 'Pigmy', which entered the bay together, one from the east and the other from the west. Side by side they bore down upon him, priming their carronades

— short, large-calibre ship's guns. Instantly Yawkins ceased discharging and weighed anchor. Piling on the sails he headed straight down the bay for the open sea. But this time it seemed they had him: whether he passed to port or starboard in the muddy channel he must take a damaging broadside as he came abeam. At the last second, however, he jinked course, and slipped between the two cutters like an eel through the neck of a bottle, so close that he was able to fling his hat on the deck of one and his wig on the deck of the other. Then, to show still further his contempt for their challenge, he hoisted an empty cask to the masthead and bore away under full canvas past little Ross Island and out into the Solway, showing the cutters a clean pair of heels, for the 'Black Prince' with Yawkins in command could outsail the fastest of them.

The Manx Bridegroom

On the eve of his wedding day a spirited young man from Ramsey on the Isle of Man determined to run a few bags of fishery salt across the Solway, where he knew there was always a ready market. He went against his family's advice, but the profits he thought would help to pay for the wedding feast, which they could ill afford, and a few articles for the house. It was to be a surprise present for his bride. He was accompanied by one man only, the bride's brother.

A fair breeze and gentle sea gave them a good crossing and their patched little scout was nearly to Heston Island when they were suddenly ordered through a loudhailer to stand to. The command came from the cutter 'Prince Ernest Augustus' which had been anchored out of sight in Balcary Bay. Pretending to misunderstand or not hear the order they continued innocently on their course for Port o' Warren, a noted landing place for contraband. They had gone only a matter of yards when without any further warning a shot was fired from the cutter, which was quite close at hand. It struck the young groom in the breast. He was dead even before he slumped into the bottom of the boat among the bags of salt.

Stunned at the tragedy and terrified for his own life, the bride's brother ran for the nearest point of land below Rockliffe, and deserting the little scout took to his heels inland. Behind him, bearing down fast, came the 'Prince Ernest Augustus'. Reaching the shore the sailors dismissed the fugitive as just another smuggler and did not pursue him. Tipping the groom's body out on to the sand, they ran a line to the scout and towed the few bags of contraband salt to the Custom House in Kirkcudbright.

Local people, having heard the shot and seen the chase, hurried down to the shore. Shortly afterwards, when no-one came to claim the young man's body, they buried him by the edge of the sea, where one

or two drowned seamen had on another occasion been buried by them. Later, under a warrant from the sheriff, his body was removed to the churchyard at Colvend nearby.

When the survivor reached home, long after the wedding day, the dead man's father was distracted with grief. It was decided that the body must be brought home to the graveyard of Kirk Christ Lezayre. If permission could not be obtained, then they would retrieve it secretly. The bride's brother accompanied them despite some danger to himself, and the bride insisted on going as the chief mourner.

It was a sad group of relatives and friends that sailed across the Solway to Colvend. They had no difficulty with the magistrates, and soon the young man's body was raised from the grave and laid in the bottom of the boat. Though the weather was bad they set sail once more for Ramsey. Alas they never arrived. Even before they reached Heston Island, where the young groom had been shot, their boat was overwhelmed by the sea and the entire funeral party was drowned.

Sir John Reid, commander of the 'Prince Edward Augustus', was summoned before the High Court in Edinburgh on a charge of murder for this event, but he was acquitted. For many years the first burial place of the young Manxman, beneath the farm of Glenstocken, was pointed out just above the shore.

Big Maggie

One fine morning a party of three or four smugglers pulled their boat into Dally Bay, three miles south of Corsewall Point on the far north-western coast of Galloway. Feeling they were secure they carried the brandy, wines and tobacco ashore, then climbed South Cairn above the bay and sat in the sunshine to wait for the men with packhorses who would transport the cargo inland. They were careless, and lolling in the warm heather were surprised by an excise officer accompanied by a single soldier. The smugglers ran away down the hillside, and soon were standing off into the Irish Sea. Pleased with his capture, the officer sent the young dragoon to commandeer men and horses in the king's name from the nearby farms and clachans. When they arrived he would transport the contraband to the customs house at Stranraer.

Left alone, the officer paraded round and round the stack of liquors and tobacco above the shore, a pistol dangling from his hand. He was quite delighted with himself.

Across the hillside came Maggie McConnell, a buxom young queen of the district. She sauntered over to the officer, a fine figure of a young woman. Admiring the stack of contraband she bid him good morning and held out her hand. Little suspecting what lay ahead, the excise officer took it gladly. Before he knew what was happening his arm was flung up, the pistol went flying, and he was struggling in the young Amazon's arms as helplessly as if she had been a boa-constrictor. With a thud that knocked the breath from his body she threw him down in the heather and pinned him there by sitting on his chest. Then she adjusted her apron so that it covered his face, and waited. The officer kicked and swore and struggled, but all to no avail.

After a long, long time, she stood up and let him pull himself from the heather. The contraband had gone, the hillside was empty.

For a while young Maggie McConnell remained, engaging him in light, bantering conversation, and not too many minutes afterwards the dragoon returned with a party of men and the ponies he had requisitioned. Maggie excused herself, and bidding the officer farewell was soon gone over the hill. The poor man stood by the crushed heather, picking bits of stalk from his uniform and wondering how he could explain the missing contraband to his young assistant and the men of the district.

Remember the Sabbath Day

It was the Sabbath and a fine midsummer evening. In the twilight a revenue officer was riding through a quiet stretch of country not far from his home. Suddenly, to his misfortune, he found himself among a crowd of smugglers, some of the most desperate on that stretch of the coast. At the time the contraband trade was at its height, everyone was caught up in it, and he had offended the smugglers by the zeal and success with which he had tracked them down. Instantly he was recognised and pulled from his horse. Some were for thrashing him there and then, but other more bloody ruffians restrained them and indicated that the revenue officer should accompany them. He had no alternative, but asked that a boy should be sent to tell his wife he would be delayed, for she was expecting him any minute and would have a meal prepared. Realising that this would be to their advantage also, they agreed, and a boy was dispatched with the bare message.

The officer accompanied the desperadoes to a poor house or barn quite close at hand, which was a regular haunt of theirs. Thrusting him into a corner from which he had no chance of escape, they produced some spirits and began to drink. From the very beginning he was the butt of their jokes and rough insulting treatment. He bore it with pretended good humour, for he did not wish to trigger off the violence that simmered just below the surface, and was now boiling up as they drank and their speech and gestures grew wilder.

It was not long before it became apparent that they were going to beat him severely, and very likely kill him, in reprisal and as a warning to other revenue men not to be too conscientious in their work. The smugglers' ferocity increased, but true to some remnant of their boyhood training and superstitious regard for the church, they were reluctant to lay hands on him while it was still the Sabbath. As the time drew towards midnight they repeatedly consulted a watch, laughing cruelly and making jokes about how long he would have to wait.

There were not many minutes to go when a noise was heard a little distance away. It grew louder and could soon be distinguished as men's voices and the trampling of horses. They heard an order. It was the redcoats. The revenue officer's wife had summoned them at once on receiving her husband's message and hearing the boy's description of the men who were with him. The smugglers scattered into the darkness leaving their tankards and bottles tumbled on the floor.

The Minister

On a night of foul weather, with a storm blowing from the south-west, a lugger carrying a cargo of spirits and wine was driven on to the rocks. It was not long before the shore smugglers, like a flock of vultures, were swarming over her. The casks of brandy and crates of wine and other valuables were carried clear, and soon, under the influence of the heady spirit, a bacchanalian orgy was in full swing. A traveller coming upon the scene was appalled.

"Good gracious!" he exclaimed to a man keeping lookout a short distance away. "Are there no revenue officers in the vicinity?"

The man shook his head. "None, thanks be to God," he replied.

"Well, is the minister not available?"

For answer the lookout pointed to a man in black in the midst of the orgy. Long hair tossing about his face and black cape flying, the minister cavorted among the smugglers like a bedraggled crow, torch held high, helping a band of wild men to drive the bung from another keg of brandy.

The Salt Smugglers

A Manx boat with a cargo of bulk salt had moored in the small port of Carsluith on the eastern shore of Wigtown Bay, two or three miles to the south of Creetown. Word was brought to Mr McLaurin, senior excise officer in Newton Stewart, and he set off with some junior officers and a party of redcoats to seize the vessel and its cargo.

They arrived as the smugglers were shovelling the last of the salt into bags, while horses stood ready on the shore to carry it away. There was no trouble, the vessel and salt were appropriated and the smugglers dispersed angrily but quietly into the district round about. Pleased with his success Mr McLaurin instructed that the salt should be transported to the old wool mill on the Balloch Burn at Creetown and placed under lock and key. Guards were to be posted on the door.

Later in the day a dozen of the smugglers met at an inn they frequented and wondered what to do. They were disappointed at their loss and reluctant to give up so valuable a portion of the cargo without some attempt to reclaim it. At length they hit upon a scheme. Gathering a number of empty salt bags, of which there were plenty around Creetown, they filled them with sawdust. Then the first man, carrying the bag on his shoulder, walked down the road near the soldiers on guard at the mill. They watched with interest as he turned over the twisting bridge and continued towards the middle of the little township. He was followed by two more smugglers with salt bags, and then a party of half a dozen.

Thinking that a second vessel must be in the neighbourhood, the redcoats called on the men to stop. The smugglers walked on, disregarding them. At this the redcoats gave chase, and the smugglers fled away through the town.

It was a long, hot chase, for the running smugglers were the strongest and fittest young men among them, and the soldiers in their tight uniforms and boots could not run very fast. At last, however, one of the smugglers was overtaken. Panting, he demanded to know what they wanted, and told them to take their hands off him. They accused him of carrying smuggled salt. Hot words developed into a struggle and the bag of sawdust fell to the ground. One of the soldiers kicked it to demonstrate what he meant — but the bag yielded, softer than salt. It was untied and the yellow gleam of sawdust showed within. They tipped it into the road — it was all sawdust. The smuggler could not keep the grin of delight from his face.

Realising suddenly that they had left the mill unguarded, the redcoats raced all the way back again, but they were too late. The back door stood open, the wood splintered about the smashed lock. The salt was gone.

Mr McLaurin was very angry, but there was nothing he could do about it. Though they hunted, they had no chance of finding the salt, for it had been transported to the garden of Cassencarie, half a mile away. Empty-handed and dispirited the redcoats returned to Newton Stewart.

The Fairy Pipers of Cairnsmore

Billy Marshall's tinkler clan ruled a large part of the inland moors of Galloway. Here they were safe among their own people and unmolested. They were deeply involved in the smuggling trade, and strings of as many as eighty loaded ponies wound through the glens and across the hillsides of the Marshalls' territory. In a cave high on the slopes of Cairnsmore some portion of the smuggled goods was often laid aside for their own use.

One evening two pipers, travelling that way, came by chance upon the cave and thought it would make them a good shelter for the night. Discovering the smuggled tea, tobacco and spirits, they were somewhat apprehensive, but considering that it was almost dark and there was a bit of a drought in their bellies, they decided it was worth the risk.

They had not been settled in long, however, when they heard the noise of a large company approaching. They were frightened, for they knew that the very least they could expect from the ruthless tinklers was a sound beating, first for having discovered their hiding place, and secondly for having broached their cask of best quality brandy.

What should they do? One of the pipers had a desperate idea. He threw the bagpipes to his shoulder and motioned his comrade to do likewise. They waited until the shadowy forms of the tinklers came close to the cave entrance, standing tall and black against the starlight. Then they broke into a wild pibroch, the glittering cascades of notes ringing in the confines of the cave.

The tinklers, thinking only of rest at the end of a long journey, were startled and sprang back. They were superstitious people, and there were many tales of subterranean fairy pipers, pipers from the legions of the Devil. At the wild, martial music, rising from the very earth at their feet, they panicked and fled. A little distance away they halted, and looked at one another, but still the music rose from the depths of Cairnsmore. Too frightened to return to that magical place on the mountainside, they continued their journey.

As soon as the pipers thought the coast was clear they gathered their belongings and crept away in the darkness, taking a bit of tobacco with them, and a small keg to keep them going through the long night.

Granny Milligan's Porridge

A little old cofter's widow named Granny Milligan turned a blind eye when the lingtowmen borrowed her horse. Toddling out to the stable in the morning she would find it gone, but a day or two later there it was again, very tired, and a few bottles of rum — of which she was inordinately fond for one of her advanced years — had been thrust into the bottom of the cornstack.

One night the smugglers had gone a little way past her cottage when a neighbour who accompanied them called out to one of the tinklers: "Hey, did you remember Granny Milligan's rum?" The man had not, and they returned to the old lady's cottage.

That night, however, they were not carrying bottles, the rum was all in casks. None the less they determined to leave her some. Without waking her they pushed open the door, which led directly into her cluttered kitchen, and as always in those days remained unlocked. A large can of water stood against the wall. Slinging the water out of the door, they half filled the can with rum and put it back where it had been, with the enamel lid on top, and quietly departed.

In the morning the old lady was pottering about the kitchen making her morning porridge. Without really knowing what she did at that hour she poured the rum over the soaked meal and set it on the fire. When she carried her bowl to the littered table and took a mouthful she was stunned. Then she ate on. It was the most remarkable breakfast she had ever tasted.

From that moment it became her favourite food. She took it every morning and lived to a great age. Nothing, she swore with a gummy grin, set you up for the day like a good dish of rum porridge.

A Channel Forced

A Manx lugger, laden with contraband goods, was standing off the Mull of Galloway early one morning when she was surprised by a government cutter under the command of Sir John Reid. The lugger bore away to the east under full sail with a following wind, and the government cutter gave chase.

Even though the lugger piled on sail beyond the point of danger, it soon became apparent that she was being rapidly overhauled. None the less the captain held his course across Luce Bay for Cairndoon, his intended port of discharge, five miles to the north-west of Burrow Head. As they drew towards the land, neither vessel easing sail, there was little distance between them.

With a gale blowing on-shore and the tide setting strongly around the headland, with high waves, fierce currents and broken water, it seemed certain that the lugger would not even attempt to round Burrow Head, but must soon stand to and accept capture. Sir John Reid was pleased to contemplate yet another smuggling vessel to his credit.

He had reckoned without the courage and skill of his quarry, however, for swinging to starboard the lugger's captain set his heavily-laden vessel straight into the Burrow Head sea. With equal pluck Sir John Reid turned his cutter in pursuit.

It was a hair-raising forty minutes, both vessels rearing to the dizzy crests and plunging into the troughs of the waves, which close at hand exploded into spray up the hundred and fifty foot cliffs. Lugger and cutter survived, however, and at length turned north into the sheltered waters of Wigtown Bay.

Though the cutter had lost a little distance, her passage round the headland being less desperate, she was still not far behind. And as the lugger came opposite the Isle of Whithorn it seemed that she was giving up the flight, for she shortened sail and turned in towards the harbour. The revenue cutter drew rapidly closer then shortened sail in turn and followed in a more leisurely and cautious fashion.

But on rounding a knoll, and preparing to moor and send a ship's boat or force across to take the lugger captive, Sir John was astonished to discover that there was no sign of the smuggling vessel anywhere in the harbour. Officers and seamen scanned the rocking hulls and nodding forest of masts, but there was no doubt of it. Then a seaman in the rigging called and pointed through an opening in the rocks through which the Solway was visible. Following his outstretched arm Sir John was filled with chagrin to see the lugger standing away from the coast and setting full sail for the English shore.

For there was a second channel into the Isle harbour in those days, a narrow and shallow passage that was used by very small vessels at high water. Never had a vessel of such tonnage as the smugglers' lugger even contemplated it. But with full sails set and a south-west gale piling up the water in the Solway, the lugger had driven a passage straight through.

It was too late for the cutter to give chase and the lugger got clear away. Later, when the tide had fallen, they were able to inspect big boulders which had been thrust aside, and a deep furrow a hundred yards long which the lugger's keel had gouged in the shingly bottom of the channel.

It was a famous escape, spoken of for many years in the south-west and all around the Solway.

Sawney Bean

Sawney Bean was the son of an East Lothian hedger and ditcher, born in the early fifteenth century, during the restless reign of King James I. He was from the start a wastrel, and his father's industrious manners being uncongenial to him, he left home and began wandering the countryside. He was a brute, a young man completely lacking in moral sense and apparently with a psychopathic instinct. Soon, with a woman whose character was as vicious as his own, he had established himself as a robber, and then a cannibal, in a cave on the western shore of Galloway.

At that time the greater part of the Scottish population lived in clachans and small villages scattered thinly among the mountains and rough wilderness, and somewhat more densely throughout the regions of good agriculture. Pockets of habitation sprang up, others were abandoned, the houses crumbled into earth and soon vanished beneath the long grass, whin thickets and birch copses that extended for miles in every direction. They were troubled times, and whilst the local forces kept order as they could, much of the country was remote, the roads were little better than potholed tracks, authority was largely centralised at a considerable distance, and in any case the court itself was in a state of great unrest. Many of the great Highland chiefs were executed in Inverness: ultimately the king himself was assassinated at Perth. The local landowners kept order among the poorer people as they were able, but whole tracts of land were beyond their jurisdiction and control, and there the footpads and lawless brigands did pretty much as they pleased.

In such a place, a lonely shore not far from the western road, Sawney Bean and his loving, fertile spouse settled down. They had a living family of fourteen, eight sons and six daughters; and from an early age, incestuously, eighteen grandsons and fourteen granddaughters. Never did they mingle with other society, but were entirely sufficient unto themselves. In fact they lived like animals, by tooth and claw, and that seems the best way to visualise and understand them. For they lived greatly on human flesh, setting ambushes for single people and even small parties on the lonely tracks and roads of the district. Realising something of what would happen to them if they were caught, they were very careful, setting additional members of the family to either side of the spot where the ambush and slaughter were to take place, so that any victim escaping from the first assault would be caught and dragged down before he had gone many yards.

For a quarter of a century they inhabited the cave, and no-one ever escaped. Neither was any trace found. A poor workman, or a lady on horseback accompanied by servants, set out on a journey and did not arrive at their destination — that was all.

It is not quite accurate to say that nothing was ever seen again, for though the murderers grew to a family of considerable size, and there were many young stomachs to be filled, there were often some bits of their victims that were not eaten or wanted, and these were thrown into the sea at a good distance from the cave. Occasionally they were washed up further along the coast, causing great horror and speculation. Searches were carried out, but in that wild and waste land nothing was ever discovered.

For years it continued, and so great at length became the popular outcry that it reached the ears of the court far away in Edinburgh. Spies and investigators were sent into the south-west to find out the truth. The best they could discover was that people had sometimes stayed at inns on their travels, and in a number of instances the landlords were so trapped by circumstantial evidence concerning missing travellers that they were arrested and put to death. Travellers also were executed, on the flimsiest of evidence, they, like the innkeepers, protesting their innocence to the very end. But the authorities were determined that the outrages must cease, and hoped, by a ruthless repression, either to destroy those guilty or so frighten them that they would cease their activities. The only effect, however, was to scare away a lot of the innkeepers, so that there was nowhere for travellers to stay, and consequently fewer people came to the district. Cut off, to a large extent, and doubly frightened, many families moved to other areas. But still men and women continued to vanish. A number of the king's spies, searching the countryside, were never seen again.

As Sawney's family grew in size and strength, occasionally a group as large as five or six would disappear on the road — though they would never tackle more than two if they were mounted. The cannibals were unable to eat as much as this, and whilst some was thrown into the sea, quantities of limbs were pickled in brine or hung to dry from the roof of the cave — legs and arms, haunches, neck joints, ribs and backs. Though they did not bother particularly with their dress, and the children went naked, there was no shortage of clothes, nor money either, for by the time they were captured — after twenty-five years of cannibalising the district — it was estimated that they had killed and eaten more than one thousand people.

On the day of a fair a man and his wife were returning home on horseback when they were set upon by the ferocious gang. The woman was riding pillion behind her husband, and while he drew his sword and fought the murderous cannibals off, clinging to the saddle and his feet set firmly in the stirrups, she was largely unprotected and clutching hands broke her grasp about his body. In the struggle and dusk he saw her dragged to the ground, her head yanked back by the hair, and her throat slashed open with a big knife. Then the women fell upon her and began squabbling over her blood, drinking it as fast as they were able. She was disembowelled. It happened in an instant, like a nightmare. The man, seeing it, fought in a frenzy.

Doubtless he would have suffered the fate of all the other victims if a party of thirty people, also returning from the fair, had not at that moment come down the rough track towards them. For the first time finding themselves outnumbered, Sawney Bean and his family made their escape, dragging with them for some distance the body of the dead woman. Her husband cried to the approaching company and told them what had occurred, which at first they could not believe. Then they followed the retreating family and found the butchered body of his wife lying on the ground. There seemed no doubt that they had discovered the fate of the missing travellers.

Some members of the party escorted the man to Glasgow, more than seventy miles away, where he told his tale to the magistrates. Immediately the king was informed. Three or four days later a party of four hundred men, led by King James himself (James II or III), set out for the lonely district where the cannibals were thought to live. With them they took bloodhounds. It was the king's determination that once and for all the murderers must be brought to justice and destroyed.

They reached the place of the attack and saw the blackened blood on the earth. They scoured the surrounding countryside, but no trace was to be found that gave any clue to the family's whereabouts. Descending to the shore they examined a number of small caves and viewed water-filled caverns, but nowhere did it seem remotely possible that as many people as would populate a small village might live. They departed and searched again inland.

When they returned to the shore the tide was low, and they saw that now some of the larger sea caves were just accessible, black above the rocks and lapping water, or sea-rippled sand. No-one, they thought, would inhabit any place so awful, and did not even bother to search them, but continued along the shore. By chance, however, two or three of the bloodhounds entered one of the caverns and set up a tumult of baying. Some of the king's party followed and entered the dripping dungeon. Ahead of them a grim, twisting tunnel retreated into blackness. Bloodhounds strained at their leashes, and those running free pressed on ahead into the darkness and would not come back. Their baying and yelping was deafening in the confined space. Filled with foreboding the men retreated to the entrance and sent for torches.

Holding the blazing brands aloft, with swords at the ready, the soldiers and bold spirits from King James's court advanced into the tunnel. The tide, they saw from barnacles and sea-wrack, ran into it for two hundred yards. They advanced further, beyond the weedy pools, and still further, by many labyrinthine twists and turnings, until it seemed they must have travelled a full mile underground. Then the cave ahead opened out into a chamber.

As the flickering light of their torches touched the rocky walls and shadowy recesses of the roof they stopped, horrified. For there the ghastly, gibbet-like larder of human limbs and parts hung drying on cords and ropes; and pickled in barrels of brine against the walls were the inner organs, hands and feet, and still more human flesh. Clothes, taken from their victims, lay strewn and piled in the corners, with mildewed scabbards and thigh boots, and a welter of rusting swords and muskets. A rocky shelf nearby was piled high with glinting coin, and handfuls of other possessions, rings and watches and brooches, which fell in confusion to the ground. And beyond, where the tunnel resumed at the inner end of the chamber, were the first watchful, crouching, silent members of Sawney Bean's family.

After desperate fighting and pursuits, men and women acting like wild animals, the children writhing and struggling, biting and stabbing ferociously with bits of sharpened bone, the entire family was captured and bound. They numbered forty-eight. The king's men were appalled. The human remains were carried to the shore and buried in the sand. The valuable spoils were tumbled into sacks and money bags. Then, the cannibal family securely tied in single file, King James led his party inland, eastwards towards Edinburgh.

News of their progress went before them, and crowds gathered in the streets to see the cannibals pass through. They were not disappointed,

for though they might be sullen, to the very last they acted like wild things.

In Edinburgh they were imprisoned in the Tolbooth. The following day, trial being considered unnecessary, they were taken to Leith and executed. Almost all died without showing the least sign of repentance, struggling and cursing their captors to the very end. The men were dismembered, their private parts, hands and feet being severed from their bodies so that they bled to death in a short time. The women, having been made witness of the men's fate, were burned alive in three fires.

FOOTNOTE

The first written account of Sawney Bean's family seems to have been a broadsheet dated about 1700. Interestingly, for the time, this claims that the king was James VI and I — remembered as the witch persecutor and rooter-out of evil. The key version, however, appeared in *Historical and Traditionary Tales connected with the South of Scotland* — better known as 'Nicholson's Tales' (1843). This sets the story two centuries earlier, in the suitably more remote reign of James I.

There is some disagreement, too, in the location of the cave. Several have been proposed, but that most commonly accepted is below Bennane Head, three miles to the north of Ballantrae — eight miles from the Wigtownshire border. Nicholson, however, describes it as 'a cave by the seaside on the shore of the county of Galloway', and since it is among the most famous of the local tales, it is included in this collection.

The Crook and the Cairn

Sandy Maxwell sat by a cairn on Dundeugh Hill, islanded by the Water of Deugh and the Water of Ken, and stared moodily up the glen towards the last houses in Carsphairn. It was the middle of the afternoon and it was hot. He was bored up there with the sheep. Being the Sabbath he could not even take up a stocking and do a bit of knitting. Idly he poked at the ground between his knees with the point of his crook, scratching patterns in the dry earth.

Though he was a middle-aged man, he became engrossed in the patterns he was making. The spike of his crook dug deeper, gouging a stony trench. With pebbles from the cairn he built a little rampart against it. Like a boy at the beach he was amused and pleased by the toy fortifications, but they were not big enough. He thought he would extend them all the way round the cairn, as if it was a castle. As these things go, soon his jacket was off and he was hauling great boulders from the heart of the stone mound, constructing a solid dyke in a circle around himself. His shirt and kilt and legs were dusty with dry earth. He was completely rapt, hot and happy, playing by himself.

In an hour the dyke was higher than his knees, but the pile of stones was nearly exhausted. As he heaved a large boulder from the earth, he was surprised to see that the cairn had been built above a heavy flagstone. For a minute, sweating and scratching his head, he looked at it, then made haste to remove the last of the rocks that covered it.

The flagstone was heavier than he had expected. Settling his feet and bending his knees, he heaved with all his might, and slowly it swung up on one edge. For a moment it balanced, then toppled and landed slap on the earth, almost to the rim of the dyke. There was a hole beneath. With growing excitement Sandy looked down, and in the shadow saw some kind of stone container covered with a big slate. Rather nervously, putting his fingers to his mouth, he reached down and lifted the slate. A great wide-mouthed crock jar, full of gold coins, winked up into his face. Amazed, he sat back on the edge of the hole, surrounded by his dyke, and gazed down at it. It was a treasure, but it smacked of witchcraft or fairy work, and for some minutes he did not like to touch it.

As he looked in wonder, he recalled that that very Sunday morning, while his wife, a sharp-tongued quarrelsome creature, went about her work, there had been a knock at the door. She had opened it to a tiny, bent, fairy-like old woman, brown-faced and shabbily dressed. She had begged a cup of meal, and his wife, with unaccustomed good nature, had given the little creature a whole basin full. Perhaps this had something to do with his present find: if so, then she was a kindly spirit and he need have nothing to fear. Gingerly he reached down and touched the gold coins, soft and chill to his fingers. He took a big handful and cautiously withdrew them into the late afternoon sunlight. The coins shone in his hand and one falling jingled musically on the ground. There was nothing to fear — it was treasure! He was rich! Rich beyond his wildest dreams! Digging his fingers deeply into the crock, he heaped the gold before him on the grass and stony earth.

Suddenly he realised that someone might be watching. He looked around secretively, but the hillsides were deserted, he was quite alone. Carefully he lifted the crock from the hole and began to pour the pile of heavy coins back in, to carry them home. Then he stopped. It was the Sabbath! No good would come of gathering such worldly treasure on the Sabbath. Every second word the minister preached told him that. Disappointed he stared down at the heaps of wealth. Still, he could bury it again and return first thing the following morning. It would be safe enough.

Slipping three coins into his pocket to show to his wife, he buried the crock once more, jingled the beautiful gold back in, replaced the slate, and toppled the heavy slab over the hole. Then, staring round him all the time, fearful that he should be disturbed, he rebuilt the cairn, and with his boots scuffed away all sign of his ditches and dykes.

By the time he was finished the evening was well advanced, but he was satisfied with his work. Carefully he stuck his crook deep into the earth to mark the cairn, so that there should be no mistake when he returned in a few hours' time. As he set off for home there was just enough light for him to see the whins and tussocks of heather at his feet. Fingering the three coins in his pocket he paused half way down the hill and looked back regretfully. There stood his crook beside the cairn, silhouetted against the night sky.

His wife was prepared for his return, her sharp words carefully chosen, her anger kindled to a hot flame. Patiently, smug within himself, Sandy waited until her tongue had run its course and she turned to the oven where he knew the hot meal was waiting for him. But as she laid it on the table with last bitter recriminations that it would be ruined and it was his own fault, he told her to hush, and not make such a fuss over a plateful of food. Reaching into his pocket he laid the three gold coins down on the scrubbed boards. With delight he saw her words dry up.

She was speechless, and for the first time since they were married Sandy enjoyed the luxury of talking freely without being interrupted. But when he told her that he had left the gold on the hill, her tongue was loosened, and instantly she began to berate him for a fool. He placated her with reassurances that no-one had seen him and they would return at first light to dig up the crock once more. Then they would be rich beyond their most extravagant daydreams — richer than the greatest landlord in the district! Screwing her fingers into her apron, sweating with avarice, his wife sat opposite him, and Sandy tucked into his dinner.

She told him that they would build the finest house in the village of Carsphairn, where she had lived until she was married. How she would show off before all those snooty neighbours who now looked down on her as the wife of an idle, drunken wastrel of a shepherd! Her snapping eyes shone at the prospect. Sandy, however, with unusual authority, informed her that he was the master of the house and they would do no such thing. He was buying Dundeugh Hill! He would rebuild the castle and there they would settle down in real style, with shepherds and ploughmen and so many servants that they wouldn't need to lift a finger until their dying day. But his wife would not have any of it, and she was accustomed to having her own way. He could buy Dundeugh if he wanted, but first they would build her house in Carsphairn — and she lingered over the luxuries she would have installed, and how she would walk down the street in gowns of silk, with an elegant parasol, and all the neighbours would look from behind their curtains and as they trailed past in their dowdy frocks, pea green with envy. Sandy finished his dinner, wiped his mouth with the back of a hand and pulled out his cutty pipe. Well, she could dream, but that's all there was to it. They were buying Dundeugh Hill, the matter was settled.

They had never had such a disagreement! For hours the hot words flew, calming momentarily as one or the other had a new idea that was worth considering. The summer dawn was lightening the sky before, in a final firework display of temper, his wife gathered the dishes together and took them to the sink to wash up. Sandy lay back in his chair and gazed towards the brightening window. The entire Sabbath night had passed and not once had he thought of opening the Bible. Even now, as he sat at peace, his thoughts drifted through a landscape of glittering, golden coins. Behind him the dishes clattered about the sink with unusual violence.

Thin lips pressed together, the washing-up finished, Sandy's wife seized the bowl of dirty water and carried it to the door. But as she reached it there was a knock. Flinging the door wide, she found the little, brown-faced, fairy-like old woman standing on the threshold.

"Yes?" she said rudely. "What do you want?"

"Mistress Maxwell," said the little woman. "I wonder, would you mind throwing your dirty water in the drain across the yard. Tipping it down the ditch here, beside the house, it runs along and wets my baby's bedclothes. It makes such a mess."

Sandy's wife was ready for a row with anyone. Her thin nostrils widened.

"Indeed I do mind," she snapped. "Who do you think you are coming here, to my house, and telling me where to throw my dish-water. Watch your tongue, you impudent old witch, or I'll throw it over you instead."

So saying, she flung the greasy water into the ditch at her feet, splashing up on to the ragged hem of the old woman's dress.

"Very well, Mistress Maxwell," said the little woman. "I sought to do you a good turn. It's just as easy to do you a bad one."

Turning on her heel, bent and with rapid steps, she walked away around the end of the house.

Shortly afterwards, calling their son from his bed, Sandy Maxwell and his wife set off up the slopes of Dundcugh Hill. It was not yet four o'clock in the morning. The Water of Ken, wandering down from the morning-misty hills to the north-east, shone pink with the first light of the summer day.

In half an hour they were approaching the crest of the hill. There was the cairn, with Sandy's crook standing at the end of it, just as he had left it the evening before.

Pulling the crook from the ground and casting it into the heather, the three set to and tumbled the rocks aside. It had been a clear night and the morning was chill, but soon they grew hot. Sandy's wife, less strong than the two men, heaved at the boulders, tearing her nails, kilting her skirts above her thin knees. Soon the cairn was demolished, but to Sandy's amazement and dismay, the stone slab was gone. How could this be? He looked around, wonderingly, and pushed back his bonnet.

Somehow, however, they had gone to the wrong cairn, for there, not a hundred yards away, his crook stood above the very pile of rocks he had dismantled and then rebuilt the day before. Not knowing how they could have made such a mistake, and cross from having wasted their efforts, the three left the strewn boulders and hurried towards it, their plaids and shawl and a sack they had brought to carry the treasure, bundled in their arms.

But when, now sweating and breathing hard, they had pulled that cairn also to the earth — no flagstone was revealed! Sandy was still more puzzled.

Then his son pointed back a little way, and there, not far from the cairn they had been to previously, stood a cairn Sandy had not noticed, with his crook planted invitingly into the ground at the end of it.

"Good sakes!" his wife cried in exasperation, as they hurried through the heather, her dress gaping wide at the throat. "Will you be sure this time."

Sandy examined the cairn carefully. The stones were loose, little tufts of grass and clods of dry earth clung to some of the boulders. He recollected the shape of one or two.

"Yes," he told them. "This is definitely the one."

Their confidence refreshed, they set to, and with grunts and cries as fingers were squashed and shins raked, they dragged the rocks apart, sending some rattling away down the hillside into the whins and thin scree. To Sandy's horror, the earth beneath the cairn was dry and bare.

Dragging off her bonnet his wife struck him across the head with exasperation. But she, too, saw that there was fairy work about it somewhere. And a minute later, as they all lay back sweating and panting in the growing heat of the sun, she saw her husband's crook standing like a flagpole above a cairn quarter of a mile distant.

Dispirited, but still with burning hope, they hurried again across the summit of Dundeugh Hill and began to tear the cairn apart. Then there was another — and another — and another. Their dander was up. Like furies they flung themselves at one cairn after the other — their son, after a time, standing back and giving the orders. Great boulders, heavy enough for three men, flew away down the hill, scattering sheep for their lives. They sweated like badgers. The summer sun rose in full heat. Midday came, and passed. And at length Sandy could do no more.

"Oh!" he cried, falling back in the heather, kilt sprawling above his knees. "It's a nightmare, a nightmare!"

Some distance away his wife, stripped to her damp, earthy bodice, lay among a pile of rough boulders, unable to speak.

A minute or two later, while still they were panting, a sudden cry from their son made them sit up. For the first time in hours they looked about them. All over Dundeugh Hill a thousand — ten thousand — cairns had sprouted, and at the head of each Sandy's crook nodded in the wind, mocking them. Though they laboured until the earth was gathered into the sun they would never have been able to search so many.

Sick at heart, and hardly able to set one foot before the other with fatigue, they set their faces down the hill. In their minds the bright, foolish visions of the beautiful house and splendid castle mocked them as they went.

When they reached the door of the cottage the little, brown old lady was waiting for them.

"Well, Mistress Maxwell," she said, "it was a grand, fine morning for your tantrums. Maybe now you'll learn it pays to be obliging to a neighbour like myself."

And Sandy's wife was too tired even to strike at her with her bonnet.

Young Maxwell could not keep his mouth shut and soon the story was known all over the district. They were a laughing stock. But throughout that whole hot summer Dundeugh Hill swarmed with prospectors, like the later heyday of the Yukon goldrush. The hillsides were littered with boulders, more like the surface of the moon than a Galloway sheep pasture. And with all their dodging the sheep became so agile that they had no trouble at all in outstripping Sandy's dogs. But for all their work, not a brass penny did the prospectors find. Only the three fat golden coins that he had brought down the hill on that Sabbath evening, remained to tell the truth of Sandy Maxwell's crock of gold.

The Wigtown Martyrs*

In 1685 Margaret Wilson was eighteen and her sister Agnes was thirteen. They were sensible, well-educated girls, the daughters of a well-to-do farmer, Gilbert Wilson of Glenvernoch in the parish of Penninghame, to the west of Newton Stewart. During those troubled Covenanting times Gilbert Wilson and his wife had conformed to the Episcopalian dictates of the king, and were regular attenders at the services of the curate of Penninghame. Their daughters, however, remarkably for girls of such youth, refused to conform, and would not accompany their parents to church. Their failure was punishable by a fine; and worse, suggested that their religious principles and political allegiances lay elsewhere, in illegal and traitorous secret gatherings. Even at that age they were required to take the Test.

Knowing that the eyes of the curate and soldiers were upon them, the two girls fled from home with their brother, a boy of sixteen, and made their way with others into the sheltering hills of Galloway. There they survived as they could, and attended conventicles both in the open air and the homes of courageous Presbyterians.

Gilbert Wilson and his wife were held responsible for their children's nonconformist beliefs. In consequence soldiers were billeted freely on the farm, up to a hundred at a time. They demanded money; Wilson's possessions and stock were arbitrarily confiscated and sold; he was summoned to courts in Edinburgh and Wigtown. From a state of comparative affluence he was eventually reduced to dire poverty.

The winter was cold and the caves of Carrick, Nithsdale and Galloway were bleak homes. When the group of Covenanters with whom the young Wilsons were residing heard of the temporary lull in the persecution that came with the death of Charles II in February, 1685, they were glad to descend to Kirkinner near Wigtown, and the home of Margaret MacLauchlan.

She was an elderly woman of about seventy, sensible and well-informed, the widow of a carpenter, and a staunch Presbyterian like themselves. For years she had been a firm attender of conventicles when the opportunity arose, and on a number of occasions had given

* See 'The Covenanters'.

300

her own house to the use of a field preacher and the Covenanters of the district. But her sympathies had not gone unnoticed, and more than once her home had been ransacked and her goods appropriated by the soldiers. She knew the Wilson girls well. When times were hard she had by her words and faith strengthened their conviction and resolve.

On this occasion, however, when the girls were sheltering beneath her roof, they were betrayed by a friend, and soon a troop of soldiers was knocking at the locked door.

For a time the girls were thrown into a place known as 'the thieves' hole'. Then they were transferred to the prison where Margaret MacLauchlan was confined. The old woman had been treated harshly, denied any fire or bed although it was winter, and kept short of food. With them in the jail was a twenty-year-old servant girl by the name of Margaret Maxwell.

They were required, brusquely, to take the Oath of Abjuration, declaring themselves against the 'Apologetical Declaration' — the Cameronian's challenging and unfortunately over-stated manifesto, which proclaimed the two Covenants, disowned the king, and threatened punishment, even death, to the enemies of Reformation. To have taken the oath would have been to deny their convictions and disown their fellow-sufferers. They refused, and accordingly the four were brought before the commission for Wigtownshire — consisting of Sir Robert Grierson of Lagg, Colonel David Graham (brother of Claverhouse), Major Windram, Captain Strachan, and Provost Coltron of Wigtown.

They were indicted with rebellion, having been present at the battles of Bothwell Bridge and Airds Moss, and having attended twenty field and twenty house conventicles. So far as the latter charges were concerned, doubtless they were largely guilty, but the first were foolish, a total fabrication. As the Session Records of the Parish of Penninghame state: 'It was well known that none of these women were ever within twenty miles of Bothwell or Airds Moss.' And even supposing they had been present, what part would have been played by three girls aged fourteen, twelve and seven, and a woman of sixty-four?

Margaret Maxwell, found partially guilty, was sentenced to be flogged by the public hangman on three successive days, and subsequently to stand in the pillory for an hour. Margaret MacLauchlan and the two Wilson girls, however, were proclaimed guilty on all charges, and sentenced according to the new decree that female traitors in Scotland should be put to death by drowning. More precisely, as the Session Records of Penninghame express it: 'the judge sentenced them

301

to be tied to palisadoes fixed in the sand, within the floodmark of the sea, and there to stand till the flood o'erflowed them.'

The sentence, as doubtless had been intended, sent a great wave of shock and dismay through the countryside. Gilbert Wilson, having scraped together every farthing he could muster, travelled to Edinburgh, and on payment of one hundred pounds Scots was able to redeem the life of his younger daughter.

In Wigtown, meantime, the prisoners were assailed by their friends to take the Oath of Abjuration. They persisted in their refusal. Then Margaret MacLauchlan, possibly wishing to save the young lives of the girls, professed herself ready to take the Oath, and on that ground petitioned the Privy Council to recall the sentence upon her. Apparently the application was successful. Similarly, due to the efforts of Gilbert Wilson, a reprieve was obtained for his older daughter also. The Privy Council document is dated 'Edinburgh, April 30, 1685' and commences: 'The Lords of his Majesty's Privy Council do hereby reprieve the execution of the sentence of death, pronounced by the justices against Margaret Wilson and Margaret Lauchlison, until the . . . day of . . . and discharge the magistrates of Wigton from putting the said sentence to execution till foresaid day; and recommend the said Margaret Wilson and Margaret Lauchlison to the lords secretaries of State, to interpose with his most sacred Majesty for the royal remission to them.' Thus they were granted a reprieve to an unspecified date. Unfortunately no record of the reprieve can be traced beyond the council chamber, and the process of law continued.

In the case of Margaret Maxwell, the servant girl, the hangman was merciful. She was brought from the jail, stripped to the waist, and tied to the back of a cart for whipping. No sooner had she appeared in the street, however, than the citizens of Wigtown pulled together the shutters of their windows and retreated indoors. The pavements of Wigtown were deserted. Then the hangman used her very gently, and sought to release her from the pillory — or 'jougs' — before the hour was up, but she insisted that she was 'neither wearied nor ashamed' and the time was completed.

Agnes Wilson was released.

On the day appointed, 11th May, 1685, Margaret Wilson and Margaret MacLauchlan were conducted by a troop of soldiers under Major Windram to the sands at the mouth of the River Bladnoch, just below the town of Wigtown. It was low water. They were tied to stakes, the older woman further out, since it was hoped that seeing her death struggles the younger might yet recant. A great crowd gathered on the shore. As a bystander described it: "The sands were covered wi' cluds o' folk, a' gathered into clusters, many offerin' up prayers for the women while they were bein' put down."

As the tide came in Margaret MacLauchlan, who had wavered in the jail, gathered strength. Seventy years old, she prayed and recited passages from the Bible as the lapping water, still cold from the winter, rose up her body. At length it was at her face, and in not many minutes was above her head. Her struggles were over, she was at peace.

Margaret Wilson had been tied in such a position that she must see the drowning of her companion. As she watched the old lady's brief struggles she was not frightened. "It is Christ wrestling there," she said. And when Margaret MacLauchlan was dead, the pale water was only just rising up her body. She did not flinch in her resolve. Bound to the stake she sang from the 25th Psalm:

'To thee I lift my soul:
O Lord, I trust in thee:
My God, let me not be ashamed,
Nor foes triumph over me.'

In a voice calm and clear, even cheerful, she recited a portion of the eighth chapter of the Epistle to the Romans: 'Who shall separate us from the love of Christ — shall tribulation, or distress, or persecution, or famine, or nakedness, or peril, or sword? . . . Nay, in all these things we are more than conquerors, through him that loved us.' She sang and recited many extracts, and engaged in fervent prayer. Not for one moment did she turn from the path she was following, though the people who crowded nearby, soldiers among them, pleaded with her to say the few words that would have secured her release.

At length the rising Solway was about her face and she was drowning. A soldier pulled her face from the water. Then, to give her yet more opportunity to recant, her bonds were untied and she was carried to the shore. She was nearly unconscious. As she came round, Major Windram asked if she would now pray for the king.

"I wish salvation for all men," she replied meekly.

The crowd appealed to her yet again to save herself. Voices cried, "Say God save the king, say God save the king!"

She replied, "God save him if he will."

"Oh sir, she has said it!" cried her friends.

But it was not enough for the authorities. Lagg, it is said, came up,

and with an oath of his own instructed that the Oath of Abjuration be put to her once more. She heard the familiar words , but when she was asked to swear, she replied passionately: "I will not, I am one of Christ's children. Let me go!"

Accordingly she was taken out to the stake and bound afresh. A second time the water rose to her face. This time there was no reprieve.

They were buried in Wigtown churchyard, where the first of a number of tombstones, bearing an epitaph detailing the martyrdom, was raised above them twenty-six years later. Nearby were the graves of three other martyrs, William Johnston, John Milroy and George Walker, all of the Parish of Penninghame, who were hanged for their beliefs in the same year — three tragedies just as great, though less notice has been taken of their history.

Today the graves of the five are marked with three white stones surrounded by a railing. Nearby stand the shaggy, ivy-clad ruins of the old church, and the present Church of Scotland. Above the graveyard wall there is a fine outlook to the far-off hills of Galloway which the Covenanters knew so well.

There has been a great deal of controversy about the Wigtown Martyrs. Some accounts differ from the above in minute details, others in more important facts. It is claimed, for example, that Margaret Wilson was not brought ashore: a tall dragoon waded out and raised her head from the water to give her that moment longer, whereupon she uttered the words that have been recounted. Margaret MacLauchlan's age, though commonly accepted as 'about seventy', varies between sixty-three and eighty. The date of the drownings is given as both the 2nd and the 11th May. Some historical commentators do not even accept that the drowning took place, though it seems impossible to discount the weight of evidence. And as might be expected, there are many peripheral tales.

The memory of the events died hard, and without forgiveness. As much as two hundred years after the martyrdom, in the last decade of the nineteenth century, a minister of the district overhead a quarrel which was concluded with the damning thrust: "I wadna like to have had a forebear who betrayed the martyrs! I wadna be coomed o' sic folk!"

According to one account, Grierson of Lagg gave the women a last opportunity to take the Abjuration Oath at the stake, which they refused to do. At this an officious town sergeant thrust down their heads with his halberd and cried with savage glee: "Then tak' another drink o't, my hearties!" The words returned upon him, for later that same day he found himself consumed with an unquenchable thirst, which pursued him for the rest of his life. It was a disease, an unnatural craving which compelled him to carry water wherever he went, to stop and drink at every ditch, stream and tap he encountered from that afternoon onward. He became famous for it. His friends deserted him: he was pointed out with abhorrence everywhere he went.

In the evening following the drownings, a constable by the name of Bell, who had helped to tie the two women to the stakes, and had carried out his duties with notable lack of feeling, was asked by an acquaintance how the women had behaved as the water rose about them. He replied jocularly, "Oo, they just clepped roun' the stobs like partans (crabs) and prayed." Now the word 'clepped' means 'web-footed' in addition to 'moving like a crab'. Shortly afterwards the constable's wife was brought to bed with child, and upon taking up the infant the midwife cried out in horror: "The bairn's clepped!" And so it was, the baby's fingers were webbed. During the next few years a second and a third child were born, and each was discovered to be clepped like the first. By superstitious people it was seen as something worse than a mere deformity; it was the mark of the Devil or an evil fairy, and looked on with some dread. More generally, however, it was taken in the town as a sign of providence, that the sins of the father had been visited upon the children. They were known in the neighbourhood as 'the Cleppie Bells'.

'Craigwaggie's Meikle Chuckie'

Every fortnight Jock Mulldroch from Craigwaggie laid an egg. When he felt the fit coming on him he would climb the ladder to the peat-loft, and sitting on his hunkers among a scattering of dry bracken make low crooning notes. Then, when the egg was laid, he would break into a loud cackling crow of pride and triumph. When his mother heard this she came running with a basket to collect the egg. They were a good size, larger than goose eggs and speckled with black and yellow. Still, his mother sold them as bonny goose eggs and got a fair price for them. Then, to Jock's great pleasure, she set a couple beneath a broody hen.

It was a long, long wait. Even the hen seemed to think things had gone on long enough, and increasingly used to rise and look circum-spectly at the unusual eggs beneath her. But then, at last, the shells cracked and chipped. Out popped two little lads, dressed in green.

Under their grannie's care and good feeding they thrived, and although they grew bigger, it was not much bigger. They were known throughout the south of Scotland as Willie and Wattie Birlie, and were well liked by everybody. Really they were more like brownies or urchin fairies than people. They seemed to have the wanderlust and led some-thing of tinkers' lives, though they always returned to Craigwaggie and their loving father and grannie.

At length, sad to say, in the great snowstorm of 1740, they vanished. Some said they went into a snow-wreath and never came out again, others that they sank in one of the great quaking bogs on the moors. They were never seen again.

Their father went on laying eggs, sitting in the peat loft.

Bibliography

The following is a list of the principal works I consulted during the preparation of this book. There were, in addition, many articles and papers, handbooks, guides and other minor publications.

Andrew Agnew: *A History of the Hereditary Sheriffs of Galloway*, 1864.

John Gordon Barbour: *Unique Traditions chiefly of the West and South of Scotland*, 1833.

Alexander Christie: *Pages of Rerrick History*, unpublished.

C. H. Dick: *Highways and Byways in Galloway and Carrick*, 1916.

Ian Donnachie *and* Innes MacLeod: *Old Galloway*, 1974.

The Gallovidian Magazine, 1899-1919.

The Gallovidian Annual, 1920-1933.

Malcolm Harper (Ed): *The Bards of Galloway*, 1889.

Malcolm Harper: *Rambles in Galloway*, 1876.

Andrew McCormick: *Galloway: the Spell of its Hills and Glens*, 1932.

Andrew McCormick: *The Tinkler-Gypsies of Galloway*, 1906.

Andrew McCormick: *Words from the Wild Wood*, 1912.

Walter McCulloch: *The Galloway McCullochs*, unpublished.

James Mackay: *Robert Bruce — King of Scots*, 1974.

William Mackenzie: *The History of Galloway*, 1841.

Donald Macniè (Ed): *The New Shell Guide to Scotland*, 1977.

I.M.M. MacPhail: *A History of Scotland*, 1954.

John Mactaggart: *The Scottish Gallovidian Encyclopedia*, 1824.

Herbert Maxwell: *A History of Dumfries and Galloway*, 1896.

John Nicholson (Ed): *Historical and Traditional Tales connected with the South of Scotland*, 1843.

The Reader's Digest Association Ltd (Ed): *Folklore, Myths and Legends of Britain*, 1973.

Rossell Hope Robbins: *The Encyclopedia of Witchcraft and Demonology*, 1959.

John Robertson: *The Story of Galloway*, 1963.

Sir Walter Scott: *Minstrelsy of the Scottish Border*, 1803.

The Third Statistical Account of Scotland: the Stewartry of Kirkcudbright and the County of Wigtown, 1965.

R. de Bruce Trotter: *Galloway Gossip: Wigtownshire/Kirkcudbright-shire*, 1901.

Elizabeth Whitley: *The Two Kingdoms*, 1977.

J. Maxwell Wood: *Smuggling in the Solway*, 1908.

J. Maxwell Wood: *Superstitious Record in the South-West of Scotland*, 1911.

J.A. Wylie (Ed): *Scots Worthies: their Lives and Testimonies*, edition undated.